Book 1 of the award-

Historical Novel Society Editor's Choice
Winner of *the Global Ebooks Award for Best Historical Fiction*
Finalist in *the Wishing Shelf Awards, the Chaucer Awards* **and**
the Kindle Book Awards

'*Evocative and thoroughly riveting. A vividly-written, historical saga.*' The Wishing Shelf

'*A walk through time! That is what it was like to read this fine novel. It drew me into the pages and would not let go of me until done! Bravo for a wonderful read!*' Arwin Blue, *By Quill Ink and Parchment Historical Fiction blogger*

'*A remarkable achievement.*' Deborah Swift, *Pleasing Mr Pepys*

'*You will not find any better historical fiction, nor a more powerful evocation of a vivid past than in Gill's brilliantly written series.*' Paul Trembling, *Local Poet*

'*The whole quartet is well written, well plotted and beautifully composed... highly recommended.*' Cristoph Fischer, *Ludwig*

'*A thrilling page-turner and very hard to put down.*' Deb McEwan, *Unlikely Soldiers*

'*Gill's skill at moving from culture to culture, savoring the distinctive colors of each, is breath-taking.*' Elizabeth Horton-Newton, *Carved Wooden Heart*

'*Fascinating history – the plot was terrific.*' Brian Wilkerson, *Trickster Eric Novels blogger*

JEAN GILL

SONG AT DAWN

1150: PROVENCE

THE TROUBADOURS
BOOK 1

Cover design by Jessica Bell

Jean Gill's Publications

Novels
The Midwinter Dragon - HISTORICAL FICTION
Book 1 The Ring Breaker (The 13th Sign) 2022

The Troubadours Quartet - HISTORICAL FICTION
Book 5 Nici's Christmas Tale: A Troubadours Short Story (The 13th Sign) 2018
Book 4 Song Hereafter (The 13th Sign) 2017
Book 3 Plaint for Provence (The 13th Sign) 2015
Book 2 Bladesong (The 13th Sign) 2015
Book 1 Song at Dawn (The 13th Sign) 2015

Natural Forces - FANTASY
Book 3 The World Beyond the Walls (The 13th Sign) 2021
Book 2 Arrows Tipped with Honey (The 13th Sign) 2020
Book 1 Queen of the Warrior Bees (The 13th Sign) 2019

Love Heals - SECOND CHANCE LOVE
Book 2 More Than One Kind (The 13th Sign) 2016
Book 1 No Bed of Roses (The 13th Sign) 2016

Looking for Normal - TEEN FICTION
Book 1 Left Out (The 13th Sign) 2017
Book 2 Fortune Kookie (The 13th Sign) 2017

Non-fiction

MEMOIR / TRAVEL

How White is My Valley *(The 13th Sign 2021) *EXCLUSIVE to Jean Gill's Special Readers Group*

How Blue is my Valley *(The 13th Sign)* 2016

A Small Cheese in Provence *(The 13th Sign)* 2016

WW2 MILITARY MEMOIR

Faithful through Hard Times *(The 13th Sign)* 2018

4.5 Years – war memoir by David Taylor *(The 13th Sign)* 2017

Short Stories and Poetry

One Sixth of a Gill *(The 13th Sign)* 2014

From Bedtime On *(The 13th Sign)* 2018 (2nd edition)

With Double Blade *(The 13th Sign)* 2018 (2nd edition)

Translation (from French)

The Last Love of Edith Piaf – Christie Laume *(Archipel)* 2014

A Pup in Your Life – Michel Hasbrouck 2008

Gentle Dog Training – Michel Hasbrouck *(Souvenir Press)* 2008

for Kaye and her John
who know the meaning of romance
and who will find no derring-don't in this book

CHAPTER ONE

S he woke with a throbbing headache, cramp in her legs and a
curious sensation of warmth along her back. The warmth moved
against her as she stretched her stiff limbs along the constraints of the
ditch. She took her time before opening her eyes, heavy with too little
sleep. The sun was already two hours high in the sky and she was
waking to painful proof that her choice of sleeping quarters had been
forced.

'I am still alive. I am here. I am no-one,' she whispered. She
remembered that she had a plan but the girl who made that plan was
dead. Had to be dead and stay dead. So who was she now? She
needed a name.

A groan beside her attracted her attention. The strange warmth
along her back, with accompanying thick white fur and the smell of
damp wool, was easily identified. The girl pushed against a solid
mass of giant dog, which shifted enough to let her get herself out of
the ditch, where they had curved together into the sides. She recognized him well enough even though she had no idea when he had
joined her in the dirt. A regular scrounger at table with the other curs,
all named 'Out of my way' or worse. You couldn't mistake this one
though, one of the mountain dogs bred to guard the sheep, his own
coat shaggy white with brindled parts on his back and ears. Only he

1

wouldn't stay with the flock, whatever anyone tried with him. He'd visit the fields happily enough but at the first opportunity he'd be back at the chateau. Perhaps he thought she was heading out to check on the sheep and that he'd tag along to see what he was missing.

'Useless dog,' she gave a feeble kick in his general direction. 'Can't even do one simple job. They say you're too fond of people to stay in the field with the sheep. Well, I've got news for you about people, you big stupid bastard of a useless dog. Nobody wants you.' She felt tears pricking and smeared them across her cheeks with an impatient, muddy hand. 'And if you've broken this, you'll really feel my boot.' She knelt on the edge of the ditch to retrieve an object completely hidden in a swathe of brocade.

She had counted on having the night to get away but by now there would be a search on. If Gilles had done a good job, they would find her bloody remnants well before there was any risk of them finding her living, angry self. If he had hidden the clues too well, they might keep searching until they really did find her. And if the false trail was found but too obvious, then there would be no let-up, ever. And she would never see Gilles again. She shivered, although the day was already promising the spring warmth typical of the south. She would never see Gilles again anyway, she told herself. He knew the risks as well as she did. And if it had to be done, then she was her mother's daughter and would never – 'Never!' she said aloud – forget that, whoever tried to make her. She was no longer a child but sixteen summers.

All around her, the sun was casting long shadows on the bare vineyards, buds showing on the pruned vine-stumps but no leaves yet. Like rows of wizened cats tortured on wires, the gnarled stumps bided their time. How morbid she had become these last months! Too long a winter and spent in company who considered torture-methods an amusing topic of conversation. Better to look forward. In a matter of weeks, the vines would start to green, and in another two months, the spectacular summer growth would shoot upwards and outwards but for now, all was still wintry grey.

There was no shelter in the April vineyards and the road stretched forward to Narbonne and back towards Carcassonne, pitted with the holes gouged by the severe winter of 1149. Along this road east-west, and the Via Domitia north-south, flowed the life-blood of the region, the trade and treaties, the marriage-parties and the armies, the hired escorts sent by the Viscomtesse de Narbonne and the murderers they were protection against. The girl knew all this and could list fifty fates worse than death, which were not only possible but a likely outcome of a night in a ditch. What she had forgotten was that as soon as she stood up in this open landscape, in daylight, she could see for miles – and be seen.

She looked back towards Carcassonne and chewed her lip. It was already too late. The most important reason why she should not have slept in a ditch beside the road came back to her along with the growing clatter of a large party of horse and, from the sound of it, wagons. The waking and walking was likely to be even more dangerous than the sleeping and it was upon her already.

The girl stood up straight, brushed down her muddy skirts and clutched her brocade parcel to her breast. She knew that following her instinct to run would serve for nothing against the wild mercenaries or, at best, suspicious merchants, who were surely heading towards her. She was lucky to have passed a tranquil night – or so the night now seemed compared with the bleak prospect in front of her. What a fool to rush from one danger straight into another, forgetting the basic rules of survival on the open road. To run now would make her prey so she searched desperately for another option. In her common habit, bedraggled and dirty, she was as invisible as she could hope to be. No thief would look twice at her, nor think she had a purse to cut, far less a ransom waiting at home. No reason to bother her.

What she could not disguise was that, common or not, she was young, female and alone, and the consequences of that had been beaten into her when she was five years old and followed a cat into the forest. Not, of course, that anything bad happened in the forest, where she had lost sight of the cat but instead seen a rabbit's white scut vanishing behind a tree, as she tried to tell her father when he found her. His hard hand cut off her words, to teach her obedience for

3

her own good, punctuated with a graphic description of the horrors she had escaped.

All that had not happened in the dappled light and crackling twigs beneath the canopy of leaves and green needles, visited her nightmares instead, with gashed faces and shuddering laughter as she ran and hid, always discovered. Until now, she *had* obeyed, and it had not been for her own good. Fool that she had been. But no more. Now she would run and hide, and not be discovered.

She drew herself up straight and tall. No, bad idea. Instead, she slumped, as ordinary as she could make herself, and felt through the slit in her dress, just below her right hip, for her other option should a quick tongue fail her. The handle fitted snugly into her hand and her fingers closed round it, reassured. The dagger was safe in its sheath, neatly attached to her under-shift with the calico ties she had laboriously sewn into the fabric in secret candle-light. She had full confidence in its blade, knowing well the meticulous care her brother gave his weapons. As to her capacity to use it, let the occasion be judge. And after that, God would be, one way or another.

By now, the oncoming chink of harness and thud of hooves was so loud that she could hardly hear the low growl beside her. The dog was on his feet, facing the danger. He threw back his head and gave the deep bark of his kind against the wolf. The girl crossed herself and the first horse came into sight.

Dragonetz considered their progress. They had been seven days on the road since Poitiers, and many had objected to the undignified haste. Such a procession of litters, wagons and horse inevitably travelled slowly but they had kept overnight stops as simple as possible, resting at the Abbey and with loyal vassals, strengthening the ties. Apart from Toulouse of course, where Aliénor had insisted on a 'courtesy visit', her smile as polite as a dog baring its teeth. It had taken all his diplomacy to talk her out of instructing her herald to announce 'Comtesse de Toulouse' among her many titles and she had found a thousand other ways to throw her embroidered glove in the young Comte's face.

It was no easy matter to be in the service of Aliénor, Queen of France, but he would say this for her; it was never dull. The Lord be thanked that she had decided to insult Toulouse by the brevity of her stay or he could not answer for the casualties that would have ensued. Two more days of travel should see them in Narbonne and safe with Ermengarda and then he could relax his guard to the usual twenty-four hour check on every movement near Aliénor.

He was aware of the bustle behind him, wheels stopping, voices raised, and he slowed his horse almost to a standstill, anticipating the imperious voice beside him. Aliénor had tired of the litter and, mounted on her favourite palfrey, reined in beside him. He declined his head. 'My Lady.' Queen of France she might be but like all born in Aquitaine, he had sworn fealty to Aquitaine and its Duchesse, and France came second.

'Amuse me,' Aliénor instructed her companion, her pearl earrings spinning. The Queen's idea of dressing down for travelling might have included one less bracelet, a touch less rouge on her exquisitely painted face, and a switch of jeweled circlet, but there was little other compromise. The fur edging her dress could have been traded for a mercenary army. And that was exactly as it should be, she would have told him, had he questioned the wisdom of flaunting her status on the open road. She might have been spoiled as a child but she had been taught that a Lord of Aquitaine commanded respect as much through display and largesse as through a mailed fist, and she had learned the lesson well. In Aquitaine, she was adored. France, however, was a different country and they did things differently there.

'Once,' he began, 'there was a beautiful lady with red-gold hair, riding a white palfrey between Carcassonne and Narbonne, unaware of the danger lurking on the road ahead...'

She laughed. The pearls on her circlet gleamed and the matching ear-rings danced. Some red-gold hair escaped its net and coils under her veil. Everything about Aliénor was impatient for action. 'We have travelled more dangerous roads than this, my friend.' She was referring to their trek two years earlier, when they took the cross and the road to Damascus, the road paved with good intentions and finishing as surely in hell as anything either of them had ever known. A Crusade started in all enthusiasm and finished in shame. Each of them had good reason to bury what they had shared and he said nothing.

She rallied. 'Wouldn't you love to deal with monsters, dragons and ogres instead of Toulouse and his wet-nurses?' Her smile clouded over again. 'Or the Frankish vultures, flapping their Christian piety over me. Do you know how Paris seems to me? Black, white and grey, the northern skies, the drab clothes, the drab minds. All the colour is being leeched out of my life, month by month and I cannot continue like this.'

'You must, my Lady. It is your birthright and your birth curse. You know this.'

'I cannot exercise my birthright when I am relegated to embroidery and garden design. It is insufferable.'

'Power does not always shout its presence, my Lady, and each of the two hundred men armed behind you on this road represent a thousand more ready to die at your command. Every word you speak has the weight of those men.'

'Tell that to my husband, the Monk!' was the bitter reply. Her companion knew better than to reply to treason, especially when it came from a wife's mouth. 'Oh to be free of Sackcloth and Ashes, to hear a lute without seeing a pursed mouth or hearing that bony friar Clairvaux invoke God's punishment on the ways of Satan.'

'Clairvaux,' her companion mused, 'Bernard of Clairvaux, now what was that story about him? No, I mustn't say, not to a lady.'

'But you must, my wicked friend, that's exactly what I need, gossip. The more scurrilous the better.'

'Scurrilous gossip? About the saintly Clairvaux? How could that be possible? Anyway it's an old tale so you'll have heard it before,' he teased.

'I want to hear it again,' she ordered.

'As my Lady commands. But don't blame me if you have nightmares.'

'I already have nightmares. And Clairvaux is the least of it, curse his skinny, goose-pimpled arse.'

'You've stolen the best of my tale, my Lady, for it does indeed concern his skinny, goose-pimpled arse.'

'Tell anyway.'

'Once –'

She cut him off. 'No troubadour tricks. No romancing the rogue. He doesn't deserve it.'

'So then, even Bernard was once a young man and his body was supple, muscled, toned, bronzed and –'

'For shame!'

'You prefer I leave out some of the detail of a young man's body? I've only just started.'

'The only toned bit of that man's body is his knees, for he is always on them, and it was ever so, whatever age he was. No, I shall have no description of him as a beautiful young man. Next part of the story, if you will.'

'I have to mention one part of the young man's anatomy, my Lady, for therein lies the story and the problem, from Bernard's point of view. He had stopped at an Inn and was served by a beautiful young serving girl, skin transparent as lace, hair golden as –'

'Yes, yes, a pretty girl. On!'

' – and poor Bernard found that part of his anatomy preferred to follow its own will rather than God's. Horrified at this inappropriate rectitude in the only situation where he would rather have been less rigid, he raced out the Inn as one possessed by a Demon, tore off his clothes and jumped into the freezing water of the village fountain, extinguishing all rebellious behaviour from his shivering, goose-pimpled body. And so ended the one and only moment when Bernard of Clairvaux wondered what a warm body would be like against his own. From then on, his body was ruled by icy regime.'

'It's not true.' Aliénor was rueful. 'He never took his clothes off.'

'My Lady, how can you doubt my word?'

'Your word as my Knight or your word as a troubadour, teller of outrageous tales?'

'The latter, my Lady,' he concurred sighing. 'But don't you think it makes a satisfying portrait – the shivering, naked monk in the fountain?'

'To the life,' she agreed. 'But I am no Bernard of Clairvaux and there are times, I too wonder what it would be like to hold a warm body against my own.' If this were an invitation, he gave no sign of taking it as such and she returned to the more entertaining subject. 'And did you hear the other one, how he ran into the street shouting that someone was trying to rob him –'

' – and it was some sinner after his virginity!'

'Must have been a blind, desperate sinner!' Aliénor called over her shoulder to the four Ladies-in-waiting keeping a discreet distance. 'Ladies, come join us. We are engaged in character destruction and the more the merrier.' As the other horses were jostled near enough to take turn-about beside the Queen, her companion's attention shifted to the road ahead, where a slight movement stabilized into an unmistakably human figure.

'Sire?' the alert came from one of his men up front.

No longer teasing, he ordered, 'My lady, you must fall back with your women. Keep to the middle. No-one sane walks this road alone and there is likely a trap ahead.' He had already moved ahead, throwing orders behind him as he caught up with his hand-picked vanguard. He glanced over his shoulder, satisfied that Aliénor was already invisible in the middle of a thick shield of armoured men.

Swords out, reins tight in one hand, they advanced on the lone figure standing at the roadside, who seemed to get smaller as they grew nearer.

'It's a woman, Sire!' his man exclaimed.

'Be on guard, Danton, a woman can have a band of cut-throats on hand as easily as a man,' but there was as much chance of hiding men in the open vineyards around them as behind a molehill. He sheathed his sword, and a signal passed back along the line in a wave of relief.

The Commander reined in beside a girl who stood stock-still, a great hound at her side, growling menaces. The entire procession ground to a halt behind its leader and Danton jumped out the saddle, sword unsheathed, eyes on the dog.

'No!' came instinctively from the girl, who stepped forward, interposing a reckless arm between Danton's approaching sword and the growling dog. Her other arm clutched some sort of large bundle close to her chest.

'No,' agreed the Commander, looking fixedly at the girl. 'Danton, I think the puppy would benefit from some space while we decide whether to slit its throat or not.' Danton backed off but kept his sword ready. It was obvious to all there that his leader was not only referring to the dog. 'You see,' he said gently, 'we can't be sure that you won't run across the fields, then get ahead of us and prepare your bandit-friends to slit our throats and steal our valuables. And that just wouldn't do.'

The girl looked at him, astonished. 'But I'm on my own!' Topaz eyes, like those of the hunting leopards in Alexandria, green shadows and muddy depths, sparks where there should have been fear. Topaz eyes and black hair, silky as the tents of the Moorish armies. Olive skin like a slave girl but smooth, unpitted, ripe. Her clothes spoke of the servant but the fire in her eyes did not.

Even more gently, he told her, 'We just can't take the risk. And so that gives us two choices.' She didn't move but he could see the movement of her long throat as she swallowed. 'Either Danton here is allowed to exercise his duty and his sword —' She neither flinched nor spoke. Interesting. Physical courage combined with the good sense not to provoke him. ' — or we must invite you to join our company.' Was that a frown? There was definitely some mystery here.

'What *is* going on?' Aliénor pushed her horse through to stand shoulder to shoulder beside the Commander's. 'Can't we just get on with the journey?'

'We can, my Lady, as soon as you tell me whether I must have this maid run through or packed with the other baggage.'

For a heartbeat he thought he had misjudged his Queen and that finally her wildness had overcome her humanity. Aliénor studied the girl. Then, after a tortuous pause that stabbed a hundred times, 'She has something to hide,' Aliénor stated, in a tone that reminded everyone present why they followed her. 'Muddy servant's clothes, alone by a ditch on the busiest road in Occitania... Who are you and what are you doing here?'

The girl looked down but she said nothing.

'No! Don't hit her,' the Commander and Aliénor spoke as one to prevent Danton showing what he thought of dumb insolence to the Queen. 'If you are told to hit her, you must deal with the dog first, not second, I think you'll find,' the Commander added unnecessarily, as the dog snapped the air where Danton had nearly been.

'Quite,' said Aliénor, her gaze level and merciless on the girl. 'As you see, it is dangerous to ignore me, and suggests guilt. What is in that package?'

'My belongings,' the girl muttered.

'Well, that wasn't so hard to say, was it,' Aliénor's eyes narrowed. 'Now open it up,' she ordered. The girl hesitated and Aliénor's voice steeled further. 'Either you open it yourself or Danton kills the dog, which he is very keen to do, and then it is opened by force while you are held very, very roughly by the arms. And then it gets worse, much worse. Am I clear?'

The girl's answer was to lay the brocade down on the rough stone. As she bent down, her hair swung clear of her neck and the Commander revised his first impression. Her skin was not flawless; a badly healed scar marred the clear skin of her left shoulder. His professional eye judged it to be deliberate, and whip rather than blade. With tenderness, she unwrapped her precious object until it was laid bare on the outspread brocade.

The musical instrument revealed was of reddish wood, so highly polished that the girl's figure gleamed dully in the deep, pear-shaped bowl. Three circles of cream enamel inlay decorated the wood, each with a design of arabesques and interlaced points. Eight strings, frets, a bent peg-board for tuning.

'Al-Oud,' he breathed.

She looked puzzled. 'It's a mandora.'

'And obviously stolen.' One of Aliénor's Ladies had edged forward. At first sight, she was no less magnificent than her mistress, but whereas Aliénor's finery was merely the setting for Aliénor herself, this Lady was diminished by her trappings. Her painted face seemed set as a mask, her fur trimming too broad as if to compensate for lesser quality, her jeweled ear-rings too glittery, obviously paste to a connoisseur. 'Cut off her hand and let's be done with her.'

'And your reasoning in this?' Aliénor asked quietly. No-one doubted her willingness to judge and, if that be the judgement, sentence as proposed. No-one questioned that the girl's hand was forfeit for her theft. Most would have judged this lenient, for such an instrument was a unique treasure. Had they not been on the road, the girl could be an example to others, could be caged, and tormented by the public before the next phase of a long, slow death. No-one present would have flinched at such a necessity, although some would have enjoyed it more than others. However, they were on the road and there was no time for such deliberation.

'My Lady, how would a servant come by such a thing, except dishonestly – and servant she clearly is, by her clothes. And I can think of only one thing a woman might be doing alone on this road! My guess is that she has stolen this instrument and fled, offering her legs in the air, until she can sell her other goods at market. She couldn't even tell you her name, my Lady! What more proof of guilt do you need!'

The girl's eyes blazed but she just picked up the mandora and clutched it to her. Aliénor's eyes met those of her Commander as the fingers of the girl's left hand found their habitual place on the frets and she cradled the instrument in the position they had seen a thousand times, in every banquet hall of the civilized world.

'The proof is easy,' Aliénor declared. 'If the instrument is yours, play for us, girl.'

Amid the jangles and snorts of restless horses, the mutterings of people impatient to get on, and the birdsong of amorous April, the girl closed her eyes. She thrummed the strings, adjusted the pegs and cleared her throat. Then she sang a scale. The sweetness of the simple ut re mi fa so la already held promise and when she opened her eyes and wound her voice round the strings in perfect harmony, the company around her hushed. The well-known words of the Aubade, the Dawn Song, floated like apple blossom on the breeze and the dog lay down, silent, beside the singer.

> 'A-bed beside his lady-love,
> Her own true knight stopped kissing.
> 'My sweet, my own, what shall we do?
> Day is nigh and night is over
> We must be parted, my self missing
> All the day away from you.'

> If only day would never come
> If only night could spare the pain
> Of each new parting, little Death
> That leaves enough to die again.

> The Watchman calls the hour of Dawning
> Bids me stand and face the day,
> Exiles me to constant Morning
> Grieving that I must away.

> Know that whereso'er I wander
> Never shall I find true rest
> Without the circle of your kisses
> And may you love your Night the best.

> 'My sweet, my own, what shall we do?
> Day is nigh and night is over
> We must be parted, my self missing
> All the day away from you.'

The last notes of the mandora hung plaintive in the air as Danton sheathed his sword.

'You have answered the charge of theft and we find you innocent,' Aliénor's measured voice broke the spell. 'What have you to say, that you refuse to give your name to me?'

'I do have a name to give you, my Lady. My songster's name is Estela de Matin.'

'Then Estela de Matin it shall be and such a musician is always welcome at my court, whether man or woman. If you would like to join us, we can explore the mysteries surrounding you at our leisure.'

If the girl saw the mailed fist in the glove of this 'invitation' she gave no sign but curtsied acceptance and wrapped up her instrument again in its brocade.

'What do you think?' Aliénor asked her Commander.

'A sweet voice but empty,' was the verdict. 'It lacks the maturity the song needs.'

'What made you choose that one, of all the songs?' Aliénor asked the girl, who had looked down, hiding her flushed face, but now raised her eyes to meet the Commander's.

'I love the song,' she said simply. 'It is the work of a Master and it seemed right to me and I thought everyone would know the song...' she tailed off.

'You chose well,' Aliénor told her. 'And yes, we know the song, don't we.'

'Too well, my Lady.' The Commander excused himself and rode back down the line.

A bulky man, with wild black hair and beard, pushed his horse to the front. 'My Lady, I am sent for the girl.'

'Take her, Raoulf and see that she is comfortable.' Raoulf dismounted, took a step toward Estela and the dog half-rose. 'No, dog,' she told him. 'Go! You are not my dog! I don't want you. Go away!' The dog watched but made no move as she went towards Raoulf. He lifted her onto his saddle, with her mandora, as easily as if she were a puppet, then he jumped up behind her. A dainty boot lashed out at Estela's shins as she passed, with a murmured 'So sorry,' that dripped poison and smelled strongly of musk. Estela would remember the smell but for now she was beyond caring. There was just one question to resolve before she gave in to an overwhelming weariness, of body and spirit.

'Who is your Commander?' she asked Raoulf.

'You're not going to pretend you don't know,' was the strange reply.

'Truly,' she pressed.

'Dragonetz los Pros, of course,' he stated, as if it was obvious. And it should have been.

'I thought he would be older,' she said. Dragonetz, Aliénor's knight, who had earned his title 'los Pros', 'the Brave', as a Crusader, when so many had come home with titles like 'Brown-britches.' Dragonetz, the Master Troubadour, the writer of the song she had presumed to sing in front of him. And the inanities she had come out with! He would think it deliberate! Her cheeks burned and she was only too pleased to be unloaded like a sack of corn onto a simple mattress in a wagon. When Raoulf pulled a coverlet over her with his calloused hands, and told her to rest now, she responded automatically, 'Thank you, Gilles,' and drifted with the bump bump rhythm of the wagon into deepest sleep.

CHAPTER TWO

E rmengarda, Viscomtesse of Narbonne, glanced idly through the narrow window, over the city wall to the River Aude, swollen with winter rain and snow melt flowing down from the mountains. Another few weeks and it would be time for the sheep to go back up from the plains to the heights for summer grazing. The reckoning from the harsh winter was being tallied daily in the ledgers of the clerks, who reported conscientiously to their mistress. They had no option as Ermengarda knew every last solidus in her coffers, and if Narbonne was the richest city in Occitania, it was in no small measure due to its ruler.

Today, however, Ermengarda had more pressing and personal concerns. Within the next day, few days, week, depending on how the journey went, she was expecting the Duchesse d'Aquitaine with a full entourage of Ladies and men-at-arms. The Palace had been preparing for weeks, storing grain, wine, hams; sweeping and strewing herbs in bedchambers; laying straw and placing troughs by empty stables. No detail was too small, from the Narbonne coat of arms on the heavy fabric newly draping the windows of Aliénor's chambers, to the phials of oriental perfume by the bathing tubs.

Like the ducks. Ermengarda watched as a group of mallards seemed to float along with the current while their little legs were paddling for all they were worth. And the paddling would continue for as long as Aliénor honoured Narbonne with her presence and with the requirement that Narbonne feed, quarter and entertain four hundred personnel. Ermengarda sighed. The timing was not good. Apart from the disastrous winter, her people were suffering in the wake of the great failure known as the Second Crusade. Also considered by some, more specifically, as Aliénor's great failure.

Narbonne relied on trade, and trade relied on trust and security. The sea-captains needed to set sail from their safe harbour without fear of being attacked by Genoese pirates when they'd barely left the bay, and in the certainty of re-victualing and repairing boat damage while they bought Moorish goods in the spice ports of Oltra mar. In addition to the sea-ways, overland routes had to be safe from thieves and brigands. And now look at the state of things! Every day her captains and merchants brought Ermengarda new problems; news of peaceful traders imprisoned, tortured and disfigured in deliberate reprisals against any Christians; news of safe routes barred by weather and wreckers. Everywhere, the balance for which she worked so hard shifted into insanity. Soon the trading season would begin in earnest and she must use all of her connections to repair the damage as best she could.

So, how did she feel about Aliénor coming? They had last met before the Crusade, Aliénor blazing with the passion of her adventure and Ermengarda full of misgivings, like a spectre at a wedding, a crone spreading ill-will and evil omens with her caution and reservations. Having been right gave her no pleasure now and she was slow to judge Aliénor as harshly as much of the world judged her. This elegant woman, her senior by ten years, had dazzled fourteen-year old Ermengarda with her intellect and exquisite taste, had shared her inside knowledge of the most powerful men in the land along with her secret recipes for cheek rouge, had called her a friend – and still did.

But even at fourteen, Ermengarda had her own hard-earned understanding of powerful men – and women – and she never forgot that Aliénor's authority, over however great a realm, was harnessed in uneasy pairing with the King of France, Louis, while she, Ermengarda, *was* Narbonne. There was no doubt that Aquitaine was Aliénor's but to what extent did Aliénor belong to Aquitaine? Her eye had roamed to France and rumour said she was still not satisfied.

Rumours. Ermengarda collected rumours along with the daily reckoning of accounts. It was impossible that Aliénor could have carried out half that she was credited or blamed for Oltra mar, overseas, but even so she had played a part that ran to twenty verses in the latest songs, some versions of which had been banned for the coming visit. Although Aliénor might be amused by the stories of herself riding bare-breasted with her Amazons to hack down the Infidels, Ermengarda did not think that a kind hostess would encourage the singing of 'the whore of Antioch' in which Aliénor's trips to her uncle's bed became increasingly lewd. Whether she had actually made those trips to her uncle's bed was one of the many little details that might become clearer after Ermengarda saw Aliénor again. Could it have happened? It seemed more likely to Ermengarda than the tale of the Amazon army. It was important to know what you were called behind your back and Ermengarda knew perfectly well that she was 'the shopkeeper' and Aliénor 'the whore'. To some extent she *would* always be a shopkeeper, Ermengarda acknowledged.

Her thoughts flowed downstream with the Aude. The ducks' apparent serenity had been short-lived and five male mallards were attacking each other viciously in their attempt to mate the one female. Ermengarda watched as two males, still fighting each other, held the female underwater in their mating frenzy and drowned her. *Be careful, Aliénor, be very careful. Not all lovers go down on their knees.*

A respectful knock called her attention. Time to attend to the shop window and make sure that Narbonne looked every inch the jewel of the Mediterranean. She hoped Aliénor would have the good sense to send riders ahead that would give her at least one day's warning of the onslaught.

But of course. She smiled. That charming Dragonetz would be the one to send ahead. And he would be sure to remember the sort of courtesy that put her in a good mood.

'Rabbi Abraham ben Isaac, you may enter,' she instructed. *To business.*

'Have you sent ahead to warn the Lady Ermengarda?' Dragonetz asked Raoulf, as they checked wagons and horses on the grazing land outside the castle of Douzens. Only a select few humans and animals would pass the night inside the security of the walls and Dragonetz clearly wanted to be sure that the party outside was as well-protected as possible.

'Michels the Weasel and Gervais went this afternoon with your message, Sire. Tonight we halt at Douzens, tomorrow night with the white friars at Fontfroide and we should reach Narbonne after noon on Wednesday.'

'Good man. Let's hope the road continues trouble-free. And the girl? What do you make of her?'

Raoulf pursed his lips, considering. 'I can fetch her for you if you have time for a tumble…' He felt a point of pressure at his back, a tease of steel suggesting he'd said enough. But he hadn't said nearly enough. 'You're a man, you can't carry on like this.' The pressure made its point a fraction clearer and Raoulf was careful not to move. 'Take that damn thing away from me, Dragonetz, unless you're really going to knife someone who knew you when you were a mewling puppy.'

'You really shouldn't test my temper with your cesspit wisdom. You're too slow to stop me leaving a lesson across your clothing if not your skin.' Dragonetz returned his dagger to wherever he secreted it. 'My mewling days. Thank you for reminding me. Unless of course, you are referring to my more recent behaviour?'

Raoulf would by far have preferred the dagger to the jagged words. 'Enough, Dragonetz! Leave it behind. What happened, happened. People die in a war and you can't punish yourself forever.' *Mistake,* he thought, the moment he spoke. He had been wrong in thinking the tone could not chill further.

'Thank you for that reminder too. And as I've made clear enough I think, I always appreciate opinions on my conduct.' Raoulf knew better than to interrupt the silence. Amid the clanking of harness and metal, creaking of wheel wood, human bustle, a clear soprano voice lilted a song over to the camp from somewhere near the river.

Raoulf nodded approval or gave curt instructions as they rounded each wagon. He gestured at empty buckets and men scurried to refill the water for the horses. One look from Dragonetz was enough to correct anyone mistaking this stop for journey's end. 'And?' Dragonetz prompted, his jaw setting in even more severe lines.

'And, Sire?' Raoulf countered.

'I believe I asked you a question.'

'The girl.'

'Quite. And it's a military question not a man's.'

'Your loss,' Raoulf couldn't resist but carried on quickly. 'I don't think she's playing a game of bait and rob but she's not telling the truth either. I'm sure she's alone – good, that means no cut-throats round the next bend. But there again, she's alone – bad. Why is she alone? Her hands say she's no servant. I'd say that all she knows of the world came to her by songs and travelers to wherever she lived. I don't think she's ever left there before. Seems innocent, sheltered, behind that air of know-all. Didn't even know you. And the way she sings says she's no ordinary girl. She was exhausted when I laid her in the wagon and when I covered her up, she called me Gilles.'

'A lover, a husband...' Dragonetz wondered. 'Someone who'll come looking for her, someone who'll want recompense for his damaged goods.'

'She's not damaged by me! Yet!' Raoulf retorted. 'I was waiting for your word first but if you don't want her –'

'And neither do you. Nor any of the men.' It was an order. 'If she's not what she seems, we should be all the more careful that she *isn't* damaged by any of us. I want her chaperoned by the Ladies.'

'Purely as a military consideration?'

'Purely. I'll have enough problems caused by Lady Aliénor

amusing herself politically without adding some enraged Castellan from the back woods chasing my hide.'

'Not lover, if you want my opinion, nor husband, this Gilles person. She might have been tired but she still knew it was me, or rather someone like me, serving her I'd have said. Yes, someone like me.'

'*Is* there another one like you?' Dragonetz was sardonic. 'Then God help us all.'

'Thank you, Sire.'

'Raoulf, don't you ever get tired of people under-estimating you? The big black bear lumbering after young Dragonetz?'

'Have you seen a bear catch a fish, Sire? The slower people think me, the more I can find out and the easier I can catch them.' He hesitated. 'There's something I've been meaning to say to you –'

'What, still more? Thank the Lord the journey will be over soon if it ferments so many thoughts. Well, go on. You might as well spit it out man, now you've started.'

Raoulf was conscious of the need to choose his words carefully but finally he came out with, 'You know Lady Fortune and her wheel?' Dragonetz nodded impatiently. 'Well, it doesn't do to bind yourself to the Lady on the way up or she won't let you go on the fall. So if you're bound, now is the time to loose the ties.'

The bustle was dying down around the camp as men settled to chew the fat round camp-fires in the waning light. Pink rays from the setting sun glinted off abandoned armour and swords. An assailant would have to be foolish or very strong to chance his arm against two hundred fighting men and a Templar stronghold, even in a surprise attack. The Watch was sound, no sign of danger anywhere. Dragonetz sighed.

'You care about me, Raoulf, don't you.'

Although it was expressed as a statement, Raoulf answered all the same, his matted black hair blowing back from his face as he looked down at Dragonetz, eyes tinged blood-red from the sun. 'I swore an oath, Sire.'

The two men held each other's gaze and it was Raoulf who

dropped his first. 'You take second watch,' Dragonetz ordered. They both knew that if trouble was coming, that's when it was most likely. 'I'd better oil my charm for dinner with our hosts.'

'No harm will come, Sire.'

'That you still believe so, Raoulf, is only one of the differences between us. Until tomorrow.'

'Sire.'

Dragonetz watched the broad back retreating, heard Raoulf's coarse remark and the laughter in response as he mingled with the other soldiers. It was a pity but Raoulf would have to go. He had become a liability. Dragonetz refused to be loved by anyone, man, woman or child. Never again. He would indeed loose the ties, all the ties, including those with the Lady whom Raoulf designated Fortune. But first he had business to conclude.

So she must think of herself as Estela now. She splashed her face in the stream, which was already losing the warmth of the afternoon sunshine. Downstream, men were taking their horses to drink, easing into the routines of setting up camp. The usual pack of dogs that hung round human dwellings was scrounging for scraps round the cook-fires. If there was a flash of white fur among the blacks and browns, Estela didn't notice. Beside her, other women were dabbling feet and arms, gossiping about laundry and kisses; no time for either until they reached Narbonne and then it seemed that they would catch up on both.

Guillelma paid her no attention as she chatted to her friends but the girl knew that however sympathetic the raw-boned servant had been, she was also her prison-warder. Not that Estela had anywhere to run to, nor that she even wanted to run. It was soothing to flow with the river, follow Guillelma to do 'what we women do', be given bread to eat and water to drink. Perhaps she would be a servant after all, she mused. Laundry and kisses.

Was it possible to begin life at sixteen? It had to be. 'Estela de

Matin', the Morning Star, could be whoever she wanted to be. She wouldn't be the first troubadour to hide behind her chosen name. Forget the laundry. She would be famous like Cercamon, 'Seek the world', and no-one would care what she had been before. Cercamon's childhood was buried with him. Whether he had been a pot-boy or a Castellan's son, no-one knew or cared but everyone sang his songs and his name would live forever.

Estela sang the Cercamon opening *'Ab lo pascor m'es bel qu'eu chan'*, 'At Easter time 'tis joy to sing,' and flushed as she realized the chat had stopped and she was the centre of attention.

'I told you so,' Guillelma informed the others, as if she'd won a wager. 'Don't stop, pet, it's lovely. A real breath of spring, you are.'

'You carry on,' encouraged a woman whose body seemed about to explode from her coarse burnet gown at any moment. As the sun burnished the distant hills, the women were gilded statues, sitting by the rose-gold water, listening to the unaccompanied, plaintive solo. Inevitably the song darkened, turned to infidelity and loss and when Estela reached the lines

'Miels li fora ja non nasqes
Enans qe'l failliment fezes
Don er parlat tro en peitau'

the sun dipped and Guillelma shivered.

'Very nice but we'd best be getting dry and warm,' she interrupted Estela, who stopped on a false note that jarred her entire body. She blinked, still lost in the world of the song. Guillelma took her by the arm and led her back to the wagon that seemed to contain whatever meagre possessions the woman had. Satisfied that they were alone, Guillelma shook her head and glared at Estela. 'You'll get yourself killed, you will!'

Estela just looked at her wide-eyed.

'And you really don't know why, do you!' Guillelma whispered. 'Singing about her being better off not born than sinful,' Estela still looked blank, 'and that people were talking about it all the way to

Poitiers. Who do you think the song's about! And what do you think she'd do if she heard you singing it!'

Understanding dawned and Estela wished it hadn't. Poitiers, the capital of Aquitaine. 'But I didn't!' Estela exclaimed.

'Well, that's fine then. You didn't.' Her voice was its usual matter of fact tone. 'And we'll all keep it like that. You didn't. And we didn't hear you. And hope to God it stays like that! But I won't be there with you this evening so just keep your mouth shut and learn everything you can, quickly. '

'What do you mean?'

'The Lady Aliénor has taken into her head that you should eat with your betters in the keep this evening, at the bottom table of course, but I've been asked to make you respectable all the same.' She frowned and studied Estela. 'Silk purse and sow's ear come to mind but we'll do what we can.'

'You know how to make me ... respectable?' Estela didn't know how to put the question tactfully.

Guillelma threw back her head and laughed without restraint. 'You mean how can a peasant like me fit you up as more of a lady?' Estela flushed. 'Because, my dear, this peasant looks after the Queen's wardrobe and when we're not on the blessed road for weeks on end, this peasant dresses herself up a bit too. But yes, it's my needle not my good looks that got me where I am.'

'I'm sorry,' Estela couldn't meet the other woman's eyes.

'Like I said, you'll get yourself killed. But you might as well have some fun before then.' She motioned Estela into the wagon and the girl could now see open boxes piled with bodices, shoes, furs, head-dresses. Guillelma seemed to see order in this chaos and almost disappeared into a trunk, muttering 'gold, yellow... scarlet too osten-tatious... pretty but not standing out too much... impossible...'

When she came up for air, Guillelma was holding three gowns, which she placed on top of a pile while she searched for shift and bodice. Then five pairs of soft leather boots were added to the pile after a calculated glance to estimate Estela's shoe size. While her own clothes fell at her feet, accompanied with clucks and mutters of 'a tuck there, no flesh on the girl, none at all,' Estela wondered what was going to be expected of her. And what more she could get wrong.

'And if I get asked to sing?' Estela stammered. 'What shall I do?'

'Sing,' was the short answer then Guillelma relented. 'If you want advice from a peasant,' she looked up from lacing a boot, 'don't take your instrument and do make yourself invisible. And if the worst comes to the worst, you already know two songs not to sing, so I should try a third one. Who knows, even you might be third time lucky.'

Oh, Lord. She had forgotten Dragonetz and he would be there too.

And Aliénor and their Templar hosts. Dear God, were there any problems with 'Assatz es or' oimai q'eu cha,' 'Now it's time to sing'? She checked the lyrics mentally. One reference to Saint John. That would be all right in front of the knights, wouldn't it? Well, it would just have to be! Singing never used to be this complicated.

April evenings were still cool enough for the heat from the blazing logs in the great fireplace to be more than welcome. Shadows flickered on the stone walls from the torches lit at intervals in the sconces round the Hall. The Commanderie at Douzens was less than twenty years old but of basic military construction and rarely saw guests of this rank. Luckily, the well-stocked cellars, the well-staffed kitchens, and the tables laden with fresh bread and hams, richly confirmed the Templars' reputation for hospitality. From the High Table, Aliénor scanned her company.

Her gaze travelled below the salt, where she noted and approved her little protégée, black hair gleaming against a tawny gown, sitting quietly among the lower household personnel. To one side of her, was the distinctive headgear of a dark-skinned Moor, no doubt brought back from the last Crusade. Estela's eyes were cast down, showing no preference for one companion over another. There would be no music tonight but Aliénor was not impatient to launch her new star. Dragonetz could refine the youngster first. And then there would be the pleasure of watching Ermengarda's face when she heard that voice. It was surely fate that had brought such a jewel to her and she intended to set it off to advantage.

She continued her appraisal of the gathering. Various knights of the Brotherhood, and some minor landholders attached to the Commanderie, with their wives or sisters. At the High Table, the Master, Peter Radels, red-faced and sweating from exertion or wine, or both; the joint commanders, Isarn of Moleria and Bernard of Roquefort; another powerful Brother, Bernard of the Casul Revull; two of her Ladies, Philippa and Sancha, the latter in a teeth-grinding glitter of blue beads and scarlet satin that clashed not only in itself but also with the brilliant red of Aliénor's own garb; and then, of course, there was Dragonetz.

Aliénor's knight was the model of courtesy, bending his head as he passed two words in exchange with one lady, three words in exchange with the other, then in an animated lengthy conversation with the Master. Aliénor smiled. There was little doubt where Dragonetz' interest lay and she guessed from the few words she could overhear that he was drilling for information on water power and mills, light relief to him, no doubt.

'My Lady, we cannot leave Damascus and Edessa in the hands of Infidel.' Isarn was waiting for her response and Aliénor returned to her duty. There would be no light relief for her.

'That is why I took the Cross,' she replied. 'And we have not forgotten our lands Oltra mar, however hard the last lesson we took there. It must steady our hand and thought for a more successful venture.'

'My thoughts, exactly, my Lady. Perhaps you can convey some of our suggestions to King Louis.' If Aliénor flinched at being taken for a mere messenger, she gave no sign, but continued in her discovery and analysis of the strengths and loyalties of the knights of Solomon.

The Master leaned confidentially towards Dragonetz, who poured him another cup of wine – good, local red wine from the Corbières, fruity and warming. 'You should join us, Dragonetz.'

'I did consider it. Last time I was asked.'

'You should,' Radels persisted.

'The vow of poverty concerned me a little.' Dragonetz swirled the wine in his silver goblet, mischief in his eyes.

Radels just laughed. 'We should have had a whole Kingdom when Alfonso died but as it is, we've not done too badly.'

Dragonetz was well aware of the fiasco sixteen years earlier when Alfonso el Batallador, King of Aragon and Navarre, had died heirless, leaving his entire estate to the knights Templar. In such a manner did a rich man buy his welcome to the next world, while alienating the people he left behind in this one. Wisely, the knights had negotiated their way out of their inheritance, avoiding decades of bloody warfare and adding to their already legendary treasure store. And, according to an increasingly loose-tongued Radels, Douzens had gained its share of the booty, including some very interesting vassals, who were next on Dragonetz' conversational list, after just one or two more questions for the Master while there was still some chance of a lucid response.

'And I'm sure you will continue to do well, with such a head for business,' Dragonetz assured the other man, whose head was thrown back more and more frequently in the business of his cups. 'Perhaps you can enlighten me on one such business matter. Let us suppose that a man had a promissory note from the Brothers of Antioch, and he wished to purchase land in this region, would such a note be acceptable to the vendor?'

The glint in Radels' eyes suggested that he was not too far gone to understand the situation. So much the better. 'A note of some value, I take it?'

'Indeed.'

'Then that would depend on whether the vendor is a Brother, an associate or completely other. '

'Suppose that any of the three is a possibility.'

'If, for example you – sorry, I mean, such a man – were to buy, for instance, a stretch of the Aude where a mill might be built,' Dragonetz acknowledged the hit and wondered just how much wine it took to blunt this particular brain. More, evidently. He topped up both their cups and beckoned a servant to refill the pitcher. 'and if this man were to buy his land from the Brethren, the note would be as good as gold from al-Andalus.' Dragonetz nodded, concentrating. 'And if this man were to approach our neighbouring brethren at the Abbey, who might also have such land for sale,' Dragonetz took a thoughtful sip. Now he was getting somewhere! 'then they might be willing to accept the note if it were accompanied by a personal signature, say, of a local Commander, making it even more flexible as currency, but they will of course fleece this man to his naked hide in the name of God and the Abbey.'

So the wine was having some effect. 'And in the name of God and the Commanderie, this man might get a bargain?' Dragonetz queried smoothly.

'Indeed.'

'And the third situation? Of purchase from one without connections to the Brotherhood?'

Radels pursed his lips. 'More tricky. Some men of affairs understand the benefits of our notes, particularly if they can read. Others stay behind the times and prefer oxen and fishing rights. Believe me, Dragonetz, the day will come when promissory parchment will be current, universally.'

'But meanwhile?'

'Meanwhile, the note promises to pay the bearer the sum stated and any Commanderie will honour that note in solidi, so if this man needs to pay in weight of silver he would need to present me with the note in proper manner.'

Dragonetz had been through the options a hundred times during the journey and needed only the facts he had gleaned from Radels to come to a decision. He knew what he wanted, he knew who had it and he knew how to get it, and in return he had given away only what he intended to – not a bad evening's work. He stretched his long legs under the table and eased muscles a little weary from saddle and wooden bench.

'A personal note from a Commander would indeed be a great favour.' Radels' eyes gleamed, 'That could be arranged.'

'And of course, as a little thank you to the Commander we could conclude the other purchase of which we spoke. My word on that and let's forget this dreary subject.'

'You will not regret it. Send the note to me and I will issue a new one for the reduced sum, with my personal guarantee for the note.'

'So be it. Now, tell me where this excellent wine is produced and how we convince my Lady to stay here instead of invading Narbonne, where embroidery and dress fashions will surely numb my brain. And for God's sake, no Crusader's tales, if you wish me to stay awake.'

Radels laughed and needed no more encouragement to vaunt the gustatory pleasures of his domain. Long after he'd agreed that the wine was a perfect combination with the strange salty taste of a blue cheese from the caves of Roquefort, which Radels insisted was a local treasure, Dragonetz excused himself and joined the increasingly free movement round the Hall, as, the meal over, people sought particular conversations. Making brief obeisance to Aliénor, Dragonetz told her, 'I shall make your wishes known to the girl, my Lady, then please excuse me. I would check the camp before taking whatever sleep this night gives me.' She waved and smiled her approval, as relaxed as if they were alone, both of them knowing that every gesture was marked and analysed.

Estela couldn't be unaware of Dragonetz' approach. He was unhurried and polite but somehow there was never anyone in his way, and the conversation beside her stopped as smoothly as he did.

'My Lady,' he greeted her. She flushed. 'May I?' He waited for her assent and then took a place that became magically vacant on the bench beside her. Almost gently, he continued, 'That's better. I see no reason for you to crick your neck looking up at me. The Lady Aliénor wishes me to tutor you in music. We will reach Narbonne the day after next and can begin then but if you wish to ride with me tomorrow, we can make arrangements. You ride?'

'Yes.'

His voice was even gentler and lower. 'Al-Hisba al-Andalus.' She looked at him, startled, then realised that he was no longer speaking to her but to the Moor, although he barely turned towards him.

'Sire,' the man responded.

'You know who I am?'

'Yes.'

'It seems I have bought you.' The man's face remained expressionless, his sharp cheekbones, hooked nose and firm lips slashes of deep gold in the flickering torchlight. 'There is only one problem,' Dragonetz continued. 'I don't have your consent.'

'You don't need it.' The reply was a fact, stated like any other.

'But I do, you see.' Dragonetz kept his voice low, smiled and looked at Estela. Anyone watching would think his conversation with her. She was mesmerised, like a deer startled in the woods. 'I will not have you, unwilling.' His eyes were still on Estela and she shivered, the small hairs on the back of her neck prickling.

'If I say no, I will be punished.' Even Estela knew what that meant and that this choice was no choice, like her own she thought. Between the Devil and the deep sea.

But the Devil spoke again. 'If you say no, I shall tell them I miscalculated, that I cannot afford a new man as well as another little matter that I have in hand – no blame on you.'

The whites of the Moor's eyes shone and met the unreadable black in the other man's. 'If it is Allah's will, so be it.'

'Be ready to leave tomorrow morning after Tierce. Al-Hisba al-Andalus,' he mused, 'the man from Andalusia. What is your given name?'

'That, you have not bought, my Lord.' Estela held her breath. There could only be one reaction to such insolence.

Dragonetz breathed out hard. Then he laughed. 'Be there, tomorrow,' he said, his eyes still on Estela as he stood abruptly, moved further down the table and spoke to some of the men attached to the Commanderie, tenants and small land-owners.

By the time Estela worked out what she should have said, Dragonetz had left the Hall. As had the Moor.

CHAPTER THREE

E stela had slept badly again. Her straw mattress was comfortable enough and Guillelma's snoring was mere background noise, as were the grunts and shifting of the two other women sharing the wagon space. The fact that she had dozed off and on during the day would not normally have prevented her catching up on much-needed sleep, especially now she seemed safe from pursuit. No, the problems were in her own head, thoughts chasing each other like frantic mice when the cat is loosed among them. *You wanted to be a troubadour. You dreamed of learning from the best. Why do you feel like a smacked child? Because he treated you like a nothing? Used you as cover? Like a jongleur throwing a ball in the air with one hand while magicking a rose from the other. Throwing you in the air and magicking the Moor. What was that all about anyway? And yet, he trusted you to watch and say nothing. And you have the chance to perform at court. But what if your voice and fingers let you down? What if you're not good enough? Why did he look at you like that?* The complicity disturbed her as much as the intensity of a steady, black-eyed gaze, meant only to misdirect. She had been cheated. But of what?

She heard the call to prayer at prime, imagined the knights in silent progression to their Chapel. What would it be like to be part of an Order, follow the Rule, obey without question? For a moment, she imagined the relief of letting go, giving up responsibility for her life, responsibility for life itself, to something higher. Poverty and chastity seemed to be her doom anyway so why not in a convent? The grey of pre-dawn outlined the shapes in the wagon, women and baggage. There had to be something more than this! A verse ran through Estela's head as Guillelma stirred.

'Aissi-m te amors franc
Qu'alor mon cor no-s vire...'

'Love holds my heart so clear and true
That I see no-one else but you...'

Would she ever know love like that, true and hers alone, or was that just for songs? She sighed. At least she had the songs – until of course Dragonetz destroyed that too. Not that she contemplated ducking his invitation. She was experienced enough to know that the only sure way of failing was not to try, and an invitation from Dragonetz was a summons she knew she had to face. The first rays of the sun found their way under the improvised curtains and Estela joined Guillelma in the morning routines, as all around her soldiers struggled into chainmail hauberks and coifs, while servants carried pots and stoked the cooking fires, and horses were led to the stream before saddling up.

When the last cooking fire had been stamped out, the last knife and water-bottle stored in a provisions wagon, and when Guillelma had assured Estela a hundred times that the mandora was safely locked in with Aliénor's jeweled accessories, the company was ready to break camp. The moment Aliénor and her Ladies finally appeared, still paying the necessary compliments as they said farewell to their hosts, Dragonetz signaled the vanguard and another day on the road began. Aliénor chose to travel by palanquin this time, with one of her Ladies, and the others followed her example in wagons rather more luxurious than the one in which Estela had spent the night.

A breeze freshened Estela's cheeks and she forgot to protect her skin from the sun, enjoying the exercise as she walked with Guillelma and the other women, at the back of the procession. The vineyards gave way to copses and more undulating countryside, and in the rhythm of the march, Estela lost track of time. Once again it was the way the general chat stopped that alerted her to Dragonetz' presence before he was physically before her, this time on a black destrier rather than the palfrey of the previous day, and leading a placid grey mare.

'My lady,' he bent his head to her, then jumped out of the saddle. 'Would you care to join me? Guillelma?' He passed the reins of both horses to Guillelma, the destrier shying nervously at the new situation. 'Shush, my Seda,' he soothed the horse, and explained to Estela, 'he's been attached to a wagon too long and needs his master.' Dragonetz bent and cupped his hands.

Without thinking, Estela placed a booted foot onto the offered step, as she had always done, and hoisted herself sideways onto the saddle. Guillelma passed her the grey's reins and she took them easily in her right hand, still looking at the stallion. 'He's beautiful, just like silk.' Seda was high and finely boned, a black shimmer. Of course, a palfrey ambled comfortably for a long journey whereas Seda was built for a tourney and too highly strung for riding mile after mile. It would be like using the silk of the destrier's name to wash dishes. Presumably, Dragonetz thought he would need his destrier at journey's end. Or didn't want to leave him behind. Such a horse was worth more than most men's land.

Dragonetz stroked the horse's neck, downwards, along the rippling muscle. 'He is beautiful,' he agreed, as he swung himself into the saddle and carved a path through to the front. The mare didn't need pressure on her side to follow the big black placidly. Estela let her mount have her head. 'Tou', Dragonetz called back over his shoulder when Estela asked her horse's name and was told, 'Tou.' Gentle.

'Well, Tou,' Estela murmured, 'looks like it's you and me now.'

They threaded their way to the head of the main procession, a vanguard of five soldiers just within sight, checking out the road ahead. They had already given safe passage to some merchants and their wagons and exchanged news briefly with a troop of Ermengarda's patrol en route to Carcassonne. Estela felt a lurch of disappointment that the Moor was also there, waiting for them, on a horse much like her own. It seemed she had hoped for some undivided attention as much as she feared it and the anti-climax thudded dully when Dragonetz said courteously, 'Al-Hisba al-Andalus is willing to share his learning with you. Please excuse me.' With that he wheeled and was gone back into the body of the company. She could hear his voice, efficient when checking on his men, light with laughter as he spoke to Aliénor or her women, and then nothing.

Into the silence, the Moor spoke, first in some other language, then in Occitan.

'What is past cannot be changed
Remorse brings only sorrow
And nothing can be re-arranged
So waste not your tomorrow.'

The words hit Estela straight and true. It was as if he had read her inmost thoughts and given her advice all in one little quatrain. Intrigued, despite herself, Estela searched her repertoire of songs. She thought she knew them all, certainly all that were widely known. Finally, while al-Hisba al-Andalus rode in patient silence, Estela admitted defeat. 'Who is it?'

Al-Hisba al-Andalus, smiled. 'Omar Khayyam, Omar the Tent-maker, the great Persian poet.'

'But I've never heard of him!'

'You mean you have heard of all the other Persian poets? And the rhythms of al-Andalus when we sing?'

'Should I have?' Her outward defiance hid Estela's sudden sense of her own ignorance, a sensation discovered in the last two days and previously unknown. She who had always been proud of her learning! The world was bigger than she thought. She could either sulk and pretend the little cage in which she lived contained all that she wanted or she could go through the open door and fly, however badly at first.

'Tell me,' she said, 'everything about al-Andalus.'

'*Everything* might need another journey, my Lady, but let me explain to you that hundreds of years ago, when my people came from Oltra mar, as you call it, to al-Andalus, or Andalusia as you might know it, we brought our books, our poets, our engineers, our doctors, our astronomers, and our music. Where would you like me to begin?' he teased her.

'Books?' asked Estela.

'You have heard of the Great Library of Cordoba?'

'I know what a library is,' Estela was quick to reply, 'why, there is a library in Avignon with two thousand books.' She waited for him to be impressed and was pleased with his long pause.

Finally, 'My Lady,' he said, 'The Great Library at Cordoba had four hundred thousand books.'

It was her turn to be silent. 'I can't imagine such a big number,' she said.

'It is the difference between the sheep in those fields,' and indeed there were flocks of leggy, woolly beasts in the surrounding pastures, 'and the stars in the sky.'

'Have you seen all those books?'

'Cordoba itself was destroyed but other libraries remain – Toledo, Seville,'

'I would love to see so many books! I can read,' declared Estela, knowing full well that this was a rare skill, rarer still among women.

'In Arabic, my Lady?' was the gentle query in response.

'Does Lord Dragonetz know Arabic?' she retorted. If she were hoping to rescue her self-esteem, the attempt was doomed.

'Yes, my Lady. To read the ancients, on medicine, on astronomy, on music, Arabic is necessary.'

'Music.' Estela turned firmly to the topic where she at least knew a little and therefore she reasoned, could also learn most. 'I am sure my Lord Dragonetz has told you that I sing and play mandora.'

'A mandora, al-Oud,' al-Hisba al-Andalus confirmed.'

'That's what he said!' exclaimed Estela, remembering the moment when her instrument had been revealed to Dragonetz and Aliénor.

'My Lord is well-travelled. Yes, what you call a mandora started life as our Oud. Eight strings?' he queried and Estela was only too happy to launch herself into a discussion of the tuning, chord variations and rhythms that she achieved with her playing.

So lost was she in the new possibilities that al-Hisba al-Andalus opened up that when Dragonetz returned, she was actually disappointed. She needn't have worried. Far from spoiling the discussion, Dragonetz extended it to lyrics and poetic forms, until Estela felt her brains overheating to explosion. As if he had sensed this, Dragonetz switched the conversation to channelling water and building mills. As she took no part in this increasingly technical exchange, Estela allowed her thoughts to wander pleasantly, lulled by views of sheep and woods, sun and blue skies. For a better view, she held Tou back a moment and moved to the outside of the two men, her back to them as she breathed in the morning.

She had no warning of the blow from behind that knocked her cleanly off her horse, accompanied with a shouted 'al-Hisba!' and a horse's scream. She sensed Seda rearing up beside her and the shiver of panic through Tou as Estela flew out the saddle. There was some whizzing around her. Later, she would realise that her side-saddle position might have saved her life or at least prevented limbs tangling and breaking as she fell. Instinctively, she threw her hands out in front of her to stop the fall before her face hit the weathered gravel. The shock jarred up both arms, twisting her wrists and burning her palms as they scraped the rough ground and she crumpled momentarily, too close to frightened hooves. A last burst of energy rolled her to the verge. And there she lay, panting. Winded beyond speech, she tried to make sense of what was happening.

The procession halted, horses restless with fear, people yelling 'What's happening?' and the snap of orders in response. A soldier was holding the reins of both al-Hisba's horse and Tou, shushing them, but it wasn't the sight of Tou that wrenched Estela's guts. Al-Hisba al-Andalus and Dragonetz were bent over a black body convulsing in the dust and al-Hisba had unsheathed a long, curved blade. For a moment, Estela thought he was going to murder Dragonetz and then she understood. Al-Hisba put his hand to the stallion's neck and Seda stilled, with no need of the sword at his throat. The metal bolt protruding from his head had finished what it started, the work of a crossbow.

'Go with your God, wild friend,' the Moor said, smoothing the arched neck, still gleaming with health even as Seda's eyes dulled. Al-Hisba sheathed his weapon and shook his head at Dragonetz, who stood tall and silent, then turned on his men.

'One? Ten? Three hundred? How many are out there in Jesu's' name! What in hell are Arnaut and his men doing? Picking daisies?' His tone rivalled al-Hisba's blade.

A white-faced Raoulf was the only one who dared answer. 'They chased into the scrub, my Lord. I'm waiting the signal.' He hesitated. 'What alerted you? You know what they're going to find, don't you?'

Dragonetz smeared mud and blood across his forehead with an unheeding hand. 'One person,' he conceded, 'so it's likely they'll survive the encounter. Until I deal with them.' The silence chilled the very sunshine. 'When the first bolt was shot, I saw it glint. My guess is five or six bolts in about a minute. Perfectly possible for a reasonably competent arbalestier, hand-spanning to keep weight down. If there had been more shooters, there would have been more bolts. One arbalestier means one target...'

Raoulf was already scanning the ground for more bolts. He looked up. 'An assassination. Your assassination.'

'That's my guess,' Dragonetz confirmed calmly.

Two men picked up bolts and Raoulf piled up the third and fourth. 'Five,' he stated.

Dragonetz nodded. 'Let's hope the daisy-pickers get their man, alive. I want to know who, I want to know why and I want another horse.' He didn't look once at Seda as he gave orders that the stallion's body be shifted to one side. Someone brought him the same palfrey he had been riding the day before and waited.

Estela had risen to her shaky feet, brushed down her tattered dress and was suddenly aware of the damage to her own body. It didn't feel like she had escaped being kicked by a horse, more that selective kicking had been only one form of the battering she had undergone.

By the time Dragonetz turned his attention to her, she had to concentrate to remain upright.

'I am sorry for being so rough,' he told her. 'There was no choice.'

'You saved my life.' In saying it, the full realisation of what might have been came to her and she staggered, catching the arm he held out to support her.

'I nearly cost you your life.' There was a bleakness in his words that she didn't understand. She took Tou's reins and leaned against the horse, breaking the contact with Dragonetz.

'You should lie down.'

Even though the statement carried no hint of criticism, Estela felt stung by it, and rallied. 'I shall be better for riding,' she declared. 'Perhaps you would help me up.' He held her gaze in his for a long moment, unreadable. Then, without any further attempt to convince her otherwise, Dragonetz cupped his hands, and if he noticed her wince as she hit the saddle with rather less grace than usual, he gave no sign. He mounted his own palfrey and rode ahead, to meet the vanguard of six, who were returning from the woods, with something trailing on the ground, tied to one of the horses.

Within sight of the company but well out of earshot, Dragonetz cantered up to Arnaut and his men, meeting them before they joined the road. For Arnaut's ears only, he muttered 'Feet out of stirrups,' then, for the second time that morning, Dragonetz knocked someone out of the saddle. This time it was a mailed fist to the stomach and Arnaut landed cleanly on his back, sprawled on the bare ground among tussocks of grass. His men hung back, keeping a healthy distance between themselves and the mailed fist. 'Now, tell me why you ignored a crossbow in the woods and don't waste my time pretending you didn't see it.'

Arnaut sat up, doubled over. 'You mad bastard,' he gasped. 'You could have broken my legs.'

'Only if you disobeyed orders.'

Arnaut raised clear grey eyes to his. 'That's your answer.'

'You were obeying orders.' It made no sense. Dragonetz could only think of one person whose orders would matter to Arnaut. His men were hand-picked. Which meant. 'From me,' he stated bleakly.

'Yes. Last night at dinner. A message from you by a servant. Your password and your instructions to ride on. 'Arbalestier friendly,' were the words, 'say nothing.'

'And this servant is no doubt long gone from Douzens. And I expect you're also going to explain why the friendly arbalestier, who could answer some rather important questions, is a mashed corpse putting an unnecessary strain on Martis' horse.'

'He did answer the questions. So I had to kill him.' This time Arnaut couldn't meet Dragonetz in the eyes.

It made no sense. Orders he hadn't given, answers that couldn't be spoken to him in person. 'Out with it,' Dragonetz told him.

'Aliénor.' The name was spoken so low that Dragonetz thought he'd misheard but the second time there was no mistake. 'Aliénor ordered you killed. We dashed into the woods when we saw the bolts fly, heard you shout and what we found was the crossbow abandoned and the flattened grass where he sat to shoot. He made little effort to run, he was so sure we'd let him go. This man,' he jerked his head towards the body, 'gave us her token for safe passage.'

'And the token was good.' Dragonetz already knew the answer.

'Unmistakeable. Her seal. The man believed absolutely that he was following my Lady's orders and his last expression was disbelief when I killed him. Dying eyes don't lie.'

Dragonetz only hesitated a second. 'So he believed it. Just as you believed in my orders. False, both, or stolen.'

'It seems so.'

'But the attempt is from inside.'

'That's why I had to kill him. Whatever happened, the tracks are back in Douzens and he knew no more than he told me. Further talk would only weaken the company and that one would not have kept quiet!' He spat.

'Yes. Your men?'

'Will hold their tongues and accept what I tell them.'

'And you?'

'Will hold my tongue and accept what you tell me. As long as you don't hit me again.'

'Would you rather I let your father punish your incompetence?'

Arnaut winced. 'Christ, I'd rather you hit me again.'

Dragonetz motioned the other five men to join them. 'Unhitch that carrion-fodder, for God's sake!' he told Martis. 'By rights you should be in his place, you useless bunch of witless, eyeless sots. You're lucky it's only a horse that's dead. This could have been my Lady Aliénor.'

'Sire, you think this was an attempt on my Lady?' asked one of the men.

'You've already heard it was an attempt on me and why am I so valuable? Use what little brains your mongrel parents gave you!'

'You are my Lady's Commander, so killing you is a threat to her and her stay in Narbonne?'

Dragonetz rolled his eyes. 'The Lord be praised! It would also be very inconvenient to me if such an attempt succeeded so I'll have the stones off the next one of you cretins who fouls up. Is that clear?' He made a last mental inventory of the human remains dumped where the rope had been cut and said, 'Leave it there. It's off the road. Now get to your place before a hundred English archers appear in the woods ahead!' All but Arnaut galloped off to overtake the procession and regain their position up front.

'Do you trust the Moor?' he asked.

'No.' Impatient at stating the obvious, Dragonetz fidgeted with the reins.

'There is no easy way of asking this,' Arnaut began, 'but I need to know. Do you trust Lady Aliénor?'

'You don't need to know.' Dragonetz was curt as he wheeled round to rejoin the company. 'But I trust no-one, including you. Now get to your position – and tell Raoulf only that you killed the man in youthful enthusiasm.'

Arnaut grimaced and galloped off. Dragonetz could see him reining in beside Raoulf. When the father's mailed fist punched his son, hard, in the arm, Dragonetz hid a smile that quickly faded. There were too many who cared too much about him and each other, hostages to Dame Fortune. Did he trust Aliénor? As much as he trusted himself, he thought bitterly, as much as he trusted himself.

Every bump of the road told Estela that her aches and bruising would be worse the next day. If only she had her collection of salves. A compress of comfrey and some arnica salve would make a big difference.

'I have some thyme oil among my belongings, my Lady. That will give some relief.' This time, Estela saw nothing magical in the way the Moor had apparently read her thoughts. Her discomfort must be obvious enough.

'Yes, that would work. Thank you.'

'We will be stopping soon for lunch.'

Thank God! Estela gritted her teeth and drew on all her reserves to keep going. Her restless mind offered little help, picturing again and again what she hadn't seen, along with what she had; Dragonetz flinging himself and her off their horses, the black stallion rearing, the lethal bolt, Seda's eyes misting like mirrors. She spoke as much to still her own thoughts as to gain a response. 'Animals have no souls.'

'So your Church teaches.' Al-Hisba apparently agreed.

'But not yours.'

'No. For me, all living things contain Allah.'

'Every living thing dies. That crossbow – it should have been my Lord Dragonetz.' *And it could have been me...*

'Perhaps. And perhaps it was not meant for my Lord Dragonetz. Perhaps for once a Christian was obeying his own Church Law. Perhaps he wasn't using a crossbow against another Christian.'

She considered the implications. 'Is there someone who wants to kill you?'

'Are there flowers in springtime?' She had to be content with this enigmatic response but the question resonated. She asked the same question of herself. *Is there someone who wants to kill you? Oh, yes.* They wouldn't care about church edicts, that was certain. And it didn't take as many as flowers in springtime to succeed. Surely they hadn't caught up with her already?

When they stopped for lunch, Estela allowed herself to be fussed over by Guillelma, who made use of al-Hisba's thyme oil, rubbing it none-too gently into Estela's knees and arms. It stung where it touched grazed skin.

'The fall hurt less than the treatment!' she complained.

Guillelma ignored her. 'Look at that gown – ruined! Slashes might be in fashion but not ragged and muddy. It's all well and good finding clothes for you but twice a day and throwing them away when you've worn them will make somebody poor before the week is out and it won't be me!' She grumbled on, a soothing background that allowed Estela to drift away from the day's events and just follow orders to move a leg, an arm, to lie down 'just for ten minutes'. The cart was rolling again when Estela awoke. It seemed to be her lot to slump in a wagon during the day, she thought ruefully, but the rest and treatment had given her enough relief that she could jump down from the wagon, untether Tou and complete the march on horse-back, with the Moor as silent company. One last climb, up a wooded hill-side, and the Abbey of Fontfroide came into view.

This time, Estela, Guillelma and many of the women shared a dormitory inside the Abbey, which was bigger and better equipped for guests than the Commanderie at Douzens, and with a separate building specially for that purpose. The graceful proportion of the cloisters and soaring arches made little impression on Estela, too tired and sore to wonder whether architecture had a soul, a question that the Abbé would have eagerly debated had he, too, not been otherwise engaged.

While some of Aliénor's company were allocated rooms inside, and those less privileged set up camp outside the Abbey, the white friar inspected a promissory note for a very large sum of money. He then debated the precise terms of a contract to purchase land and river rights, came to an agreement and instructed his scribe to draw up the terms. He took the proffered right hand in his own and shook on the agreement, but the modern chivalric gesture of good faith was backed up as soon as possible by the gesture preferred by the monastic orders – two signatures on two identical pieces of parchment, properly witnessed.

There were no witnesses later that night, when a man went alone to the Chapel, a parchment still tucked inside his jerkin. He made a reverence, then knelt before the altar, which was decked in Lenten purple. Hour after hour, the knight kept silent vigil, his head bowed. He only spoke one word, 'Seda.' If he thought about religious doctrine, the question for Dragonetz was not whether horses had souls, but whether men did.

CHAPTER FOUR

No degree of bruising would have prevented Estela being on horse-back for her first sight of Narbonne but she could hardly take up the privileged position at the front that she had occupied the day before. Instead, she was trying to keep on the outside of the press of soldiers, women and servants, some on horse, some on foot, that brought up the rear. The mood had changed completely from the journey's mixture of tense surveillance for the men-at-arms, and relaxation for the rest, to relaxation for the men-at-arms and the pomp of procession for the rest.

Estela felt the collective gasp reach her before she caught a glimpse through the crowd of the great Perpignan Gate ahead and felt her own breath catch. It was so wide that six men-at-arms were vanishing side by side through the archway, three times the height of the mounted soldiers, and above that was a tower, set in the fortified wall. Aliénor was mounted near the front, a respectful space surrounding her and her chosen women, and Estela could hear the cheering as the Queen entered the gate and vanished into the darkness.

Men and wagons jostled into place as they approached the city wall, where some of the City knights kept the Toll Guard company and paid respects to the visitors. A straggle of shopkeepers and ragamuffin children had come out to see the show and gave a half-hearted cheer as the last of the company reached the Gate. Estela craned her neck upwards to see the stonework, strange foreign evocations of bull-heads and chariots, crescent moons and scrolls on niches, then she too was eaten up by the dark narrows of the city streets, following blindly past tall houses that leaned towards each other.

After endless small streets, Estela was confused to see the city wall again and the procession apparently going out of Narbonne. She blinked in the brightness outside, dazzled further by reflections from the river that was the next obstacle. Like a trick of the light, another identical city wall, with a plainer gate, faced them across another bridge. Bemused, Estela was swept along with the others, past yet more cheering tradesmen and workers sneaking time to see the spectacle. Into the dark again but this time the turn to the right opened up a view of no ordinary building. Ermengarda's Palace was magnificent beyond anything Estela had ever seen and on the steps were gathered a hundred or more Narbonnais as welcome party. There had been plenty of time from their entry through the South Gate to get word to the Palace and there was no doubt that they were expected.

At the head of her people was a golden figure, radiating light as if she were giving out the sunbeams rather than catching them in her headwear and her attire. Estela suddenly realized how ordinary her evening gown for Douzens had been. Its tawny yellow would have faded like a dead dandelion beside this cloth of gold, embroidery glittering like the real gold in the circlet retaining her veil. Estela suspected that the white fur edging was ermine, chosen for softness and to set off the flushed tease of the skin revealed. Even from a distance, Estela could guess at the delicate rose and gold beauty of the Viscomtesse of Narbonne and she suddenly felt coarse and brown, in a way she hadn't beside Aliénor's red-headed fairness of skin. There was no chance that Ermengarda's creamy skin sported the sun freckles that marred Aliénor's wrists after days on the road. No doubt some serious application of lemon paste would be part of the royal sojourn at Narbonne. Estela sighed, knowing that she could scrape her skin to the bone and it would remain the same smooth olive she was born with.

A sign from Ermengarda's right-hand man and then the drums rolled and trumpets sounded while it was Aliénor's turn to capture all eyes. To her left, the scarlet St-Denis Oriflamme pennant with its flame edges flickering in the breeze and to her right, the lion passant regardant of Aquitaine on his gules background, observing the crowd with disdain as he too shimmered with each movement. Poised at the foot of the steps, her Ladies and knights around her, Aliénor let the soaring notes announce her. The conventional rise of the fanfare dipped into a well-known phrase, an allusion to a troubadour melody, one composed by Dragonetz for Aliénor, and the Queen acknowledged the tribute with a nod to the crowd and a graceful wave of her hand towards her knight, at her side. Then the trumpets merged again to build up to the last crescendo, one note ensemble. While this echoed against the stone, Aliénor glided upwards as if airborne, towards Ermengarda, her standard-bearers in step.

The ensuing silence marked the moment even more than the fanfare and Estela felt a lump in her throat at being there as witness. In years to come, the children peeking through the legs of their grown-ups, and pushing to get a better view from the front, would tell *their* children of the ceremony, of the time Ermengarda of Narbonne welcomed the Queen of France and her retinue. Marvellous as they found Aliénor, trailing legends of the Crusades and of northern politics, these same children would leave no hearer in doubt that their Lady Ermengarda was her match, just as Narbonne was a match for the Kingdom of France and that to be Narbonnais was to live in the centre of the civilised universe. Estela almost cheered with the mob, suspecting that her eyes shone just like those around her, as strangers smiled at each other, muttering every word they knew for 'wonderful'.

And so France came to Narbonne. The steps gave her the advantage but Ermengarda did Aliénor the courtesy of walking down to greet her so that the two rulers met half-way, their long trains covering several steps, guarding the inner circle formed as the women embraced, once ceremoniously, and again with what seemed to be genuine affection. Now that Aliénor was on the same level, her superior height showed, but Ermengarda's regal stillness drew the eye as much as Aliénor's quicksilver movements. The latter's emerald gown rivaled Ermengarda's in gold embroidery, with lace flounces where the other wore fur. Her coronet was not short of either gold or jewels, emeralds to match her gown, emeralds in rings and bracelets that flashed as Aliénor's expressive arms conjured up a sunny journey that had passed without mishap but with stories to tell.

Estela shook the dazzle from her head. Honours even, one-apiece, she judged, as the tally boys would have reckoned in an equal joust. Once, when she was a little girl, she had been given a lesson in glamour by Gilles. He had let her come with him to the smithy and, while his horse was being shod, he had told her about the weapons that were there for making and for mending. He lingered over one weapon in particular, then he whispered in the blacksmith's ear, got a grunt in reply and picked up two knives. One glittered with stones around its hilt and had a fancy knot design. The other was plain and the edge had a notch in it, interrupting the run of the blade. Easy choice! Estela was young and chose the pretty one, which of course bent when, as instructed, she tried to cut bread with it. She watched as the blacksmith whetted the blade of the plain knife back to a perfect edge and she ate the little end of bread that she sliced as if it were air.

A few weeks later, she was ready for the revision and when Gilles gave her the choice of another bejeweled knife and a plain rough one, she chose the plain without hesitation. He laughed and once more Estela tested the knives, this time throwing each in an arc to land point-first at a wooden door-frame, a bull's eye game Estela had been playing from the age of five. The fancy knife was stuck so deep in the wood that Estela had to twist it out but even so, the blade was true – unlike the plain knife, so old and brittle it snapped.

'So?' Gilles had asked her.

'So, you can't tell,' she had sulked.

'But you have found out the difference each time,' said Gilles. 'Think about it.'

She was still thinking about it, hard, eight years later. Her fortunes had joined Aliénor's. Was the glitter gold or dross? The lion of Aquitaine rippled again in a gust of wind, its upraised paw changing from dog-like offering to a raking death-blow as the claws sliced downwards. Perhaps tawny could be more than dead dandelions after all.

Estela was tired of everyone rushing round. The Palace was ten times, a hundred times the size of the fortress she grew up in, and its outbuildings formed all of the Cité that she had seen so far. She joined in, carrying boxes and goods out of the wagons into the great kitchens or the ante-rooms where yet more servants sorted and carried. Unlike the others, she had no idea what she was supposed to be doing and it was almost a relief when Guillelma, now wearing a respectable if dowdy dun gown and wimple, tutted and told her that she should be in her own room, unpacking.

'Obviously you don't actually have anything *to* unpack,' Guillelma clucked, taking her arm and guiding her through the bustle of goods marching in all directions in front of invisible bodies. 'But I will send everything you need to your room and you must behave like a lady because that's what the Duchesse wants.' Estela noted that for Guillelma, Aliénor was always the Duchesse d'Aquitaine before being Queen of France. 'If my Lady wants you to shine in front of Narbonne, then shine you will!' Doubt entered her voice. 'You do know how to behave like a lady?'

'Yes,' but that didn't mean she would always do so, Estela promised herself. 'A room to myself?' she queried.

'I know. Double-checked it myself when they told me, but it's right. Orders from my Lady were that you be treated like you're Dragonetz' jongleur, because that's what you're going to be.'

Estela stifled the quick resentment at this dictation of her life and reminded herself that three days earlier it would have been her dream to play the role of jongleur to one of the finest troubadours in the country. Not all song-writers could perform well and the best troubadours were often accompanied by the best singers, jongleurs who did not compose themselves but interpreted the other's work. And here she was, being taken seriously as a singer, provided with clothes, food and lodging by a royal patron, about to work with the troubadour she had most admired long before she met him. Why then was she disappointed?

Stone steps twisted and turned, ducked under low lintels and climbed again, until eventually they reached what Estela was told was her chamber. A good size, swept clean and strewn with – she sniffed – lavender, pennyroyal and rosemary, she guessed, good against fleas, moths and diseases. She sat on the fur bed-cover and felt the luxurious movement of feathers inside the mattress. An empty chest was open, ready for her garments, two stools stood against the wall and a window-seat offered another option.

Estela regarded the view through the narrow window, shivering pleasantly as the breeze tickled her skin. She was above the entrance to the Palace and she could see people scurrying below like worker-ants with a haul of dropped crumbs, taking their cargo to the nest. Among them was Guillelma, who seemed to be involved in some dispute by the stores wagon, where barrels and bread rations were being taken out of the wagon by one party, then put back into it by another group. It seemed likely that it would be some time before Estela could unpack, as ordered, and she needed to relieve herself.

There was no reason to abuse the chamber-pot under her bed and she traced her way back along the corridor to a right turn, into the garderobe situated in the thick of the wall. She made use of the hole overhanging the river, then was about to return to her room when she decided that a little exploration would be more interesting. Turning right instead of left, and keeping careful track of the turns in the narrow stone corridors, she noted the wash-basin and water on her level, and then she continued.

Steps down to a door on her left suggested that there was a public passage there rather than a private room, so she creaked open the heavy oak door and went into the gloom of a dark, narrow passage, more like a cave than a corridor. She continued, hoping that the passage would connect to a wider way but if anything, it grew darker as it bent round away from the door. Suspecting that it would lead nowhere, she was about to turn around when she heard voices, distant, echoing voices but voices all the same, so she continued. The passage carried on and on but as long as she could hear the voices growing louder, Estela forgot about turning back. She would find a way out by the voices.

When she could hear every word spoken by two female voices, that she had no problem identifying, she finally turned a corner, expecting to see the women in front of her. Instead, her only reward was a small prick of light through the wall on her right. She put her eye to it and realised that she had found a squint, one of the peep-holes favoured by suspicious lords.

There had been a squint at home, hidden behind a tapestry on the wall of the upstairs chamber her father had built so he and his new wife could move out of the Great Hall. He didn't want anything happening in the Great Hall that he didn't know about so the squint had been part of the design. Estela's mouth twisted at the thought of all that her father had not wanted to know about, and at the memory of being shown that other squint.

In the chamber below her, where she glimpsed rich brocades and solid oak benches, two women were seated on stools, clearly alone together to judge by their open-ness.

'Dragonetz says there was an attempt on his life, by crossbow, meant to implicate me as murderess.' There was no mistaking Aliénor's tones.

Ermengarda was just as direct, wasting no words on womanish sympathy. 'Who?'

'The list is long,' a shoulder-shrug, 'and you know it as well as I do.' An expressive hand waved in the air as the other tallied off the suspects. 'Toulouse,' she began, 'who sits on what should be my estate, and who would sit more comfortably if the gall under his saddle were removed. '

'And do you gall him so much? What is he like, our new Comte? I heard you called on him, on your journey.'

'Fifteen.' Aliénor dismissed the Comte de Toulouse with another airy wave. 'His voice barely broken and compensating for that with a penchant for persecution. He has some grudge against the Cathars and is already stirring up those who prefer their religion sanctioned by Rome.'

'I am not so much older,' came the quiet reminder.

'You were born to Narbonne. He just clutches like a greedy child what his father stole from my grandmother.'

'And you would like it back. Which makes you a threat.' A pause while Ermengarda thought it through and the silence told as much of the relationship between the two women as their free speech. Engrossed in her eavesdropping, a tiny scuffle behind Estela alerted her too late to avoid the strong hand clamped round her mouth and an arm imprisoned her.

'Be still,' she was told as she struggled, but she had twisted round enough to recognize Dragonetz and she calmed. Or rather she seemed to calm until she felt his right arm investigating her skirts and further. Then she took advantage of his distraction to bite into his left hand, which dropped from her mouth as she drove her elbow back as hard into his guts as she could manage, trying for a side-step to turn and follow up with a knee or foot. He was too quick for her and even with one arm, his body-check held her helpless. 'Little bitch,' he muttered and when she saw what was in his other hand, she realized she had mistaken his intentions.

'I should kill you,' he said, holding her own dagger close to her throat, 'before this finds itself in my Lady's back!'

Being crushed against his body hampered the effect but she managed a muffled, 'Go on then, if you're that stupid. Don't you think I'd have used it by now if I was going to!'

He released her so quickly she fell back against the wall. 'Should have killed you first time I saw you,' he murmured, then, inexplicably, 'too late now.' In the dim light she saw his finger go to his lips and, over her heart thumping, she heard Aliénor. 'And if someone knows I carry the heir to the throne? How many more does that add to the list?'

Estela felt the hilt of her dagger pressed into her hand. 'You've just been given a keener weapon,' breathed Dragonetz. 'Either I kill you or I trust you.' Estela said nothing but returned her dagger to its sheath in her under-shift, all ears for the conversation below.

The news was too important for congratulations. 'How long to go?' asked Ermengarda.

'In October, the King can announce to his people that his duty is done.'

'Is it so bad between you?'

'You know that we asked our dear Pope for a divorce in the autumn?'

'And instead, he calmed Louis' fears that he had angered God by knowledge of his cousin, then Innocent blessed your marriage and blessed the bed he showed you to. Yes, word reached me.'

'If only Louis *did* know me! Or was less a Saint and more a man! He looks at me with big eyes and is afraid to touch me without permission from a bevy of Bishops. It's like being married to a puppy! It took me months to convince him that our marriage was against God, the only way I can see to get out of it! And now the Pope himself has condemned me for a life-time!'

'But this —' Estela imagined the glance at Aliénor's secret belly, rounding underneath her voluminous skirts, '— this changes everything.'

'Yes, I shall be mother to the King of France! Then we shall see!'

'So you think someone might know and have tried to kill Dragonetz? To get to you? There is no sense to this — why not kill you?'

'And if that is to be next? Easier with Dragonetz out the way.'

'What does he think?'

'He thinks some plot was hatched at Douzens, involving someone in our company, but he's not sure who's behind it. In fact,' she hesitated, but continued, 'in fact, he has told me to consider that it might be your doing, as you knew all the details of the journey and Narbonne's power over even the Templar purse-strings could squeeze tight enough to hire such a man.'

Dragonetz snorted a laugh beside Estela, 'By the Christ, she's good! She's even made me believe I suggested such an idiocy. There's a nice wedge to drive between me and Ermengarda —and she wanted me to know it!'

'I have as little reason to account for my actions as I have to wish you dead.' Ermengarda's tones were measured but had dropped from cool to sea-freezing. 'I admit I feel temporarily motivated to have a cross-bow aimed at Dragonetz but no doubt the urge will pass. For curiosity's sake, why exactly am I supposed to have engineered an assassination attempt on the chief protector of my friend and ally?'

'Forget it,' Aliénor waved the silly idea out of the room. 'I told Dragonetz how foolish a thought it was. He thinks of nothing but trade routes and inventions these days.'

'Bravo,' admired Dragonetz, sotto voce, so close behind Estela that she could feel his breath, 'two birds with one stone. Discredit me and remind Ermengarda that her trade routes are shaky after the Crusades.'

'It is always possible that the shot was meant for Dragonetz himself, some private quarrel.' Ermengarda steered the conversation back to safer waters.

'Indeed. He is a troublesome man,' Aliénor agreed.

'No saint, and not one to wait the approval of a bevy of Bishops should he want something – or someone.'

'So I have heard.' Aliénor was unperturbed.

'And speaking of Bishops, top of my list if there is an attempt against you, my dear friend, would be the clerics. The Pope might have blessed your marriage but there will be much disappointment at your happy news, well hidden of course. There's Clairvaux, which puts all the white friars into the picture – and you stayed last night with them. And Archbishop Suger would be free to advise Louis to a more suitable queen if you were removed. As we said at the start, the list is long and I shall double the guard around you. If I receive any pertinent information, I shall let you know at once.'

'If you tell Dragonetz, then you've told me.'

'Indeed,' was the ironic mutter beside Estela.

Aliénor reached out to take Ermengarda's hand. 'Now, let us talk of trade. Did you get the goods I had shipped to you from Oltra mar?'

'The sacks of sugar? Yes, and I think you're right. It stores better than honey and is an excellent sweetener. Our merchants are already trying to organize future purchases.'

'I knew you'd like it! The moment I tasted it, I thought how useful it would be here and that you must have trade options on it as soon as possible. They use it all the time Oltra mar. Now tell me, what news from Tortosa?'

'Trade needs trust,' Ermengarda sighed. 'And the world is in turmoil. Even al-Andalus is full of unrest. Before, our merchants were safe there whatever their faith. Now it is difficult for Christians and even for Jews. Rabbi Abraham ben Isaac has told me that the Jewish Quarter is overflowing with Spanish Jews, no longer left in peace by the Muslim Moors in al-Andalus and seeking a new life here. We are still counting the cost of the last Crusade.'

'And shall do until we regain Edessa and all of Antioch!'

'I'd be happy to regain cotton and carpets! But tell me, were you really bare-breasted and leading a horde of Amazons against the city of Edessa?'

Aliénor's laugh was full of mischief. 'We didn't even fight against Edessa.' Her tone became bitter. 'Louis thought Damascus was more important.'

Estela's wrist was pulled so that she had no option but to follow Dragonetz back along the passageway, until the voices sank to an echo in the walls and then disappeared, and the two of them emerged from the doorway into the still-bright daylight of the stairwell.

'You heard nothing.' Dragonetz' eyes burned into hers. 'You weren't there. We'll start lessons tomorrow. I'll send a man to fetch you to me. Bring your mandora.' And then he was gone, just when

Estela had thought of something to say. Was it always going to be like this?

Lost in thought, she traced the way back to her own bedchamber, where Guillelma was waiting for her, red-faced and irritated. It would take some hours of sorting through chemises and veils, gowns and boots, and discussing the relative sparkle of citrines against topazes before Estela had smoothed the ruffled feathers.

CHAPTER FIVE

Abraham ben Isaac, also known as Raavad II, a short form of his rabbinical title, was also considering the implications of recent developments. He had just closed a meeting of the nine members of the rabbinical board and he could not remember such arguments in all the time that he had lived in Narbonne. It was true that the influx of Sephardic Jews from al-Andalus had upset the balance of the community. The newcomers had different ways of worship and, more disconcerting still, their own interpretation of how to put this into daily practice.

All those years the nine had discussed the Halakha, the Jewish way, and, with Raavad's guidance, led the community into a way of life in which families and fortunes had flourished, and now it was back to rifts and rivalry. Worse still, tensions within the city between Christians and Jews, Christians and Muslims, even Jews and Muslims, were exploding into isolated incidents.

Oy vey, the young! Raavad raised his arms to heaven and shared his frustration with his God; the young, Yahweh bless them all, were saying that it was unfair that the laws of Narbonne discriminated against them. No matter how often the Elders asked, 'Do you love your family? Do you prosper? Do you walk the streets without being kicked or spat on?' the young always wanted more. Fairness! It had been a long time since Raavad had such illusions. They had no idea how lucky they were that they lived under Ermengarda de Narbonne and not Raymond de Toulouse, who was already making life unpleasant for the Jewish community, and there were rumours of worse to come.

However, there were limits on how far Ermengarda would go to preserve his people and their rights within Narbonne. She had made it clear that if the current troubles continued, someone would have to pay, in bloody and public manner, and it would not be Christians dancing by the neck after some Old Testament justice. Out of respect for him personally, Ermengarda had offered him the great favour of nominating, now, the Jews who would be found guilty and made a public example should there be one more complaint of sabotage or fire-lighting. Raavad and Ermengarda had shared a smile over some of the sabotage; mice loosed in the cellar where a particularly unpleasant merchant had fruit stored; 'accidental' holes in barrels of wine; moths hatching and holing in carpets from which all the dried lavender had disappeared. Such incidents were soon smoothed over with compensation but the atmosphere of distrust was escalating and no trust meant no trade. Ermengarda was very clear on what 'no trade' would mean for Narbonne and for all its citizens and travellers, Christians, Moors and Jews alike.

As for fire-lighting; there had been no smiles exchanged over a torch being thrown into a shop doorway. No trade would slowly throttle Narbonne over months, perhaps years; fire would burn her alive in an hour, along with most of her citizens. 'I do not have a hundred years to rebuild Narbonne!' Ermengarda had told him. 'And believe me, I do not care who lights the next torch, or what the intended victim has done, it will be shouted from the walls that the criminal is a Jew and he will pay for it! Do you understand!' And her eyes had blazed with all the fire of the imagined roof-tops of Narbonne showering sparks and ashes on her screaming citizens.

Should he have told her this was not fair? Should he have asked why it should be a Jew that paid? He did not need to. He understood the role of scapegoat very well. He also understood what it meant for

Ermengarda to keep the balance that allowed a minority people to live in peace in Narbonne. No, in times like these, it was never the majority who paid, not if a ruler wanted peace. The only choice when it came to it was between wholesale massacre, as apparently Raymond had in mind, and public examples as proposed by Ermengarda. No, that was him being unfair. Ermengarda had actually made a third choice. She had offered them both the possibility of prevention and this is how he had presented matters to the nine, underplaying the alternative. They did not need to be told how serious it was.

Curse the Crusade, curse the stirring up of hatred and curse these new words coming into everyday relations. Only yesterday, he had heard a new troubadour song in the streets, a rousing Crusade lyric about 'lavage', washing the world clean. The shock as he realized that he and his fellow Jews were among the dirt that was to be washed away in this cleansing, made him spit the foul taste out of his mouth, just to remember it. Where would it all end?

He knew perfectly well that the taste was all the more foul because he was just like the rest of them. He would draw up the list of twenty names that Ermengarda wanted, every man on it guilty and condemned should the need arise – Ermengarda's need. She had pre-empted his first thought by telling him that his own name would not be acceptable. Apart from the fact that he was too valuable to waste, no-one would believe that he was a criminal and she didn't want martyrs. His second thought too, was crushed when Ermengarda told him that there would be no buying of pardons, no escape from Ad Fiurcas, where the public gibbets marked the way to the leper-house. Raavad had bowed acquiescence and it was the speed with which the names were in his head that shamed him most. Of course he must choose trouble-makers, and of course they must be recent immigrants, from among the Sephardic Jews from al-Andalus.

If the list were ever used, the al-Andalus Jews would see just one more instance of Christian persecution against them and his own community would believe they were guilty and deserved it. Everyone would accept it. Apart from a few mothers, wives and sisters of course, and that could not be helped. He might even be able to raise support for the bereaved. If it came to pass. He would make this list to protect his community, who would be none the wiser. But Yahweh would know and could judge him no more harshly than he judged himself.

Set-faced and alone in his Inner Sanctum, Raavad unlocked a wooden chest, reached below the garments neatly folded there and carefully took out a package of oiled sailcloth, which hid and protected a book. He placed this with care on his desk and opened it with the familiarity of one who could go straight to a favourite passage. He read and re-read a verse, nodded at its wisdom, then replaced the book in its hiding-place.

Narbonne was no longer a safe place and he must think again as to where such a treasure would be out of harm's way. His son-in-law, Abraham ben David in Nîmes? No, if Narbonne had troubles it was likely that Nîmes and all of Provence had the same or worse. Further afield? There were possibilities. But how to get it there? So far, he had confided in no-one but he was increasingly afraid that, if something happened to him, the book might fall into the wrong hands. Or just be destroyed by accident. Would Yahweh let the book burn? That was another question a young man might ask. Abraham ben Isaac knew perfectly well that earthly fires were more predictable than divine miracles.

Like the wise man he was, Raavad postponed the decision until he could see his options more clearly. Instead, he turned his attention to the business of the day. If the Lady of Narbonne valued him highly, it was not for his learned interpretation of the Torah, it was for his contribution to the life-blood of her city and for his freedom as a Jew to do what she could not, as a Christian. So now he must think about loans, percentages and number of years for repayment, factoring in the insecurity of the city and the impact of the Crusade. It was a very very large sum of money that he was being asked to find, and quickly. That too should be part of the calculation. When the servant announced a visitor, Abraham ben Isaac was ready for the man who entered, cloaked and ordinary.

'My Lord Dragonetz,' Raavad greeted him. 'Please, sit down.'

While the tall, young soldier removed his cloak and took the stool offered, the Moneylender took the chance to observe his customer. His garb was in the usual garish colours of his people but Raavad had learned from his mistakes that this popinjay appearance didn't imply the brain of a bird. He deplored the showy taste and their need to wear their wealth on their sleeves but it was useful professionally, enabling him to glean information about his clients.

He smoothed his own black robes and tried to read the other man's face. Loose black curls gave a typically Christian impression of girlish softness but the jaw and cheekbones, however fine, were strongly delineated and carried just a slight shadow from his fashionable shaven look. His skin showed traces around the chin and cheeks of adolescent ravages, weathered into rugged character. When he returned Raavad's gaze, his eyes were clear black, calm and deep as a mill-pond.

One more advantage of Raavad's long business experience was that he knew how to vary his tactics according to his client. Generally, Christians hated haggling whereas Jews and Moors would have felt cheated if they didn't. Dragonetz, however had seen the world and might either be more entrenched in his own culture or more open-minded, depending on his own nature. Some men liked to build up to a loan with discussion of the weather and others preferred their business brief and to the point. Let the game commence, thought Raavad, making first move. 'A thousand solidi is a lot of money...' He left the implications dangling.

'And you're not going to waste my time by telling me first that you can't get hold of so much, then that because it will be difficult I must pay even more for the privilege, and then finally you will give me terms and we will either take five minutes or ten hours to agree. So, shall we take all that as read, you give me fair terms, I agree them and we both leave the room happy men.'

So, someone who liked to be in control, a man who knew what he wanted and who preferred to be direct. At least on this occasion. But Raavad was not one to be pushed anywhere he didn't want to go. 'Forgive me, my Lord,' he looked anywhere but at Dragonetz and

wrung his hands in the manner he knew that Christians found annoy-
ing, 'but as the risk is mine, so is the need for certain questions... and
of course if you prefer to discuss your business with other,' he paused
' – men of affairs, then that is your right and we can still part – how
did you put it? – two happy people. I keep my money and you are
saved the tedium of discussing business with me.'

To his surprise, Dragonetz grinned. 'Touché,' he acknowledged.
'You know very well that if I am here, it is because I have been turned
down by the Lady Ermengarda and the Abbey or because I didn't ask
them.'

'And?' prompted Raavad.

'The latter.'

'Because?'

The tiniest hesitation. 'In truth,' Raavad nodded encouragement,
knowing the phrase often preceded a lie or a sin of omission, and
Dragonetz continued, 'I would prefer ties of money interest to
returning a quarter of my produce each year.'

Now this was becoming intriguing. 'Forgive me again, but this is
beyond my experience in a Christian. However polite you may be –
and I find it surprising just how polite people wanting money can be!
– surely you feel the distaste that is proper at the very thought of
usury!' He could not help the downturn of his mouth in bitterness at
the thought of the double standards, a reminder of his problems, and
his grip on the wings of his stool tightened.

'I am here to put myself in debt,' Dragonetz said quietly. 'This I do
freely to make a dream come true that I have long held, to enable a
project that is practical and will make money but is beyond my
capital and I have told you I would rather render interest to you each
year than produce to someone else. I have seen worse than usury in
the Holy Land and if I am here it is because your reputation for a fair
– if hard – bargain is known in Narbonne. I have no doubt there are
those who shear a sheep till it bleeds and if I'm mistaken in you, then
I bid you good-day.' He reached for his cloak but was stayed by a
gesture from Raavad.

'Forgive me,' he said, this time meaning it. 'I have to judge what manner of man you are and I'm sure you understand that I need to know what the loan is for.'

The younger man leaned forward, his brows knitted in irritation at having to explain himself. 'My project is a mill on the Aude. I already own the land and the river rights and I need to acquire workers, to build it and to run it.'

'How practical – a woollen mill! You are not the first to see the potential of the fleecing business and you are right, there are big profits to be had. I was expecting something more out of the ordinary, I must admit, but a mill will do well.'

'But you see, I *am* ordinary.' Dragonetz looked straight into Raavad's eyes with the gaze of an honest man who, when he does lie, is very convincing indeed.

'Yes, yes,' Raavad rubbed his hands again, 'a mill will do very well indeed. And now for security. You can show me the land rights?'

Dragonetz fished in the folds of his cape, pulled out a scroll and passed it to Raavad without comment. The money-lender unrolled it, skimmed the Latin phrases to find what he was looking for, 'the area bordered by the land of Sgnr de Craboulesto the north, Sgr de Floralys to the south and Sngr de Mandirac to the west, all river rights within that boundary.' He checked the signatures. 'A pretty piece of land, my Lord and you are getting in at the start, while the industry is still new. Yes, yes. So we have some choices for security,' He rolled up the scroll and returned it to Dragonetz. 'The easiest one is for your father to under-write your loan.'

The sudden flush beneath the swarthy skin gave Dragonetz' response before he put it into words. 'No. This is between you and me, not between me and my father, nor you and my father.'

'A pity, a pity. That would have been so easy. There is no question that my Lord Dragon has the wherewithal.'

'My project will pay for itself.'

'Indeed, indeed.' Raavad gave the impression of thinking carefully, having in fact made his mind up before the interview as to what he wanted. He had of course known about the land purchase and guessed at the mill but there was something missing here. What you don't know today, he told himself, might bite you tomorrow, but he knew he would find out nothing more and his instinct was to conclude the affair. For suitable profit and security of course. 'The security must be the land itself, Lord Dragonetz. You will understand that, for a sum of this kind, my brethren are digging deep in their pockets, very quickly, and can only do so if they, in turn are offered security, so my conditions are these – one,' he ticked them off, 'that in the event of non-payment of dues, the land itself is forfeit; two, that the dues shall be a payment of 15% in six months' time, on – let me see.' He consulted a chart. 'The Kalends and Nones of October will be on a Sunday, so that's no good for you, the Ides will be on the Sabbath, so that's no good for me, but the Kalends of November will be a Wednesday, which is perfect. And then thereafter there will be an annual payment of 15%; and three, that the contract shall be drawn up by my scribe, duly signed and witnessed.'

Dragonetz too gave the appearance of reflecting and Raavad looked down to hide the approval in his own eyes. His feeling that this was a young man who had learned the game was confirmed when Dragonetz offered, '10% annually and we are in accord.'

Hesitating just enough to make them both feel happy with the outcome, Raavad agreed, 'Done!' and accepted the knight's hand in his own. This strange new practice of shaking hands was taking hold – before long it might even be tenable in a court of law. What was the world coming to!

In the time it took for the scribe to draw up the contract and for it to be signed, matters were concluded and Dragonetz left with a second scroll to add to the first. Raavad watched him go, wondering why such a man would speak of a mill project with barely contained passion, as if he were realising the dream of a lifetime rather than joining the ranks of Narbonne's well-padded land-owners. Dragonetz was an adventurer; where exactly was the adventure in sheep? Abandoning the mystery, Raavad ordered a servant to let in his next client, who had been patiently waiting in the next room, where he had heard every word of the previous interview, which was as it should be given that he had paid very highly for the privilege. Raavad sighed. Another client whose religion forbade usury and who was very very keen to talk about money with a Jew.

'Welcome al-Hisba al-Andalus. Come in and sit down,' he told the Moor.

After a couple of hours organizing a stone-mason and a carpenter, who were willing to begin work straight away, Dragonetz was only too pleased to have the distraction of an hour in the music room ahead of him. The 'room' was an alcove in one of the Palace halls, giving a sense of seclusion, some pretty acoustics and a window onto the street, but in sight of those either passing through or themselves finding a corner for conversation. Al-Hisba and Estela were already settled, discussing the tuning of the mandora, when he arrived and Dragonetz gave the barest greeting and let them continue. He sat on the window-seat, closed his eyes and let the two voices make melodies in his head instead of words. Sweet and true mingled with baritone, spring and autumn, the present and the past. He had started to fit new words to the duet in his head when he realised that sweet and true had become sharp and insistent.

'Are we boring you, my Lord Dragonetz?' asked Estela.

He opened his eyes and stretched out his legs, focusing completely on this unexpected, unwanted apprentice, who was glaring at him. 'I want to teach you everything I possibly can,' he told her simply and saw the irritation dissolve. 'Do you want to learn or to be a table decoration?'

For answer she picked up the mandora, teeth gritted. 'Al-Hisba has been showing me how they do it differently in al-Andalus.' She strummed a few chords conventionally then marred the harmony with dissonance, which moved again to harmony as she played, her slim fingers curling and flexing, stroking the strings as if a cat's fur or a man's skin. Her cascade of black hair had been bound in a long plait that swung over her right shoulder. Her forehead shone high and clear as she concentrated on her instrument, no need of shaving her hairline or other artifice to accentuate her looks.

'And how would you use that?' asked Dragonetz.

'I don't understand.'

'Let al-Hisba play so you can listen,' and this time the alien sequence was transformed even further with a hiccup in the rhythm. 'Shut your eyes,' Dragonetz told Estela. 'And tell me what you hear.'

'A perfect fourth,' replied Estela.

'So you were schooled in music. Forget your schooling. What do you hear?'

Al-Hisba repeated his performance. 'A dispute,' Estela murmured uncertainly, then with more conviction, 'plates dropped in the kitchen.' She flushed and her eyes flew open. 'I'm sorry, that was so stupid, it just came to me and I don't know why.'

He rewarded her with one of his rare laughs. 'And I heard the clash of swords. So we have slightly different experiences of disputes but if I heard this music in my head, it would need a disagreement in the lyric.'

'Oh yes,' she had caught up with him now and the words came tumbling out, 'and I'd write the moment where the Lord caught his Lady a-bed with the young hired man, and there *would* be the clash of swords and then the next passage – play it for me, al-Hisba, please, like you did before, the harmony afterwards, yes, that would be the harmony afterwards in the story, order restored.'

'Husband and wife happily reconciled,' he teased.

'But how could that be?' Another golden look came his way. 'No, they must both die of course.'

'Naturally,' he agreed, 'the husband and wife.'

'Now you're just testing me! No, the husband must kill the lover, who will not apologise, and the wife will not say she loves her husband better, so he must kill her too, and order is restored. The harmony tells us that this is beautiful.'

'Of course,' he concurred, still twinkling, 'if a little painful all round. Do you think it might have been more enjoyable if the hired man and the wife had concealed their amour successfully?'

Her brow furrowed. 'Then there would be no story and now,' she accused him 'you are just teasing me. I am telling *you* how to write songs,' she realised.

Al-Hisba had slipped into one of Dragonetz' melodies, the one that had been used to mark Aliénor's arrival in Narbonne.

'Sing it for me,' he told her gently and then he shut his eyes again, caressed by a voice and his imagination. And then he made her work. What was she doing trilling like a bird at dawn? Why was she breathing in between 'his' and 'heart'? Couldn't she hear that it turned the words to nonsense? Why was she singing the beginning as if doom was at hand? What emotion had she saved for the end? Estela took it all, did it again and again, worked until she was getting worse instead of better and then Dragonetz produced a flute and a tambour and while he took on the flautist's role, al-Hisba played his wild Moorish rhythms and Estela was told 'Play! Like a child would play! Just have fun!' The lesson finished with the two men on their feet, skipping and dancing to the mad music that reached wilder and wilder crescendos until Estela admitted defeat and banged one last chord. 'Enough, I can't keep going any more.'

But Dragonetz was still twirling like a top. He took his lips off the flute long enough to say, 'You heard her al-Hisba. We win!

Al-Hisba shook his tambour dramatically above his head, drumming the side to a climax and then dropped it in front of him, bowing his head, so that only the flute played on. 'You win, my Lord.'

One last high note, sustained to the last of his breath, and Dragonetz too stopped. 'I do, don't I!' he crowed and then realized that their antics had attracted the attention of a growing number of onlookers, one of whom was rustling her skirts towards the musicians.

'My Lord Dragonetz, how entertaining!'

'Lady Sancha,' Dragonetz returned, drawing ragged breaths. Now, there was a lady who had not only just shaved her hairline but had also dyed the hair above it, a bilious yellow.

'May I sit and listen?'

'Sadly, my jongleurs lack stamina and are a great disappointment to me.' Dragonetz shook his head in his great disappointment.

'Then, my Lord Dragonetz, I shall have to make do with just you,' Sancha delivered an arch death sentence to his afternoon and pulled up a stool.

'My pleasure, my Lady,' was the chivalrous reply as Dragonetz kissed her hand. All he could hear was a discord on a mandora accompanied by a girl's low giggle. He shut his eyes. Water, cool and clear, a mountain stream with snow still in it.

'Oh, my Lord,' fluted Sancha as he straightened from a moment too long over her hand. Dragonetz looked past Sancha to where Estela stood, straight and slim, waiting to take her leave, her eyes dancing and her face still flushed from their enthusiastic music-making.

'Tomorrow,' he told her. 'Be here.'

She dropped a respectful curtsy. 'My Lord.' The barest flick of her eyes towards Sancha. 'I am full of admiration for your stamina.'

'My Lord,' al-Hisba too was breathing heavily as he bowed and left. Ahead of him, Estela's train swept a graceful wake. Dragonetz reluctantly brought his thoughts back to his companion and caught her too following the girl's exit, with a calculating look that quickly returned to meet his, when she sensed his attention.

'Pretty girl,' she commented.

'A dark lady.' His voice was expressionless.

Her hand flicked up to stroke a newly blonde curl and she smiled, clearly taking the comment as critical. 'Very dark,' she agreed, 'as are her origins. No doubt we shall find out more about her before people tire of their new plaything.'

'What shall I sing for you?'

'Sing to me of love, Lord Dragonetz. Of love...and then we will talk of politics.' She leaned towards him, invitingly.

And so Dragonetz sang of love.

CHAPTER SIX

E xhausted at first by the novelty of everything that was expected of her, Estela quickly slipped into the ways of the Palace. Much of her day was spent among Aliénor's women, a flutter of gaudy birds who chattered with Estela and each other, so alike that she muddled Alis and Elena, Philippa and Adorlée. Every time Estela plucked up courage to talk to one of these creatures of sugar-icing, she stammered her way into a world of hair-pieces and sleeve-tassels, where servants were 'impossible', chambers 'provincial' and the husbands, who were clearly imminent, a source of giggles and specu-lation. Estela did try.

Alis – or Elena – told her about 'the best hand cream' but as soon as Estela tried to ascertain which herbs gave the cleansing properties and which scented the product, Alis – or Elena – gave her a strange look, said 'It's just nice' and distanced herself as quickly as possible from Estela. No wonder that Aliénor herself found Paris limiting if these were her companions. And no wonder that she sought out men like Dragonetz and women like Ermengarda! Of Aliénor herself, Estela saw little and she might as well have been invisible as far as the Queen was concerned, pre-occupied with more important matters. Estela wondered whether any of these women knew of Aliénor's pregnancy? She found it hard to believe that they would hide such knowledge if they possessed it! Unlike herself. She had not mentioned their eavesdropping to Dragonetz nor he to her but it was an unspoken bond between them. He must know that until the pregnancy was public, Estela held dangerous and valuable knowledge. He must know it was crazy to trust her. And yet.

Estela passed the time observing all she could, deeper than hair braids and ribbons. Her respect for Lady Sancha grew – or rather diminished on the level of hairdo and ribbons, which revealed their full potential for garish artifice in Sancha's experimentation. It was on a deeper level that Estela's respect grew. While apparently at one with the bevy of Ladies, at ease in exactly the sort of conversation where Estela floundered, Sancha managed to gather more interesting information at the same time.

Estela heard the way a conversation with Sancha would include the health of Alis – or Elena's –'Uncle Roger' and the progress of his building work, 'Uncle Roger' who just happened to be Roger Trencavel, ruler of Carcassonne, and ailing, but whose city walls were nearly completed to form the strongest defence in Occitania. Or in a conversation with someone else, Sancha would comment artlessly on the pretty pink stone walls they had seen in Toulouse and discover that Alis – or Elena – had spent her childhood there as a ward to Faydida of Uzés, wife of Alphonse Jourdain, father of the current ruler.

Gradually, Estela realised that all of these women were highly connected and that from news of their aunts and uncles, cousins and siblings, an intelligent woman could piece together more important news than any pigeon could carry. Lacking the skill to play the same game, Estela took to listening-in to any conversations Lady Sancha was involved in, and she was soon capable of sifting chit-chat from pieces in the puzzle of politics.

As she began to distinguish Alis from Elena by virtue of their connections and usefulness rather than by their own personalities, Estela also started taking more notice of a young girl who was always with the women. Too self-conscious at first herself to realise that someone else was feeling awkward and left out, Estela now sought out the girl and encouraged her to talk. Apparently Bèatriz was from the mountains north of Provence, sent by her parents to be educated at the court of Narbonne. While Ermengarda was occupied with Aliénor, she had entrusted Bèatriz to the Ladies.

'Where I am being educated most wonderfully,' concluded Bèatriz, only a trace of a twinkle in her demure expression. Her face was a perfect oval, too large for her twelve-year-old body but Estela thought that there was promise of beauty here, seen to more advantage away from Ermengarda's golden elegance and Aliénor's fire.

'I am to return this autumn to my marriage,' she informed Estela, who listened to information about one more imminent husband, a local lord about whom the girl knew little else but trusted her parent's judgement. What she modestly held back, but Lady Sancha was happy to tell Estela, was that Bèatriz was heiress in her own right to one of the richest lands in the Vercors mountains, bordering the Holy Roman Empire and a draw to many greedy, neighbouring eyes. It was not needlework and household management that she had been sent to Narbonne to learn from Ermengarda.

The complicity between Estela and Bèatriz entered a new phase when the topic of music was raised.

'You sing and play mandora, don't you?' Bèatriz asked in her direct way, cutting off Adorlée's explanation of the benefits of linen underwear.

Outranked, and therefore too well-bred to show her irritation, Adorlée smoothly continued in the new conversational direction, 'Yes, she does and I've heard it's very nice.'

Ignoring Adorlée completely, Bèatriz told Estela, 'I sing too. And I compose songs. I shall be a troubairitz.'

Before Adorlée could earn the attention that she deserved for the patronising 'Very nice' that was on her lips, Estela jumped in with, 'Why don't we play together. That would pass the time –' she glanced at Adorlée and smiled sweetly – 'nicely. I'm sure we could find some alcove where we wouldn't disturb the other Ladies.'

There was no mistaking the enthusiasm in Bèatriz's response and it was quickly settled between them that they would make music together the following day. If Estela thought she would have an easy task playing teacher, she quickly realised her mistake. The benefits of a courtly education were soon clear but they were no mere veneer and within minutes Estela told Bèatriz, 'You have a gift.' Estela played for Bèatriz while she sang and very soon there were Ladies cooing their appreciation. For once, neither Estela nor Bèatriz objected to the word 'nice', and as the Ladies grew accustomed to the music-making and returned to their previous activities, there was a chance for Estela to pass on some of what she herself was learning daily, and the lessons leavened the tedium of 'women's matters' for both of them.

The evening meal in the Great Hall also enriched Estela's day, with a chance to guess at the goings-on amongst the great and the good seated at the High Table. Perhaps not so many of the good, Estela suspected, although she saw the white robes of a Cistercian Abbé and the black of a priest, appear and disappear among the dinner guests on different occasions. Perhaps a hundred people were seated at the trestle tables round the Hall, dozens of servants scurried from the Hall to the kitchens and back with flagons and dishes, the huge fireplace blazed with the last flames of a spring night and the curs tussled over crumbs and left-overs, tossed to them in quiet corners. The braver dogs crawled between the legs of the diners and at one point Estela recognized a large white acquaintance.

'Useless,' she greeted him as he crammed his body under the table like sausage meat into skin, bumping the table up as he settled underneath, to shouts of annoyance from Estela's neighbours. 'You don't fit in, do you,' she murmured, 'but you just keep on trying.' She slipped a lamb-bone under the table, felt a wet tongue run over the place where her indoor slipper left her foot bare, and then felt the silent radiation of companionship sent by a dog gnawing contentedly at his master's feet.

'Nici,' she named him in Occitan, 'Big idiot,' and she felt the beat of a thumped tail, the song of the happy dog, as Nici accepted the verbal caress. She slid her feet onto his great flank and rubbed in circles, feeling less alone. It became a routine to let the huge patou go under the table and settle there, to give him morsels and know his pleasure. It could hardly be surreptitious with such a big dog and among those who looked their disapproval was al-Hisba. 'You shouldn't encourage him,' he told her. 'He's a pest with his begging.'

She shrugged. 'Animals might or might not have souls but they certainly have stomachs. He is easily pleased.'

'He's just a dog.'

'A horse is just a horse and a man is just a man,' Estela retorted, rinsing her greasy fingers in the bowl of water provided, wiping her mouth with her wet hand and repeating the process.

'A horse, my Lady, is a thousand years of service to man and a pureblood is both beautiful and valuable. That,' he looked at the offending beast, who gave a hesitant tail-wag, just in case, 'is just a dog.' Al-Hisba bowed and found a place elsewhere, free of under-table beggers.

Wherever he might roam during the day, Nici was always there in the evenings with the Palace pack and Estela saw no harm in letting him keep her company. She started to seek an end position on the bench to make it easier and avoid upsetting other people, either mentally or physically, and Nici was surprisingly agile when he realised it would increase his food rations. Apart from people-watching and dog-company there was little other entertainment during dinner. So far it had been low key, some pretty songs by pleasant voices and competent musicians, but it was as if both Ermengarda and Aliénor were holding back their best for a big occasion. Estela dreamed of being part of it, planning every move in her imagination as she mentally assessed the Hall, the lighting, the acoustics, and the seating arrangements.

What Estela really lived for was the two hours a day that she spent on music. Sometimes Dragonetz would be absent and she would quiz al-Hisba about al-Andalus. In between chords and discords, she learned about gardens; hanging planters that spilled flowers like unrolled bales of patterned silk; trees planted in multi-coloured pebbles, in paving more intricately patterned than the stained glass of a church window; raised beds that shot flowers heavenwards like strange birds; tilled earth gardens, watered by pumps, pipes and channels, that produced succulent fruit and vegetables she had never heard of, figs and oranges, aubergines and almond nuts. Estela found that her knowledge of herbs and spices, like her knowledge of music, had huge gaps and she made mental notes on the medicinal properties of garlic, saffron, ginger and cumin. Al-Hisba responded enthusiastically to her questions on herbal remedies and even complimented her on her knowledge, which warmed her as much as a smile from Dragonetz while she sang.

From the way al-Hisba spoke of it, al-Andalus sounded like paradise but when Estela asked him why he had left, he was much less keen to respond than to discuss the efficacy of thyme infusion for coughs. 'Home is like spring-time, my Lady, full of a promise that stirs the blood, a promise that can only lead to disappointment.' He *was* willing to tell her that he had been contracted as homo proprius, bondsman, to a Lord in al-Andalus, under whom he had prospered as a land-owner and businessman. He then formed a very small part of the price for which the knights Templar relinquished their crazy legacy from King Alfonso and he had worked at Douzens for six years, advising the Brothers on their use of the land, introducing irrigation and horse dung. Al-Hisba was as happy to talk about water channels and what he called fertilisation as he was about herbs and medicine, but his expression closed down again, his eyes hooded, when she said, 'You don't talk of people, of your family.' He was silent a long moment and she knew she had gone too far when he replied, 'And neither, my Lady, do you.' The moment passed and once more they lost themselves in discussion of rhythms as Estela put names to al-Makhera and al-Takil, and could play them both.

Estela no longer noticed the Moor's scarf wound round his head, an asymmetric bandage with an end free to one side. She no longer noticed his loose robe and strange accent, his flat way of walking, his curved sword, his oiled beard. He was no longer a foreigner and no longer a stranger. She trusted him as her teacher and more, as her friend, so much so that she risked one more dangerous question. This time she was careful in her phrasing of it. 'Al-Hisba, will there be a time when you will trust me with your given name?' The answer came quickly, with a bright flash of teeth. 'I believe there will be such a time, my Lady,' and he made no reciprocal challenge to her. In truth, she often forgot she had ever had another name and it was certainly not one she wanted to reclaim.

Sometimes, it was al-Hisba who was absent on affairs and only Dragonetz was there. He seemed more distant when it was just the two of them, less likely to move her fingers into place across the frets, less likely to help her breathe correctly by placing his hand flat across the front panel of her robe and lifting the pressure to remind her when to breathe in. He was more likely to gaze out the window as if he had forgotten she was there and then she could observe him unheeded, the tight fit of his hose around muscled calves, the short tunic which flared full from his hip in the fashionable bliaut style, wide sleeves revealing broad bracelets and long, tapering fingers, hair falling free to his shoulders in black curls, impossibly lustrous.

She guessed at the habits he had picked up during the Crusades, among them bathing as often as he could. Al-Hisba had shocked her with his view on the general lack of hygiene of her people and had told her that one of the joys of Narbonne was its civilised bathing rooms, with several hot tubs for purification. Estela had suddenly felt grubby and added physical inferiority to her growing list. Dragonetz gave every sign of having made frequent use of the bath-tubs and yet he looked the picture of health. So much for her grandmother's warnings! Estela wondered whether anything she had learned as a child was still true but she was too interested in all that was offered to her hungry mind to take refuge in the coward's fear of the unknown. She added bath-tubs to her mental list of prescribed experiences.

On this particular afternoon, Dragonetz seemed abstracted and then, as if he'd made up his mind about something, he said, 'Aliénor keeps asking me when you'll be ready and I'm going to tell her she can show you off any time she likes. I want you to be prepared any evening now.'

Estela felt her stomach churn. She wanted this so much it hurt but what if she should disappoint? There had been some background music after meals but so far Dragonetz had not performed, nor any star of Ermengarda's, although Estela had heard the gossip and knew that the Viscomtesse de Narbonne had a surprise entertainment planned for her guests. During every meal in the Great Hall, she had imagined a message from Aliénor, the walk from her place at table to her chosen spot, near the High Table, with some torchlight on her. She heard the flutter among the audience, the hush and the first strains of her mandora. She had planned a million times what she would sing, repeating Guillelma's mantra, 'Third time lucky.' And now it was really going to happen. Her stomach dipped again.

'*Do* you think I'm ready?' she asked, with her whole heart hanging on his response. She had learned to read his face and his tone, not just the words he chose.

When he turned to her, his black eyes blazed with passion, 'Estela,' he began and her own name brushed her skin like the wild Mistrau wind, raising the soft down on her arms. Then something he saw in the hall behind her darkened his mood and he murmured, 'Meet me at the stable in ten minutes,' then he snapped, loudly, 'You sing of death and lovers parting, as if it's a jolly trot to a picnic, fast and merry. Don't you understand the words? Don't you have any feelings? We are done for today!' He smashed his hand against the innocent woodwork and Estela's instinctive jump backwards led easily into her covering her face with her hands and rushing distraught away from the alcove, avoiding Lady Sancha and leaving her angry tutor to complain about young students and pressing business.

Bemused, Estela left her mandora in her chamber, grabbed a cloak, changed into riding boots and headed from the Palace towards the stable block where Tou could be found. The stables had always been her sanctuary, leather and beeswax mingled with horse and clean straw, people who talked of bot-flies and saddle burn, the friendly harrumps and whooroos of her own grey mare, the ring of a hoof on cobbles. A stable-hand already had Tou outside and was saddling her up.

'Has she been ridden lately?' Estela asked, knowing that even a placid mare like Tou could be frisky after being cooped up for days.

The lad straightened up. He was about Estela's height and probably her age too, wearing the rough jerkin and britches of his trade, his hair a ragged mop of curly brown and his eyes brightest blue in a face that still had more curve than angle. His shoulders and arms were bare, the muscles gleaming and restless in the sun as if he too fancied a gallop in a spring field. The pit of his arm was dark with soft hairs and sweat and Estela leaned closer to breathe in the scent of male animal. She almost shut her eyes to turn it into music. What was the matter with her today? She only had to see a young man to follow her fancy to... to places she was not going to follow her fancy to!

He lowered his eyes, respectfully. 'As ordered, my Lady. She's been exercised every day. Should be sweet as a nut for you. We just had the message to saddle her up so I haven't finished... if I can carry on?'

'Of course.' As he bent down to tighten straps, she watched his broad wedge of back, working, the inward curve at the base of the spine visible below the jerkin, rounding out again below. What was it al-Hisba had said? Something about spring stirring the blood. That must be it; she had a touch of spring. She cleared her throat. 'What's your name?'

He looked at her with those amazing blue eyes, cornflowers and sapphires she thought, trying out a line of verse in her head. 'Peire,' he told her, 'Peire de Quadra.'

Peire the Stable. Of course. She smiled graciously at him, quite the lady. 'Well, Peire de Quadra I shall remember that name. You have done a good job and I will ask for you by name next time.'

His face lit up. 'Thank you, my Lady.' It was like giving a bone to Nici. She had no time to consider why this was a worrying thought as the sound of his voice told her that Dragonetz had come. Her giddy mood lifted even further. Perhaps it was only spring and the freedom of the stables that lifted her spirits so but she suspected that the disease was catching. She had never seen Dragonetz like this, boyish and wild, lit with mischief, his lop-sided grin tilting her world.

'People will talk,' he told her, crouching and cupping his hands.

'People always talk,' she replied. It felt the most natural thing in the world to mount from his hands, as if they had performed the little ritual a hundred times instead of three? Four? Only once she was on Tou's back did she register the disappointment in Peire's eyes. It was his job to help her mount, not for a Lord to bring himself down to the level of a working boy. Next time, she promised Peire with her eyes and a smile, next time, and his expression lifted again, smoothed by a compliment from Dragonetz who took his own mount, jumped into the saddle and called to her 'Come on then!' She didn't have to be asked twice.

CHAPTER SEVEN

E stela followed Dragonetz out of the city gate but instead of crossing the river to re-trace the route by which they had entered Narbonne, Dragonetz turned right, following the course of the river along a well-used path between the Aude and the walls. Once they reached the guards' tower that marked the boundary of the Cité, the path widened enough to ride side by side, still heading north along the river bank. Yet another sunny, spring day made Tou almost skittish but following Dragonetz' mare at a steady pace calmed her quickly and Estela could now let her attention wander.

'Where are we going?' she asked.

'What a dangerous childhood you must have had,' he teased. 'Do you always follow strange men into the unknown?'

'If I judge it to be safe,' she replied coolly. 'Are you reliable?'

'As a blacksmith's hammer, as a washerwoman's hands, as a cooking pot...'

'As a rabbit's tail,' she supplied drily. 'And where are we going?'

'To Matepezouls.'

'Of course,' she said, none the wiser. 'Because?'

'Because it is a beautiful day, because you need to get out, because I need to get out and because Lady Sancha's jealousy is dangerous.'

'But she has shown little interest in my singing and playing. And even when Bèatriz sings, Lady Sancha has no more concentration than the others. She's good you know, Bèatriz. She would be better than I am if she had someone like you to teach her.' She faltered.

'Someone like me,' he mocked. 'Did you have someone in mind? And it isn't your music that Sancha's jealous of.'

'I can look after myself. I always have.' She was starting to get irritated at being treated like a child and it must have shown because he switched to the one, forbidden topic that would revive the feeling of parity between them.

'Do the Ladies know of Aliénor's pregnancy?' No title in front of the Queen's name, just a bald assumption that he and she could openly share their views on a topic that many would call it treason to discuss.

'No, I don't think so. And she hides it well, none of those little give-away gestures, you know, the way they fold their hands across their belly and smile, long before their gowns grow more voluminous.'

Dragonetz laughed easily. 'No, I don't know, but I bow to your obvious experience. I'm hoping that you can keep an eye on things, let me know if there's strange talk or behaviour around her.'

'You're thinking of the crossbow attempt? Any idea as to who was behind it?'

'Some creature of Raymond's is my guess. Toulouse has a long grudge against Aliénor and killing me to frighten her is the way he would think. From all I hear, he is not such a boy as Aliénor hopes him to be. But someone knew my password and used Aliénor's seal so that means someone close to her, and sharp.'

'She's hardly with us so there's not much I can do. I can't say I blame her either!'

'Bored, are you?'

She could hear the laughter in his voice. 'It's not funny. You have no idea how tedious it is!'

'But I do. That's why I am offering you a diversion. Welcome to my little world. This is Matepezouls.'

A bend in the river opened up a view of unexpected industry

around a working watermill. As they drew nearer, Estela could make out a dozen men in a work chain unloading goods, adjusting machinery and supervising. She recognized the robes and headgear of al-Hisba, striding from one area to another, apparently giving orders. Raoulf was there too, his muscles bulging as he lowered a huge metal hammer into a big vat, which seemed to be full of white material. Helping him was Arnaut, stripped to the waist and taking the weight of the hammer as it was lowered into the vat, still attached by a leather thong to a spar. The sun gilded Arnaut's back, bronzed and smooth, seeming slight and boyish beside his father's massive bulk but showing no strain as he completed the movement, straightened and turned. Catching Estela's eye, he grinned and wiped his hands on his britches, then came over to join her and Dragonetz, who were still mounted. When Arnaut offered her his arms to help her dismount, she accepted yet another spark to her spring fires and let him clasp her waist as, just for three seconds, she felt his sure hands burning through her embroidered belt and she slipped, drawing a sharp breath against his bare chest before he respectfully took a step back.

Dragonetz glanced at Estela, his mouth twisting in amusement as if her thoughts were written on her pink cheeks. First Peire, now this! Did she only have to smile and the world was full of beautiful young men? Ah, terrible fate. She smiled at Dragonetz, smiled at Arnaut, and smiled at Raoulf, who also came to join them. She smiled at al-Hisba, who was the only one not to smile back.

'We have come to annoy you,' Dragonetz told his men. Apparently unaware of his half-dressed state, Arnaut smiled again, with another glance at Estela, who was only too aware of this, to the very hair on his chest in a curly golden v. 'My Lady is here to learn about the mill,' Dragonetz continued smoothly, 'and I want an update. Al-Hisba?'

The Moor bowed. 'Two full loads of rags have been processed, my Lord. The rags in the vat are under the hammers and we are trying different hammers to reduce the rags more effectively to pulp and fibre.'

'I thought you said it worked like this in al-Andalus?' Dragonetz was sharp.

'Even in al-Andalus these are new techniques and I think we can improve on them.'

'Show me.' Beside the vat, al-Hisba pointed out the way the hammers smashed into the vat as their thongs were raised and dropped. Estela traced the route of the thongs to the spar, and the spar to a turning shaft. At that point, leaf-shaped irregularities arranged in pairs round the shaft, bumped the spar and caused the hammer movement. Three pairs of bumps, three hammers, rising and falling at different intervals. Estela shut her eyes and heard the music of the vat, the creak of the turning shaft, the squish and smash of the hammers on the rags and water mix in the vat. When she opened her eyes, she caught Dragonetz looking at her intensely, as when he tried to find and correct her breathing or her fingers on the frets. She tried her magic smile to see if it was still working and earned a tilt of his mouth and a wink.

'It sticks a bit,' Arnaut was saying. 'And we don't know what to season the wood with to make it stick less.'

'Or rub on it,' Dragonetz suggested.

'Goose fat,' Estela declared and faced four stares. 'Well, in the kitchen,' she faltered, 'they rub goose fat on the iron pans to season them and after that they don't stick so I just thought,' she petered out.

There was a silence, broken by al-Hisba. 'It might work,' he said. 'And I haven't heard a better idea.'

'Or metal instead of wood. What about iron?'

'Maybe,' al-Hisba responded cautiously to Dragonetz' suggestion. 'We'd need to talk to the blacksmith about which metal.'

Pretty *and* serviceable, Estela thought automatically, then realised that 'pretty' probably wasn't important in this instance. She had the sense to keep her thoughts to herself as the talk went way beyond her capacity to follow. She continued watching the moving rags, back through hammers, bumps, shaft, along the shaft to the hub of the mill wheel, turning and churning, powered by the Aude itself, or rather a culvert of the Aude, siphoned off and rejoining the river lower down.

The river itself was protected from the mill-race and the wheel was protected from variations in the river's flow.

When there was a gap in the men's debate, Estela ventured the question that had been on her mind from the beginning. 'It's not a woollen mill. What are you making here?'

The others looked at Dragonetz. 'The future,' he told her. 'One day, everyone will read and everyone will write. Because of this man and his people,' he gestured at al-Hisba, 'because they have given us paper. We are making paper and it will get cheaper and cheaper to make it until one day even the poor will wipe their hands on it and throw it away!'

'You're a dreamer,' Raoulf shook his head and even Arnaut looked sceptical while Estela, none the wiser, asked, 'What is paper?'

'Alchemy!' was Dragonetz' unhelpful response and it was al-Hisba who explained, 'The rags get turned to pulp by the hammers, then dried and pressed very thin. The thin sheets get cut into squares and you have writing material, like parchment.'

'But at one hundredth of the cost! And in quantity!'

Estela was shocked. 'But if this is true –'

'And it is,' both al-Hisba and Dragonetz assured her, one calm and self-assured, the other barely containing his excitement.

' – then it should be the Church producing this... paper, shouldn't it, so that the scribes can use it.'

'That, my sweet Estela, is the beauty of it! I shall sell paper to the Church for enormous profit and I shall be fantastically rich! As shall my workers.'

Estela chewed the side of a finger, a bad habit she had kept from childhood. 'The Church won't like it,' she stated.

'No, they won't.'

'That makes a dangerous enemy.' Estela stated the fact.

'We've told him,' Raoulf was gloomy. 'But you can see what he's like. The future pff!' and he spat, coarsely. 'The future will be my Lord's body with a bolt through it!'

'Ever the optimist!' Dragonetz clapped Raoulf on the back. 'That's what you're here for, you and your men, to watch my mill and watch my back. Speaking of which, this should make things even.' With which enigmatic statement, he tore off his doublet and underthings so that he too was bare to the waist, then he grabbed Arnaut's hand and dragged his unwilling man into a run. Shouting, 'I said I owed him a ducking,' Dragonetz ran the two of them straight off the edge of the bank into the river.

'You mad whore-son,' burst from Raoulf as he rushed after them to the bank, anxiously scanning the murky water for signs of life. Estela counted to thirty before two heads burst up above the surface, gasping, spouting and followed by thrashing arms. Arnaut twisted underwater, avoiding Dragonetz' attempt to duck him again and came up at a safe distance, both men treading water and spluttering. 'Come and join us, Estela,' Dragonetz called to her.

'Can't swim,' she yelled back.

'What are you thinking of, bringing a Lady here!' Raoulf shouted, purple with annoyance.

'A Lady! I'd forgotten!'

'Oh my God, no,' groaned Raoulf.

'Estela, my sweet, Arnaut wants to do combat and regain his pride – throw us a token.'

Without thinking, Estela pulled the bangle off her arm and threw it in a high arc to land equidistant from the two men. Neither wasted words but dived underneath, rippling the surface as they carved the water underneath. Another count, thirty, forty, Estela thought that Raoulf would explode, holding his own breath to see how long it was possible, then Arnaut broke surface, gasping, followed quickly by a triumphant Dragonetz whooping and waving the bangle in the air.

'She's not an ordinary Lady,' he yelled, 'she's a Troubairitz! Ask her!' And then he struck out for the bank, Arnaut following at a safe distance and after some horseplay with Dragonetz trying to prevent Arnaut getting out of the water, both men stood dripping and laughing, pushing each other. Dragonetz waved the bangle, taunting and Arnaut stood, bent double, getting the words out with difficulty. 'You always have to win, don't you, even when you don't want the prize!'

Dragonetz' eyes glittered. 'Always, Arnaut, always,' and then he knelt in front of Estela, offering her the bangle back. She looked down on the black curly hair, bent in mock homage, the broad wet shoulders, the long tapered fingers reaching out to her, returning her token. She felt Arnaut's stillness, the sunshine, the moment to which this day had been leading all along. She thought of Peire, his disappointment over something so small, so easily given, so wrongly with-held. It was her moment and she could do anything she liked with it. She shut her eyes and felt for the lyric. If this were a song, how would it go? And then she knew what to do.

She laid a hand on his head, felt the hair wet and cold, saw the goose-pimples forming on his arms and she spoke for everyone to hear. 'My Lord Dragonetz, I thank you for your skill in returning me this token. I will never forget it. You do great honour to the name of your lady, the Duchesse Aliénor. Please rise.' She did not wait for Dragonetz to stand nor look at him before she turned to Arnaut. 'This favour is mine to bestow where I will. If your spirit is free, would you wear this for me, in token of your loyal service, be willing to protect me should there be need, whether my name or my body, and,' she paused and looked him straight in the eyes, 'and expect nothing in return, nothing whatsoever.'

There was not one second's hesitation as Arnaut sank to his knees and Estela saw the golden head where earlier had been black curls. She saw him swallow hard as he said, 'My Lady, always.' She put her hand on his head, a benediction this time with no regret, gave him the bangle and raised him to his feet.

'Well, that was fun, wasn't it.' Dragonetz bent his head and shook the mop of wet hair. 'Shall we shake off the wet like the dogs we are, Arnaut?' He imitated the drying technique of a large dog.

Arnaut laughed. 'I know why dogs don't wear shoes,' he admitted holding a dripping boot in the air.

'Well either we must remove all our clothes for drying or some kind person must find us some dry ones,' Dragonetz informed the world, starting to remove his hose and smiling at Estela.

'Enough, you puppies!' Raoulf growled. 'God's death! I'll fetch you some clothes before you shame me any further!'

The warning shout 'Dragonetz!' which made him whirl round, came simultaneously with an unsheathed knife, swinging from one hand to another, mere yards from Dragonetz' naked chest, too close to him for Raoulf or any of the other armed guards to interfere. Just behind Dragonetz, Estela and Arnaut stood, motionless. Nothing moved but the knife glinting in the sunshine, closest to Dragonetz.

'So you'd have had me in the back,' Dragonetz spat.

'How doesn't matter,' was the response between gritted teeth and the man took a cautious pace forwards. 'And you're still unarmed.' Anonymous in his working clothes, the assailant could have been any one of the men who had been unloading and carrying goods. Estela looked for something remarkable in this face, something evil in this, the man who would murder Dragonetz in cold blood. And she saw nothing, nothing at all, which chilled her more than any sign of hatred. Lack of feeling made for an effective killer. The man took another pace forward and Estela felt Arnaut stir beside her, gathering himself. Dragonetz must have felt it too, for he grabbed Estela and pulled her in front of him, too quickly for the knife to reach him first. Estela felt Arnaut move, and stop dead at Dragonetz' bizarre murmur of 'Feet out of stirrups!'

The man bared his teeth in no smile, 'You think I would hesitate to kill the woman, then you, my Lord? What a fool,' and Estela shut her eyes, with no thought for the music of the moment, feeling rather than seeing the knife stop in one hand and arc towards her at the same time as the hand rifling her under-shift found what it sought and an elbow pushed her roughly to the ground, following through to lodge Estela's dagger into the surprised attacker. Dragonetz disarmed him with the other hand, booted him to the ground and leaned over him, so close that only Estela and Arnaut could hear the question 'Who paid you?' and the answer, gasped so low Estela wondered whether she had heard right. But there was no mistaking the plea for mercy that followed, 'Don't kill me,' she heard as her dagger hovered above the man's throat.

Al-Hisba's voice floated cooly across the scene, naming the man on the ground. 'Isaac ha-Levi.'

Estela saw her dagger raised slightly and screamed, 'No!' but there was no hesitation as Dragonetz plunged the weapon into the man's neck. Estela saw the spurt of blood and rolled on her side to vomit. Arnaut helped her get up and held her arm until she shook him off. 'Why?' she accused Dragonetz. 'You didn't have to kill him!'

'Oh, but I did. He was Jewish,' was the short reply. Without looking her way, Dragonetz took her dagger to where the water flowed back from the mill-race to the river and he washed it clean, then wiped it on the jerkin he had discarded on the grass before jumping in the river, a life-time ago. He gave it back to her, set-faced. 'This is becoming a habit,' he tried but she took the dagger in silence, a man's needless death between them. Although that's what she carried a dagger for, wasn't it? She sheathed it back in its hiding-place. 'Arnaut,' he ordered, 'Accompany Lady Estela back to Narbonne and see her safely to her chamber, preferably with a woman to tend to her while she recovers. Al-Hisba, I want you to take a message to Abraham ben Isaac. Raoulf, move this body to the wagon shed. It can stay there till his people come for him.' He surveyed the gathering. 'There will be no talk of this incident. There was no attempt on my life. A man was attacked by thieves on his way to his work here, we found the body and brought it here, in common humanity. Is that clear? Al-Hisba?' He took the Moor to one side and gave him further instructions then al-Hisba mounted and rode off towards Narbonne, vanishing quickly out of sight in front of the slower pace of Estela and Arnaut.

Estela looked once behind her but the mill was exactly as she had first seen it, workers once more busy in the process of making paper. Nothing had changed.

The ride back was sombre, the silence broken only when Estela asked, 'What does it mean 'feet out of stirrups'?'

'He's warning me of a feint, a jongleur's tricks, not to believe what I see.' Estela said nothing. 'He will have a reason, you know.'

'You trust him, don't you.'

'Yes.' Estela remembered that this was a soldier, this beautiful young man pledged to her honour and riding at her side. A soldier who had seen battle, to whom the spurt of blood from a man's throat was nothing. A soldier whose first allegiance was to his Commander.

They rode on without a word and it seemed to Estela that Arnaut was glad to leave her, to have done his duty and to return to the action. She, on the contrary, had decided she would try the hot tubs in the time that remained before evening meal. What was it al-Hisba had said about them? Cleansing, relaxing, purifying – that sounded about right.

An hour later, Estela was soaking in steaming water so hot it reddened her skin. After being taken to the Ladies' baths in a room beside the kitchen, she had dismissed the servant, preferring to be alone, the other two tubs being unoccupied. Towels were left to hand, her clothes neatly arranged on a bench at the back of the room and three drops of lavender oil added to the water. She took the little stool out of the tub and placed it on the tiles. She preferred to lie back, letting her hair float around her in the water, her feet up against the other side of the great half-barrel that served as a tub. She washed the day from her system with soft olive oil soap, imported from the Moorish south – what paradise al-Andalus must be! – and, even from the soap, the scent of lavender impregnated her skin and her brain, lulling her into non-being. She shut her eyes, submerged her head, so that all she could hear was the sound of her blood pulsing, her heart beating.

She had no sense of falling asleep nor of waking but the cooling water told her she must have done so and she shivered. Time to dry herself, to return to the world. She stood up, held onto the edge of the tub, thinking perhaps she should have kept a servant to hand after all and she placed a tentative foot on the floor beside the bath. She put her weight onto one foot to climb out of the tub and cried out with pain, trying clumsily to reverse the weight, adding more slicing pain to the foot outside the tub before she could draw it over the side and back into the bath where the blood tricked in swirls into the water. She inspected her foot and saw the cuts, some still with splinters of glass protruding from them. She picked out the splinters, dropping them over the edge of the bath away from her intended exit.

Kneeling, Estela looked over the tub at the floor where she had put her foot. Broken glass. She looked all round the bath for a clear space but there was broken glass everywhere, all round the bath, in a ring two yards or so wide. There was no way she could jump over it, assuming that she could bear to stand on the glass beside the bath and then jump. The very thought made her wince. The bath stool? No. Whoever had strewn the glass had also moved the stool to mock her at the back of the room, beside where her clothes should have been. She took in this new piece of information. Clothes gone. Towels, towels... she scanned the room, knowing already what she would find. No towels. But there was no point worrying about that until she had actually got out of the bath in the first place.

She yelled for help and heard the echoes disappear into the steamy acoustics, the thick walls and no doubt into the clatter and chatter of a grand kitchen before evening meal. Maybe after the meal, or maybe not till the morning, if then, someone might hear her. She shivered as much at the thought of a night in cold water as because she was already cold. There was no way to get rid of the water unless she could make a hole in the tub and use a chunk of the bath itself as a board to walk across the glass? Puncture the solid wood tub with what, exactly? Estela had a bar of soap and her own body. There was no way of scratching or kicking her way through the tub. Think again.

She hated the only plan she could come up with but she had to get out of the tub and there was no other way. Once more she knelt in the bath, leaning over the side so that she could drop her waist-length hair over into a pool on the floor. Contorting herself to reach the hair with her first foot, she climbed out of the bath, bent double all the time, to place her feet on her hair.

Then, little by little, she shuffled hair and feet forward, one at a time, in a monkey-crouch that strained her knees to shaking point. An occasional splinter would pierce through the hair into a foot but it was bearable and she kept going until she was sure that she was past the broken glass, when she straightened up with a groan of relief and complaints from her aching muscles, Her swinging hair caught her side and again she felt stabbing pains. Stupid! Her hair was a torture-machine, spiked with splinters of glass.

She gathered her hair in one hand, near enough her head to be above the glass splinters and she held it in a pony-tail as far out from her body as she could. Now there was nothing for it but to go out the door, stark naked, holding her hair where it could give her no covering at all. She could only hope that the first person she met would take pity on her. She swallowed hard at the thought of walking through the door into the busy kitchen and her hand was on the latch, ready to face the music when she heard a voice she knew well, on the other side.

'Estela, are you in there? It's me, Dragonetz. Aliénor wants you to play tonight and you're going to be late.'

Help from Dragonetz or face a kitchen-full of curious eyes? Some choices are quickly made. Estela lifted the latch, opened the door enough to hiss round it, 'Come in here!' She stepped back quickly so no-one could see her through the doorway as Dragonetz entered the bathroom. 'Shut the door!' If she hadn't been cold, anxious and humiliated, she would have enjoyed the momentary shock in his expression but he mastered himself quickly.

'It seems you wanted a swim after all,' he drawled. Then he saw the glass in the hank of hair swinging beside her. 'What happened?'

'Turn your back,' she told him.

'It's a bit late for that! You have two breasts and the place of Venus, like all women. I'm not going to ravish you and you're going to tell me what happened. Let me hold your hair while you put this on.' While talking, he had removed his tunic and passed it to her.

'My feet hurt.'

He picked her up in his arms and carried her over to one of the tubs with no glass around it. 'Can you kneel and lean into the tub?' he asked her quietly and on her assent, he swept up her hair and unloosed it into the clean water in the un-used tub, swishing it back and forwards so that the splinters were dislodged. He took off the belt round his undershirt and used the buckle like a coarse comb, grooming the hair for more splinters. And finally he ran his hand over the hair, combing it with his fingers, checking that it was clear and clean. He squeezed the water from the tresses, asked Estela to sit on the edge of the bath and inspected her feet. Little trickles of blood and water still ran from the cuts.

'Painful,' was his judgement, 'and the less you walk on those the better, but nothing serious. Let's get you out of here. 'Put your arms round my neck.' She was beyond protesting and curled up against the fine linen undershirt, pulling the tunic to cover her knees as best she could, hiding behind her hair as she was carried out of the bathroom. Dragonetz gave a few curt orders to the first servants he passed, to clean the bathroom and fetch al-Hisba to Estela's chamber, then he strode through the back ways of the Palace, picking out the route with the ease of a man who could find a spy-hole in a secret passageway.

He laid her gently on her own bed and told her, 'I'll have my tunic back now, if you please. I don't feel I am dressed for dinner and neither are you.' He then turned politely to look out the window, while Estela ignored her feet to grab clothing out of the trunk, throw it on and return the tunic. Then she sat down on a stool and filled up with tears.

Dragonetz toyed with her bangles, abandoned on the table top, then picked up her brush and, as if it were the most natural thing in the world and she were not sitting there crying, he drew it lightly through her hair.

'The bottom first,' she managed to say, 'or you will force the tangles to the roots and never get them out.'

'You see what you bring me to?' he asked her.

She felt the weakness of her smile but at least the tears were drying up, thank God. 'Your training as a lady's maid is sadly lacking, my Lord, but with some practice and effort on your part, I believe you could pass muster.' She felt his breath on her hair.

'Shall I make your excuses to Aliénor?' he asked her softly. 'It is too much for you, I think.'

'No,' she said firmly. 'I will not lose Aliénor's goodwill and throw away my own future for some scheming sneaky evil-doing stab-in-the-back – oh,' she stopped short, remembering an actual attempt to stab in the back. 'Could it be they want me too?' she wondered aloud.

'More likely to be some jealous creature of Aliénor's. Cut feet don't kill.'

There was a polite knock on the door and Dragonetz answered it to al-Hisba, who tutted over Estela's feet, then applied a salve and some bandaging. When he had finished, Estela made sure her face was wiped clean. She must be glowing after all this soap and water! No time to apply make-up in the style the Ladies had taught her. She picked up her mandora and, slowly so as to spare Estela's feet, the three of them went down together to the Great Hall, looking as if they had not a care in the world.

CHAPTER EIGHT

F orgetting, Estela idly stroked Nici with her foot under the table and winced. She was too much on edge to feel hungry and toyed with her food. She sipped a little wine, enjoying the warmth and trying not to think of the day's crazy events. She only had to think of water and she saw blood, a Jew's blood wiped from a dagger, and her own blood, and she felt chilled to the bone. At least she was sitting down for a while so her feet didn't hurt as much. The walk to the Hall had never seemed so long and she knew the two men had talked to make it less obvious that they were slowing down for her, offering to carry her instrument and taking an arm each to support her, support that she reluctantly accepted. The talk had made no sense at all. Al-Hisba had passed on the thanks of Abraham ben Isaac to Dragonetz for saving the lives of so many Jews and said he would make arrangements for the body to be delivered to the man's family, something he did not deserve. Dragonetz grimly replied that the respite was temporary and that the choice of a Jew had been deliber-ate. Apparently, Abraham ben Isaac agreed. Estela might as well have been invisible except for the strong arms on which her own rested and once again she wondered at being trusted with such a conversa-tion, even if she didn't understand any of it. She would, she swore to herself, she would understand it all, but for now all that mattered was walking.

At the entrance to the Great Hall, Estela took her mandora and walked away from the men, proud and alone, but sank gratefully to the nearest corner of a bench, quickly joined by Nici, who sniffed obsessively at her feet and tried licking her boots. The smell of blood, Estela realized, and the urge to lick the wounds of a pack member. She told him no but caressed his big head and he flopped, sighing and contented. Waiting on a bone, Estela told herself. If only people were as straightforward.

There was an air of expectation round the Hall during the meal and Estela noticed some new figures at the High Table. Someone sober as a cleric in plain grey frowned at some men strangely attired in cream linen tabards, which had necklines like keyholes and were edged with broad bands of multi-coloured embroidery. The guttural sounds of their language when they spoke to each other added a liquid note to the chat around the hall, nothing that Estela could iden-tify, not French, not Latin, not Arabic, not the Jewish languages, nothing she had heard around Narbonne.

The Chief sat beside Ermengarda, hairy and immense, with a shaggy mane of red hair and a long beard to match. Round his neck hung a gold chain worth the price of a hunting lodge with a huge hammer-head hanging below it. If that too was solid gold, as Estela suspected, it was beyond price. Nor was that all. He wore a large golden clasp fastening the tunic, which crossed over to one side, and when the plain trumpet sleeves fell back, they revealed chunky torques around the massive arms. Never had Estela seen so much gold on one person.

However, she could not say that he displayed the most wealth, without a professional evaluation of the jewels worn by both Ermen-garda and Aliénor. If those were real diamonds in the gold net sparkling over Ermengarda's hair, then surely that put her slightly ahead of Aliénor's emerald-studded coronet, but then there was a broad embroidered belt, also studded with emeralds, and the bracelets, to be added to the reckoning. Estela was dizzy with the sparkle from the High Table glinting in the torchlight and she had forgotten her nerves in her speculation about the barbarians until a drum roll interrupted the conversation and Ermengarda stood up to address the Hall.

'In honour of our visitors, Aliénor, Duchesse d'Aquitaine and Toulouse, the Queen of France,' Ermengarda waved a gracious hand towards Aliénor, who had smiled like a cat with cream at being given her disputed title of 'Toulouse'. 'And of Jarl Rognvaldr Kali Kolsson.' The massive barbarian beat the table with one fist to show his appreciation of the somewhat superfluous gesture in his direction. The hammer round his neck took on a whole new meaning and there was little chance of mistaking who might be the Jarl. 'Prince of Orkney, on his way to the Holy Land and calling by chance at our fair port, where he is learning what welcome we in Narbonne give to those from over seas.' Her last words were drowned by the drumming of booted feet on the ground, surprisingly loud for only six men, who added some table-banging for good measure. An enthusiastic group, that was certain.

'In honour of our visitors,' Ermengarda continued when she could be heard again, 'I declare a Torneig of Song.' More stamping and banging. 'To the winner I offer this prize.' Ermengarda clapped her hands above her head and a servant ran to her, knelt and held out something that rested on a tasseled cushion. Once more the Viscomtesse raised her arms but this time to display a sword belt and scabbard. 'In the most supple leather from al-Andalus, tooled in designs of the south and with my pledge that the finest leatherworker in Narbonne will add the blazon of whoever wins.' General murmurs of approval and of course some stamping. Just what she'd always wanted, Estela told herself, a man's leather sword-belt. Not that there was any expectation at all that a man would win, like, say, Dragonetz for example! She knew perfectly well that she was not in his class yet but one day she would be, she vowed.

Aliénor was on her feet now beside Ermengarda. 'And from me, the winner shall have this.' She too clapped her hands and there was a gasp as a servant brought her a suit of chainmail, which she could hardly lift to show the assembly, to yet more noise of approval. The two women were about to sit when Jarl Rognvaldr heaved to his feet. 'And I,' he said in a heavy accent that still carried the gulping sound of his native tongue, 'offer this!' In one swift movement he pulled the large golden clasp from his own tunic and thumped it down on the table in front of Ermengarda as if it were a piece of meat. His followers hammered and stamped enough to test the Palace foundations. The Viscomtesse picked up the circular pin like the treasure it was and held it high. 'It is a Viking luck rune,' the Jarl explained, 'and has been with me since I was a boy.'

Ermengarda turned to him but spoke for everyone in the Hall to hear. 'You do us too much honour, my Lord. Such a prize carries a piece of your heart with it. Choose again, please.'

And everyone in the Hall heard his reply, deep and strong. 'I leave all of my heart a willing prisoner in this hall, my Lady Ermengarda, whether I give away a trinket or not. Narbonne keeps me stronger captive than a man chained inside Cubby Roo's Castle, where the walls are as thick as a boat is wide.' There was a heartbeat pause and then he roared, 'Let the Torneig begin!' Amid the stomping and banging, Ermengarda gave the official signal, leaned to catch something Dragonetz was telling her and nodded. Estela's stomach dived again and instinctively she looked to Dragonetz for reassurance. Was it her imagination or he did he look her way as he raised his glass in a barely perceptible toast? She felt for her mandora and touched its angled peg-box, ran her fingers down the neck.

A hush ran round the Hall as the first troubadour took his place, exactly where Estela had thought she would go, when she rehearsed the moment mentally. Her stomach looped once more, like a swallow over the river. A page announced 'Marcabru' as the man dressed like a cleric took a stool and now Estela knew who he was, as did everyone else in the Hall. Better known even than Dragonetz, and older than him, people said he had been left on a rich man's doorstep, nicknamed 'Pan Perdut', 'Left-over Bread', and then called Marcabru, some said named after the woman who'd left him on the doorstep but no-one really knew. Since then he'd performed for the Lords of

Gascony and the Lords of Aragon and it was quite a coup for Ermengarda to produce him out of her sleeve like a jongleur. Estela ignored a reminder from her insides that he would be a hard act to follow and concentrated on Marcabru.

The man had presence. From the first notes of his lute and his voice, he spun a mood and a story. He took his audience to the Crusade in his opening verse, made them fight alongside him for 'Peace in the Name of God.'

'Pax in nomine Domini.
Fes Marcabrús los mos e'l so;
Auiatz que di:
Cum nos a fait per sa dousor
Lo Seignorius celestiaus
Probet de nos un LAVADOR,
C' anc for outramar non fon taus,
Endelai envés Josaphat,
E d'aquest de sal nos conort.
Lavar de ser e de maití
Nos deuríam segon razó'

'Peace in the Name of the Lord
to the tune called by Marcabru

In shock and in awe
Hear of his mercy too
Who gives us the Way to Cleanse
A Way first found Oltra mar
From the Valley of Josaphat
A Way to Cleanse here
As we should, to be good
Morning and evening
I tell you this clear
When he rises, each hale man
Should go to the Lustrum

Elixir of Life
Preventer of Death.'

In complex, clever rhymes and soul-wrenching drops in his melodies, Marcabru reminded everyone in the audience of his Christian duty, moving easily from what they should do to what 'others' did, in vicious accusation. More than one shifted guiltily as Marcabru sang of

'The lecherous wine-slurpers
Dinner-gobblers, fire-stokers, hearth-hoggers
Who stay behind and shame us.'

'E ill luxoriús corna-vi
Coita-diznar, buffa-tizó
Crup en cami'
Remanran e feran pudor
Qu'en sai cum es
Antiocha pres e valor
Sai plora Guian' e Peytaus
Diau Séigner, al tieu LAVADOR.
L' arma del comte met' en paus
E sal gart Peitieus e Niort
Lo Séigner qui resors del vas.'

'For I know well the score
Of one's valour In Antioch,
His soul now far from men
Mourned by Poitou and Guyenne
In your heavenly Lustrum. Then
I pray, my sweet risen Lord
Guard always Poitou and Niord.'

Estela felt the swell of the music and the rising baritone calling her to arms, firing her with the desire to do God's work and reclaim the

Holy Land, kill the enemy, cleanse herself of impure thoughts and cleanse God's own country of the Infidel Moor. She would not be one of those lashed by Marcabru for being too cowardly – she would go to war against these foreign dogs! And the climax in praise of Raymond of Antioch's brother in arms, Baldwin, was a deft touch, uniting the themes of purification with the Crusade and of course pleasing Aliénor without touching too closely on her beloved uncle.

'He's good, isn't he,' a voice whispered beside her and she flushed as red as if, once more, al-Hisba had read her thoughts.

'In his way,' she responded cautiously, too conscious of the lyrics. 'He asks a lot of his audience, and it's all very clever. The rhymes are perhaps too clever for taking it in at one hearing. Of course it is a couple of years old so some will have heard it before. But the Master's performance...' She shook her head, having no words for the level of artistry she had witnessed. 'Are you going to sing?' she asked him.

'I think I will keep my Oltra mar face in the shadows. I think the welcome here is only for red-headed Vikings.'

She could think of nothing to reply that wouldn't make things worse. At that moment Arnaut joined them. 'He's good isn't he.' Estela and al-Hisba exchanged glances and Arnaut continued blithely, 'and Aliénor will enjoy all the Crusading vigour but I can tell you now that Dragonetz hates it. Not that he's adjudicating so I don't suppose it matters what he thinks.'

'Why?' demanded Estela. 'I thought he gained his title 'los Pros' in the Crusades.'

'Hush,' rebuked their neighbours, as Marcabru once more strummed an opening note.

'Cowards' as a term of abuse faded to a pleasantry against the insults to which Marcabru treated his audience in his next song. This time he launched into a blistering satire against idiot lovers who put sensual pleasures above the love of God, all delivered in that deep voice of his, which made you believe in retribution and hell-fire.

Estela shivered as the final notes tolled but part of her still analysed how the feeling was created. 'A servantes,' she commented to al-Hisba, 'even though he calls it a vers, he's using all the tricks of the trade. My, but he's vicious. And they love it.' She looked around at the faces shining with fan-worship. 'The nastier he is, the more they like it. He's sure to win.' She had a sudden desire to swim upstream. 'Al-Hisba, will you play tambour for me when I sing?' She imagined the Moor taking the floor at her side, the reaction of the audience.

'No,' he stated baldly and he looked at her as if she were in their music lesson again and he were testing her, to see if she understood, to find out what she had learned and how far she had yet to go. She was disappointed at not being able to make her public gesture of friendship for the Moor but there was no time for debate.

'I will,' jumped in Arnaut enthusiastically and she smiled at him. Of course he would.

Then the maestro started his final song, a personal embroidery on the themes of his second.

> 'Marcabru fills Na Bruna
> fo engenratz en tal luna
> qu'el sap d'Amor cum degruna
> escutatz
> quez anc non amet neguna
> ni d'autra non fo amatz.'

> 'Marcabru, son of Marcabruna
> Was born under such a moon 'a
> Knows
> of love its rotten heart
> So never will become a part
> Of being loved nor loving show.'

'Well, you can't say he doesn't know his own talent!' Estela muttered to her companions as the applause echoes round the Hall. 'But there's no doubt about the talent.'

'Cheerful soul,' was Arnaut's verdict. 'Bet he's fun in the bedchamber.'

Estela laughed, which was exactly what she needed to calm her nerves as Dragonetz and Aliénor stood and looked in her direction. A page walked in front of the High Table and announced, 'Aliénor, Duchesse d'Aquitaine and Toulouse,' *Never miss an opportunity*, thought Estela, 'and the Queen of France, presents Estela de Matin.'

Another tummy flip but Estela picked up her mandora and stood. She had forgotten about her feet and had to force herself to walk to the stool where Marcabru had been sitting. Arnaut followed just behind her, stopped and collected a tambour from the group of Palace musicians who were ready to accompany a troubadour on request. Estela sank gratefully onto the stool, told Arnaut her programme and tuned her mandora, controlling her nerves.

She shut her eyes, shut out the Great Hall, the lords and Ladies, became the little girl who had sung for her parents and then for their assemblies, seen the pride in her mother's eyes, tuned in to the mood of the audience. She could do this.

Eyes wide open, she started the love songs she had chosen, now an ironic counterpoint to Marcabru's vitriol. She couldn't compete with him, nor was she trying to, but she knew that she could use the contrast to advantage. She must be sweeter than honey, a nightingale after a bear, her black hair silk rippling over her shoulder as she strummed the chords and plucked a plaintive melody. With Arnaut at her side, his perfect profile, his blonde hair, his lithe rhythm as he held high the tambour and beat the stresses for her, she knew they looked to be all that she sang of, all that Marcabru had mocked, a young couple passionately in love. She played to that too, exchanging long looks with Arnaut, who warmed quickly to the game and dropped to his knees to rattle his tambour wistfully at her feet.

She strummed one last sad chord and ended, drooping with suitable melancholy as the song finished. She had sensed the mood of the audience changing as she sang, from the belligerence aroused by Marcabru to gentler emotions. More than one couple were exchanging glances full of promise. If life was short then there was one sure way of making it enjoyable. Estela noted one lady wiping her eyes.

'Wonderful.' Arnaut bowed to the audience and gestured to her as she curtsied and took the applause. 'You were wonderful.' As he bowed, she glimpsed her token dangling on a chain beneath his tunic. 'It was an acceptable first performance,' she judged, trying not to be smug. She would have liked a more impartial verdict but she had not dared look at Dragonetz during her performance and she felt too vulnerable for criticism, however constructive, Now was not the time to seek him out, even with her eyes, for she would know his thoughts straight away from his expression. He would be preparing mentally for his own songs. How was he going to compete with the virtuoso performance by Marcabru, master of lyrics, musical composition and a voice to chill a graveyard, deep and true and haunting? Good as Dragonetz was, how could he make a bigger impact? Surely he would be on next? The butterflies had flown her stomach as magically as they arrived there and instead a flutter of compliments alighted as she made her way back to her seat, bringing a flush to her cheeks.

'Mmm,' said al-Hisba, with a nod that she took to be approval. 'Not bad but still a bit thin.' She remembered Dragonetz' comment when he first heard her sing. 'Lacks experience,' and the criticism stung. Still a girl.

Once more there was a fanfare and a page announced, 'Jarl Rognvaldr Koli Kolsson, Prince of Orkney.' General amazement quickly hushed to anticipation as the Jarl lumbered to his place, throwing the stool out of his way, one of his men behind him, one to the side.

The latter addressed the Hall. 'Jarl Rognvaldr wishes to honour Lady Ermengarda with a skald, a poem in the style of my people, Our Prince is renowned for his verse and tonight he draws inspiration from my Lady, his host and from the songs of love that he has heard so sweetly sung.' The Norseman had bowed towards Ermengarda and towards Estela, who rose to accept the compliment, curtseying. So not everyone had been over-awed by Marcabru.

And then the Prince of Orkney claimed all eyes. He recited on his feet, letting the music of his language roll slowly over his audience, not caring that they didn't understand a word. Instead he paced back and forth, used his hands and his voice to throw emotions to the gods and catch them again. Estela could feel the alliteration and the rhyming, could sense a technical cleverness to match Marcabru and his presence was like a stormcloud, threatening and blasting them with words. A strange sort of love poem. And strange to have only the music of the words. Although the other Vikings were holding strange instruments, they moved not a muscle while their Lord declaimed.

When the poem ended, the Viking who had introduced his lord returned to the front. 'My prince has asked me to explain some of his skald in your language. It is our way to make pictures with kennings so that 'skorò haukvallar', the pillar of the hawk-plain, means 'sleeve'. We paint pictures and make names with sounds so that listening to our poetry is part of making the meaning. My Prince would like you to know that the 'Ern' in the poem is an eagle and 'ogeroa' means 'lets down her hair' so you should hear these two words together as we would do.' He bowed towards 'ERMenGARda' and made his meaning clear. 'And when my Prince uses the word 'ogeroa' we hear also geroa and geroi, the last meaning the ships propped up round the shore, perhaps propped up by this same name we hear in the music of the line.' This time it was the Prince himself who bowed to Ermengarda and she acknowledged his poetic tribute and practical hope with a serene smile and nod.

It was not clear whether the Norseman intended to continue educating the Narbonnais or not because at this point, Arnaut started clapping with mad enthusiasm, joined quickly by someone at the High table – Dragonetz, of course, Estela noted – and then, as is the way, the whole audience had joined in, spurred on to more clapping by Arnaut and Dragonetz every time there looked to be a lull. Only when the two Norsemen bowed their thanks did Arnaut mutter, 'Thank God for that,' and let his hands drop.

'A man can die of boredom,' Arnaut explained to Estela, and he waved cheerful thanks to Dragonetz, who bowed, the movement imperceptible to anyone not watching closely. 'Sometimes you clap because they *have* finished, thank God, and sometimes, you clap to make them.'

'I'll bear that in mind,' Estela said ironically.

'You were different, everyone clapped you because they loved you.' Arnaut's lack of guile was impossible to resent. He made Estela smile and it was her turn to feel like an old cynic.

Luckily for Arnaut's health, the Vikings had finished their declamation and the Norseman who had been in the background gave a rousing tune on a sort of guimbarde, although Estela had never before seen one with a bamboo frame, nor heard a man get the sound of a horse's hooves from twanging the metal tongue, clacking with his teeth. This time Arnaut's applause was genuine and the Vikings left the floor to the stamping, banging and shouting of their fellows left at table.

'Dragonetz los Pros' announced the page and Estela's stomach dipped stupidly. She watched Dragonetz say something in Ermengarda's ear and then he was walking round the table, not to the place where the stool was once more waiting a troubadour, but over towards her. At the same time, Ermengarda rose and spoke. 'My Lord Dragonetz apologises but, owing to a minor injury to his hand, he cannot play for you tonight, so will instead sing with the accompaniment of his student.'

'My Lady Estela?' Dragonetz held out his hand and she once again picked up her mandora and allowed herself to be led, slowly, with all eyes following them, back to the floor. Her sore feet reminded her exactly how Dragonetz had hurt his hand and she flushed, switching her thoughts to the question of what on earth he was going to sing. She reviewed all his songs in her mind, confident that she knew them all but when she sat on the second stool that had quickly been drawn up, and he whispered his choice to her, she looked at him wide-eyed and said, 'You can't!'

'Watch me,' he grinned and so she tuned up, and in front of Marcabru, three rulers and a Hallful of the Great and – God forgive her – the Good – she accompanied Dragonetz in three of the crudest, most lascivious songs ever composed. She had known that the key to winning would be contrast, she told herself as his beautiful rich voice – another baritone, incapable of Marcabru's thunder but with a range of feeling that Marcabru would not have wanted to convey, given the likely cost to his immortal soul. Dragonetz took his audience under the bushes looking for the prettiest 'hares' a girl might show and when he sang of 'country matters' no-one doubted the pleasures on offer.

Then his lusty male voice reprimanded a friend for being unwilling to satisfy a Lady in the manner she liked best, all described in physical detail as he declared himself more than willing to do what his friend would not. Estela glanced around the Hall, measuring the levels of sophistication, the evident enjoyment at the High Table – apart from a scowling Marcabru of course – the downcast eyes of some of the Ladies, feigning pudeur, the smiles and laughter that lit up faces red in the torch-light.

Estela could sense the rush of energy in Dragonetz, a different kind of virtuoso performance to Marcabru's certainly! But inimitable and at the top of his form. Her fingers played to his jokes, pointed out the puns, danced with and around his voice.

After two such songs, surely he would switch genre? The audience shuffled in anticipation and Estela smiled to herself, knowing what was coming, hoping he could carry it off. There was a little breath of disappointment as he started a third song, unknown to most in the Hall, but clearly in the same vein, where he declared himself ready for fun, with 'ab mazer viet de nuill aize en despan', his donkey-size dick, but then, just as the audience felt out of laughter, Dragonetz switched into a perfect falsetto and gave the woman's reply. Estela had to fight to control her own giggles and she could see tears streaming down people's faces as Dragonetz acted the woman. When he threatened the crude lover with a good kick up the backside, his voice trilled with feminine rage.

'*Q'eu vos farai lanzar par le culada*
Tals peitz que son de corn vos semblaran
Et ab tal son fairetz aital balada !'

'So then you will blow your own trumpet yet more,
Take a trip on your hot air to render it pure!'

He ended triumphantly, shaking his fist towards the imagined villain, who happened to be in exactly the same direction as Marcabru. Everyone was standing, holding hands high, clapping, shouting, the Vikings louder than ever and it was beginning to turn into a potential threat to Arnaut's health when Dragonetz himself bowed yet again and called for quiet.

'I've asked Lady Estela de Matin to close our entertainment,' he told the assembly.

Estela had been warned of this when Dragonetz told her his programme and she had racked her brains for a way to avoid following his performance. She stood up and projected her voice, as she had been trained.

'My Lord is kind to his student and I would like to take the chance to introduce mine.'

'You continue to surprise me,' Dragonetz murmured, as Estela invited Bèatriz to the floor, where Dragonetz ceded his place and the girl sang a simple, well-known melody to Estela' s accompaniment.

'I will never forget your kindness,' the young heiress of Dia told Estela, eyes shining as she accepted her own share of appreciation.

No-one objected to Dragonetz being declared the winner and accepting two prizes from Ermengarda and compliments from Aliénor, who oozed smug satisfaction, but the evening still held one surprise. Ermengarda turned to the Prince of Orkney, who held up the prize he had offered at the start but not given to Dragonetz.

'I laud the winner,' he declared, 'but I have asked him if I may give this in his honour to his student, for the pleasure she has given us.'

Estela stumbled her way to the High Table, half-hearing comments as she went past, 'Sweet voice' (but thin, Estela added in her own mind), 'Pity she walks like a duck'. Afterwards, Estela would wonder which of Aliénor's Ladies had made the remark, and why she should scent musk strong and repellant, but at the time she was too busy concentrating on reaching the Jarl without falling over.

He presented her with the great gold clasp and she gasped at the weight of it. 'It is the rune of signs,' he told her and when she looked at it close-up she could see that the design was circular but with sign-posts like the spokes of a wheel or the feathers of arrows stuck in a wheel.

'Wherever you go, you will never be lost,' he told her. 'When you seek direction, the Pathfinder rune will answer you. Odin and Thor will recognize you from now on.'

Overcome, Estela stammered thanks. When she raised her head, it was to seek out Dragonetz, who was already surrounded by Ladies but who caught her eye. 'Well done,' he mouthed and her stomach warmed as with wine, but he had already bent to whisper some obscenity in a pretty ear and she could hear the tinkling laughter in response. Marcabru was also surrounded, by men wanting to discuss vers clos and technicalities of form, from what Estela could hear of the conversation. And so, of course, she joined them.

CHAPTER NINE

Dragonetz was aware of Estela leaving the Hall, Arnaut and – inexplicably – a large white dog at her side. Whether she slept with either was none of his business, he told himself, twice. Young, idealistic, beautiful Arnaut. It was a toss-up which had been the more dog-like in devotion during the evening, the hairy white hound or Arnaut, but it was none of his business. His thoughts wandered freely while his mouth responded automatically to coy feminine comments on his choice of songs or on the other singers.

'Such a miserable man, that Marcabru,' commented Marie or Sylvie. He found them all the same.

Losing patience, Dragonetz said shortly, 'He is a genius. Excuse me, my Lady Aliénor needs me.' He had indeed been summoned, which saved him from inventing an excuse to escape.

Aliénor was clearly pleased with herself and with her troubadours but after lavishing compliments she drew him out of earshot and got to the heart of what she wanted.

'I need to know more about Ermengarda, bind her closer or know how far she'll go. I want you to tell her that I was the one who had Toulouse disposed of, poisoned, for her sake, and I want you to tell me how she reacts. Obviously you won't tell her that I sent you. You will make it seem part of your own search for information.'

'Obviously.' Dragonetz smiled and nodded for public view, as if she were still paying him compliments and pointed out, 'That won't be easy, given that I'm supposed to think she's trying to murder you.'

'You'll think of something,' was the airy reply and Aliénor dismissed him with a gracious nod.

Dragonetz was still mulling over the implications of this conversation when he finally went to bed, alone. Alphonse, the father of the current Comte de Toulouse was called 'Jourdain' because he was born to his crusading father in the Holy Land and allegedly baptised in the River Jordan. As an adult, he returned to rule Toulouse. Like Aliénor, Alphose Jourdain had accepted the cross from Bernard de Clairvaux in 1146 and was ready to follow in his father's footsteps as a soldier of Christ. He met up with King Louis, Aliénor and their allies, and went with them to the Council of Acre. Dragonetz steeled his mind away from events following that and from his own part in them. After the disastrous battles, Alphonse had gone on to Caesarea, where he had died in 1148, poisoned. Dragonetz put the question to himself that he had not asked Aliénor. It was not the sort of question that people answered honestly. *Had* she murdered Alphonse Jourdain?

There was no doubt of her hatred, not just for him but for any Comte de Toulouse, usurpers of her birthright, all of them. She had even talked the King into laying siege to Toulouse to win it back for her but he had not succeeded, one more nail in the coffin of their marriage. With Jourdain dead, only his thirteen-year-old son stood between Aliénor and Toulouse itself and rumours had certainly accused her – or credited her, depending your viewpoint. Dragonetz didn't doubt for a minute Aliénor's capacity for a politic murder but she was not the only suspect. And she had not benefited. Two years later, she was no nearer claiming Toulouse in more than words at a banquet.

Top suspect on most gossips' list was the Queen of Jerusalem, to gain control over Tripoli for herself and her sixteen-year-old son, already King of Jerusalem jointly with his mother. If the motive were not gain but mere vengeance for long-standing quarrels, then you could add the Comte de Barcelone and the Comte de Béziers, and even Roger and Raimon Trencavel of Carcassonne. And, of course, Ermengarda herself. What enemy more implacable than an ex-wife?

Dragonetz contemplated the early history of the golden ruler of Narbonne. Viscomtesse at four years old, swept into marriage to this same Alphonse, Comte de Toulouse, when she was twelve. This allowed Toulouse to claim Narbonne and then one year later, in 1143, he became the target of every Narbonne ally striving to support the young heiress in getting rid of this same parasitical husband. Whether from support of Ermengarda or from concerns over the fast extending power of Toulouse, action was swift and effective. Alphonse was ousted while he was away from home, backed into a corner by the Catalan alliance that left him only too happy to agree to the divorce. He could not outface the armies gathered against him and he retreated to Toulouse, to lick his wounds and fill his son's head with his hunger for Narbonne, stolen from him when he had it in his grasp.

What if Ermengarda, now grown into her power, had taken the quickest route to eliminate declarations in Toulouse of its rights to Narbonne? Was her arm long enough to reach Caesarea? Undoubtedly. The ruler of the greatest trading state on the Mediterranean could reach wherever there were spices, carpets and silks. Had she gained from it? Not politically, if the young Comte de Toulouse fulfilled his promise of being twice the tyrant his father was, with the title of Narbonne as loudly proclaimed in his city streets as was the title of Toulouse proclaimed hers by Aliénor. But personally? That depended on how deeply the marriage had touched the young Ermengarda, a marriage that had supposedly touched her so little it could be dissolved for non-consummation. But you never knew. Alphonse would have accepted any terms and Ermengarda was hardly likely to protest a convenient lie. Besides which, she was quickly married again, this time a wise alliance to Bernard d'Anduze, a respectable nonentity who left the city as soon after the marriage as possible, leaving Ermengarda the freedom of a married woman without the inconveniences. Oh, how Aliénor must envy that! D'Anduze's brother, the Archbishop of Narbonne, might be less enthusiastic about the freedom given to his sister-in-law.

Dragonetz chased the speculations in circles. Why did Aliénor now want to raise the spectre of Alphonse between her and Ermengarda, with himself in the middle? He sighed and shifted sleepless position one more time, no nearer untangling the knots. Perhaps sleep would bring counsel if he ceased to worry at the problem. He willed his brain to leave the day behind, bring on the void, but as soon as he let his thoughts drift, they homed to the one place he dared not go. In a giant wave sweeping him under, he smelled lavender on wet skin, he felt the weight of black hair running through his fingers, he saw the welt of a scar and his own words 'just a woman' moved beside him on the bed until he rolled over and took what comfort he could from his own imagination.

His last thoughts before he finally slept were that Raoulf might be right, and he was going crazy from doing without a woman. He would choose among the Maries and the Sylvies, someone dispensable, someone who knew the rules. And the interview with Ermengarda would give him the answer to a question of his own as well as to Aliénor's, With Ermengarda's help, he would no longer have to wonder what to do about Estela to keep her safe. *It cannot happen again. I won't let it happen again.*

Dragonetz spent the day at the mill, putting as many miles between himself and Estela as he could. Every turn of the wheel and every hammer-drop had smoothed one more wrinkle from his brow until Palace politics was as irrelevant as a woman's touch. All that mattered was the exact calibration of a mechanical system and the best way to use it to produce paper.

'It's ingenious,' he told al-Hisba, who had also given music lessons a wide berth.

'The brothers used one at Douzens to wake them for midnight

mass. One of the brothers was in charge of maintaining the water in the system and that's all it takes to keep it going.'

'A water-powered timepiece,' Dragonetz mused, on his knees, inspecting the bowlful of water with the levels marked for the hours. 'How did you fix the markers?'

'I calibrated them with the markers on a sundial. This is a simple version. The one at Douzens used a gear to ring a bell for wake-up and I have heard of more complicated movements activated by the water level dropping.'

'Same as our hammer system.'

'Similar,' agreed al-Hisba. 'As we have no shortage of water this is an easy way to work out the timing of the hammers, and to keep a record – or at least it would be easy if anyone here had been taught some basic arithmetic and recording! So this is what I have found.' He picked up a charred stick and wrote in the earth.

'Ten,' he told them.

Raoulf held up ten fingers and looked with disbelief at the ground. 'A stick and a wheel!' he said. 'It doesn't even look like ten! And he's been writing this sort of Arabic in the ground all the time and expecting us to understand it. I've told him to get an abacus like any civilized person but no, he says that one day we will understand Al-Khwariz-mi's geometry if we only persevere. I tell you, Dragonetz, I don't mind helping with the stones but this is going too far into foreign ways!'

'You see,' al-Hisba looked at Dragonetz and shrugged his shoulders. Sighing, he told Raoulf, 'This, the stick, represents the number one....'

'A minute ago it was the number ten! Next you'll tell me that the wheel,' he scuffed his foot near the circle, 'magics the one into a ten.'

'Something like that,' Dragonetz laughed and cut off Raoulf's spluttered reply. 'Never mind the magic, Raoulf, just listen. So, ten what?' he asked al-Hisba.

'I calculate that there are ten turns of the wheel –'

Everyone ignored Raoulf's pained, 'I told you that was a wheel –'

'–every minute.'

Dragonetz took the charred stick. 'So every rotation has the three hammers fall twice, because there are two cams per hammer.' He scored the sum in the dirt,

3 + 3

6

'So one rotation has 6 hammerfalls and there are ten hammerfalls each minute.' Dragonetz used his stick again.

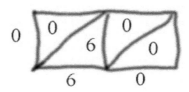

'So that's 60 hammerfalls each minute.'

'As you say,' al-Hisba bowed his head, acknowledging the other man's education, while Raoulf crossed himself and shook his head.

Dragonetz gave his own men the chance to redeem themselves. 'So what would improve this? Arnaut? Raoulf?'

'Faster of course!' Raoulf was contemptuous. 'Why didn't you just ask me that in the first place! If the hammers go faster they'll do more work. Same as men.'

'Yes, but without al-Hisba's calculation you wouldn't know how fast they are going now and you wouldn't be able to measure the difference and see what happens.'

Never one to give up easily, Raoulf grumbled, 'You can see how fast the hammers move and you can see if they speed up!'

'Not if you're in Aquitaine, you can't! With al-Hisba's measure anyone can check up on the hammer-speed and we can make comparisons, even if we're not here.'

'So,' Arnaut chipped in, 'the question is *how* we speed up the hammers.'

'Lighter hammers,' suggested Raoulf.

Arnaut shook his head. 'No difference. It's the wheel that sets the turning time and the water turns the wheel. We could take the river directly into the wheel, then when there's floods and rapids it would speed up?'

'Too dangerous. No, we have to stick with the culvert and channel, which gives us control of the water. So it has to be us who speed up the water... Raise it? Start with a wide channel and narrow it over a drop in height to increase the flow and move the wheel faster. I know, we could put a drop-gate in the channel, raise it to decrease the flow, lower it to increase it. Al-Hisba, will it work?'

The Moor bowed. 'My people have been doing this for thousands of years to irrigate the crops, Yes, it will work.'

'So, show me how we can organize this drop-gate. Where shall we put it?' In his eagerness, Dragonetz was already walking along the cut which channeled the water from the river to the wheel and the others had no option but to scurry in his wake.

By the time he found himself outside Ermengarda's chamber, keeping the appointment made earlier that day, Dragonetz felt thoroughly refreshed, as much by cogitations on cogs as by a long soak in a hot tub, where he kept his thoughts firmly on paper-making. He had eaten with the men at the mill, stayed away from Palace people and felt all the readier to face what was likely to be a delicate conversation. The very fact that Ermengarda had arranged it for late evening, in her ante-chamber, suggested that she too was prepared for a very private exchange.

His light knock was answered straight away and he slipped into the room. The torchlight flickered over draped stools, emblazoned with fleur de lys, rich navies and reds, their mistress poker-straight and still, standing, waiting for him to enter.

'Dragonetz,' she said simply and sat down, indicating a stool in front of her, lower than hers he noted.

'My Lady.'

'You wanted to see me,' she began. 'Was this to tell me about your paper-making mill in my domain?' He took a sharp breath while she continued. 'To claim a reward for killing a Jew? Or to claim a reward for saving the lives of the Jews I'd have had to hang if you'd made the murder attempt public? No? Then perhaps you want to check whether I intend to repeat my attempt to murder Aliénor, as she would have me believe you see me as the most likely suspect?'

Dragonetz stood up to leave. 'Your spies are efficient and you seem to have covered it all,' he said, 'so perhaps I should go.'

'Of course I know what happens in Narbonne! Sit down, Dragonetz.' He sat. 'Just don't play me for a fool.'

Then he did meet her eyes, grey, measuring him. If he had doubted his best way through this maze of a meeting, he no longer hesitated. 'You know I never suspected you.' She waited but he had no intention of exposing Aliénor's subterfuges. Or at least, not those ones. 'So we won't waste time on that. But you are nearest the mark with your last suggestion.' One finely plucked eyebrow, the fair hairs barely visible, was raised. 'I would indeed like to talk of a real suspect, the menace in the south-west…'

'Toulouse,' Ermengarda acknowledged. 'Go on…'

'A young viper it seems, likely to bite those who take him to their bosom as well as spit his venom further afield. I have the impression that my Lady Aliénor regrets that his father's death has not removed this poison from her life and yours. She hoped so very very much, for your sake, that the removal of Alphonse Jourdain would remove this threat to Narbonne once and for all, and all unpleasant memories with it.' Dragonetz waited and watched.

'So I am to believe that poison was a just means to remove poison, is that it Dragonetz?' He gave no response but waited. 'And it was just because it was by Aliénor's hand, you would tell me, for my sake what's more, not because Aliénor calls herself Toulouse by right.' Her tone was light and ironic but grew less controlled. 'And I am implicated because I had no reason to love the dear first husband who saw his chance at Narbonne through marrying a young girl and stealing her birthright. The Toulouse claim now frets away at me like a half-healed wound and no, Dragonetz, I did not mourn Alphonse Jourdain. Do I wish his son dead? Is that what Aliénor wishes my connivance at? Or even that I should take the name without the act?'

Dragonetz schooled his face and his thoughts to give nothing away but his heart jumped when she took both his hands in her own and held his gaze. 'Dragonetz los Pros, if Narbonne truly needed the death of Raymond de Toulouse, I would have it done tomorrow, as surely as I would sentence twenty innocent Jews to the gallows to preserve the peace of my city. You know this already and you would do the same. You have done the same, or worse.'

His eyes dropped but she would not let his hands escape. 'This is what we do, what we must do, our birthright and our burden. But I do not poison men on a whim! Only a fool takes a sword and cuts through the knots in a rope, and loses the rope along with the knot. Raymond creates knots I must untangle but I would have to kill a great many men to cut through all my knots. And, as you said, the death of Alphonse Jourdain created as many problems as it solved so,' she gripped his hand firmly before she released him, 'I want no part of any murder. And you can tell Aliénor that.'

'My Lady,' he murmured, knowing the question she would put to him.

'This is a puppet-show, Dragonetz. Let us stop competing to pull the strings. Was it Aliénor? Did she have Alphonse poisoned?' Ermengarda asked him.

'I don't know,' Dragonetz admitted, honestly, holding nothing back. If he had not already sworn his oath of fealty to another, he would have been on his knees offering his sword. The least he could offer was the truth. 'It angers her that Louis' attempt to regain Toulouse for her was as feeble and half-hearted as everything he does. Alphonse was alongside us in Constantinople, in Acre, fretting at her like a half-healed wound.' Ermengarda acknowledged the reference. 'And he was not a man to underplay either his petty triumphs or his great ones. Yes, he got under Aliénor's skin and although he was miles away when he died, in Caesarea, Aliénor could have reached that far. I don't know whether she did.'

'And Aliénor will tell you what suits her from one moment to the next.' *As will you, as will I.* Dragonetz kept the thoughts to himself. 'It seems the man too monk-like for Aliénor has not been so half-hearted on one occasion and France will have an heir. Or is it indeed his?' Ermengarda asked innocently.

Luckily, honesty and self-protection gave the same answer. Dragonetz' 'Yes' was emphatic.

'I had heard that Aliénor sometimes compensated for her husband's short... comings,' she teased Dragonetz, who knew full well the rumours that he himself warmed the Queen's bed when she so wished. But it was not of him that Ermengarda posed the question, although her eyes told him she might have. 'The timing does not of course work for it to affect the fatherhood of this infant but I heard that Louis was not best pleased with the ... relationship between Aliénor and her uncle, Antioch. Is this true?'

Dragonetz knew that he could dance a politic answer and keep Ermengarda at a distance, at the distance proper for a man who followed his liege Lord blindly. It had been two years since Dragonetz was that man and he would never follow Aliénor blindly, never again. If he kept his oath and followed her, it was with his eyes open, and with a promise to the dead that he would make the right choices, not Aliénor's choices and if this promise clashed with his oath, the dead claimed first allegiance, whether he paid for eternity or not.

So it was with open eyes that Dragonetz answered bluntly, 'Yes, Aliénor and Raymond were lovers and Louis knew. I'm not sure that shipping her off to Tripoli by force was the best way of dealing with it. She will never forgive him.'

'Not even when their little Prince-son is playing hobby-horse in front of his doting parents?' Ermengarda hadn't even blinked at the allegation of adultery and incest on the part of the Queen of France.

'Never. Aliénor will mate with a king to make more kings, *her* kings, but she hates weakness and she cannot bear to be thwarted. Louis is guilty of both in her eyes. Worse, he humiliated her.' Dragonetz remembered Antioch, Aliénor crazy with Crusade, with satiated desire, while Louis stumbled around in a living nightmare, his pilgrimage become the road to hell.

What he and his wife then argued about was whether to re-take Aleppo for Raymond, because Louis could not say the words of their real argument. Unable to watch his wife leaning against her uncle, laces still loose from clothes thrown on in haste, but unable to speak or hit back, Louis fought over Aleppo, tried to prove his manhood by sulking and sailing off, had Aliénor bundled aboard a ship by his soldiers and her men told curtly to join their ships. A fine start to a fine campaign! 'She loved him, her uncle, Raymond of Antioch,' Dragonetz told Ermengarda quietly. 'They were made of the same substance, pure fire together. When the news came that he was lost in battle at Aleppo and that Nur ad-Din had sent Raymond's head to be paraded by the Caliph at Baghdad, Aliénor stopped eating. She was desperately ill for months, recovered only at the thought of a divorce. It was Raymond who suggested that the Pope would divorce her for consanguinity with Louis but the Pope was only too pleased to bless the marriage, and the result of that, you know.'

'Why are you telling me all this?' The room held its breath.

'I have served Aquitaine from boyhood. I've been at my Lady Aliénor's side through trophies and tragedies and I wish her well.'

'But,' prompted Ermengarda.

'But I really don't give a saint's relic whether a man – or a woman – is a Christian, a Jew or a Muslim.'

'That's a dangerous statement. Even more so for a knight who's taken the Cross and fought in the Holy Land!'

'And will do so again, should my Liege Lord demand it.' Dragonetz couldn't keep the bitterness from his voice. 'But I will also lead *my* life and I will rescue all I can from this destruction we wreak on each other in the name of religion!'

'A paper mill?'

'A paper mill,' Dragonetz confirmed. 'If we take knowledge out of the hands of the Church and disperse the real treasures of the Moors and the Jews, we could become –' and for once, words failed him. Her silence told him he'd failed. No-one could understand what he'd seen, what he'd done, a brute among brutes. No-one could see how it could be different.

'Civilised,' offered Ermengarda and his heart lifted. 'Yes, I know the treasures brought to my city by the Jews and the Moors, from al-Andalus and even our enemies in the Holy Land, who all know secrets of medicine, arithmetic, astronomy, engineering,' she too ran out of words.

'Of which we know nothing!'

She corrected, 'Which we are learning. The more Narbonne trades, the more she grows in this learning. Trade is more than daily bread! And the Jews I protect in my city are more than coin-spinners! Abraham ben Isaac has been useful to you.' Was there nothing about him she didn't know? 'One day this same Raavad will be remembered by his people, perhaps by everyone, for his wisdom, when I will be forgotten.'

'Never forgotten, my Lady, and if Narbonne will help me in this paper trade, your name will be writ large across the world!' He knelt in front of her, taking her hands in his, the ceremonial gesture of oath-taking. 'I am sworn to Aquitaine and cannot offer my sword elsewhere but I offer you a future in which Aquitaine is tiny, the future of knowledge shared and traded, the spread of reading and writing on paper!'

'It is a good dream, Dragonetz,' she said gently, her hands small and motionless in his grasp. 'Yes, Narbonne will support you in this but I will not do so openly. The Archbishop is far less a brother-in-law to me than his good brother is a husband, for Bernard keeps to the letter of our agreement and we have a clear understanding. Our Papal Nuncio, however, fights me at every turn over his share of dues from tolls and justice and this paper business will unite clerics everywhere against you. It will be hard enough to dig ourselves out of the problems that the Crusades have caused, trade routes damaged, trust broken, Jews and Moors persecuted, without drawing the fire of the Church as well. Should the Friars close the doors of hospitality on our trade routes we will suffer and that's the least of the weapons they hold! So, my support can only be in private, Dragonetz.'

'I understand. And I am grateful.' He bowed his head.

'And however charming you are, there will be no reduction in taxes.' Her voice was grave but he looked up and caught the sparkle in her eyes. 'Now, we can talk of paper and mills another time.'

'There is one more thing. You were right. I would like a boon.'

'Say on,' her voice was colder but when he had detailed his request, she warmed again. 'I understand,' she said. 'Your concern does you credit and I too know the... caprices of my Lady Aliénor. The girl will be safe, I can promise you that.'

'Thank you.' Her fingers curled and she extricated her hands from his. 'We could make better use of this night,' she said, stroking his hair and following the curls down to the opening of his jerkin, tracing the line of his neck with her index finger. 'Rise, Dragonetz.'

'It's a little late for the command, my Lady,' he smiled at her as he stood, allowing her into the circle of his arms. He loosed the pins trapping her coiffed hair, found the pale rose of her mouth and shut his eyes.

'You're trembling, Dragonetz,' she whispered.

'It's been a long time, my Lady. I won't be able to stop, once we begin...'

'We've already begun,' she murmured, unlacing his jerkin and teasing the black hairs on his chest between her fingers, then searching lower, loosing the ties in her way. 'I want you to explain to me some of the finer points of your recent songs.'

'Your Viking will kill me,' he tried.

'Only if I tell him.'

It took all his self-control to resist just a few seconds more, holding her away from him, warning her, 'I won't last long... this will be a disappointment for you.'

'Then,' she said, pressing closer, 'We will pleasure you first and I will wait the second time for my jouissance.' *Raoulf would approve* was Dragonetz' last coherent thought before he let go, dissolving into the scent of Eastern oils and the smoothness of translucent skin. Shaking free of her own clothes, she stood pearl white and naked before him, smooth golden hair above and crinkled golden hair below. He reached out to touch the small breasts, firm as apples, and she caught his hand, drew it to her mouth and explored his fingers with her teeth and tongue.

'Come' she said, leading him to the canopied bed, and he did. Three times that extravagant night, leaving the rich fabrics of Narbonne crumpled and discarded and their mistress pink, gold and sleeping.

CHAPTER TEN

Aliénor took advantage of being alone to lean against the wall and ease her aching back. She was hoping to hide her pregnancy until after she returned to Paris, preferably until after the baby was born. From the moment it was public knowledge, she would be penned in like a prized brood-mare, banned from breathing in case it hurt the baby, subject to every passing whim of court priest or astronomer. She already had to fight for any say in matters of state and her growing belly would weigh in against her. She didn't have to imagine the thousand slights expressed as compliments from important men to a woman whose worth was in her belly. She had heard them all last time around, had lived the nine month speculation on the heir-to-be, had dreamed her future as the mother of the King of France, finally able to achieve all of which she was capable. And then she gave birth to a daughter.

Nothing had prepared her for the disappointment, for the eyes that didn't meet hers as they offered hypocritical congratulations. The southern whore had failed. She read it in every gesture, especially in Louis'. His first words were, 'Never mind, there will be another,' and she knew when he sighed that he was thinking of the devil's work he would have to do in her bed to get a second.

Her own disappointment blazed into bitter resolve. She would show them all what a woman like her could do; a woman with all Aquitaine at her lightest sway. Her first move was to ensure that baby Marie was well-placed, her wet-nurse healthy and loyal, first link in the chain that would grow a royal princess. Little Marie's mother would not underestimate the potential of the right daughter, brought up the right way – the southern way – and married to the right title.

So, while Louis put on his long-suffering face and girded up his loins for another attempt, Aliénor ensured that her daughter was surrounded with hand-picked women from Aquitaine. The less interested in her that Louis and his frocked advisors were, the more time Marie would spend in Poitiers, enjoying her childhood and imbibing Occitan. In absence, Aliénor would bind her daughter to her so tightly that no-one would ever come between them, however many miles separated their bodies. By the time Marie's betrothal was discussed, she would be Aquitaine's forever. Her baby born and kissed good-bye, Aliénor had been swept up in the wave of Crusading fervor.

Shifting uncomfortably in the window seat, her thoughts swerved from the two years abroad back to her womb. She was past the dangerous time at three months, and she carried well, so she was more irritated than worried at the thought of 'being careful' on grounds of her or the baby's health but she knew that she had other reasons to be careful. They were no further forward in finding out who was behind the crossbow attempt on Dragonetz but it underlined the point that her knight was threatened, and so she was threatened. A warning? A first move? No-one could have known about the baby then. But now? Had anyone guessed? And if they did, what would they do? Instinctively she clasped her hands on the bump hidden beneath her gown.

Of course, Dragonetz knew. And – she faced the unpleasant truth – he was drawing away from her, had been ever since Damascus. Just as she had left some part of herself bleeding on a stick, paraded on the battlements of Jericho along with Raymond's head. But whatever the changes in herself, in Dragonetz, she was sure of his loyalty as her knight. She pondered his report on Ermengarda, the other person

Aliénor had told about the baby. Like Dragonetz, Ermengarda seemed to be slipping away from Aliénor, and there was no question of binding the Viscomtesse of Narbonne with an oath of fealty to either Aquitaine or France.

Three years had changed them all and Ermengarda, who knew nothing of desert or night ambushes, except what her merchants told her, had hardened into leadership in that time, in a different way from Aliénor but just as strong. It was no good harking back to the young girl who had swung on Aliénor's arm, asking for advice on everything from perfume to judicial procedures, open in her admiration. When Aliénor looked at Ermengarda gravely explaining the organization of Narbonne to Bèatriz, she saw how they had been, herself and Ermengarda.

Broody mare, she told herself as the loneliness threatened tears. *This is why pregnant women cannot be trusted with affairs. Tears and smiles for nothing. And you know that Ermengarda had Advisors from the age of four, was born to Narbonne as you were to Aquitaine, was no naïve girl swinging on your arm but already back from leading a successful campaign. Ouch. That hurt. No-one would ever say that she, Aliénor had led a successful campaign.*

Goading herself away from self-pity, Aliénor considered what Dragonetz had told her and it fitted. Ermengarda was too much the ruler to assassinate her ex-husband on personal grounds and too much the trader to assassinate him for political reasons. 'And that's two weak spots, my Viscomtesse,' murmured Aliénor aloud, 'should ever I need them. Trade before politics and you hesitate to kill.' She had smiled mysteriously when Dragonetz told her that Ermengarda was happy to have Toulouse gone, however it might have happened. He had made this a question and in the pause he left, Aliénor carefully said nothing, leaving her smile to say that perhaps a man's murder was her doing and perhaps it wasn't, much the way she presented it to herself. With a shrug, Dragonetz had told Aliénor that Ermengarda would not entertain for a minute the idea that Toulouse was dead by Aliénor's order. 'And that's the third, my friend,' Aliénor told herself, 'You judge others by yourself.'

And Dragonetz' conclusion had been? That Ermengarda's interests ran alongside those of Aliénor. She would keep a hold in the south against the new Toulouse while Aliénor was busy elsewhere and at such a time as it became practical, Narbonne would welcome a new Toulouse, the rightful heir.

None of this was new. 'What are you not telling me, Dragonetz?' Aliénor asked herself. 'Practical' to Narbonne would always mean 'good for trade' so perhaps the support for her claim was qualified? Was Ermengarda tempted to an alliance with young Toulouse? Dragonetz was definite on that, a resounding never, to the extent that Ermengarda feared Raymond more than his father.

Even though it was exactly what she had asked him to do, Aliénor wondered how Dragonetz was so sure of Ermengarda's thoughts. She guessed at that answer too, putting to one side a memory of a young knight and her hands shaking as she took his oath and claimed him. Dragonetz had grown away from her and she was Duchesse d'Aquitaine and Queen of France. There was no room in her life for complications.

But still. 'What are you not telling me, Dragonetz?' was still echoing in her head when Ermengarda announced herself and entered, with a request that made Aliénor forget Dragonetz completely.

After a minimum of politeness, Ermengarda came straight to the point. 'My friend, I know you have taken to this little would-be troubadour, you have showered her with gifts, treated her as a lady in your entourage and there is no questioning her talent – what a voice! – that, thanks to you, she has developed…'

'But?'

Ermengarda nodded, 'She is treated as a lady but she is not living as one. Certain of my women are unhappy that someone who behaves as she does should be mixing with them, and in particular with my Lady Bèatriz.'

'Who behaves as she does? Has she been rolling round the tables drunk or arm-wrestling your Vikings and I haven't noticed?' Aliénor laughed off the accusations.

'Far from it,' Ermengarda continued patiently, 'in fact, in a married woman her behaviour would be considered perfectly acceptable but as a single woman, she should not be riding out alone with men or even singing and making music in a corner with two of them. I know,' she cut off Aliénor's protest. 'I agree with you. The constraints are ridiculous. Estela is an artist, she *should* be free to learn, to discover the world for herself and to share her gift with the world. But if the Ladies are making malicious gossip, it isn't good for Estela and it isn't good for you. Here in Narbonne, neither of you can be hurt by a few nasty comments, there is space for you to breathe here, to enjoy some freedom, but in Paris?'

Aliénor's hand tightened on the stuff of her dress. She knew exactly what sort of malicious gossip flew round the streets of Paris and who was its target.

'In Paris,' Ermengarda continued inexorably, 'you are not treated with the respect you should be. You cannot afford the accidental damage Estela will do to her own reputation and to yours. Imagine this beautiful girl at court talking freely to whoever she likes, as she did to Marcabru? It won't work, Aliénor, you know it won't! And you'll just be giving more ammunition to your enemies while Estela herself becomes more and more unhappy.'

'So you think I should get someone to talk to her, ensure she is chaperoned?' Aliénor sighed. Why was everything she did weighed down by other people's rules? Weariness flooded her at the thought of dealing with something so trivial. No-one would think she had ridden at the head of an army, faced Saracen blades, put fear in fighting men's eyes. Give her a clean fight any day instead of struggling like a fly in the strands of court intrigues! 'Or tell them go hang themselves!' she rallied. 'To hell with them!'

'Or let me keep her in the south, for Narbonne,' Ermengarda suggested quietly. 'Protect her by finding her a suitable marriage. There is a merchant I would like to reward, a widower with children, who would be happy to render this service in return for securities for him and his family. Estela could stay here when you leave, continue her tuition of Bèatriz, become the troubadour *you* saw she could be, fulfil the promise *you* saw in her.'

'Sing my praises all over Occitania,' Aliénor smiled weakly, 'instead of having her wings crushed in Paris. I see.'

'And?' prompted Ermengarda.

'Yes,' was the tired response. 'Go ahead.' And then finally, because she had to say it aloud, to someone outside her own head. 'Oh, Ermengarda what if it's a girl?'

'It will be a boy,' Ermengarda told her firmly. 'Now, would you and the future King of France like to accompany me to the Viking Games?'

'He hasn't!' Aliénor felt her spirits rise.

'He has,' Ermengarda confirmed, tight-lipped but laughter in her grey eyes. 'Dragonetz los Pros has accepted a traditional Norse challenge from the Prince of Orkney.'

'Oh, my sweet Lord!' blasphemed Aliénor. 'And what exactly led to this challenge?'

'I am reliably informed that Jarl Rognvaldr Kali Kollsson chose Dragonetz los Pros as the most worthy.'

'And Dragonetz?'

'Says it will be fun.'

Aliénor sighed.

'Quite. So I take it you would like to go to the quayside?'

'It is clearly our duty to be there,' was the regal response. 'Let's inform the Ladies.'

Estela had a privileged vantage point in the front row with other Ladies, seated on rough benches that were themselves raised on trestle tables, hastily erected round a makeshift arena on rough ground near the docks, close enough to see the ships soughing and to hear the metallic clank of anchor chains tensing and relaxing in the swell. The Viking ships looked sleek and sophisticated, unmistakeably alien even without the dragon prows rearing up, and dwarfed by the sturdy Narbonnais merchantmen. Estela shielded her eyes against the glare, which was intensified by the glitter from the water, and she made out the figures of Dragonetz and the Jarl, gesticulating and presumably giving instructions, surrounded by their men. The full company of Vikings were ashore for the spectacle and Dragonetz had an equal number of his men-at-arms. Estela picked out Arnaut, Raoulf and some others she recognized. There was no sign of al-Hisba, probably in among the spectators somewhere.

Three young page boys hastily lined up at the side of the arena with their trumpets and blew a fanfare, which lost a bit to the breeze but achieved its aim and attracted everyone's attention. The same Norseman who had interpreted the Jarl's poetry came to the front of the arena to address Ermengarda and Aliénor, with Arnaut at his side.

After enough formal compliments to satisfy everyone round the ring who might consider him or herself deserving of them, and when Estela had lost concentration on the strange accent, her attention was caught by the words, 'The Individual Challenge will consist of three parts; spear throwing, Glima wrestling and swimming. Does Dragonetz los Pros accept the challenge?'

'He accepts!' Arnaut's reply rang out while beside Estela someone whispered, 'Wrestle against that? He's crazy!' Estela looked at the Prince of Orkney, now in the Arena, colossal, shaggy-haired, Zeus in bull form and she looked at Dragonetz beside him. 'He's crazy,' she confirmed.

Lady Sancha added, 'They tell me that the Jarl started the competition earlier with a little appetizer. He made his oarsmen man their places, then he skipped along the oars over the ocean and juggled three knives in the air, balancing on an oar-tip.' Her eyes glittered with excitement, the pupils huge and shiny.

'And Dragonetz?'

'Walked along an oar, stood on his head and asked Arnaut to pass him a full horn of wine, which he downed in one. The Jarl promptly summoned another, bigger horn and downed it, standing up.'

'And here they are, still standing up,' Estela mused.

'All praise to Dragonetz los Pros,' continued the Viking. 'And to show how highly he esteems the men of this region, Jarl Rognvaldr Kali Kollsson offers a challenge from his men to conclude the sports with a game of Knattleikr. Does Dragonetz los Pros accept the challenge?'

'On behalf of his men, he accepts the challenge,' shouted Arnaut and the trumpets were accompanied by all the noises that can be made by approximately two hundred people hoping for a great sporting occasion, otherwise known as broken bones and a blood-bath, on a fine spring afternoon.

Dragonetz and the Jarl then came forward to make a formal obeisance to Ermengarda. They were so close that Estela could see the sweat glistening on the men's foreheads, both of them dressed Viking-style in the plainest of leather jerkins and britches. Did she imagine Dragonetz glancing her way with a quarter-smile that chilled on his lips and glanced over her to ripen for some other woman nearby? She certainly didn't imagine Arnaut's lips tightening in disapproval as his eyes dipped towards her waist and he instinctively raised his own hand to the chain around his neck, attached to her own token.

Estela's hands followed Arnaut's eyes and she cursed her thoughtlessness as she felt the embossed surface of the Pathfinder Rune clasping her sashed waist. Whether it was magical or not, it was the only possession that was hers by right, not by charity, and she wore it always but of course it must seem a public declaration of support for the Prince of Orkney. Her cheeks flamed but there was nothing she could do without making things worse and anyway, it could hardly matter to someone as important as Dragonetz. It was Arnaut who cared too much and she could easily explain to him, later.

And then the competition began in earnest. Accompanied by trumpet-bursts, chatter and then silences in anticipation, servants brought four javelins and cleared any bystanders from a wide arc in front of the royal stand. It seemed to be Dragonetz' right to go first but whether this was a good thing or bad, Estela could not decide. She had of course witnessed tourneys and also less chivalrous games among the pages at her father's castle but nothing like this.

'Does anyone know what the rules are?' she asked Lady Sancha.

'I believe the Vikings know.'

'So what will Dragonetz do?'

That unnatural brilliance in her eyes even more evident, Lady Sancha replied, 'What he always does.'

'Make it up as he goes along,' murmured Estela, not needing confirmation as Dragonetz took his spear, now identified with a blue ribbon. He paced out a run-up, turned and took his run, stopping at the mark. Sideways on, his right shoulder muscles glistening as his body curved into the throw. He hurled the spear in a perfect arc, scything the blue skies like a blade to land point down so far out that Estela had to shade her eyes to see it.

Then it was the Jarl's turn. He moved lightly for such a big man, at ease with his own weight and power. His run-up gathered such speed that it seemed impossible for him to stop short at the marker but he did, transforming all his energy into a throw that seemed to hardly test his giant physique. Another right-handed throw. Estela followed it with her eyes, a more upward trajectory, curving down and true but – she held her breath – just short of Dragonetz'. One-nul. There were some words exchanged between the men, explaining some aspect of the rules probably, as Dragonetz nodded acceptance, and then he took his second spear – in his left hand. The run up was identical but his movement was more awkward and when he turned to throw, the inverse position of the first time, Estela could feel the lack of fluidity, could see the hesitation in his shoulder, before she noticed the flight of the spear, long but low and straight so that it shaved the ground and landed flat. A mis-throw.

The Prince of Orkney gave one nod and then followed with his second spear, in his left hand, as fluently as with his right, following an identical arc to his first to land beside it, just short of Dragonetz'.

Amongst the clapping and cheering, Estela hissed, 'Do we have any idea who has won?' No-one answered her. No doubt it would be revealed at the end. The servants were herding spectators back into a closer ring around the arena, where the Jarl and Dragonetz donned leather garments not unlike a blacksmith's apron but shorter and joined like underclothes, with a strap at the waist and a strap at the thigh. They wore these on top of their britches but had taken off their shirts.

At a signal from one of the Vikings, the two men went into a clinch, one hand in the other man's waist strap, and one hooked into the thigh-strap. The size difference was obvious when the two of them were in this strange embrace. They moved together as if at the start of a dance, the feet mirroring each other's moves.

Then there was a whistle blown and the dance changed into a frenetic blur of moving legs, each trying to hook the other and bring him down. Pushing, pulling, still gripping each other's leather straps, the men's feet stamped, kicked and twisted into impossible positions as each tried to turn the move back on the other with a shift of weight. A feint, a sideways pull and a deft foot put Dragonetz on his back. 'Nul-one', muttered Estela, unconsciously clenching her hands.

The Jarl stood to one side and waited politely, until Dragonetz rose, walked back to him and once more they clutched each other by the straps. Again the dance, the signal and the struggle, this time for longer as Dragonetz used his balance to mislead and counter-attack the bigger man, who could not lean as far or as flexibly as his slimmer opponent. 'Ouch! declared Estela, and 'One-all,' as a swing from one side to the other, accompanied by a neatly placed foot, dropped the Jarl on the ground with a thud.

Then they were into the third bout. Estela noticed that all Dragonetz' actions were with his right side and right foot and she thought of the spear-throwing. 'Hide it!' she instructed him, jarring an imaginary opponent with her own left shoulder and earning 'hrumphs' of disapproval from those around her.

Inevitably, the Jarl tried to force Dragonetz on his left side, expecting weakness. He must have been disappointed. The knight's training might have left him one-sided with a spear but not in muscles or defensive skills. Having thrown himself into a failed attempt, the Jarl was caught off-balance at the strength of the riposte and, spinning out of control away from Dragonetz, he hit the ground a third time, shaking his head, annoyed with himself at falling for the trap.

Dragonetz bowed, the Jarl dusted himself off and joined him, then there was a short break for the men to take off their leather wrestler costumes and refresh themselves with water brought out to them. At least Estela assumed it was water. Lord knew what the effect of more wine would be and she had already witnessed Dragonetz at play in a river. She did not fancy the idea of him testing the Prince of Orkney's capacity to hold his breath under-sea. So far, the contest had been fair, but she could see how heavily the two men were breathing, how high the colour in their faces. Pride was at stake in this last event and there was no doubt they both wanted to win. What did 'swimming' mean exactly?

She was still wondering this as word went around the crowd that they must go down to the docks to watch the next event. And so she joined in the milling, moving throng making its way across the arena that had once again become wasteland. She passed a spear, still stuck in the ground, its little blue ribbon still tight around the shaft and she had an idea. Minutes later she'd lost sight of the Ladies and was mixing with the townspeople and the men-at-arms, less attractively scented but more interesting in conversation. 'Arnaut', she called as she recognized him and caught him up. 'What's happening? What's this swimming competition? Who's winning anyway? Is he all right?'

'Who?' He gave a sarcastic glance at her clasp. 'The Prince of Orkney?'

'It doesn't mean anything. It's just a pretty ornament. Now stop fooling around and tell me.'

'He's a bit bruised,' Arnaut admitted, 'and I don't know when the alcohol will wear off. I just hope it's before he starts swimming so that he knows when to stop.'

Estela's stomach clenched. 'It's a distance swim,' she guessed. Arnaut nodded. 'And there's a marker?' There was no answer and the feeling of panic deepened. 'Arnaut, tell me there's a marker.'

'The only marker is common sense,' he told her bitterly. 'They swim out to open sea and the first one to turn back loses.'

'You've got to stop him!' she said. 'Common sense? Dragonetz? And the Viking's as bad. You can see it in their eyes!'

'You know I can't do a thing when he's like this.'

'Al-Hisba, he's here somewhere, get al-Hisba.'

Arnaut took her arm gently, spoke to her as if she were a startled horse. 'He'll be fine, Estela. He always is. And no-one can stop him anyway. You have to let a storm run its course.'

Dazed with a sense of wrongness, Estela allowed Arnaut to lead her to the front of the crowd, find the other Ladies, now accompanied by various of Ermengarda's advisors and town nobles. Arnaut leaned towards her so that she could hear above the noise. 'And it's even. He won the wrestling, lost the spears because of the left-handed mis-throw so it all depends on the swimming.' Then he was gone.

Before Estela could think of anything she could do to prevent it, two wild figures, stripped to work-britches, ran towards the sea and threw themselves off the jetty. Now, all there was to do was to wait and hope that two wild figures returned at some time, presumably loser first but who knew what Viking rules decreed!

Meanwhile, the tradesmen were making the most of a captive crowd, offering pastries and honeyed water at exorbitant prices. Estela suddenly felt very hungry and even knowing that the pastries were likely over-salted to sell more drinking water, she succumbed to the urge and withdrew her purse from its hiding-place next to the reassuring weight of her dagger.

As a spectator sport, the distance swim left a lot to be desired and some of the men in the crowd had rushed to commandeer whatever skiffs and rowboats they could, to head out into the bay and hope for a glimpse of the competitors. Probably run them both down and kill them, thought Estela cynically. Chewing layers of fatty dough had restored her spirits and it was hard to believe in danger while the sunshine glinted on the water, the children played tag in and out of adult legs, and the breeze caressed her skin.

'My Lady Estela.' The deep voice startled her. She had been too far away to notice the approach of a man in church robes but she had seen him at High Table often enough to recognize him straight away and wonder why he would seek her out. His manner suggested business. 'It is a pity that men should spoil a beautiful day with their rivalries and attempts at self-glory,' commented Pierre d'Anduze, the Archbishop of Narbonne.

Now that her own reservations were expressed in such a fashion, she found she objected violently. What was she supposed to say? Nothing, seemed safest.

'You don't agree?' he pressed.

Saying nothing was not going to be an option and this was the Papal Legate, the most powerful prelate in Occitania, backing her into a conversational corner. Why? Her mind raced as her mouth responded, 'I'm sure your Grace's presence reminds us all of a higher purpose in life.'

Then he did look at her, weighing her up. She returned the favour. He was much of a height with her, showing signs of his advanced age. His hair was silver, thinning over skin mottled with age spots, his eyes lightly clouded with cateracts, but his carriage was erect despite his bulk, and his voice that of someone used to deference. She forced herself to look away, let him think she was over-awed. Pretend your left side's weak, she told herself, and make him give away all his tactics.

'You are new to Narbonne,' he continued smoothly. She kept her gaze demurely lowered. 'But have already made quite a stir.'

'I am flattered, your Grace.'

'Don't be. Flattery is only one of the dangers to your immortal soul in this frivolous court where you play the songbird and keep bad company.' It was hardly a surprise to Estela that the Archbishop disapproved of games, secular music, in fact every sophistication of Ermengarda's court, and his animosity towards Ermengarda herself was well-known. From the gossip that Estela had picked up, d'Anduze had not leaned as far towards Toulouse as his predecessor but in the eight months he had been in power he had already challenged the ruler of Narbonne over judicial rights, land rights and of course the state of her immortal soul. No, the Archbishop's disapproval was no surprise but why in heaven or earth was he bothering to express it to her personally, a nobody?

'I have a lot to learn, your Grace.'

'Evidently. And you are young enough to benefit from wise counseling.' Estela could guess who the wise counseling was likely to come from. 'You would do well to find a more responsible patron, one more sensitive to your reputation, something which is only possible in one who takes care of her own reputation.' So this was about Aliénor? It still seemed strange that the Archbishop would take such an interest in the well-being of Estela's soul! 'And the young man, our Champion of the Games,' he sneered, 'he also could do with some counseling. From someone who knows about milling. You've seen the mill I believe?'

'Yes,' Estela began enthusiastically, 'it's taken a lot of work to set it up.'

'A paper mill,' prompted d'Anduze. 'Ingenious as an experiment – but of course, it won't work in practice though.'

'Oh it works already,' Estela responded heatedly, 'Now that they've regulated the hammers,' and then she tailed off as she sensed the heightened interest and belatedly remembered that paper production would not go down well with the church.

'Really? And these hammers do what exactly?' d'Anduze smiled, encouraging her to continue.

Estela returned his smile with one equally false, an *I'm just a girl* smile. 'I have no idea. I heard one of the men say it. I think the workers bring hammers to repair the water-wheel or something like that. I have no idea how it all works but I'm sure my Lord Dragonetz would be only too happy to discuss his mill with you.'

The smile disappeared. 'Don't play games with me, little girl. You are as far out of your depth as that devil's spawn out there.' He jerked his head towards the ocean and prodded a podgy finger into Estela's throat. Her hand tightened on the handle of her dagger but she held still, as she would with any snake rearing its head. 'As far out of your depth and just as likely to drown. Remember that,' he told her, then he left, cutting a stately swathe through the crowd, distributing verbal largesse right and left as he disappeared from view.

Estela's sense of foreboding was back with a vengeance. She hoped she had given nothing away that could be used against Dragonetz and she searched the water anxiously, stupidly hoping to pick out two heads amongst the bobbing boats and spume. It could only have been twenty minutes that the men were away and they were both strong swimmers, so there could be hours to wait. They'd have swum beyond the harbour to the open sea and she broke out into a cold sweat at just the thought of the monsters lurking in the depths, serpents and krakens, sharks and leviathans.

Her knotted stomach insisted that something had gone wrong and when she heard the shouting coming from the small boats and rippling up through the crowd at the quay, she knew it was not a homecoming triumph. Gathering her skirts, she punched, kicked and fought her way to the front of the crowd that was quickly forming round a small group of men. In the centre was the Prince of Orkney, on his knees, head hanging forward, his huge body heaving with the effort of each breath. Beside him lay the inert body of Dragonetz los Pros.

Pushing through to get to the two men, Estela saw that Dragonetz was breathing, however raggedly, and his eyes were open. It was his body that had given the impression that he was lifeless, lying limp and somehow smaller than it should be. She crouched beside him, startled by the fact that his body convulsed, then stilled. She tried to remember everything her mother had taught her, keeping her emotions to one side as she observed the feverish hue, the dilated pupils, the sweat pouring in rivulets over his neck and chest and the wild irregular thumpings of his heart underneath her hand.

'Get al-Hisba, find him wherever he is and tell him to bring his medicines,' she threw out, hoping that someone was capable of action. 'Can anyone tell me what happened?'

Between gasps, the Jarl answered, 'He was ahead of me, swimming like Loki in salmon form and then – we hadn't been swimming long – he slowed. I nearly caught up and he started thrashing the water, shouting as if some monster was fighting him. I thought he was fooling around but then as I reached him, he went under. I grabbed for him but he started lunging at me, screaming nonsense about darkness and enemies, so,' the Viking shrugged, 'I knocked him out and brought him back to shore, where he came round but is like you see him. There is some magic at work here, something evil.' He spat on the quayside and made some sign.

Against magic, she had no remedy. As Estela studied Dragonetz' face again for clues, his eyes stopped roving some imaginary landscape and focused on her. She saw the recognition kick in, despite the wild dilation, and he clutched her hand, still resting on his chest, transmitting the pounding wrongness in his body. He had trouble speaking, as if his mouth were dry instead of sea-wet but one corner made a feeble attempt at the smile she knew so well. 'B'ooful,' he announced, patting her hand. 'Going to be married. 'Gratulations.'

'Estela?' queried al-Hisba's voice at the same time as Arnaut said, 'What in Christ's name have they done to him!'

'Fish,' was Dragonetz' helpful contribution and Estela could see by his unfocused eyes that he had left them again. Dilated pupils, she told herself and suddenly she knew. If someone took the drops internally, or was given them, instead of merely enhanced shiny eyes and dilated pupils, the latter would occur alongside fever, hallucinations, dry mouth, racing heart and death. 'Sweetheart,' her mother had told her, 'I know it's fashionable and it looks nice, but I don't think you should put something in your eyes that is so toxic inside the body. Please don't.' And she hadn't. But most of the Ladies at court did.

'Al-Hisba,' she turned urgently to the grave Arab. 'I think he's had belladonna poisoning. If I'm right, I don't know what we can do! Make him sick? Will that do it?'

Al-Hisba took her place beside the shaking body, opened Dragonetz' eyes wide with his hands and looked at them, felt the heartbeat, nodded at her, was already searching in his pouch, pulling out a powder. 'Arnaut, can you get some water? It is from Esere beans, the 'ordeal beans' of the Kanem people in Africa,' he told Estela. 'It is a poison but if we are right, it will work as an antidote.'

Arnaut handed a flask to al-Hisba and someone shouted, 'The Moor is poisoning him!'

Estela stood up and while al-Hisba administered the drug, she and Arnaut faced the men pressing tighter round them. 'You idiots, he's saving his life,' she shouted but the sheer panic might have spread further had not the Jarl heaved to his feet and swayed beside them, calling something in his strange tongue. In seconds, the other Norsemen were through the crowd and formed a guard around Dragonetz, soon joined by his own men-at-arms, who forced the mob back. Estela turned her attention back to the patient. He was still flushed and feverish but then, she chided herself, it would take time for any medication to work. She was sure it was belladonna and she trusted al-Hisba's lore. The wandering eyes found her face and focused again. Dragonetz reached out and touched her hair with his hand, noticing what Arnaut had not. 'B'ooful,' he said, 'blue ribbon in her hair. 'S my ribbon.' And then his eyes closed.

'He'll sleep,' al-Hisba reassured her. 'Nature's way.'

The crowd was already dispersing as word went round that the game of Knattleikr would start in the arena as soon as the two teams were assembled. That cleared the remaining spectators in seconds. A litter was organised to take Dragonetz and al-Hisba back to the Palace and Estela allowed herself to be caught up in the buzz of speculation amongst Ermengarda's Ladies but her thoughts were elsewhere. She responded briefly to Aliénor's keen questions and noted the exchange that followed between the Queen and Ermengarda but it was as if her own head was befogged with belladonna and what she saw around her had no substance.

In a trance, she saw Raoulf and Arnaut attend to the pressing matter of handing out curved sticks to nine chosen men, including themselves, who rewarded the crowd for their patience with a display of the most brutal lack of ball control ever seen in Occitania. Dragonetz' men had no need of another team to injure themselves, thwacking sticks against each other's shins with pleasing regularity, blissfully unaware of any rules apart from the aim of getting the ball between the posts of the opposition goal.

Bemused by the ineptitude of their opponents, the Vikings lost all their own capacity to pass and shoot but were not to be outdone on thwacking shins or aiming the ball at undefended human parts rather than at the goal. The Jarl was not playing, in deference to Dragonetz' forced absence, but he hurled what were presumably instructions from a position that was sufficiently in the way to allow him to smack a fist into a passing player from time to time. A hot dispute over an own goal led to one-on-one fisticuffs that lit the match across both teams. Spectators took the chance to stream onto the field and take part themselves in the great sporting occasion. The Jarl took a break to bow to Ermengarda and, barely audible above the row, to formally declare the games over and honours even. Then he returned to the fray. At this stage, the Ladies left, Estela among them, desperate to return to the Palace for news.

CHAPTER ELEVEN

'Did I win?' Dragonetz asked Estela and she knew he was himself again, however white and drawn, as he lay in bed, attempting a crooked smile for her.

She had pulled a stool over to sit near enough the bed that she could observe his physical state, surreptitiously. Arnaut was standing, shifting about restlessly, still grumbling that it wasn't seemly for her to be here at all and that no, no-one else would consider him perfect as a chaperone.

'The Jarl declared one broken leg, two broken wrists, multiple sprains and bruises, enough bloodletting to purify an entire city and an overall draw,' Estela told him. 'And that's really not the most important thing!'

'Civilised man, the Jarl,' Dragonetz reflected. 'So tell me who slipped me poison.'

Arnaut stopped his pacing. 'You can talk about that when you're feeling better! And Estela shouldn't be here at all. It doesn't look good.'

Dragonetz waved a weak hand, dismissing any idea that they should leave him to rest. 'Brain's working fine, just the body needs a bit more time. Aliénor and Ermengarda will sort out Estela's reputation.'

Estela bit back her reaction to his airy assumptions, reminded herself that he was still ill and told him about the conversation with the Archbishop.

'Could he have meant me to drown?' wondered Dragonetz. 'Not very good for his immortal soul.'

'That's two attempts on your life now,' Estela pointed out.

'Was it an attempt on my life? Or a threat? Both times? And the attack against you in the bath chamber? Connected or not? Do you have enemies of your own, Estela?'

She ignored his last question. 'Belladonna is extremely poisonous if taken internally, would show its effects in about a quarter of an hour, depending on the dose. I don't need to tell you what the symptoms are!' He winced and screwed up his face. 'So my guess would be that the belladonna was in the water you drank after the wrestling and intended to impact while you were swimming. If the Jarl had been ahead of you instead of behind, you'd have drowned fighting imaginary sea-monsters. And if al-Hisba hadn't used his talents, you'd have died from the poison itself.'

'So you think the dose was meant to kill?'

'Yes!'

'Maybe,' al-Hisba contradicted, as he came into the bedchamber. 'Estela is right that belladonna can kill but in careful doses it is used as a sleeping potion –'

'If he'd fallen asleep in mid-ocean that would have killed him too!' Estela interrupted.

'– and again, in a careful dose it can boost energy. You were winning until you started hallucinating so it is possible that someone was trying to make sure you won and thought the drug was easier to control than is the case.'

'Had a bet on you myself,' Arnaut commented, 'but if I was trying to fire you up, I would never have thought of belladonna!'

'No,' agreed Estela, 'I think it's more likely that it was used as a poison – a lethal poison.'

'You are probably right but you should know the other possibilities. If I know them, so do others.'

'What about access to belladonna?' asked Dragonetz. 'Anyone could have put it in my water flask but who could have got it in the first place?'

'Any lady who makes big eyes at you,' Estela told him, then explained. 'Ladies put drops in their eyes to make them shine. You can tell because as well as being shiny, the pupils are bigger than normal.' He stared intently at her. 'No,' she said shortly. 'Someone told me it might not be safe.'

'So, any lady could get belladonna drops.'

'And any servant could get them from any apothecary on behalf of any lady and anyone could take the drops from any lady. The stuff is everywhere – it's impossible to track it down!' Estela chewed the edge of her fingers.

'That's a terrible habit, you know,' Dragonetz told her.

'I know, my – someone used to tell me all the time.' She ignored Dragonetz' raised eyebrow over her stumble. 'What if –' she started, '– no, it's too fanciful.'

'Go on.'

'What if it *is* a Lady. That doesn't mean it's not Toulouse or the Archbishop or both behind the scenes but it could be one of the Ladies who put the drops in the water. Could it have been a Lady involved in the cross-bow attempt?'

Arnaut and Dragonetz exchanged looks. 'It's possible that one of the Ladies stole Aliénor's seal, overheard our password and used it.'

'Not one of Ermengarda's Ladies then but one of Aliénor's, who travelled with us.' Estela nodded at the confirmation of her suspicions.

'You have someone in mind.'

Estela hesitated. 'Lady Sancha,' she said. 'She's clever enough, she's always snooping and,' she murmured quietly, 'she doesn't like me so it might have been her with the broken glass.' If only she had identified the voice in the Great Hall, the one commenting on how badly she was walking, the voice that knew why and took pleasure in it. Then she could be sure.

'No,' Dragonetz surprised her with his certainty. 'It isn't Lady

Sancha. She wouldn't have visited the communal bath-chamber even with her clothes on. You'll have to look elsewhere.'

'How can you be so sure?'

'I am. And that doesn't concern you.' Estela felt like he'd slammed a door in her face. She rose to leave.

'Arnaut's right. You need rest now.'

'Thank you for coming.' His eyes were trying to reach her but she couldn't respond. She couldn't ask him the question burning in her own mind, what he'd meant in his delirium with his talk of marriage and congratulations. Was he getting married? Did he want congratulations? Somehow she'd pictured a beautiful high-born wife looking after the babies back in Aquitaine while her adventurous husband was on his travels. Perhaps it was a remnant of the Dragonetz that had formed in her head when she first heard his lyrics sung by her father's troubadour.

She'd imagined a middle-aged man, carefully crafting his past experiences into poetry that churned the heart. She hadn't imagined this wildfire companion, whose abilities to churn the heart weren't limited to his poetry. She wasn't sure whether she was more disturbed at the thought that he wasn't married or at the thought that he was about to be. And she didn't want to think about why she was disturbed at all.

A formal interview three hours later, with Ermengarda and Aliénor, clarified for Estela exactly who was getting married.

'My Lady Aliénor, my Lady Ermengarda, you do me too much honour.' Estela hid her confusion in a curtsey. 'I am overwhelmed.' She spoke nothing but the truth. Weeks ago she had faced destitution in a ditch and now she was being offered financial security for life along with a place among the troubadours at Ermengarda's court. Everything she'd ever dreamed of. She had always expected to marry one day and from the sound of him, this respectable burgher would be everything her mother would have wanted for her. There could be no question as to her response and she did not disappoint the two rulers in her gratitude. Both of them glowed with the self-satisfaction usual after an act of great charity.

Taking Estela's arm as she rose from her curtsey, Ermengarda gave her a warm smile. 'We can discuss the details another time. You will soon realize the freedom that marriage gives you.'

Looking at the dazzling confidence of the ruler of Narbonne, Estela could believe it but the older woman's face darkened and Aliénor's softly spoken 'Not always,' was the last thing Estela heard as she made her escape.

She headed straight for the stables, the instinct to get away from the Palace taking over her feet, leading her blindly through hallways and courtyards. A familiar white form bounded up to her as she rushed along, butting her thigh with his great head. Without thinking, she clicked her fingers for him to follow her, a habit she had grown into in the evenings since the broken glass. She felt safer with the massive dog blocking the way into her bedchamber and he seemed happy enough to accompany her when she called him or pad off with the pack when there was nothing on offer from Estela. 'Come, Nici,' she murmured and carried on towards the stables.

The musty smell of straw, sweat and dung acted on her like a somniferous herb and she was relieved to see the broad back and chopped hair of Peire, bending over a pitchfork as he mucked out. She was not in the mood for long explanations or social niceties. Peire would not ask her difficult questions or express views on Ladies riding out alone. 'Peire,' she called. His face opened to hers, guileless as a daisy in sunshine. 'I need you to saddle up for me. If Tou's not ready, I'll take another.'

'My Lady, I can get Tou ready but I need a little time. Do you want to come back?' He flicked a flustered lock of hair away from his eyes, reminding Estela strongly of a restive colt irritated by flies. Even his hair looked more like a docked horse-tail than any human style.

'I'll wait,' she said. 'It does me good to be here. Take your time.' She remembered to smile, that a Lady's smile was currency for a poor stable-hand, but she was grateful that he nodded, and responded to her mood with action and silence. The blue eyes were more shrewd than she had given him credit for. Peire came and went with tack, then with Tou, murmured to the mare as he deftly tightened girth and adjusted bit. His hand spanned Tou's neck in a flat caress and Estela shivered. She stopped fondling Nici's ear and the dog complained in his throat and butted her, to no avail.

'My Lady.' Peire offered her his hands and she mounted, crushing a totally unsuitable gown against the horn of the saddle. What did it matter – soon, she would have as many gowns as she wanted. She gave curt thanks and kicked Tou into action. Nici loped alongside, in the easy pace of his enemy the wolf, and Estela ignored the stares of Narbonnais as she walked Tou out beyond the city walls, out beyond the people. As soon as she was in open space, she kicked Tou to the fastest pace she could manage but it was like the motion of a fat kitchen-maid running to catch the baker before he closed shop. Tired of the rolling gait, Estela brought Tou back to a walk and let her thoughts drift to the amazing interview with the two rulers.

Estela reviewed the facts of her future, as they had been presented to her. She would be married to Johans de Villeneuve, a land-owner and widower with four grown children, a man comfortably off and about to become more so after generous recognition by Ermengarda of his services as an adviser and negotiator. Some of this generosity would be Estela's dowry, her private fortune at her own disposal, giving her independence for life. She would remain living at the Palace as one of Ermengarda's entertainers, among her Ladies but with the extra privileges and freedom required to develop her talent. She would continue teaching Bèatriz and would herself benefit from the mentoring of Marcabru. Why did the idea of learning from Marcabru fill her with disappointment?

Independent for life. Singing at the court of Narbonne. Able to follow her dream, develop her own composition and maybe one day even perform her own songs. She was sixteen and had an amazing future. Her mother would have been so proud of her. So what was the problem? Or rather, the problems.

Marriage scared her. She thought back to the few, precious conversations with her mother about managing a household, about supporting her husband politically, about bearing him an heir. Surrounded by farm animals in her childhood, Estela knew exactly what would be expected of her on her wedding night and although she felt nervous, she acknowledged some curiosity and the desire to become a woman – and to be recognised as a woman. Her mother had no need to warn her that songs of romance were not the daily fabric of married life, even of happy married life, and it was no coincidence that lovers in songs were never married, or at least not to each other.

No, Estela was not likely to confuse overheated blood with a decision on how she would live the rest of her life. But who was this Johans de Villeneuve? He was obviously old, at least forty, to have children her age and older. Was he ugly? Why did he want to marry her? What would he expect from her? Had he even seen her? It was obvious that he was Ermengarda's man and this marriage, with all the promised bounty, was a sign to everyone of the Viscomtesse's favour.

Was Estela ready to be Ermengarda's woman? She was just getting used to belonging to Aliénor and now she had been given away. Her momentary resentment that Aliénor should part with her so easily disappeared when she remembered the Queen's words. 'Paris is a form of imprisonment for a woman of spirit and the days vary only in the forms of torture. I do not wish on you what I cannot escape. This proposal is as much my gift to you, for the glory of your voice and of your future, as it is that of my Lady Ermengarda. I hope you will take this life we offer you in both hands and soar, take flight for me too. I have chosen a different path but I envy you.'

It was clear that Johans de Villeneuve would accept an absent wife, given that Estela would live at the Palace and have court duties. Her mother's advice on household management would not be put to use, not yet at least. Would he then visit her at the Palace? For duties of the bedchamber? She supposed so. And although he had heirs already, no-one could suppose he had enough children, having only four. With one sweep of plague, mortality ended all plans. Yes, she was nervous at the idea of having children but she was more than old enough, so she would do her duty. She would be the woman her mother had hoped and her questions would be answered after her marriage, when she would truly find out what manner of man Johans de Villeneuve was. Until then, she must trust to Ermengarda to have chosen with Estela's interest at heart. There was no doubt that Ermengarda believed she had done so. Estela fingered her Pathfinder rune, tracing the graven paths.

'This is the one I must take,' she whispered. 'Ermengarda, Narbonne, a future with music. And Johans de Villeneuve.' And the path not taken? Her fingers traced an opposite path on the clasp and she saw a blue ribbon, a crooked smile and a song at dawn as two lovers parted. She flinched away from the clasp as if it were white-hot and as soon as she broke the contact, the images left her. She shook the silliness out of her head and thought about the one problem that she really must resolve, and before the wedding. A woman could not marry under a pseudonym.

Her thoughts were interrupted by hooves thundering towards her and for a crazy moment she thought she had conjured up the man in her head, come to sweep her off on a black charger.

'Estela!' Arnaut greeted her, out of breath, his cheeks pink and his grey eyes shining. His blonde hair flew out like a halo and he looked like a beautiful avenging angel in his working armour. His horse was not black and was not a charger. It was slightly overweight and puffing hard from the unaccustomed labour. It skittered a little at the sight of Nici as Arnaut pulled up. 'Dragonetz sent me after you.'

'Did he now,' she said drily.

'It's not safe, riding round on your own!'

'According to Ermengarda's Ladies, being with you is even less safe!' she retorted.

Arnaut flushed. 'Normally, I would avoid adding to gossip about you but I am following orders!' Estela bit back a sarcastic response and was glad she had when he continued, 'But I would have followed you anyway. This,' he fingered the chain round his neck leading to her token, 'this means something to me. I have sworn to you and if there is any threat to you, I won't allow it.' Estela felt old beside his young man's passion but then she reminded herself that however young he sounded, he had seen action Oltra mar and his sword was no toy. Neither was he and she must be careful.

'What makes you think there is some threat to me?' she asked slowly.

'Dragonetz says you are to be married.'

Estela's mouth tightened in annoyance but she answered the man who was beside her not the one who wasn't. 'This is true but it is... very recent news.'

Undeterred, Arnaut pointed out, 'I think Dragonetz knows about things before they happen.'

'Quite.'

'I have to ask you two serious things, Estela, and I want you to think before you give me an answer, not to tell me today. You don't have to marry this man if you don't want to.' Estela's heart dipped as she guessed what he was going to say. 'I would be honoured to have you as my wife.'

'Arnaut,' she began but he cut her off.

'Please, let me finish. I know that you said there could be nothing but friendship between us. Perhaps love on my side and friendship on yours would make a better marriage than this man you don't know!' He rushed on. 'And if your answer is still no, if you want me to kill him for you, I will.'

Estela swallowed, hard. 'Arnaut, I have to answer now because otherwise the question will just be hanging over us. My answer won't change.' She glanced at his profile, set and stern as he rode beside her. 'There is no easy way to say this. I wish I did love you but I don't, not in that way.'

'You love this man you're marrying even less!'

'So nothing more is expected and no-one will be disappointed! You deserve someone worthy of you. No, don't contradict me, I'm only speaking now of this feeling that you have. Yes, we are friends and I want us to stay friends. If we married, what hurt it would cause, to you and me as well as those around you! And that is *if* we behaved stupidly and married against all good sense so let's talk sense as well as love. Raoulf would be happy, wouldn't he, with you marrying a pauper found in a ditch! You know I would have nothing if I turned down my Lady's generosity.'

'My father doesn't have a say in everything,' muttered Arnaut.

'And I am sure your mother would welcome me to her fireside, where I would sit doing embroidery while you were following Dragonetz on his latest campaign. And I would beg your parents for a new dress or even some coin to go to market.'

'I have some income.' Arnaut's voice was low.

'Which will grow when you meet the heiress of your dreams.' Estela refrained from adding 'And the dreams of your parents.' There was no need to rub the message in further. 'We are not children and we must make adult decisions.'

'So you don't want him killed,' Arnaut stated bleakly.

'I want you to be nice to him. Unless of course at any time I change my mind and ask you to kill him.'

'You only have to ask,' he promised.

'That's very reassuring. Enough of all this. The topic of my marriage has a limited interest. Tell me how the paper mill is going.' Although she started the tangent to distract Arnaut, Estela found herself more and more involved in the intricacies of drying, cutting and shipping paper. She had not realised that things had progressed so far and it was in amicable and animated conversation about the possibility of brand-marking paper that the two of them returned to Narbonne.

In the privacy of her room, Estela shook off her amazement at receiving two marriage proposals in one day, and found that she had come to a decision. If her marriage was ordained, then so was the revelation of her name. She could ask for a small audience but she would have to be married under the name given her at birth. And she would have to take the risk that word would reach those she had so recently escaped from. This time, however, she would be ready for them. Nici belched and rolled on his back in the doorway of the bedchamber.

CHAPTER TWELVE

Ermengarda and Aliénor had received Estela in private as she requested but the air was frosty with regal impatience at spending time on trivia.

'Well?' Ermengarda demanded. 'I assume Guillelma has the arrangements in hand. I gather that next Wednesday, the seventh day before the Ides of June, is acceptable in the eyes of the Lord as represented by our dear Archbishop, who is sending a priest to bless the union. My Chancellor will officiate and I will authorise the contracts. Have I forgotten something?'

This was not going to be easy. 'I think you should know who I am, my Lady.'

The voice softened a shade. 'Don't worry. My favour, and that of the Queen of France, makes you a very desirable match, however lowly your birth. And as your liege lord, I will replace your family and vouch for you contractually.'

'Believe me, your Lady, I understand the honour and couldn't be more sensible of it.'

'But?'

'But I fear an objection from my family when they hear of it. I am Roxane, daughter to the Castellan of Montbrun.'

'God's blood and are you indeed!' swore Ermengarda.

'Montbrun?' queried Aliénor, smoothing the apron of her skirt over the hidden bump, a gesture that was becoming habitual.

'A minor noble but a noble all the same. And in the Corbières, with Carcassonne as liege not me, so that makes it more difficult – not to say impossible – for me to play Lady Bountiful over an outraged father. This smells of unpleasant lawsuits. Let me think.'

'And if I sent to your father for his consent? With news of your advancement and suitable appreciation?' suggested Aliénor.

'He'd never consent, not if a host of Turks were waving their scimitars outside the walls of his Chateau and made it their condition for lifting the siege!'

'And the reason for this rift?'

'Family matters, my Lady.' The silence spread, with its invitation to expand on this terse explanation, but Estela was silent.

'It would be irresponsible of me to deny a father's rights,' judged Ermengarda's cool tones, 'especially on such little evidence. I should let him know that you are here.'

'Others will do that soon enough once my name is known!' Estela's bitterness brought bile into her throat, the sour taste of a forced return to all she had hoped to escape. Her knees trembled and she clenched her teeth to steady herself, fixing her eyes firmly on a mottled black stain on the stone floor, which turned from a flower to a bird to a dagger wound as she tried to still her thoughts. It was the unexpected hand of the Duchesse d'Aquitaine that raised her chin and met golden eyes with intelligent green ones.

'Estela is still in my household, Ermengarda, until such time as she marries, and I am a little weary of the rights of fathers. I have yet to see the lawsuit that declares against the right of the Queen of France to marry her vassal, given the willingness of the two parties to be married of course.'

Ermengarda's brow was still wrinkled and she was forthright. 'I don't like it. This will brew trouble near enough Narbonne to be my problem.' The implication was clear – and far enough away from Aquitaine and France to allow Aliénor to meddle with impunity. 'I said to let me think! I haven't said we can't find a way. Carcassonne...' she mused.

'Roger Trencavel de Carcassonne is liege lord to Montbrun,' Estela confirmed.

'Not any more,' stated Aliénor. Estela just looked at her. 'Word came last week from Bernarda that her husband is dead.' Estela cursed her lack of attention to the Ladies' gossip. Of course this explained the absence from Aliénor's household of his niece Alis, as well as fifty other pieces of speculation which had floated over Estela while she strummed with Bèatriz. So Roger Trencavel was dead. Like so many, he had been ailing since his return from Crusades and whatever gnawed at him turned inward, obsessing about the construction of great walls around the city. With light-headed fancy, Estela hoped he'd seen the walls finished before he died. Roger dead and childless meant Bernarda relegated to second rank; no wonder she was sending messages to Narbonne. And liege lord to Montbrun was now Roger's younger brother, Raimon.

Ermengarda gave one of her rare smiles, a flicker of warmth lighting the alabaster skin. 'I do believe that Roger Trencavel, Viscomte de Carcassonne wrote to me before his death, conferring a charge on me.' Estela was lost but to judge from Aliénor's dancing eyes, she was ahead of the game.

'I believe I remember the very missive, concerning one of his subjects, a Roxane de Montbrun and giving signed permission for her to join the household of Ermengarda of Narbonne and marry according to the choice of her protectress, the Viscomtesse of Narbonne, should the said Roxane be so willing.'

Reluctant as she was to question the solution, Estela felt compelled to point out, 'My father will never believe it.'

'That, my dear, is the beauty of it.' Ermengarda was triumphant. 'Whether he believes it or not, he will get no contradiction from Roger Trencavel, whose authority he cannot but accept, and he has no grounds to challenge the word of Narbonne.'

Slowly taking in her own benefit from the death of her ostensible liege lord, Estela was still taking in the wider implications and she risked breaking into Ermengarda's smug mood with further questions.

'Raimon Trencavel is already Viscomte de Béziers and d'Agde, under the Comte de Barcelone; with Carcassonne, Albi, and Razès, that puts him under the Comte de Toulouse as well for those fiefs – an uneasy combination of loyalties!'

'Quite,' agreed Aliénor, replying to a warning look from Ermengarda with, 'The more the girl knows, the more useful she will be. Roger was solid as Carcassonne rock in separating the Viscomtesse from that predator Alphonse and has held his fortress as Narbonne's ally in Toulouse territory. Raimon is a very different case. He and Toulouse were thick as crusading thieves until their return. It seems Toulouse was unhappy with his friend's oath to Barcelone and now, with Carcassonne his, Raimon returns to the shadow of Toulouse. Which way he will jump with his new overlord, his ex-friend, remains to be seen.'

As if the shadow of Toulouse had no power to squeeze a mailed fist around the heart of Narbonne, Ermengarda said, 'I'm sure Estela has need to speak with Guillelma, the matter of a wedding gown and so forth, so we won't keep you.' Estela took the hint and curtsied her exit but there was someone else she wanted to talk to before she sought out Guillelma. Someone who might shed a little more light on an assassination attempt, or at least on broken glass. Assuming, of course, that Dragonetz was wrong.

'Aliénor didn't send for me, did she,' observed Lady Sancha, looping her skirts over her arm as she accompanied Estela across an internal courtyard.

'No, she didn't. I wanted to talk to you in private, without making others curious.

Lady Sancha's mouth pursed in unexpected approval and she nodded. 'You're learning. Shall we?' She indicated a bower seat, overgrown with a vine, in a shady corner, one of Ermengarda's experiments with Moorish gardening. They sat, spreading their silk skirts like exotic flowers against the background of stone and leaf.

'You don't like me, do you?' Estela gazed straight ahead, at water bubbling over a stone into a square pool. Al-Hisba could no doubt explain to her how the water flowed endlessly. Wheels within wheels, with hammers, probably. Estela could feel the human warmth of the body beside her on the seat. They were too close for facing each other but Estela sensed the questioning glance that brushed her face and returned to that same enigmatic pool.

'Oh, my dear,' was the unsatisfactory response, with a sigh.

Irritated, Estela continued. 'There's no point pretending any more. I know you're a spy and an assassin, and I'm going to put a stop to it.'

'And how did you make this amazing deduction?'

This was not going to plan. Gritting her teeth, Estela continued, 'I've watched you among the Ladies, gathering information, asking clever questions.'

'And no-one could accuse you of that,' Sancha interrupted drily.

Estela flushed. 'The Queen doesn't check up on you. If you ask her to give her seal to her message, she does, and I bet one of those messages was a safe passage for the arbalestier. Even Dragonetz trusts you – God knows why – so it was easy enough for you to get his password and send word to Arnaut at Douzens that there would be a friendly crossbow on the road and to ignore it.'

'And why exactly did I want to kill Dragonetz, who, as you so rightly say, trusts me? Surely he is more use to me alive.'

'Money,' said Estela succinctly. 'You need a great deal of money. Guillelma gossips, you know, and your dresses, your jewels, your finery are all beyond the means of a small estate in Provence. So someone paid you to kill Dragonetz.'

'Ouch! A hit!' Sancha laid a dramatic hand over her heart. 'And do we know who this someone is?'

'The knights. It's not about Aliénor at all. It's about the mill. The knights, the white friars, the Archbishop – they all want to stop Dragonetz at any price.'

'I haven't a clue what you're talking about but it does seem poor Dragonetz has acquired rather a lot of enemies.

'And then you tried to get rid of me from Aliénor's household. If I hadn't appeared at table when expressly summoned to play that night, I would have been dismissed by Aliénor.'

'Back in the ditch she found you in,' agreed Sancha helpfully, adding even more colour to Estela's cheeks.

'So you admit it!'

'It does sound possible, when you string it all together like that. And how exactly do you propose to stop me?'

'Your payment!' Estela was triumphant. 'I'll denounce you to Ermengarda as we're in Narbonne, and if she traces back your jewels, your income, it will prove who is behind this!'

'Very good, child. You are right – I am a spy. And you are right that I have good reason to kill Dragonetz but it's not money. You see, he is the only one who knows my secret so if I killed him, that would remove the threat to my peace of mind that he represents.'

Estela had stopped breathing. The water bubbled in the silence left after Sancha stopped speaking and a black redstart trilled as it flirted its scarlet at a mate before flying off. This was everything she'd hoped for. Wait till she told Dragonetz! Sancha took Estela's hand and in the craziness of the moment, sensing no danger, Estela let her hand be guided into the other woman's under-shift, across her lower body and placed firmly on male private parts. Flinching as if scalded, Estela's hand withdrew of its own volition to be clasped firmly in its partner. She couldn't move, could only listen to Sancha's incomprehensible words as she – he? – stood up to leave.

'So now you know my secret too, which means of course that I must kill you too.' Estela didn't budge one inch on the seat. 'The problem being, my dear, that if you trace back my income, you will find it comes from Dragonetz, and much as he deserves death sometimes, I love that boy stupidly and, as you can understand, it is unrequited so yes, I have found it difficult to like you – pure envy, my dear girl, pure envy.

If I had been born the way other women are, if I looked like you, or had half your talent... But envy is not green enough to take me near a public bathchamber! So, you can either spend your days expecting me to murder you or you can accept that we're on the same side, and you might give a bit more thought to events in Toulouse and Carcassonne. I think we've had enough melodrama for one day so I am going back to the embroidery circle. Good day.' Sancha dropped a mock curtsey and left Estela to muse on a million re-bubblings of water in the pond.

Finally, she rinsed her hands in the cool water, over and over.

Dragonetz looked at Sancha, trying to see her as if he'd just found out what she hid beneath her skirts. There were so many clues, when you knew. A squarish jaw, the hint of prominence to the adam's apple, the muscular tendencies of her arms and above all the way she tried too hard in her feminity, as is the way of men-women and ageing beauties, into both of which categories she fell. When Dragonetz found out that this Queen's Lady was not what she seemed, there had been no time for squeamish revulsion. In the massacre caused by Aliénor's worst misjudgment Oltra mar, a minor tragedy went un-noticed – except by those involved.

A husband, cornered by turbaned assailants, shielded his wife with his sword and his body, slipping on his own blood to his inevitable death by five scimitars, exposing his lady to the opening move of traditional entertainment. Still dripping with her husband's blood, a blade laid more delicate route from bodice to hem, ripping open the vision of nakedness that the Moors had hoped to slake more than battle lust upon. What they saw gave them enough pause to allow Dragonetz the advantage, as he whirled to a woman's scream, saw her husband crumple, saw the body exposed and reacted with the same instinct he would have had if it were his own mother's body assaulted.

Over six dead or dying human bodies, he gazed steadily at Sancha's naked body and said, 'That is the most remarkable distraction I have ever been offered by a comrade but it has served its purpose now,' and he had thrown her a blanket ripped from his horse, that stood wide-eyed and trembling but waiting on his master. Trembling more than the horse, she had stumbled towards him, been thrown on the horse and returned to the huddle of Ladies with Aliénor, holding the blanket as tight as if her very bones would disintegrate otherwise.

Perhaps, he thought, if he had realised the ambiguity of this woman's body in some other way, in another time and place, he would have found it shocking. But at the time it had seemed such a little thing and once known, accepted, part of what he needed to know to understand this useful underling who placed herself under his direction as his eyes and ears in the women's quarters.

There were women who found a marital partner once and once only; Sancha's chance of finding another mate was as likely as fish playing hop-skotch in the meadows and it was unspoken between her and Dragonetz that her status as widow was permanent and ideal for her work. It was one of the mysteries on which Dragonetz refused to dwell, as to how exactly Sancha had found a marital relationship in the first place.

'You did the right thing,' he told her, smiling vacantly around the hall. What could be more innocuous than a flirtation between the voracious widow and the debonair troubadour, in full view of all who passed through on palace business? 'Estela is young and naive but not stupid.'

'She doesn't lack guts,' Sancha admitted, grudgingly, 'but she has the subtlety of a boot up the arse.'

This time, Dragonetz' laugh was genuine. 'So you're going to make peace and teach her a little more subtlety. Along the lines of your little revelation?'

Sancha ignored his irony and nodded. 'Someone has to! If she accepts me.'

Dragonetz looked at her steadily then. 'What's to accept?' And he meant it. He was old enough to have met and mixed with all kinds of humanity, to know that oddness and glitter faded equally with long acquaintance, stripped to some harder and more complicated essence of character than 'that's Lady Sancha, man dressed as woman.'

'She might be chasing the wrong hare but she's in the right wood, your Estela,' mused Sancha.

'Meaning?'

'One of the Ladies is waist-deep in this business and it's likely someone with a personal grudge against Estela as well as political against you. Possibly personal grudge against you, too. A discarded lover?' she looked the question at Dragonetz.

Affronted, he returned, 'Don't expect me to remember names and faces! All of them, I should think!'

'So, political motive remains our best line. By marriage or birth, every one of the Ladies is related to Toulouse, Aquitaine, Templars, white friars, the Archbishop, even to Clairvaux! And once again, Estela is in the right that all of these would like Milord Dragonetz disposed of.'

'Instinct? Who do you suspect?'

'All of them and none of them!' Her frustration showed. 'Someone must be very clever indeed to seem as innocuous and stupid as they all seem – I don't know why Aliénor puts up with them.'

'Same reason we do – their connections and the news we get through them.'

Sancha sighed. 'No news from Carcassonne at present as Alis has gone to her Trencavel uncle's funeral. Young Toulouse is continuing to grow in size and venom but it's directed against Jews and Cathars at present, rather than in some desire to confront Aliénor head on – after all he is the one in situ so her fun with his title is merely an irritant. His desire to regain Narbonne for the Comté is perhaps more of a threat and that's where Carcassonne becomes interesting.'

'With Raimon Trencavel at Carcassonne, Toulouse might find a stepping stone to Narbonne.' Dragonetz completed the thought. 'But Toulouse and Raimon have been at odds since Raimon accepted the Barcelone connection for his other titles.'

'Self-interest quickly repairs quarrels.'

'So Carcassonne is no longer safe. And the monks? And the Brothers?'

'Clairvaux hates Aliénor, both personally and politically. The white friars would do anything for their sainted leader. Any attempt against Aliénor would have them at the top of my suspect list. The Templars are hand in glove with the white friars, allowing a little leeway for wealthy sidetracking. There again, Estela was nearly right – follow the financial gain. Tell me, what is this business of a mill that makes you so hated.'

'A project of mine, that's all.' Dragonetz waved the question aside. 'And the Archbishop stands where in all this?'

'Against Ermengarda, who steals his money – as he sees it – and corrupts men's hearts with her decadent court and her tolerance of heathens.'

'So there might be truck between the Archbishop and Toulouse? He must look with favour on the Christian cleansing there.'

'I would guess so but there's not much chance of women's gossip from the Archbishop's Quarters! You must find that out yourself.'

'And Aliénor?'

'Blooming. Recovering the roses she lost week by week in Paris, and thriving on Narbonne intrigue.'

'But she will have to go back soon.'

'Yes. No talk of it as yet but there are physical limits on how late she can leave it – another month, two months.'

'Then we shall be on top of the civilised world.'

'Or bottom of a very dreary one.'

'I must to the apex of our hopes, right now,' Dragonetz bowed an elegant leave-taking, 'but this has been most useful. My thanks will find their way to you in the usual manner.'

Sancha gave a small nod of acknowledgement but Dragonetz was already on his way. He would rather have re-played the three challenges of the Prince of Orkney, and with his head tied in a sack, than face this conversation with Aliénor, but needs must. And, sadly for Dragonetz' prospects of light relief, Jarl Rognvaldr Kali Kollsson had upped ship, sailing on to his destiny Oltra mar, with a saga in his heart dedicated in several suitably euphemistic verses to the cool goddess who had claimed his heart by a foreign shore.

Dragonetz stood stock still while an alabaster elephant hurtled past him and dinted its trunk in stone walls too thick to care what a queen threw next. It was going better than he'd expected. Two feverish spots in her cheeks were not the only signs of a royal rage in the red-head's livid skin.

'How dare you!' she screeched at him, 'I'll have you bastinadoed, flayed and quartered if you leave me!'

'That would be one way of keeping me,' agreed Draonetz calmly but this time he ducked, noting that Aliénor was running out of ornaments as a wooden trinket box with the Arabic 'good luck' motto on its lid, followed the elephant. She took to hurling words instead.

'Mill-keeper!' The occupation was injected with as much contempt as if Dragonetz had announced his intention to hire his body out on the streets of Narbonne. The Duchesse paced the chamber, kicking a chair that displeased her as she passed. 'As well put a destrier to pasture, a wolf by the fireside as a man like you turn pot-bellied merchant. No, Dragonetz, I won't have it!' He hadn't said one word but stood, grave and patient, exasperatingly so it seemed. 'And don't pull that face either! Does your oath mean nothing to you? Do you desert Aquitaine in her hour of greatest need?' And suddenly she sat, her hands on her hidden belly, her face crumpling into that commonplace, a woman abandoned.

Dragonetz was not foolish enough to sit and draw her wrath again but he had to steel himself not to kneel at her feet, to reassure her, to play once again the scene she wrote for him. Good as she was, a glance risked from under her long lashes, checking for his reaction, bolstered his resolve and he waited, silent.

'Don't you remember, my friend, what we have been through together, carnage and... gentler moments?' Although she touched so lightly on the past, she knew exactly where to press. 'Do you remember laying your bright sword in my lap?' The delicate pause allowed time for them both to read into the phrase and remember. 'And is that sword to rust by a mill-wheel? For Narbonne!' She spat the last word and allowed him to see that the hurt in her eyes was genuine. So she knew about Ermengarda. It was inevitable. She had played all her cards and she leaned back in her chair, exhausted and tearful. 'Don't leave me, Dragonetz, please.'

Then he knelt before her and took her hands in his own. 'I serve Aquitaine and its Lady, always, wherever in the world I should be. I too remember a young knight, dazzled by beauty brighter than his sword. But my sword and my spirit are dull with too much blood. I want to build, not destroy. I want to create something for the future not watch men's eyes as they die.'

And women's, and children's, he didn't say.

'Now you sound like my milksop mewling baby of a husband! You, a miller!' The fire was back in Aliénor's voice. 'And even Louis can cope with a righteous war, with God on our side! We must re-take Edessa! It is our duty as Christians to fight the Infidels and God help me, I won't be found wanting! I need time to produce this kingling,' she patted her belly, 'and then I shall be rallying the forces for the next Crusade. I want you leading my army! You can't say me nay! You don't have the right.'

'I can buy the right,' he pointed out gently, referring to the system of scutage whereby a knight could send payment instead of services demanded by his liege lord.

'By God, you'll pay dear if you refuse me!' sparked Aliénor, tearing her hands out of Dragonetz' grasp and slapping his face.

He merely looked back at her, still on his knees. There was no point answering her crusading zeal, nor explaining that this was exactly what sickened him. 'Let the future decide the future,' he closed that subject, leaving her to hope. 'And I am leading your army, here, now, looking for this threat that dogs us here and now, in Narbonne. I am hoping we can draw out the culprit and deal with him, very soon. You know you can use trusted eyes and ears in the south when you go back to Paris. All I am asking you,' he was tactful, 'is that I stay here when you go back.' They both knew that he wasn't asking.

'Leave me,' she said abruptly, ironically in the circumstances. He stood and bowed, about to leave. Then she remembered something. 'I want your services tonight. The Viscomtesse and I wish to visit a person in the city, incognito, and I want you with us for security. And we're taking your protegée with us too.'

Dragonetz could have told her the folly of risking her life and that of the unborn heir to the throne for who knows what madcap adventure, not to mention the unnecessary risk to his own life as one man against the combined forces of evil in the whole of Narbonne but he knew the response he would get and resigned himself to the inevitable, making himself a promise that he would take Arnaut with him.

'You don't make my life easy, do you,' was all he said.

'I thought that was what you liked,' she responded but her heart wasn't in the banter and he left her sitting hunched in her chair, a foreshadowing of the old woman she would one day become.

CHAPTER THIRTEEN

E stela had excused herself from duties among Aliénor's Ladies to see Guillelma but she had no interest whatsoever in veils, gloves and gowns. She would rather have been following her self-appointed task of distinguishing one Lady from the other, recording mentally the cross-connections and political implications of every chance word. She would not be happy until she could add place to name for every woman among them and she had made a good start, helped discreetly by Lady Sancha.

Estela rebuked herself. Lady Sancha *de Provence*, she told her ill-disciplined thoughts. Which meant that she could have links with Raymond and Stephanie of les Baux, self-proclaimed rulers of Provence. The rulers of les Baux cast greedy eyes on Narbonne from the east, just as Raymond de Toulouse from the west. Ostensibly it was the husband who led the righteous campaigns to regain Provence on his wife's behalf but everyone knew that Stephanie called the tune. And their allies were equally well-known. Les Baux' niggling Baussenque Wars against Ramon Berenguer IV of Barcelone, for sovereignty of Provence, were supported by Toulouse.

Despite, or rather because of, the friendship between Narbonne and Ramon Berenguer IV, Comte de Barcelone, Prince of Aragon and Overlord of Provence, relations between Narbonne and the Lordlings actually holding Provence were strained at best, likely to erupt into outright military dispute at some stage if Stephanie and her Raymond put a booted foot on Narbonne soil, and any Lady *de Provence* must be doubly suspect, by birth and by alliance.

Excepting, of course, Lady Sancha. Estela had now come to accept Dragonetz' judgement, although she was trying so hard not to stare at Sancha and think of what lay beneath her under-shift, that anyone watching closely would have thought Estela either hated or loved the other woman. If only Sancha could be trusted not to catch her eye and wink at her, Estela might be able to control the tell-tale blushes. In other ways, Estela was now sure that Sancha could be trusted, so that wrote the other two Ladies *de Provence* out of the reckoning. Sancha knew everything about them from the chickens bred by their grandparents to the stone-mason who extended their castles.

Next on Estela's list was the *de Rouen*, Aimée, What if it wasn't a southern conspiracy at all but a Norman one? What if there was some connection with the Angevins and their ambitions to add France to their kingdoms in England and Normandy? Would they gain from killing Dragonetz? The attempts and threats seemed to suggest a network of enemies, to Dragonetz or to Aliénor, or both. Not to mention some personal animosity against Estela herself. If there was a Norman conspiracy, it made no sense to spring it in Occitania, where Normans were as sparse on the ground as bishops in a brothel, rather than in Paris. It all seemed a bit far-fetched and the more time Estela spent with Aimée, the more she was convinced that the girl's innocent expression was exactly that. No, it just didn't fit. So that ruled out the other northerners in principle, too.

'Much as I enjoy your company, I do have other work to do.' Guillelma was eyeing her quizzically, as she sat on a high settle swinging her feet absent-mindedly, forgetting that Guillelma was repairing a fancy on a shoe buckle. 'In theory, it's easier when the shoe is held still by someone else.'

'Sorry.' For a moment, Guillelma had Estela's full attention. ''Don't you mind always looking after other people?'

The capable arms didn't stop working, the doughy flesh on the forearms wobbling.

'Get a life of my own, you mean?' Guillelma took the thread in her teeth and snapped it, with the ease of habit. She laughed. 'You're still the diplomat then.'

Damn it, when would she spare her own blushes! 'I meant, more...' Estela tailed off. Guillelma had her to rights and they both knew it.

'Ah, child,' Guillelma shook her head. 'I have a fine job for the Queen and I can dress up as fancy as I like, mix with high and low, and no-one thinks the worse of me because no-one expects anything of me. And I'll tell you a little secret,' large brown eyes met curious gold, 'when I'm not working, there's a fine soldier travels the same road as I do and we find a meet-up where the warmth of a man's arms is not unknown to me.'

Laundry and lovers, Estela recalled, observing Guillelma's coarse body with interest. How could a man want a woman as old as that, as dried-out, as wobbly?

Guillelma smiled at her again. 'Twenty years we've been together when we can be and you'd swear it was yesterday he brought me a hare for the pot and a kiss for the price. You'll understand, one day.'

'Will I?' Estela felt the tears pricking, her mother's absence a sudden bolt in her chest more painful than any arbalestier's.

'So let's get on with it. You shall have a little finery for your wedding day and we will drink and dance you into your new life.'

'You and your soldier?'

'For the drinking maybe but he treads a measure with the grace of an ague-ridden pig, so I'll keep my options open on the dancing. This one,' she held up a robe, 'this one, or this one?'

'Not the blue!' Estela was sharper than she'd meant to be, remembering a man's eyes, dilated with poison, noting her ribbons. 'Red,' she said more calmly. She had hardly seen Dragonetz since his recovery and only in public. Lessons had finished and there was a tacit understanding that she was busy with her wedding plans and he with... with being Dragonetz, whatever that involved.

'And I need a mask for this evening,' she said.

'Do you, now.' Guillelma refrained from asking why and Estela didn't tell her that she was being taken to have her fortune read, accompanied by a Queen and a Viscomtesse in disguise.

'It is the proper thing to do, before a wedding, a treat for you,' Aliénor had declared, but her eyes gave away whose fortune she really wanted to hear. 'Even Ermengarda thinks we should consult this Gyptian.'

'I would like to see her,' Ermengarda agreed gravely.

The pitch sputtered from the torch Dragonetz carried and he held it a little further away until it steadied into a trustworthy light. Hooded and caped, he and Arnaut might have been a picture of night criminals but there was no help for it. They could hardly tread the cobbles of Narbonne openly in full armour without attracting attention, not only to themselves. Aliénor would be the death of him, one way or another! As likely in the streets of a civilised city, for the sake of a girlish prank, as on a blood-sodden battlefield Oltra mar.

'I feel like a creeping friar,' complained Arnaut, muffled in his hood.

'You could have oiled your armour better,' was Dragonetz' response. 'Friars don't usually clank!'

'If someone's close enough to hear my steel, then they're likely to feel it too!'

The postern gate was already opened and out slipped four more shadowy figures, cloaked, hooded and bubbling with excitement.

'My Ladies!' cautioned Dragonetz. 'This affair is mad enough without you crying your identity along the streets off Narbonne. The invisible servant creaked the gate to behind them, carefully leaving it unlocked for their return.

'We will be good,' came the low voice of Ermengarda but even she showed the night's work tingling in her veins. Unmistakeable, imperial tones reminded Dragonetz of the address they sought. At least it was still the Palace-side of the river, only a few streets away, but even so this was madness. Dragonetz leading, Arnaut at the rear, the little procession followed the route Dragonetz had previously taken to borrow money, but this time they passed by Raavad's house, continuing further down the street, a left, a right and then a low wooden door indistinguishable from those beside it.

'Let me!' Dragonetz stood to one side with the torch while the Queen of France performed a coded rat-a-tat rat-a-tat knock on the door, which opened a suspicious crack and then enough to swallow them all in the gloomy interior of a low-ceilinged, hallway. They were ushered into a room that still smelled of winter's smoke and was almost filled by a large table and twelve plain stools.

The two men wasted no time in putting their hoods down, freeing their vision and scanning the room but the four they accompanied stayed silent and covered. Although the room was plainly furnished, the walls were decorated with what Dragonetz recognized as mystic symbols. The only way in was the door through which they had just come. If it was a question of dispatching incomers one at a time, so be it, Dragonetz told himself, his sword drawn and across the entrance. He took up a blocking stance, Arnaut behind him. When they heard a whirring and turned, there was a table between the two men and the moving panel, allowing two figures to step into the room beside the four hooded visitors.

Dragonetz swore but the two newcomers merely took seats at the table. One wore the beard and sidelocks unusual in local Jews but that Dragonetz had seen on his travels. The other was a woman unlike anyone Dragonetz had ever seen. She was dressed as if one of Guillelma's clothing chests had been upended over her, landing in knots and swathes of random textures and patterns, floral green over blue fustian, red diamonds kerchief-edged over yellow lawn.

The riot of colour started at the top in a turbaned swirl and finished at her feet, calloused and dusty in leather strapping. Her face, although swarthy as that of the man beside her, was wider featured, flatter than his racial type. Weathered and wrinkled, her face gave no hint as to whether she was forty or eighty – she could have been either or anywhere in between. The shake in her hands as she placed a walking stick carefully beside her at the table hinted at the upper end of the range. In any case, hardly a threat. Dragonetz lowered his sword at the same moment as the Jew spoke.

'You grace us with your presence.' The slight accent reminded them that Occitan was not his first language but he spoke it fluently. 'The Lady shall be known to you as Dame Fairnette Babtista, which is her name among the Gadze, that is, non Romani like us, and she has accepted your request that she read for you, without being told your names, although she has given you hers.' If there was a rebuke in these words, it glanced lightly off the impatience shimmering in the atmosphere round the four hooded figures.

Dame Fairnette Babtista inclined her head in queenly fashion and waved her hand to indicate the seat beside her and with the other gestured that all but the supplicant should distance themselves. A slight figure, not the tallest, Dragonetz noted, was pushed forward by the others and, giggling, took her place around the corner from the Dame. The Romani took a pack of cards out of the man's almonier, made of tapestry, that she wore somewhere around what might have been her waist, and spread them on the table. From his position by the door, half an ear always on the passageway that gave access to the room, Dragonetz could see the painted characters on the cards. He had seen others similar Oltra mar, even learned to game with them, and he knew that should a thief break into their little rendez-vous he would be better advised to steal the cards than all of the Ladies' jewels. Would there really come a day, thanks to paper mills, when every man could have a pack of cards? He must ask al-Hisba how to produce thick paper.

Dame Fairnette muttered to herself in some strange language, a disconcerting string of throaty sounds that interfered with his concentration until Dragonetz jerked into the realisation that she was now speaking Occitan and he had completely missed the switch. The low voice wheezed, 'Dark handsome man in your future, my pretty, troubles to do with water.' He hadn't missed much, he thought, as the patter ended in similar vein.

But the hooded figure stayed seated. 'Surely you can say a little more to the Queen of France,' a haughty voice declared from within the hood. So that was their little game, Dragonetz realised, not recognising which Lady spoke but knowing full well that Aliénor was the tallest in that room, sitting in the background, fidgeting with suppressed laughter and excitement.

Without missing a beat, the Dame said, 'Perhaps I can but she must sit before me in her own person then, and ask. You gave counterfeit and received in the same coin, although your proper fate is as unremarkable as your bearing.'

The hood was thrown back then and the face of Marie de Poitiers showed two bright spots of anger in the flickering torchlight. Before she could hurl what were clearly going to be insults back at the Dame, the imperial voice of her mistress was raised. Aliénor was already dropping her own hood as she spoke. 'If there is offence then I have caused it and the lady acted on my orders, Dame Fairnette. I ask forgiveness for a foolishness.'

'And you offer me true coin, Lady Aliénor.' The tone was a wheedling whine now and the shaking hand was open upon the table, waiting for the silver that was duly passed over it and back, three times before it disappeared into the almonier.

Once more the cards were laid in a pattern of three rows. Once more the muttering song commented incomprehensibly on the cards – or the weather, thought Dragonetz, but he watched and listened anyway.

You shall not bear one king, my Lady,' were the words that shocked the room and Aliénor's stillness said more than her earlier jitters. The voice continued after its dramatic pause, 'You shall bear many kings.' The relief was palpable and Marie even broke into spontaneous clapping, which quickly petered out.

'You see this card?' The Romani picked up one from the table and showed it to Aliénor, who merely nodded. 'Mark it well for this is your doom and destiny, the Tower.'

Another pause then Aliénor laughed lightly. 'Then it looks like I shall be stuck in Paris but as I shall have my King-son that doesn't worry me, one bit.'

'So, so, my Lady,' Dame Fairnette muttered, but whether in agreement or contradiction wasn't clear.

Next was Ermengarda, all pretence at disguise abandoned and even she could not school her face completely against the tension in her jawbone, the tightening of her hands in her lap.

'Trade, prosperity, victory in battle.' Just an upmarket version of the first sitting!

'Will there be children?' asked Ermengarda in a voice so quiet that Dragonetz could hear himself swallow, reminded that for at least two women in this room a baby meant more than a lapful of wriggles.

The reply was slow, lingering over the choice of each word. 'There will be a child related to you that comes into your life for good and for ill.'

'For whose good?' pressed Ermengarda. 'And for whose ill?'

'For good and for ill,' was the unmoving reply. 'The cards have spoken. But be happy in this, you shall know love, with one who sings and plays for you, my Lady Tort-n'avetz, My Lady 'You-are-wrong',

Despite Ermengarda's light-hearted response, 'Something to look forward to, then,' her instinctive half-glance in his direction gave her away. Dragonetz felt the sudden need to face the source of any likely threat and turned away from the table scenario to the passageway, that suddenly seemed the easier of the dangers that faced him. He heard Ermengarda leave the table – thank God – and a rustle of gowns as someone else took her place. He didn't have to look to know who the fourth woman was. Even when speaking, there was a lilt to her voice, a melody all her own.

'I'm no-one,' Estela told the Romani, 'you don't need to worry about me.' The other three women were already whispering to each other, having lost interest.

Dame Fairnette began her chant and the room was quiet again. 'It makes no sense!' For the first time, she sounded frustrated. 'Everything and its opposite... song and audience in great halls... but it doesn't happen and you are alone on a great journey... or it does happen and no journey.' Dragonetz glanced back over his shoulder at

Estela, her back metal-straight, the long black hair falling below the stool. The Dame was the one who was agitated. She wrapped her arms round her gown of bright patches and rocked slightly, grimacing. 'Pain, so much pain in the past... easy to see what has been before... but the future. Why can't I see? Something is blocking, something –' suddenly she stretched out a bony hand and ripped Estela's clasp from the front of her cloak and held it out of reach, high above her head like a tribute to the gods.

'It was a present. Could I have it back please?' Estela's voice was calm enough but Dragonetz could see her right hand reaching through her cloak and, he imagined, through her under-shift to the steel beneath, just in case.

'Pathfinder,' intoned Dame Fairnette. 'Now I can see! The whole world lies before you, not one path but a dozen at this crossroads. Know you are at the biggest crossroads of your life, know this and choose with care! Not one choice but many, many roads and all dangerous. You cannot run fast enough or far enough. You drag other people in your wake, the highborn and the lowborn, and someone will not survive the knowing of you.'

'That's enough!' said Estela, reaching for her clasp, but the Romani managed to keep it just out of her reach. Dragonetz had not moved but he could feel Arnaut shifting beside him, ready to put an end to Estela's discomfort. Dragonetz laid a light hand on the other's arm, warning him to stay put. Crazy it might be but there was no danger here to call for armed intervention.

'Be glad,' the tones cackled with mockery, 'for you too shall know love, with someone who sings and plays for you.' She cackled even louder, then suddenly collapsed onto her seat and gave the brooch back to Estela.

'No doubt the same troubadour who sings of love to my Lady Ermengarda.' Aliénor threw her barbs lightly and accurately into the silence. 'Somewhat free with their love, troubadours, don't you find, Ermengarda?' Dragonetz studied the door, carefully, as wooden himself, but he was so used to training Estela's every breath, that he could hear the catch that suggested the edge of tears, even though she said nothing.

It was Ermengarda who responded, rallying. 'Indeed. I think we have troubled Dame Fairnette enough and her invention begins to fail and tend to repetition.' The Romani said nothing, hunching into a wizened old woman once more, no trace of the passion that had flowed through her while she held the Rune. The Jew had said nothing but watched passively throughout and it was to him that Ermengarda spoke next. 'We thank you for your hospitality, Makhir ben Habibi, and would know more of your work.' Dragonetz' mouth curved lightly. He should have known that the Lady of Narbonne would always have a hidden agenda for joining in a playful whim of Aliénor's. Every religion had its magical margins and to hold the threads of this city meant testing the powers and the politics of all its factions.

'You are gracious, my Lady, We progress, we progress.'

'You are modest. I understand from Raavad that your work on the Kabbalah is renowned throughout Provence and further, and that you receive visitors regularly.'

However innocuous the words seemed, Dragonetz noted the sudden tension in the Jew, who nodded his head repeatedly, like a thrush after a worm, as he replied. 'We philosophise my Lady, and the power in the Torah is a meet subject for debate, as I am sure Raavad has told you.'

'Raavad has told me many things,' was the cool reply. 'Including the fact that Dame Fairnette honours you with her company to find out for herself more regarding your studies.'

The head gave more quick nods and glanced at his companion, who still sat, deflated like a flattened wineskin. 'The Romani have some knowledge and we thought to share,' he agreed.

Once more the grating voice was heard. 'Goy are not permitted to share.'

'Goy?' queried Ermengarda.

Makhir frowned. 'It is a word we use for non-Jews. Dame Fairnette is disappointed that I cannot allow her to discuss the Kabbalah with the inner circle.'

'Cannot?' the old woman challenged 'Will not!'

Makhir spread his hands wide in the ancient gesture of helpless apology. 'What can I do?' he pleaded for understanding.

'Is that true?' demanded Ermengarda. 'Do you hold back your learning from Goys?' Her lips curled round the word and Dragonetz had a sudden picture of a tinder box held to the wooden door of this anonymous house in the Jewish quarter, neighbour to every other Jewish house, all dry wood for a bonfire.

'No,' Makhir was clear and met Ermengarda's eyes firmly. His arms went out in the apology gesture again. 'But what can I do? The Tradition does not permit women to be party to our mysteries.' There was a gasp from Aliénor and Dragonetz closed his eyes, the conflagration real in his head.

Instead, the ruler of Narbonne, golden and indisputably female, accepted the insult and moulded it into a nugget of power. 'Much like the Christians then,' she observed mildly, 'and I shall bear that in mind in future.' Everyone in that room knew a threat when he heard one, including the hapless Jew, caught between tenet and termagants. 'Dame Fairnette came alone?' asked Ermengarda, politely.

'My people like not walls nor the people who believe they own them.' The old woman answered for herself. 'We camp down-river.'

'These are dangerous times and I would not have Narbonne troubled by Gorz against Gyptians, Goys against Jews, or whatever other names we call those we do not wish to share with.' Makhir winced. 'Your people are not staying long?' The command could not have been clearer.

'We go on tomorrow.'

'Good. East?' inquired Ermengarda.

'East,' confirmed Dame Fairnette and the thought of a Romani camp disturbing the settlements of Provence brought a malicious smile to Ermengarda's lips. 'East,' repeated the old woman, 'to the great wash of the salty sea. I want to die in the holy place, where my people will come every year in their thousands, not in my life-time, but in the next or the one after that and every year after, years in their thousands, in the name of black Sarah and the Maries of the Sea. It shall be so!' Then once more she crumpled back into her seat.

'Please see she is safely returned to her people,' Ermengarda ordered Makhir, who bowed obeisance. 'You will keep me informed of your studies. There is a delicate line between philosophy and,' she swept an arm to indicate the symbols on the walls, 'the dark arts. I wouldn't want it said those studying the Kabbalah are crossing that line' – Makhir said nothing but was intent –'by showing an active interest in occult activities such as fortune-telling, which is banned by both your Church and mine.' There was total silence in the room. 'But I know that we were both merely showing respect to a passing visitor and her ways, which are not our ways. Should your gatherings here be seen as dangerous, I would have to act, but if a few – and mark, I say a few! – learned men meet discreetly and discuss their faith, and I am fully informed, I see no harm in that at all. Do we understand each other?'

Makhir's bowed head was answer enough and Ermengarda's tone lightened. 'For this evening's entertainment, we thank you.'

As entertainment, it was on a par with having your face nibbled by rats, thought Dragonetz. The Jew, Makhir, caught him as he turned to go and murmured, 'We will not be ungrateful for the service you will render us nor will we forget the cost to you.'

'I have no idea what you're talking about.'

'You will. The Kabbalah satisfies its own needs and we are all her servants.'

Dragonetz nodded a curt farewell and thanked his own more familiar God that the evening was over. Whatever Ermengarda had learned or decided, she kept to herself, without looking once in Dragonetz' direction. Hooded once more, the party re-threaded their way to the Palace, without incident. Unless, like Dragonetz, you count it an incident that he quietly asked Estela if she were all right and she replied, inexplicably, 'Go to hell!'

CHAPTER FOURTEEN

Estela's husband-to-be was grizzled and lined but still kept a firm chin, she noticed, glancing at his profile. When she had swept in all her finery to the Chapel doorway, Sancha and Guillelma at her side, she had not known which of the small knot of men standing there was the man she was here to marry and sudden tears pricked as she hoped it would not be the specimen whose belly gave the lie of his belt problems, nor the one whose fight against the smallpox had left a pitted landscape of a face. How could the world be so full of ugly men and she had never noticed before? Before she could tuck her train over her arm and run for the stables, for Tou and a thousand miles between herself and this mistake, Sancha touched a man whose back was towards them, saying 'Johans' and putting an end to Estela's nervous speculation.

His smile showed good teeth, he had neither belly nor pitmarks, and his dress, although unfortunately a red that clashed with Estela's gown, showed the quiet taste of middling wealth. He greeted her with a bow and a few platitudes but her scarlet silk dress didn't seem to spark any fire in his sobre eyes. There was no sign of that second sneaked appraisal that she had grown used to from the men around her. Perhaps that was to the good, she thought, as her stomach looped like a swift in flight. Kindness was worth more than passion. So she told herself, twice.

There were perhaps ten people gathered outside the Chapel, where it was hot enough even in mid-morning to trickle sweat between her breasts, staining the sensitive silk darker, as she stood in full sunshine, waiting. Heat flashed back from the grey stone paving. Al-Hisba had told her of the lightweight fabrics, sheers and muslins, worn Oltra mar and she wished they had reached Guillelma's clothing coffers. She covered her face with the veil and felt less vulnerable, not just to the sun. A few passers-by in working clothes paused from curiosity and stayed when they saw the figures of Aliénor and Ermengarda approaching, regal even in their choice of informal apparel, turquoises and garnets glinting in the sun. Did they even go to bed be-jewelled? Estela shook off the image of Ermengarda, golden and naked in turquoises. She really must concentrate.

Ermengarda took her place of office in front of the couple at the Chapel Doorway, ensuring that the ceremony could be seen by the public. It should have been so different. If her mother had been alive, if Estela had been matched with a man from a neighbouring estate, there would have been a betrothal, rings and flowers, promises and kisses, processions and of course, music. Estela would cope with anything this day but that. Whatever the private thoughts of Aliénor and Ermengarda, they had respected Estela's wish that not one chord be struck during this most practical of small ceremonies.

In a voice projected to the Chapel courtyard and beyond, Ermengarda had finished enunciating her right as Viscomtesse de Narbonne to legalise this marriage.

'I, Johans de Villeneuve, receive you as mine, so that you become my wife and I your husband,' pronounced the stranger beside her.

'And I, Roxane de Montbrun, receive you as mine, so that you become my husband and I your wife,' declared Estela, used to an audience, used to keeping her voice clear and firm while her knees shook like mice in a cat's mouth.

'By virtue of the written agreement of Roger de Tancavel, liege Lord of Montbrun, I declare parental consent to be given to Roxane de Mont-brun in this marriage.' Ermengarda was holding aloft a scroll and Estela held her breath. Sure enough, the two witnesses carefully selected by Ermengarda received the scroll, unrolled and read it, acknowledged the signature as genuine and set their own names to the marriage contracts.

There was no denying that Ermengarda was a magnificent liar. Blindly, Estela wrote her own name where she was told. If one of the anonymous, capped workers who'd been hanging on the scene open-mouthed, left at that point, Estela didn't notice, her thoughts a mill-race. She had been wrong to see the coming night as her introduction to womanhood. She was already standing in her mother's footsteps and she could see it all now, the commitment of body and goods to an unknown man, decades of duties, the perennial disappointment, a sense of being cheated and – in her mother's case – the fever that took her to the afterlife. Which had to be a better place. Where were the songs in that?! How could she, Estela, sing while leading such a life? Let alone write the lyrics she had dreamed of writing one day! A sour weight replaced the butterflies in her stomach, sending bitter juices like aloes through her body.

Automatically, she followed Ermengarda into the Church for mass and sat beside her husband on the hard bench, while the Priest blessed their marriage and reminded them that carnal knowledge with pleasure or for any purpose other than procreation was a sin unto the Lord. She murmured the set responses, sought and found nothing in the echoes reverberating through the ancient place of worship.

Then there were congratulations from Aliénor and Ermengarda, Guillelma and Sancha, who was leaving for the family estate in Provence immediately after the ceremony. The assembly was reminded that the couple would be feted at lunch in the Great Hall, a meal that would last until dark, with tumbling and puppets instead of melody and strumming. Her hand on his arm, Estela was linked to Johans like a bit to a bridle but she had no idea who was leading or where.

In a brief moment when no-one was near them, he spoke the only words to her since the commonplaces of greeting. Looking full at her, every bit as kindly as she hoped, he said gently, 'I loved my wife. I understand the situation.' And so she understood too, that it would be duty on both sides this night, her beautiful scarlet silk notwithstanding. Unable to speak, she smiled and nodded, as she continued to do, throughout what seemed a life-time of patchwork leather balls performing ever more tedious arcs in the air between harlequined fools; of marionettes strutting their uneven walk, directed by Jews and given voices by any wit hoping to needle another; of endless dishes, oyster ragout, yellow-coloured Saracen soup, geese feet, guinea-fowl and boar, frumenty, sweetmeats and fancies.

On and on the day dragged, while Estela picked at crumbs, smiled and nodded, starting at so much as a shadow of a familiar black head with his blonde-haired Aide and Moorish companion but they weren't there. Thank God, thought Estela, her split soul resentful that not even Arnaut nor al-Hisba had thought it worth attending her wedding feast. The third absentee she didn't name even to herself.

Raymond V de Toulouse, usurped Viscomte of Narbonne, was fifteen, an orphan and a dutiful son. From his mother, he had inherited a narrow, dark face that could be traced back to the Roman origins of her home town Uzès. She had also passed on an unrelenting hatred, based on envy, of the red-haired Aquitaine beauty she had reluctantly served for years as Lady-in-Waiting.

Barely a year after his mother's death, when Raymond was only seven years old, the pink walls of Toulouse had been shaken by the same red-head's arrogant claim to his father's city. Never mind that it was Louis VII, the King of France, who bayed the challenge without their walls, Alphonse Jourdain made it quite clear to his young son that this was more mischief caused by the whore of Aquitaine. Thanks to his father's clever negotiations, and Louis' milksop reluctance to spill blood, a new treaty satisfied pride on both sides and the

French retreated. The Toulousians repeated with glee the rumours that Louis screamed at night, haunted by charred phantoms from the town known as Vitry-le-Brûlé since Louis' one attempt at exerting military discipline over unruly vassals. If Louis was convicted by gossip of cowardice, celebrations throughout the streets of Toulouse made it equally clear who the victors were in this bloodless war and seven-year-old Raymond was lifted on his father's shoulders, carried high round the Halls and announced to the world at large as the future Viscomte of Narbonne by his slightly inebriated father.

When Raymond was eight, this strange boast was made good when his father married young Ermengarda of Narbonne. Left in Toulouse with his tutors, priests and his father's advisers, Raymond was told that his father had a new domain and he had a new mother. He wanted neither. He missed his father's huge confidence, his maleness and his pride in his son. Of course, Raymond was now too old to be physically touched in affection by his father, and after the death of his mother, the little boy had lost contact with her maids and wards, as well as the rare and vinegary maternal embrace. He didn't need to be touched. In fact, he wouldn't have believed there had ever been a time he liked it.

The eight year old prayed devoutly every night, adapting the formula he had been taught to include a fervent plea that Ermengarda die as quickly as possible and his father return to him. When his father strode into the Great Hall, beetle-browed with rage at the conspiracy against him and the annulment of his brief marriage, before he had even bedded his thirteen-year-old bride, Raymond learned young that God answered his prayers, a lesson that bonded him inseparably to his Lord. It was clear to the boy that Raymond's work and the Lord's work were one and the same, and his sense of mission filled the empty space he would not admit had been there.

Six years later, it had been easier to accept his father leaving him once more because the warrior wore the Holy Cross and Raymond trusted in God to look after his own. Reports of his father's valour, his might against the Heathen, came back to Raymond in troubadours' songs and by courier, to bolster his ego while he trod a tricky measure amongst his Advisers, studying patiently how to twist them to his desires. He learned quickly that he must gain power before he could show any and instead he cultivated subtlety, playing one against another, seeding distrust, misquoting each to the other until only he kept the threads of truth in his head. Or his version of truth.

Then came the news from Oltra mar. His father, the great Alphonse Jourdain, inexplicably dead. Despite the temporary relief of having the messenger tortured by stretch and by spike, and then killed, Raymond could not pretend to himself that the message was false, and he spent dark days and nights, doubting his special relationship with God. He was already starting to think his way out of his trap, to realise that wicked men had the power to act against the Lord, to spoil His plans for Raymond, when Raimon Trencavel of Beziers, his father's comrade at arms and long time friend, called at Toulouse after his own return from the disastrous Crusade. He wanted to pay his respects to the memory of his friend, to offer his friendship to his friend's son, the new Comte, and to share some privileged detail on exactly how Raymond's father had died.

It was both a torment and a relief to Raymond to hear that no Saracen had killed his father, no curved sword but rather a sneak-thief with poison. It seared his guts that his heroic father should have died in such a manner but it also gave him, Raymond V, a renewed sense of divine purpose. There were indeed evil forces abroad. And the main one, as he should have known all along, was the red-headed witch his mother had warned him against, that his father had defeated, who had finally taken down a great man in the only way she ever could have, by poisoning him. Raymond's eyes shone with missionary fervour. He had an enemy with a name. Of course she wouldn't have soiled her own lemon-softened hands with the dirty deed, but Raymond didn't have to search far to know the other name he needed. Who else would it be but Aquitaine's much-loved knight and troubadour, never a hair's breadth from Aliénor's side? Raymond would watch and bide his time but that time would come and he would have no mercy.

It took all Raymond's exceptional store of self-control to reveal none of this less than two years later when the haughty bitch and her greasy paramour flaunted themselves at his court. At fifteen, he understood his political needs too well to draw the wrath of France on Toulouse by overt aggression to its Queen. But he had set certain actions in motion. Raymond flicked the domino beside him and stood up to watch the fall of the hundred dominoes that he had carefully set up in loops on the floor round the chamber.

Ten seconds' rattle and it was over. Perfect. A servant could pick them up as soon as he vacated the room. He had kept the Archbishop waiting long enough for his audience, and he had come to a decision regarding the other matter. Friend of his father's or not, Raimon Trencavel the new Comte de Carcassonne needed a reminder not to get too big for his boots, and for that, the girl would do nicely, very nicely now she was back for a few days. Offering a bit of sport along the way, too, although he had tired of her long ago when she had been in Toulouse to learn courtly ways. Well, he'd certainly taught her that and better than she'd learn as a Lady with the Whore of Aquitaine, although she was useful to him there. She had fallen as easily as her father for his promises of marriage and she pleaded sweetly enough when he hurt her but it was all too easy. As if he couldn't do better than a used Trencavel to bear him a legitimate son.

Raymond adjusted his clothing, which was as sober and pious as the expression he shortly presented to the Archbishop of Toulouse, who wanted to discuss their next steps against the heretics of Toulouse. A burning question, as Raymond V, Comte de Toulouse, agreed, smiling.

Estela lay awake, dry-eyed and sleepless, having listened to a thousand footsteps pass her door, and, having invented a million more, finally accepted that she would spend her wedding night alone. She had no idea when Johans had slipped away from the wedding feast and she had assumed he was avoiding any possibility of ribald accompaniment to their bedding. A sign of delicacy and tact, she had thought, having often enough seen red-faced couples sent to the consummation of their marriage with a clatter of kettles, lewd songs and even help in undressing. She had assumed that he would join her later, slip through the door like a shadow and that, all cats being grey at night, they would take what pleasure they could from each other, unseen.

Instead, her white lawn and lace were even more wasted than her scarlet wedding finery. She might as well have kept Nici to lie by the door instead of confusing him with her insistence that he go play with his own kind. He had gambolled after her at the anti-climax when she left the Great Hall, the only living creature to notice her departure. His outrage when she told him no and shut the door on him was expressed in a series of insistent barks loud enough to reach Carcassonne and only after Estela had repeatedly slammed the door just short of his nose did he accept the exclusion and slink off, his tail hanging, his shoulders slumped. Much, thought Estela, as she felt herself. What was so terribly wrong with her, she wondered, and kept wondering, through a night long with clicking insects, creaking wood, shifting wheels, scampering of four legs and shuffling of two, all the small night noises that torment the sleepless.

Inevitably, morning thumped her from deep sleep into a splitting headache, and she took an infusion of feverfew, glad that she had accumulated her own collection of fresh herbs again, alongside the dried ones she had persuaded al-Hisba to give her, once she had convinced him that she knew what she was doing with them. More than one of the Ladies had found Estela's knowledge useful. This particular morning Estela had no patience for Ladies and it was just as well no-one approached her for a little something to settle stomach, head or heart; lovesickness was exceptionally high on the list of ailments Estela did not want to hear about. Grateful to be left alone, Estela sat in the window-seat, her head too fuzzy with fatigue and vestigial headache to do anything more demanding than sit. Even so, she became gradually aware why she was being left alone. Sidelong glances and fluttering hands made it clear that she was being served up as titbit of the day and just as Estela felt she was being pecked to death by a barnyard of clucking poultry, Aimée de Rouen, fluttered onto the window seat beside her.

'The day after is always a bit of an anti-climax,' she offered, her kind smile unerringly flaying Estela's raw spot. 'The day after the wedding,' she clarified before Estela could say 'The day after what!' and announce to the world what wasn't happening in her bedchamber. But it seemed the world knew anyway, as Aimée continued, 'And observing the Tobias nights just drags things out doesn't it, when one has a life to get on with after all, marriage notwithstanding.' Estela fixed on the reddened mouth delivering the message that everyone knew she would spend two nights alone, while her bridegroom demonstrated his Christian control and chastity, observing his procreative duty on the third night, as long as this was not on a date requiring self-denial. Everyone knew but her.

'Yes, one has a life to get on with, and we are not horses and mules,' she murmured, gazing demurely at the floor to hide the blaze of anger in her eyes. What a fool she had been! But at least she could hide the fact that she hadn't known. She drew her shaking hands back up into her dangling trumpet sleeves, clenching them into unseen fists, aware how much she had come to rely on the unspoken alliance with Sancha, now that the latter was absent.

There was no-one to rescue her from her own bitter understanding. Tobias Nights had not been customary at Montbrun but she knew that there were many whose Christianity followed stricter rules and that Ermengarda's choice of wedding date had carefully avoided giving offence to the Church. Or so Estela had thought. Perhaps the date was so carefully chosen to avoid giving offence to the devout Johans de Villeneuve, who was now patiently waiting for the fourth night to take his Virgin in the Peace of the Lord. Without mentioning the fact to the aforementioned, extremely angry Virgin.

For in the words of the Archangel Raphael to Tobias, 'The devil wields power over the couple that ignores God and surrenders to lust like horses and mules. Abstain thou therefore from touching her for three days while you pray together with her. When the third night has passed, then take the Virgin unto thee in the Peace of the Lord, more out of a desire for children than out of lust.' And so had Tobias survived his marriage as eighth husband to the lethal widow Sarah, whose previous seven spouses had not survived the devil that appeared in her on their wedding night. At least Tobias had the decency to spend some time with Sarah, even if it was in prayer! Estela's own particular demons were showing every sign of an ascendancy that was likely to increase over the next two days rather than alchemise into the Peace of the Lord. If he'd just wanted to appease an over-zealous churchman, Johans could have paid the necessary dues in place of his Tobais nights but no! Not only was she married to a stranger, Estela was married to a pious stranger.

'It must be difficult being a man,' she told Aimée, sweeter than lavender honey, and ladling it on thickly. 'Always business to attend to and trying to keep track of who's conquered where in case your Lord calls you to follow him somewhere outlandish and northern.' As Aimée de Rouen turned a deeper shade of pink than her carefully applied rouge had intended, Estela hastily tinkled. 'I don't mean Rouen of course, I was thinking of true barbarian north, England for instance. Is your husband called to duty again? He must be sorry that Guillaume ever conquered that land of mud and crawling beasts. I heard they don't even speak French, let alone Occitan or Latin!' Having delivered at least four insults that she knew of, in one sweet speech, Estela felt that honour was restored and her own colour returning to normal as she inclined her head graciously to receive the next blow. It was more rewarding than expected. Aimée couldn't resist trying to score points with information that would show Estela clearly which of them moved in high circles.

'Bertrand is in England with Henri d'Anjou but,' she confided, 'he has sent word to me that he will be home soon.' Which meant that the latest attempt on England by Henri had failed and the armies were returning to his native Normandy. Son of the Empress Matilda, once Queen of the English, Henri had taken on the mission left him by his mother. While the ex-Empress Matilda mouldered in a Normandy convent, and, according to unkind gossip, her husband Geoffrey Duke of Normandy ensured that apples grew and cows were milked, their son waved his fire brand towards the country his mother still called hers. Estela had passed her time with Sancha very constructively and intended to use her methods to effect. Estela herself could now even adopt the ways of the boudoir in Feminine Camouflage, if necessary. It had just become necessary.

'They say he's some man,' she oozed insinuation at Aimée, 'this Henri.'

The other woman's eyes lit up. 'He gives that impression but actually he's not tall – not short either – but he's built like a wrestler, and you should see his thigh muscles. It's clear he's gripped a horse or two in his time.' Estela gave the expected knowing look. 'Never sits still, always on the move. A red head with a temper to match. They say that once he dreamed himself into such a state that his man rescued him from the floor, fists cramming his sheets into his mouth and legs drumming fit to burst through the floorboards. When he came to himself, he said someone in his dream had vexed him.' In the pause, Estela thought of another red-head with a temper to match. Now that would be a marriage made in hell, she mused, as Aimée continued. 'But they also say that's not the only passion he brings to the bedchamber. Not the sort to wait Tobias nights, or so I've heard, More likely to change beds several times in a night and always to a warm one.'

'It will be so reassuring for you to have Bertrand back on his estate for a few years,' Estela fished carefully and was rewarded.

Aimée's delicate face crinkled. 'I'll be lucky if it's one year,' she said. 'And the next push will do it, according to Bertrand, so who knows what he'll do then.' Henri d'Anjou, future King of the English, mused Estela, while soothing, 'Surely you'll be allowed leave to spend some time in Normandy with Bertrand, perhaps when my Lady returns to Paris.'

'You're right,' Aimée's face brightened. 'She can't leave it much longer before going back.' So, Estela registered without changing her solicitous expression, the royal baby was out of the bag and the Ladies might as well start embroidering a layette now. So much the worse for Aliénor's safety – and freedom.

'I'm sure no-one will expect you to actually live among barbarians,' she comforted Aimée, giving her hand a little squeeze as she added, 'although of course you might find it easier to get used to than we southerners would.'

'Get used to the English?' Aimée's raised eyebrows and tone conveyed her awareness of both the depravity of that unfortunate race and also the depth of the implied slur on her northern heritage.

Estela laughed lightly and gracefully. 'Impossible,' she smiled agreement. 'No, no, I was but referring to the inclement climate. One would need cloaks weathered like boots to withstand the rain.' Now that, she thought, was fun. To find out, to fence, to score and withdraw without the opposition being sure that the hit had happened. As expected, Aimée seized on the topic of travelling clothes with a detailed enthusiasm that enabled Estela to drift in and out of her own thoughts, and pass another weary virginal hour. And then several more.

CHAPTER FIFTEEN

The seven men who kept their early morning appointment and entered the bedchamber of Raymond V, Comte de Toulouse, were hardened and worldly enough to look only at their liege lord, without one glance at the naked woman chained to the stone wall. Raimon Trencavel, newly ruler of Carcassonne, feared he had particular reason not to notice the high firm breasts with bite marks just starting to blue the skin, the slim arms starting to shake from sustaining the constraints of such a position, the trickles of blood from thin whip marks across belly and thighs. No-one needed to avoid meeting the woman's eyes as her head was entirely hidden by sacking, tied loosely round her neck, in the manner of a rustic execution. Combine a monk's attitude to carnal pleasure with a fifteen-year-old's restless penis, and sex with blood and sackcloth was what you would expect. To make political capital out of it as well was the extra gift that was entirely unique to Raymond.

His face smooth and pink as scalded pigskin, his close-set eyes narrowed along his aristocratic nose, Toulouse welcomed his eight neighbour lords, whom he had summoned for discussion of 'the new situation'. Raimon noted that apart from Sicard de Lautrec, long-time ally of Toulouse, there were six of his own fiefs represented, all of them equally loyal to him and his own liege Raymond, that is to say as loyal as they were made to be, a wolf-pack. Simo de Couysan, Savaric de Montréal, Crespi de Palaja, Tibau de Montbrun and Dorde de Rennes engaged briefly in gruff nods to acknowledge each other before all eyes found and stayed with one figure. The fifteen-year-old to whom they owed loyalty took the high seat, with the leather backing and gestured them to take the stools that would give Raimon, for one, a day of cramps from folding his long legs into some semblance of formality that didn't actually break both legs. He had underestimated Raymond. Or overestimated, depending on whether you considered a limitless capacity for torture in the name of God to be a virtue or a vice. Whichever the case, it was unquestionably a show of unexpected strength that bode ill for a ruler walking the knife edge between his new liege of Barcelone and this, his old ally. Raimon suspected that he himself was 'the new situation', following his brother Roger's death. He shifted his legs sideways to ease them as Raymond thanked them for coming at such short notice and hoped that they didn't mind the informality of their reception. No-one twitched a muscle, no-one heard the choked sob behind sackcloth.

'We commiserate with Trencavel on his loss, and we know he is fresh from mourning his brother, but as men of action we welcome his assumption of Carcassonne, Albi and Razès, to which we can now offer our wholehearted protection.' Raimon inclined his head in graceful acknowledgement of the honour, sharing only with the mute floor his understanding that, under his leadership, Carcassonne was expected to throw off its alliance with Narbonne and loyalty to Barcelone for the dubious rewards of Toulouse men-at-arms in case of need. There would of course be such a need from the moment the Comte de Barcelone heard that his vassal Trencavel had given Carcassonne to Toulouse. Raimon would need to dance lightly and quickly on his knife-edge just to get home alive, never mind to avoid falling onto the rocks of Barcelone or into the whirlpool of Toulouse.

'My Lord is gracious,' murmured Raimon, steeling his heart against the twitch of recognition that he did not feel, must not feel, towards the increasingly limp body suspended against the wall. Six voices expressed their sympathies along with their pleasure at adding

Carcassonne as an ally, at extending east towards Narbonne and Provence. Talk naturally led to the latest news of Provence, the increasing spats between les Baux and Barcelone and Raimon breathed more easily as the flow of attention moved on.

'Let Barcelone and les Baux wear each other out,' was Raymond's view. 'Then, when the time is ripe, I will claim Provence.'

The cool voice of Sicard cut in. 'And Toulouse itself? What if the bitch queen goads France into another attempt on the city?' No-one referred to Louis of France as 'the monk' when speaking to Raymond, whose 'informal' attire was a long white linen tunic, white hose and plain brown leather slippers. Only the sword belt and lack of tonsure marked the difference between him and King Louis' nickname. And, of course, the body on the wall, additionally striped now by morning rays braving the thick stone through the eyelet window.

Raymond's face weaselled thinner, his lips two scissor blades shearing the words he aimed at the gathered men. 'I am dealing with France. We will not see the whore of Aquitaine outside my walls again. Or even on my wall.' His gaze moved deliberately, unequivocally, to the figure on the wall, demanding in all politeness that seven pairs of eyes followed his. Raimon clasped his big hands on his lap, refused to see a trickle of urine down between two sweetly formed legs.

There was a shift in the atmosphere as Raymond's attention moved on once more, but this time it was not a further region of Occitania that aroused his appetite. His voice thickened. 'As you see, gentlemen, I have unfinished business, so we must leave it there.' Raymond walked towards the girl's body, close enough to prod her with the haft of his dagger. 'Say Good-day to the gentlemen.' Even now, he didn't speak her name but his eyes found Raimon's, who prayed to every God that might ever have existed that the girl would not hold back any longer because he was there, risking ever worse from the sick imagination behind a dagger that turned to prod again, this time making its point with a bead of blood. Raimon knew better than to show anything, his hands behind his back, shredded by his own nails.

He held the Comte's stare as a broken voice came muffled through the sackcloth, 'Good day, gentlemen.' It changed nothing that Raimon had not known from the moment he walked in and had willed his heart to stone. Disappointment flickered in the Comte's lizard eyes but he made the best of it. 'I think we understand each other.' His stare fixed Raimon a further count of ten, then glanced lightly at his other lords.

'We understand each other,' Raimon managed and kept enough control to leave not first, but third, from that chamber of horrors, passing a few words with his peers, while no-one referred to a young, beautiful body abused on a wall by their liege. Finally, mercifully alone, Raimon de Béziers, Carcassonne, Albi and Razès took an axe to a chicken coop, leaving a confused bailiff to investigate later that day as to what sort of fox not only left dismembered chickens strewn where they landed but also reduced their shed to matchsticks, apparently using a hand tool.

By then, Raimon and his entourage were on their way back to Carcassonne. The apprehension of the journey to Toulouse had vanished. The soldiers congratulated each other on Raimon's acumen to have bearded the devil in his lair and come to no harm. The worst that seemed to have happened was that Trencavel's daughter was off colour and required the palanquin for the journey. Her father had spoken to her briefly and then left her in peace while he himself rode deep in thought, not to be disturbed, as was natural for one with his responsibilities.

'Do whatever he told you to, Alis,' Raimon advised his daughter, installed in the litter. 'Then it will be over. Leave straight away, make any excuse but come back to Carcassonne as soon as you can. Then,' he hesitated, 'I'll arrange a place for you with the Carmelites.' Her golden hair spread on the cushion, her delicate oval of a face, the slim figure tucked under a counterpane, all was as it always had been. Except that she kept her eyes shut, her face buried in darkness and he could not bring himself to touch her.

Daddy's little angel. Thanks to Roger, the walls of Carcassonne were the thickest and most impregnable in Christendom and Raimon would think twice before leaving them again, even if both his twin Lords of Toulouse and Barcelone summoned him with the horns of hell. The nuns and their God would take care of his daughter. He could do nothing. Though he could not bear to look at her, he knew that he would see nothing else, not just for the ride between Toulouse and Carcassonne but for the rest of his life.

Estela turned over once more in her irritating bed, reckoning that she was two hours into the fourth night since her wedding. She might as well have taken the valerian tisane again tonight to help her sleep as it was obvious to her that Johans de Villeneuve was not coming, not now, not ever. And neither was sleep. Burning with the injustice of it, Estela lay in yet another position glaring open-eyed at the shadows on the black ceiling. She had done as bidden and what difference had it made? Neither one thing nor the other! Was this Ermengarda's precious gift to her?

The more she contemplated the bountiful smiles of Aliénor and Ermengarda explaining their plans for her, controlling her life, the more her stomach knotted with the need to act. Other women might accept being kept in the dark but she was Estela de Matin, she was going to be a troubairitz, she had earned the rune-jewel of a Norse Prince, the fealty of a true knight and the praise of the best troubadour in Occitania. Her thoughts shied away from too deep an analysis of her relationships with Arnaut or Dragonetz and rested firmly on the notion that she was owed an explanation. She wanted to know where she stood in this strange marriage and only one person could tell her. Now!

A cloak wrapped around her white nightwear, whose lace was less than fresh, Estela donned her leather indoor slippers and trod the silent corridors to Ermengarda's rooms. Torches flared and shadows made hunchbacks and giants whose arms stretched long and wavering to grasp at the girlish form that flickered along the walls, always out of reach, but Estela was in no mood to weave fancies around tricks of the dark. Gritting her teeth, she rehearsed her demands in her head as she marched, noiseless in the smooth leather, so lost in her thoughts that she almost missed the flash of coloured movement that indicated someone else moving about the Palace this night. Estela stopped abruptly and drew back into the shadows and registered that the tall figure was knocking softly on the very door she was herself heading towards. She didn't need the torchlight to fall on the face she knew so well, deep hollows and black eyes glittering as he kept his assignation. The door opened enough for him to enter and he disappeared from view.

Estela returned to her own chamber on leaden slippers, climbed once more into her solitary bed and faced the dark. Neither one thing nor the other, when everyone else in the world lay with whoever they chose. Beautiful wives had lovers. Even ugly women, even old women had lovers but she, Estela, was sixteen and doomed. No man would put up with this state of affairs so why should she? A man would choose his partner, woo her, win her and move on. Why shouldn't she do the same? Wiping her nose dry, Estela tried to think like a man. A suitable partner. Arnaut was the obvious choice, already promised to obey her lightest wish. She shut her eyes and conjured up his fine profile, his fair skin weathered in the sun, his build light but honed, eyes moody as sea and full of his feelings for her. She imagined putting her cold proposal to the man to whom she had promised friendship and nothing more. She saw those grey eyes chill at the insult, reflect her own fall from stars to gutter, knew she couldn't do it.

Or at least she couldn't do it to a man who was in love with her. Love called to love, was the stuff of romance and tragedy but there were other songs to be sung, where animal called to animal. Wasn't that also what men did? Wasn't that what servants were for? When Estela finally slept, she dreamed she was bound in rope and someone was cramming bitter aloes into her mouth. Whichever way she jerked her head, the merciless process continued. She couldn't beg for mercy because her mouth was full and she couldn't see who was doing this to her, who could hate her so much, but even through her fear she was determined that she would escape.

Ermengarda's hair fell in a shimmer of pale gold down below her shoulders but the rest of her appearance, in high necked gown, fully laced, would have been appropriate for receiving any of her counsellors and Dragonetz knew that she had already understood. When she sat and invited him to join her, it was impossible not to remember the first time, to wonder if he were being a fool, but he knew he could not act differently. He waited, allowing her to lead, to put the face on events that she wished them to wear.

'My friend, I believe the time for night rendezvous is over and this must be our last such.' Her steady grey eyes sought his and found the confirmation they were looking for.

'You are peerless, my Lady.' He offered her all he could. 'What we have shared was a song worth the singing and what we still share will last forever. What I have sworn to you is written on my soul.'

'What you have sworn to Narbonne,' she corrected coolly.

'And are you not Narbonne?' he was equally steady.

'I am Narbonne.' Her answer was expressionless. 'I have been Narbonne since I was four years old. And Narbonne will indeed hold you to your promises.' She reached out and he let her take his long hands in her own. 'But Ermengarda gives you freedom. What will you do with it?'

Dragonetz raised one white hand to his lips, inhaling almond oil and orange-water. 'Nothing, my Lady.' There was a silence. She withdrew her hands, rose and stood with her back to him, apparently contemplating two silver goblets and a jug of wine, untouched. He had stood up the minute she did, poised, waiting, ready to give everything he owed, to the last careful word.

'If the prophecy had not been made, would you have kept on coming to me?' Her voice was the same, even tone as usual.

'The prophecy was made,' he stated flatly.

'And you reacted. I reacted. She reacted.' Dragonetz said nothing. 'And now it is not enough with me, without love. Yet you won't go where love is. Why not?'

He would have answered no-one else such a question. 'War wounds,' he answered softly. She must know – who better? – that there was no physical damage between him and his desires.

'You are wrong,' she told him, clearly, unselfishly.

'Tort-n'avetz,' he told her, turning her own favourite expression back against her, the nickname he had coined in the new songs he was writing for her, the nickname that the Gyptian had seen accompanying her into the future, when she would be truly loved.

'I am not the one,' he said. 'And you are not for taking lightly. There will be someone worthy, my Lady.'

'Tort-n'avetz,' she responded as the door opened and closed quietly and a tear dropped onto the hand that steadied itself round a silver goblet.

Estela braided her hair into two long plaits, which she coiled on each side of her head and experimentally fastened under her matron's veil and peaked head-dress. They tumbled down, failing to maintain the fiction that she was a married woman and she brushed them out again angrily, making the hair spark and frizz. She had passed her three Tobias nights as a maiden and after the fourth night she should have announced to the world that she was now a married woman. Her mouth set in a grim line as she determined that she would soon rectify anything missing from what the word 'married' implied and before that, she would confront Ermengarda over what exactly Johans de Villeneuve was supposed to be to her. She had turned his words over and over in her head, that he had loved his dead wife and that he understood the situation. She was glad someone did!

With a pleasure that surprised her, Estela noted that Sancha was back from whatever family business had taken her to Provence. She had undoubtedly brought news from the east, the state of play between the Lords of les Baux and Raimon Berenguer of Barcelone and how it had been affected by the death of Roger Trencavel and succession of his brother. In her turn, Estela looked forward to sharing all that she had gleaned on the Angevin attempt on England and her frustration at the impasse on tracking down the spy in the camp. Unfortunately, the pleasures and distractions of intelligent conversation would have to wait as it was understood between Estela and Sancha that they guard a certain distance in public, the better to draw out contradictions in the Ladies' confidences. Sancha's elegant silk back, resolutely turned towards the younger woman, was a reminder of this and Estela resigned herself to another day of embroidery talk and fruitless fishing for news of any interest in a pool she had now emptied. A servant confirmed that Ermengarda would receive her before mid-day meal, a prospect which occupied so much of her mind that she missed the warning signals when Philippa de Lyon joined her.

Early in her investigations, Estela had judged Philippa to be harmless. A dumpy, unmarried girl with a face reminiscent of the Lyon delicacies, tripe and sausage, that she spoke about with more passion than she managed for her husband-to-be, a wealthy merchant in the textile trade. Only hint at the Lyon motto, 'Avant, avant, Lion le Melhor' and Philippa would talk for hours on exactly *why* Lyon was the best but anything off her limited range of subjects left her floundering. She was not, however, unaware of more personal gossip and Estela had yet to learn that 'harmless' with regard to organising an assassination did not necessarily imply 'harmless' in more everyday interaction.

'Not yet adopting your married status,' was the opening comment, aimed at Estela's appearance and spoken apparently without guile. Estela responded to Philippa' smile abstractedly but with no reserve. 'Some of the Ladies have been taking bets as to when you would pin up your hair, or even whether you ever would.' Estela's smile faded and she clasped her hands together in her lap, waiting. 'Aimée said that you'd keep your hair down after you'd had the message.'

Even when the baiting was obvious, the options were few, if she wanted to find out what was behind all this. And Estela very much wanted to find out. 'The message?' she queried, smoothly.

Malicious eyes glinted like shiny favours in a galette des rois. 'The message from Johans de Villeneuve.'

Estela's pride would allow no other response. 'Oh, of course,' she said. 'That message.'

'I did wonder if she should have told us. I said, Aimée, I said, do you think you ought to be telling us a private message for Estela but I remember exactly what she said. Aimée said, 'Estela won't mind one bit. We are all friends here aren't we.' And that's true and of course she's right and you don't mind a bit, do you?'

Estela imagined drawing the knife out from her skirts and carving chunks out of the flesh quivering in front of her before she found something more painful to do to Aimée. She had forgotten what girls could be like, she who'd climbed trees and crossed wooden swords with the boys who peopled the courtyards and outbuildings. She'd been motherless and free, choosing fisticuffs over barbed words. Her fists curled tight as she controlled herself. One dagger might have stayed in her under-shift but she couldn't keep the others out of her eyes. 'I don't mind one bit.' She tried to keep her teeth from gritting, her voice from rasping and, truthfully, added 'that Aimée told you.' No, what she minded to the bone was that no-one had told her!

'Well, that's what I said, and of course the message was so plain. It wasn't as if he'd said lovebird rhymes like Aimée gets.'

'From her husband, I assume,' Estela saw that she'd scored with that reply as they both knew the source of Aimée's romantic little morsels, delivered by page-boy every time a certain local burgher came to market.

Philippa was shocked. 'You wouldn't expect that from a husband, not messages like Aimée gets.' Why? wondered Estela. Because she was unlovable? Because her husband was not such a man? How odd that word 'husband' continued to sound. Had she dreamed this strange wedding? The prattle continued. 'And just saying what he meant, no more than that, just telling you that he'd left for Villeneuve as planned and should you ever have business matters to contact him via his man Conti da Manho the woodseller. Of course he said sorry for slipping off at the banquet, but he hadn't wanted to draw attention to the two of you so as Aimée was such a good friend of yours, he thought you'd forgive him passing the message on that way. Nice message, wasn't it. But me, I'd have worn my hair up straight away and I lost three hair-slides to Aimée. She guessed you wouldn't!' Philippa shook her head at the amazing perspicacity of Aimée, as did Estela.

'That was just so sweet of Aimée to tell Johans,' the name stuck to her tongue, 'that we are friends. I really do owe her something.'

'Oh,' a tinkling laugh, 'don't you worry about that. I think Aimée has won enough finery to repay her fully for carrying the message.'

'No.' This time Estela knew her teeth were gritted. 'I insist, I must personally repay Aimée for her role in this message. I will need to think about it.'

Philippa was conciliating. 'If you want. The bet's over now so you might as well keep your hair down.' With that, Estela was left in what passed on the exterior for peace, as she shut out the knots of women laughing and glancing in her direction, even Sancha. If there was sympathy in Sancha's eyes, Estela was too angry too appreciate it. She jabbed a needle into what could have been a handkerchief and would certainly become a duster and at each stab she aimed at Aimée's eyes and tongue until finally it was time to place her unrecognizable attempts at entwined royal initials in the campherwood chest with the rest of the linens. She nodded a curt quittance to the Ladies, wishing them all in hell, and went to her interview with Ermengarda. This was hardly likely to improve her day.

The Viscomtesse was motionless at the window when Estela entered the ante-chamber and at first she wondered if she had misheard the command to enter, so still was the figure, stiff in blue damask with white trimmings. Like the Virgin Mary, thought Estela bitterly, then was ashamed of the thought when Ermengarda turned round. She was paler than usual, ethereal, her words weighted with the responsibility for Narbonne.

'I am sorry. I have had little time to speak to you, Estela. I think you understand the difficulties of the time. At least,' she gave one of her rare smiles, a hint of the girl she might have been if she had grown up playing in the meadows or the river shallows instead of listening to disputes over land contracts. 'At least, my Lord Drag-onetz tells me that you have a grasp of the times that will serve us both well.'

Estela had been schooled in a harder setting than ever her music mentor could have devised and she could control any sign of her reaction to his name, which came so easily to the lips that had just as easily come to his. She could not control the rage heating to white inside her from every injustice that the day could bring.

'My Lady,' she began. She could only speak straight and true then judge the response. To this fragile ruler she had offered allegiance, or rather had it offered for her. Was Ermengarda worth the candle? 'You have honoured me in bestowing my hand, in accepting me to your entourage but you will forgive me if I am bemused at finding my life unchanged – or maybe worse, as I no longer develop my skills as a musician and am uncertain as to what I owe to the man who stood beside me at the church gate four days ago.'

Grey eyes levelled with stormy topaz, read what they could. 'Let me answer the last question first. Nothing. You owe Johans de Villeneuve nothing and he expects nothing. I have granted you the privilege of a marriage as civilised as the one which my friends found for me. The freedom of a married woman.' Estela lowered her eyes to hide her knowledge of how Ermengarda took her freedom. 'Respectable status, financial independence and most of all an end to the tedium of the bidding circus, men performing like little dogs to win you as the puppet-prize, all of them hoping to jerk your strings while they rule. I realise that you do not have Narbonne to offer the highest bidder but believe me, what you have was enough to attract the dogs.' Estela had a bizarre image of Nici dancing like a bear to compete for her affections. It was silly enough to lift for a second the clouds threatening her. 'Johans de Villeneuve is a citizen I respect. He will never make any demands on you, he will never cheat you, he will never try to profit from the turn of the wheel that will take you far far above him. He loved his wife and seeks no other. He has the heirs he needs. And his existence will always protect you from the dogs. But I thought you knew all of this.' Ermengarda's forehead lined at the need to explain what had been clear in the first place.

Estela flushed, feeling naive. 'I guessed, my Lady, but it helps me to hear it said. It is not how things worked in Montbrun.'

'I can imagine. But I would rather you learned court manners and left Montbrun behind you.' However gracious, it was still a warning. Estela inclined her head. She had already said goodbye to Montbrun with all her heart. Now she was saying goodbye to the marriage she had imagined for four days. What a fool she had been and how everyone must be laughing at the rustic from the gutter.

'But in answer to your first question, I find I am at fault. I can only plead the boring, essential concerns of Narbonne that have come between me and my duties as host and patron of the arts. You have a rare talent and I have no intention of hiding it under a bushel. I would very much like you to play for me on the night of the summer solstice. It is time we celebrated love, for its own sake, for the sake of all those in love, for the summer.' Why should Ermengarda look so wistful, she who had everything? 'Yes, we shall make music for Aliénor to carry back to France in her heart, to warm her during the cold Paris nights. You and Dragonetz shall entertain me with all the new songs he promises me he has written and we will throw off our cares for one night.'

Estela was not rustic enough to consider this a request and she curtsied her obeisance, risking only, 'Is the Queen returning soon to France?'

'I think she must.' Before the pregnancy was too far advanced. And back to Paris with Aliénor would go her Commander, her Troubadour. No wonder Ermengarda was wistful and wanted a night of love songs before their parting. Estela left the ante-chamber with the fury inside her growling its need for action and she knew of only one place she could go, one place she had always gone when she had been hit, when she had been cursed, when her father had married again. She was going to the stables.

Brushing heedless past the anonymous palace servants in Narbonne livery, clerks in the same black and white as their accounts, occasional court finery of feathers, silks and lace, Estela saw nothing that she passed. Not the people, not the grand entrance with the steps on which the Viscomtesse had greeted the Queen just weeks earlier. Not the switch from palace people to trade bustle, working leather aprons and hessian jerkins, hand-carts and laden donkeys. She didn't even notice the blast of heat as she marched from the cool of the old stone, protecting the Palace interior with walls as thick as a man's girth, into the mid-day sun, merciless on the open courtyard.

Storming across the cobbles, her summer boots tapping an angry rhythm, Estela snatched at thoughts that buzzed and bit like gnats, 'Unfair!' the recurring refrain. The smell of the first stable-block reached her before she unlatched the half-door and entered the world of soft snorts and sweet straw, wax and warm leather, but it was not enough to calm her. She blinked in the sudden darkness, then, as her eyes adjusted, saw the horses in their byres, shifting restlessly, flicking at flies with tails and manes. There seemed to be no-one in the stables but her and she was gripped with a sense of anticlimax that only fuelled her bitterness. Unfair!

Then she heard regular, working sounds in the last byre, behind the partition, sounds that could only be human. Picking her way over the drifts of straw, mouth in a determined line, Estela headed towards the noise. It was always possible that it was someone else, in which case she would bid him good-day, ask after Tou and return to lunch, where anyone civilised would already be taking a seat. She was so certain that it was going to be someone else – Unfair! – that it was a shock to see the familiar chopped brown hair and bare back bending and straightening, pitching clean straw into place. Estela watched for a minute, deliberately, allowing herself the visual pleasure of muscles that gleamed even in the shadows, bronzed skin. Her eyes traced the hollow of his spine down to the twin shadows that curved into his hose and then, with a deep breath, she walked forward and placed her hand flat on the smooth tanned skin of his back, saying, 'Peire de Quadra.'

The boy straightened slowly, as if frozen by her touch and her voice, unable to pretend that neither existed. It was probably only a few seconds that they stood in this fashion but to Estela it seemed a glorious, rebellious eternity, her palm absorbing the heat from a man's skin, her senses filled with sweet animal scents. She said his name again as she dropped her hand to her side and he turned round to face her, the pitchfork like a weapon between them.

For a moment, Estela felt awkward. What would a man do? 'Put that out of the way,' she told the boy and he obeyed, his blue eyes round and wary, never leaving her face. Following the instructions of a thousand songs, she reached up to meet his lips with her own and she found a softness and willingness that lit the tinder-box of her emotions into mindless fire. She placed her hand on the light brush of hair low on his naked stomach and she moved her hand down, onto his skimpy hose, to the place she hoped would make her purpose clear. He gasped and she felt his response, a leap against her hand, like a fish in a stream.

'Do you know how to do this?' she breathed. He nodded. 'Then do it,' she ordered, running her hand once more down this male body that was hers to command. She surrendered to the sweetness of his arms around her, crushing her against him and then he turned her, pushed her prone onto the straw and the sweetness stopped. Straw in her nose made her sneeze but it hurt her neck to lift her head so she lay, her face sideways in the prickly bedding, trying to speak but too choked. What would she have said? Please stop? This isn't what I wanted? Too late to snatch the dagger from her skirts and defend her honour. Too late.

She felt her skirt thrown up, her underthings parted so the fabric rubbed one side of her sore as the battering commenced, a blind search to force a way into her. Weighed down, trying to breathe, concentrating on a tube of straw that had bent at an angle of exactly forty-five degrees, that reminded her of the discussions at the water-mill, she was shocked beyond thought by a sharp pain, by her brain screaming 'No, no, no – take it out!' though her mouth remained obstinately silent and instead of relief, there was duller, accelerating pain that culminated in the feeling that she would explode into particles, a crossbow bolt hooked through her vitals.

She gathered from Piere's groans and the change in his breathing that it was over and she clutched at this thought when, after one last intense pain, the weight lifted from her back and she felt the boy move away, stand up, lean panting against the stable wall. She had a sudden image of herself lying on the straw with her skirts and undershift around her neck, her dagger exposed and disabled, the miserable proof of her womanhood soiling her underclothes and skin. She had never felt so lonely, so motherless. Be careful what you wish for, she mouthed her mother's words, and straightened her clothes, stood and looked at a sweaty stranger, whose eyes flicked around the byre, resting anywhere but on her.

Estela held her head straight and high. She would play this scene to the end. She took an emerald pin from the front of her gown, all part of her marriage coffer. She blew the chaff off it and polished it absent-mindedly against her skirt before fixing the boy with a clear, unashamed gaze. He could not meet her eyes and stayed as far away from her as the byre would allow. When she approached to give him the jewel, he shrank back and she was suddenly aware of what he risked.

'Don't be afraid,' she told him. 'You have only obeyed orders. I will not demand such a service again.' Her lips curled and her hand shook, despite herself. 'This is in acknowledgement.' She had nearly said 'payment' but knew that he would have accepted the word with the same reaction he gave now – gratitude – and that, she could not have stomached. 'I believe it is time for mid-day meal. You must be hungry,' she said, stupidly and with an attempt at hauteur left the place, pausing to blink in the sunlight and hold back the tears as she faced the last person in the world that she wanted to see.

His eyes searching her face, dark and cold with slow-fuse anger, Dragonetz had his hand on his sword-hilt. He said, 'I shall kill him.'

'No!' she said sharply and he just stood, looking at her, reading her. She watched the planes of his cheekbones, sharply defined in the harsh sun, the sardonic mouth that turned a lopsided witticism as easily as a scathing put-down, or even a compliment, and she felt that for the first time in her life, she was going to faint. His expression shifted once more and he took her arm, supporting her.

'My Lady Estela,' said Dragonetz. 'Allow me to accompany you back to your room. If I may.' Hiding her from public view with his own tall body, he dropped her arm and blocked her way long enough to pick some straw out of her not-so-neatly coiled hair and to tuck some wild strands back into place. If a mine direct to the pits of hell had opened in the courtyard, Estela would have dived into it rather than face the solicitous attention she was getting. 'It seems,' he said gently, 'that my role in your life consists of lady's maid. Sancha tells me you have interesting gossip of Henri d'Anjou.'

She allowed politics to carry her back into the Palace, protected from curious eyes by their known relationship, by the status of Dragonetz himself, a man beyond question, but the whole time she was conscious of the sticky wrongness of her blood and the boy's stuff fouling her body. She would never be the same again. She wished he were dead.

They were now alone in the passageways leading to Estela's chamber and as if he read her mind, Dragonetz demanded, 'Why, Estela? Why rutting with a stable-hand, for God's sake?! It shouldn't have been like that!'

'And how should it have been? With silver goblets, golden hair and the magnificent arms of Narbonne all round you I suppose!' she fired back without stopping to think. 'What would you know! At least you'll find my singing has more maturity now! Oh, go to hell!'

They had reached her chamber and she'd already shrugged off his arm but she wasn't going to run away. She'd faced enough demons today not to crumple in front of some fancy-singing sword-swinger. Her chin jutted, she glared at him and his black eyes, fathomless as the pool below the waterfall at

Montbrun, reflected her own image in duplicate.

'Only you,' he murmured inexplicably, his apparent exasperation barely covering something else. He knelt in front of her, took her hand and kissed it, formally. 'To hell I duly go,' he assured her and 'I should have killed him,' he muttered to the wall as he left.

Wishing that she had a private bath-tub, Estela forced herself to make the journey to the bathroom, where she scrubbed her skin raw and red. Then she donned fresh clothing and sent every expensive stitch she had worn that morning to be burned. She told herself it was over. She had never felt more lonely in her life and, somehow, not being a virgin made only the wrong sort of difference.

CHAPTER SIXTEEN

In the time it took a small Jewish boy to deliver a breathless message to the Captain of the City Guard, remembering carefully that his mother's life depended on him not saying that the sender was Dragonetz los Pros, Dragonetz himself was already heading for the Jewish Quarter wearing mail hauberk and sword, no time for more. He had already wasted valuable minutes in dispatching trusted messengers to Danton, the knight likely to be closest and with the best chance of organising men quickly, and to Raoulf and Arnaut.

More precious time had of course been wasted in threatening the mother of his less-trusted messenger, to encourage his loyalty. Dragonetz reflected grimly on the message from Raavad, panted out in private by the barefoot lad whose mother's life might very well depend on what Dragonetz could do next, for all he knew. The problem, from Dragonetz' viewpoint, was that he had absolutely no idea what he could do to prevent a small-scale battle of Christians versus Jews turning into full-scale carnage. He very much doubted that it was small-scale enough for him to kill them all and cry 'Assassins'. Not this time. Raavad's message had inevitably been terse and the only information he had to go on was 'Three Jews. Ten Christians. Murder. My street. Now. Come, please. In force.'

As Dragonetz heard the familiar sounds of a riot, steel and shouting, screams and bangs, multiple voices, men, women, children, he heard his knight's oath mocking his brain with its impossible requirements to protect and defend the innocent. A suicide oath.

'I have come in force,' he muttered, drawing his sword as he turned the last wind of a narrow street. He hoped to the God of all oaths that his little message-boy had succeeded and his half a chance of fire-fighting would come off, then he charged in to fan the flames, running through from behind an anonymous body that crumpled on the cobbles, still gripping the stone with which its hand was smashing the face of another male frame. The man opened his mouth to thank Dragonetz but the words turned to spluttered blood as the knight's sword found another target, true in aim and dirty as war. He might not kill them all but he was going to have a good try.

Whirling his sword, hurling abuse in five languages, regretting his helmet and shield, Dragonetz found a space clearing around him, which gave him enough time to take in the scene. The women, thank God, were not on the street but hanging out of windows, hurling frying-pans and chamber-pots, with no regard to whether the latter were full or empty. In fact, it seemed to give more satisfaction to these wives and mothers turned harpies, if contents hit a target rather than the chamber-pot itself. Men were grappling with fists and whatever heavy objects they had grabbed as a weapon.

Hammers, shears, dividers, nippers, chisels, trowels, tongs, baskets and of course knives were all clashing, metal ringing, wood cracking and stone thudding in the wild echoes of the narrow street. There were a few swords, Christians' certainly, but otherwise the mass of incensed humanity was indistinguishable, enraged workers lost to reason.

Dragonetz' pause was over; a gang of a dozen, including the swordsmen, were circling him edgily, a couple feinting distraction and yelling names, while five were trying to sneak behind him. He backed hastily against a house wall, praying that neither door nor window would allow a sneak stab from within the house and that the leaning wall jutted out enough to protect him from the pleasures of a chamberpot on the head.

There was a short discussion between his would-be aggressors and Dragonetz noted the fact that they seemed to be organised, clearly knew each other, and had some control over their actions, even in the midst of this riot. He wondered if they were Raavad's 'ten Christians' and then there was no time for wondering. It didn't take a genius to realise that twelve against one was good odds if they rushed him.

It took all Dragonetz' experience to resist the first onslaught but he had been well taught, and tried against sword and scimitar from Occitania to Damascus. His true talent was unpredictability. The swordsmen against him were plodding, unable to do more than jab at him for fear of hitting each other if they approached together and quickly aware that to approach singly was suicide.

The brute workers with them were more of a threat, particularly as a swordsman continued to lunge hopefully, harassing Dragonetz enough to make it difficult to parry and duck as stones were flung or a hammer swung on the off-chance, connecting by bad luck with Dragonetz' left leg as he changed stance. Seeing him wince boosted the gang's morale and efforts doubled. Another hit, this time a flung stone catching Dragonetz' forehead, trailing blood into his mouth, a trickle of iron. Confidence high, the man Dragonetz had identified as their leader yelled at him from well behind four of his thugs.

Tufts of ginger poked out round his mail coif, and red moustache bristled round his blackening teeth as he spoke. 'Well met, my Lord. We were hoping you would come. And of course, go.' He shouted, 'Now!' and his men rushed Dragonetz in full force, intending to use their own bodies as weapons, knowing that one man's corpse full on the sword would disable the swordsman completely. When he felt the door give behind his back at the same moment the assailants rushed him, Dragonetz fully expected to be impaled in both directions, *like an abused catamite* he thought as he collapsed backwards across the threshold and the door was closed and bolted against a thud of men and weapons.

From his position on the floor, definitely without a knife in his back, Dragonetz looked up at the distinctive cap and locks of Makhir ben Habibi, the Kabbalah expert who had been with the fortune-teller.

'The door will not hold long,' the Jew told him. 'Follow me.' If the men on the street had looked up, they would have seen a man reaching out of an attic window, where the houses leaned so close to each other they seemed to be having a neighbourly chat. They would have seen another man in the window opposite and a game of knotted sheets and flying men that resulted in the complete disappearance of the knight they were chasing.

When they finally hacked their way through an oak door twelve inches thick, there was no sign of either Dragonetz los Pros nor of anyone else. They rushed out a back door into a tiny courtyard and over the wall into another back street. By the time they were resigned to the fact they'd lost him, Dragonetz was standing once more exactly where they had attacked him, but this time he could see Raoulf, Arnaut and fifty armour-clad men-at-arms wearing the red livery of Aliénor.

He could also see approximately the same number of armour-clad City Guard wearing the silver on blue of Ermengarda. And the two forces were fighting each other, accidentally dispatching any civilian who came between them. Exactly as Dragonetz had ordered. Not that the Commander of the City Guard realised this and it was presumably that same Commander, plumed and looking for trouble, who was heading straight towards Dragonetz with all the deliberation of thirty pounds of armour, reduced to the basics. The silver beast of Gévaudan stretched its rampant claws towards Dragonetz on a sea of blue silk, rippling across the armour beneath but there was no hiding the steel point heading his way, nor the expression in a face beetroot with rage.

Fortunately the Commander's sword skills were mediocre and reduced by his temper so Dragonetz was able to parry the wild thrusts, despite his fatigue. The words hurled at him were equally wild and insulted his mother in particular and his origins in general, with the fervent wish that he would return to them forthwith, preferably dead. Manoeuvring always backwards until he was at the end of the street, all the fighting ahead of him or in neighbouring alleyways, Dragonetz patiently blocked and dodged, saving his breath until the verbal and physical attack both slowed. Then he took advantage of the pause to give a high whistle, distinctively modulated. If Sicres de Narbonne had looked behind him, he would have seen red figures melting away like mice when the kitchen door opens but he didn't take his eyes off Dragonetz.

'The fight is over. Put up your sword,' Dragonetz suggested, skipping sideways as the response aimed for his left side. Then the other man stood, panting, sweat rolling down his cheeks in grimy crimson channels.

'By God, you have a nerve! And don't think my Lady's favour will get you out of this one!' The sword rose again but half-heartedly as Sicres' temper cooled and he registered his opponent's stone-walling. The blade dropped again,

'My men have gone. I can hardly fight off a hundred men-at arms.' Dragonetz dropped his own guard and sheathed his sword.

'And take me from behind as soon as my back's turned! I don't think so.' Sicres glared at Dragonetz, ignoring the classic feint of his hostage's gaze going beyond his left shoulder to something approaching his rear. Except that it wasn't a feint.

'The cowardly bastards have run for it, Sire,' announced one of the City Guard. His Commander jumped but kept Dragonetz in his sights as he spoke.

'Have we lost anyone?'

'Two. Tibaut and Simo.'

'And them?'

'One.' Dragonetz felt his chest contract. Three men too many. Who? Who had died a soldier's death for the good of Narbonne? He moved the thought to somewhere it could not affect his judgement, to be revisited later.

Sicres' eyes narrowed to pin-pricks of hate. 'Citizens of Narbonne?' he hurled the question over his shoulder to his man.

'We've seen seven bodies, so far. One wearing armour.' His voice conveyed puzzlement. 'The others I'd guess were three Jews, three Christians, judging by their clothes.' Correction, thought Dragonetz, nine men too many and one of the band of thugs who'd set on him, the ones he was convinced were mercenaries, paid to strike the tinderbox to civil war and to kill him in the midst of it.

'I'm sorry, Sicres.' He met the other man's eyes squarely. 'I was under orders. The Queen felt that her army was losing shape in the stews and taverns of Narbonne and that we needed testing. She insisted that we sharpen our edge against Narbonne's finest.' He shrugged his shoulders. 'It seems she was right and that your men had the better of mine. No-one was supposed to die but it happens, even in the practice-fields.' Another shoulder shrug, one leader to another, one who obeyed crazy orders from some mad woman to another such. Dragonetz *was* sorry but he could not gift Sicres with the truth of what they'd achieved without throwing away the achievement.

'It does seem that your men are rusty, my Lord Dragonetz.' No-one mentioned a death score of two to one. 'And what are you going to do about it? Organize another pitched battle between my men and yours in the streets of Narbonne? In *my* city streets.'

'That won't be necessary. With my Lady's permission, we quit the city for a week's training in the wild. My men will wish yours had them instead of me by the end of it.'

'Your Lady's permission?' Sicres queried, a mocking note in his voice.

Dragonetz could imagine well enough the rumours round the city. 'My Lady Aliénor,' he clarified, 'who will have only a handful of my men left for her protection, and who needs to rely on your skills, which you have proved today. And also as you so rightly imply, your Lady, who must forgive our rude soldiers' behaviour and excuse our absence.'

'I am sure, Lord Dragonetz los Pros, that your absence will be felt... deeply by my Lady Ermengarda.' There was a stifled chuckle from behind Sicres but nothing in Dragonetz' expression showed that he had scored a point, however cheap. Another thought to be filed somewhere, for later consideration, not to interfere with a satisfactory conclusion to a messy business. Dragonetz prayed to God that messages had reached their various recipients and that they were the messages he had intended.

'Gentlemen,' Dragonetz bowed and turned his back on the street and its figures of blue and silver, joined now by the householders recovering whole chamberpots and saucepans, cleaning up the smashed debris, attending to small wounds. Then the keening started that meant they had discovered their dead.

Dragonetz strode grim and alone back to the courtyard outside the Palace, where a hundred and ninety-two tired men in red waited in formation on their horses, one empty saddle at their head. He swung onto the horse that Arnaut held for him, grunted approval and chided his disobedient heart for its relief that Arnaut, Raoulf and Danton were all there. Some mother, wife, children, whoever it might be, would be grieving tonight, wondering how a soldier could die at the hand of his fellows in a backstreet of Narbonne, after surviving the scimitars and bladed wheels in barbarian Oltra mar. He had no right to feel relieved to see his lieutenants in place but he had no right to grieve either, for anyone.

He sent a message to Aliénor with one of the men detailed to remain as her bodyguard. It was too risky to send to Emengarda in case Sicres intercepted any such contact but he could rely on her intelligence to put two and two together from Raavad's message and her Commander's report. He smiled at the thought of that report. Then he gave another whistle, one of the commands perfected in the midst of sand flying like smoke when Saracen hordes appeared from nowhere, their eyes barely showing through the swathes of material wrapped round their heads and covering their faces. Impeccably controlled, his men kicked their horses into a walk, leaving the city in what could have been mistaken for a triumphant procession rather than a shameful retreat, if you didn't know any better.

A breeze flicked Dragonetz' cheeks. 'Fresh air,' he thought and that unbiddable heart soared at the thought of night camps and exercises. He'd told Sicres one truth; he was going to give his men hell. And they were all desperate for it like menagerie animals turned out in the forest. The sort of hell that turned muscles to rock, bread to a banquet and sleep-deprived bodies to simple satisfactions.

Hours later, the cookfires doused, the cicadas trilling their subdued night song, the stars promising another dry cloudless day to follow, Dragonetz eased his legs and stretched out on the grass for time with his aides before Arnaut took first watch. They had waited, patient and trusting, for the full story, and they had earned it. But first things first.

'How did two Guards get killed?' he asked softly.

Raoulf spat out a grass blade he'd been chewing to a froth. 'Don't blame the men. Some animals in anonymous armour were sneaking a sword thrust here, a dagger blade there.'

'It was one of them caught Bausas across the back of his head and with no helmet on, he had no chance,' Danton chipped in. Dragonetz grunted. He had of course ascertained earlier in the day which of his men had died and made it clear that the honour and recompense to his family in Aquitaine would be no less than if he had died fighting the Infidel, which, in a sense he had. It always depended on how you defined 'Infidel' but that was not an insight that Dragonetz shared with his officers, never mind with a troop of farm hands turned soldiers. 'We dealt with him but his mates managed their little tricks under cover of our grand show and dispatched two Guards before they ran off.'

'Dealt with him,' Dragonetz repeated and his tone warned them.

It was Raoulf who drew the fire. 'Be reasonable, man! You were there! He watched Bausas dropping to his knees and he dealt with the murdering scum before another of ours was lost. I know you'd have liked it well if we'd brought you the piece of shit to answer a question or two but there are limits to a man's self-control!'

'No,' said Dragonetz, 'there are no limits to a man's self-control only to his belief in it. The 'he' being?' Mutinous silence from all three men was the sole response. Dragonetz sighed.

'The hell with it.' Once more it was Raoulf who braved his

leader's icy scorn. 'It was me.'

Dragonetz lay back on the grass, his hands behind his head and closed his eyes, for which his men were only briefly grateful. 'Of course,' he said. 'And when I point out that you weren't even in the same street, it will turn out – amazingly – that it was Arnaut or Danton.' His switch to sitting position had the grace of perfectly toned muscles in a young body and his eyes snapped open to accuse them all. 'Gentlemen, we have wasted enough time. You have enjoyed your demonstration of esprit de corps, let us skip the denials and torture, assume just for one instant that I am a competent Commander and in fact *your* Commander. You will share with me all the information you possess and I will tell you what really happened today. Now get on with it. Raoulf?'

Reluctantly Raoulf gave the name, 'You know I'm all for disciplining the men but this wasn't pitched battle for God's sake and the lad reacted in good faith to the situation. If he suffers for it, Dragonetz, I swear...' then he trailed off under a contemptuous gaze.

'I'm sure you do,' was the cold reply, 'but I have no intention of sharing my plans for him with you. A little reminder, Raoulf.' Then his tone switched. 'I apologise that the message was so curt but every second counted and you were magnificent today. Truly. No other unit could have responded as you did.'

'But you want us to be better.' Raoulf's tone was flat, still stinging from the previous exchange.

'I want us to be better,' Dragonetz agreed and his inclusion of himself in that went a long way to soothe ruffled pride. They all knew him as a perfectionist. 'And when you don't have the whole picture, you don't know what damage can be done by one man lacking self-control. I ordered that no Guard be killed. I know it was difficult. Two guards *were* killed, their deaths put down to us. There's bound to be a reckoning for that.'

'And you're angry with Bausas' friend for killing his murderer? He probably saved the life of another Guard! Or one of ours!' Raoulf was completely lost at the reasoning.

'I know,' said Dragonetz. 'As it turned out, I wish I'd ordered you to capture or kill a bunch of thugs in armour and let none escape. But I didn't know that at the time and those weren't my orders.'

Raoulf was thinking. 'So you'll go easy on him because he reacted to what was actually happening and dealt with it as seemed best.'

'Yes, you bloody old fool, I'll go easy on him! But only because I can make better use of him that way. You *know* we can't afford to care about one casualty. Men have to be expendable and their friends have to obey orders. Now do you want to know what happened or not?'

'I got your message while supervising kit inspections and routine exercises,' Danton chipped in. 'The boy said to get the horses prepared for leaving the city as soon as possible and to take all the men on foot to the Jewish Quarter, provoke and attack the City Guard but kill no-one. So I gave orders at the stables, rallied the men and you know the rest.'

'Much the same message reached me,' agreed Raoulf.

'And me. Why was the Guard there? And why did we have to fight them?'

Dragonetz measured his words. 'Officially, and no man here but ourselves must think any different, officially we were ordered by Aliénor to test our men against Ermengarda's élite to sharpen them up.'

'And unofficially?'

'I had a message from Raavad. A brawl between Jews and Christians started presumably by some trivial dispute. Likely to erupt into civil war. He sent to Ermengarda too.'

'So you sent for the Guard.' The beauty of it dawned on Arnaut first. 'Not to keep the peace but to cover the civil brawl with our pitched and very loud battle.'

'Some anonymous citizen informed the Guard that there was a disturbance in the Jewish Quarter.' Dragonetz couldn't keep a straight face any longer. 'And then they *were* the disturbance. How,' he enquired with interest, 'did you provoke them to fight?'

'Traditional methods.' Danton grinned.

'Called their mothers and sisters whores, then prodded them a bit. Always works.' Raoulf grinned.

'Not always.' Dragonetz reflected on the prodding he himself had received. 'But often,' he conceded.

'And you'd have to be damned unlucky to get your sword through chain mail when you're trying to avoid killing, so that should have been easy.' Raoulf made a bitter concession to Dragonetz' earlier anger. 'A bit of sport all round and no harm done.'

'That's how it would have been,' Dragonetz agreed. 'A few citizens accidentally and tragically killed in a military exercise, no racial hatred, no blaming the Jews. Except that the initial dispute wasn't accidental. There was a band of mercenaries out to start civil war in Narbonne, who thought that killing a soldier or two was all to the good.' He kept to himself the more targeted attempt on his own life. 'So the question is, who stands to gain from the destruction of Narbonne? From bringing down Ermengarda?'

'Toulouse. Or the Les Baux, splitting the alliance against their attempt on Provence.

'Indeed,' said Dragonetz. 'Same old favourites. I suggest we get some sleep. Surprise attack at dawn will be sounded and we'll see how the men react. By the way, the retreat was excellent.'

'Pleased Sicres, I don't doubt!'

'Pleased me too, which is more to the point. Perhaps we'll organise a tourney when we go back to Narbonne between Sicres' best and ours, blunt some lances – lose a few men on both sides for sport and cheer up the remainder.' No-one was stupid enough to speak. 'Arnaut?'

'Sire,' Arnaut confirmed and took his position on First Watch while his comrades matched their bodies to tussocks and found unconscious communion with the earth.

With determination, Estela braided her hair in thick defiant loops and coiled them round her head in a glossy black crown, the announcement to the world that she was a married woman. Was that all there was to it? Pushing, shoving and forcing with a blunt instrument? Her mouth twisted as she mouthed the sweet lies of the songs she had learned by heart, the lines of desire and regret, of passion and parting, and compared the reality.

She tried the demure coif once more for good measure but gave up trying to arrange her thick plaits underneath it and threw the white headpiece back in the chest. Instead, she pulled out a swathe of red silk, wrapped it round as a head rail and knotted it to one side, leaving the ends trailing. Maybe there were advantages to living in the barbarian manner of Oltra mar, long robes hiding all but her eyes from the stinging glances that she was about to face. Further arming herself with a scarlet mantel, fastened with the Pathfinder Rune brooch, and a maroon cotte over her white under-shift, she smoothed her skirts and trod the route to break her fast and face the Queen's Ladies.

No-one pointed at her, no-one whispered audibly 'You know what we said about Estela, well...' no-one even smirked knowingly and finally, crewel needle in hand as she worked on yet more finery for the Queen, Estela accepted that she was last week's news. Nervous as she had been of everyone reading on her face what she had done, she was disappointed when no-one did. She had wanted everything to change, she had shattered her world and nothing had changed, no-one had noticed. She pricked her finger and blobbed a blood-flower among those planned on the fine weave in front of her. She sighed. That too was ahead of her. She was expecting her own blood-flowers in a few days and she was enough of a country girl to know what it meant if they didn't start. That would certainly show somebody something! But what exactly, she didn't know.

Gradually, her head bent over her sewing, she took in the chat going on round her, sifting gossip from news, trivia from potentially useful. It was a relief to Estela, mixed with something else that she chose to ignore, to hear that Dragonetz had taken his troops out of the city on some training exercise. More confusing was the mixture of reports on a scuffle in the streets between Aliénor's men and Ermengarda's. Word was that Sicres, the Commander of the City Guard, had beaten Dragonetz in a duel, disarming him and forcing him to withdraw his men from the city for an unspecified period.

Contradictory word was that Dragonetz had been following Aliénor's orders throughout and had not tried to fight Sicres. Speculation on what those orders might have been varied from the result of a drunken bet between Aliénor and Ermengarda as to whose army was better, to the notion that Dragonetz was continuing his crusading work in the streets of Narbonne. It had after all been the Jewish Quarter where the fighting took place and everyone knew that the Jews had fought side by side with the Moors in the Holy Land. And of course Ermengarda would order her men to protect the citizens of Narbonne. It was public knowledge that the two rulers did not see eye to eye regarding the Crusades, Aliénor's passion to redeem the Holy Land falling flat on the trader Viscomtesse.

However, the main distraction for the Ladies from the game of Estela-baiting seemed to be the return of Alis from Carcassonne, pale and thin, red-eyed from weeping her uncle's death. The Ladies leeched on others' emotion and grew fat with it, expanding in false sympathy at whatever minor horrors came their way and gasping with pleasure at anything worse. Alis was treated to much clucking of 'You poor dear,' as she related the unpleasant practicalities of a funeral in mid-summer heat, the rancid smells and flies, but the chamber positively reeked of anticipation when Alis started to detail her father's need to establish his new authority with some public spectacles. Estela drifted off into her own thoughts at the third description of a severed body part, this time a hand, moving of its own accord and pointing in accusation at the executioner before crumpling to its unnatural end.

Estela was mid-way through stabbing an imaginary gang of cutpurses when she realised someone was not merely speaking but speaking to her.

'Estela, what are you doing to that?' Vaguely, Estela followed

Sancha's gaze and saw the pattern her needle had stabbed on the cloth. She sighed.

'Here, give it to me.' Sancha bit off the thread and with her own needle started carefully unpicking the trail of destruction masquerading as laid-work. While her head was bent, Sacha added conversationally, 'New headgear?'

So someone *had* noticed. 'I thought it fitting.' At last Estela was able to give the haughty reply she had planned. Wasn't that what it had all been for?

The other woman hid her smile in the needlework. 'It is fitting,' she said gently, 'and it suits you. You don't need to prove yourself, Estela.'

Tears pricked in response and Estela stifled a sudden urge to confess what she'd done, to receive absolution. Instead she sniffed and blurted out, 'You'd be a good mother.' Even before the colour washed from Sancha's face, Estela reached out to touch her and murmured, 'I'm sorry. I forgot.'

The colour flooded back as Sancha bent lower over the faulty stitching. 'I take that as a compliment,' she replied, her voice as ragged as Estela's sewing. 'Now, let me tell you the news from Provence.' Too absorbed in her own private life, Estela had forgotten that Sancha was newly returned from the provinces and she was soon absorbed in discussion of the increasingly fragile balance between Raimon Berenguer, Comte de Barcelone, and les Baux, Dukes of Provence. Sancha was convinced that it would not be long before there was open battle over Provence, with Narbonne caught in the middle, both as Barcelone's ally and as the next treasure coveted by les Baux' greedy eyes.

'So that puts one of the Ladies from Provence into the frame as a go-between, our spy against Aliénor and Dragonetz.'

'Possibly,' conceded Sancha. 'But I have dug into the backgrounds and connections of all the possible suspects and they would have to be master spies to have hidden all the traces. There are many Provençals like me who have no desire to see les Baux gain further power, nor blood shed yet again for the sake of a name with more hectares attached. It just doesn't fit.'

'And it doesn't really tie up with some connection being made at Douzens. That argues someone from the Corbières.'

'Like you,' Sancha pointed out drily, eliciting a smile.

'Touché. Unfortunately, I don't have your contacts or status to collect the gossip in the Corbières that you can in Provence. Besides, the connection at Douzens could have been made by Templar links, or Church links – they are all traders and travellers who might have made our insider's acquaintance in Aquitaine and met up again at Douzens.'

'Possibly,' Sancha replied again, persisting, 'But you can fit more of the Corbières pieces together now. Isn't your father a Toulouse man?'

'Carcassonne and Toulouse,' Estela agreed. 'But I know nothing of him and his affairs.'

'Nor want to know. I understand. But perhaps it's time we listened to a tale of a witch hanged till her feet danced and the miraculous prophesies that came from her dead mouth.'

'Or the blind child who touched the new ruler of Carcassonne and after his miraculous cure shouted that he could see a heavenly aura round Raimon. I think I get your meaning,' was Estela's dry response.

'We can interpose some pertinent questions, I think, particularly if her father or even Alis herself paid their loyal visit to their old liege lord to reassure him now there is a new one.'

'Toulouse,' breathed Estela as both women moved their stools to join the circle round Alis, who was relating the marvellous omens of late twin births among the sheep and wells springing from dry land that had greeted Raimon Trencavel as Viscomte de Carcassonne.

In between being suitably impressed by miracles, malformations and the merely bizarre, Sancha and Estela managed to elicit the information that Toulouse had indeed required a duty visit from not only the new Comte de Carcassonne but several of his vassals and that the fealty owed by Trencavel to Barcelone, in his new role, had not yet been officially given. As far as Estela could determine, this left

Raimon Trencavel on the fence with his feet dangling well into Toulouse's playground. Carcassonne had ceased to be Narbonne's ally and it wasn't clear what Raimon would do if push came to shove over Provence. Sit on that fence as long as possible, probably. Particularly as Toulouse also had his eyes on Provence for dessert with Narbonne as his main dish.

Alis herself was little help here as, in answer to a disingenuous question from Sancha, she expressed disappointment that she had not seen the famous pink walls of Toulouse on this occasion and had only second-hand gossip of that city. She had heard that the young Comte was hoping to stamp out corruption and its heretic carriers. According to Alis, which meant according to her father, Raymond de Toulouse put religion above everything. Above, Alis murmured hesitantly, above normal human relations. At this point Alis paled, as she had not during her account of traditional flaying and quartering of a convicted traitor. Pressed by curious Ladies as to what she meant, Alis declared her knowledge merely second-hand gossip and started yet one more gruesome tale of righteous punishment.

Estela was chewing all this over, when her thoughts were once more interrupted, this time by a voice grave but still girlish. She hadn't noticed Bèatriz joining the Ladies, presumably having left Ermengarda and Aliénor with duties elsewhere. The girl pulled up a stool the other side of Estela from Sancha and she stroked her own silky brunette hair, hanging loose over her shoulders, as her gaze took in Estela's coiled braids. 'What's it like, being married?' she asked, round-eyed and serious.

Estela bit back her first three responses and thought hard, disarmed by the clear innocence in the liquid brown eyes. Perhaps something had changed after all. Was that what she had lost? Was this what they meant when they said a girl had lost her innocence? That she no longer treasured the hope of a touch like the summer breeze through a tree, of a kiss like a strawberry burst in the mouth, of words of love whispered with skin warm on naked skin. Girlish dreams.

She met clear brown eyes with honest golden ones. 'All marriages are different. For you, there will be celebration through all of Dia when you marry. Your people will bless the union of their future Comtesse and wish it fruitful. Your chosen one will be a match for you, a man to share a kingdom with.'

'And to share a bedchamber with.' Bèatriz spoke so quietly Estela hardly heard her.

'And to share a bedchamber with,' Estela replied firmly. 'And nothing to be afraid of in this. The man who is lucky enough to marry you will be as grateful in the bedchamber as in the Great Hall and you will rule both together, wisely and well. That's what you are here to learn.' She gave the most reassuring smile she could command and the girl's face glowed.

'I have been wondering about such matters,' she said, stumbling on, 'because the Queen and Ermengarda have proposed a Court of Love and they have asked me to preside over it with them and be party to their judgements.

'A Court of Love?' Estela queried.

'After the Night of Music, you know, the one planned as a last tribute to Aliénor before she must return to Paris, when Dragonetz and you, and some lesser troubadours will show their skills.'

'Yes, I have been practising with al-Hisba.' Estela tried not to think of the forthcoming performance and remained none the wiser for the Court of Love. It was Sancha who spared her the need to show the depths of her ignorance.

'It's a fancy of our great Ladies. They give audience as is customary but this time the questions must be only on matters of the heart. The more philosophical the question, the better they enjoy the debate. And their judgements are the last word in refinement on the proper comportment of lovers.'

'Well,' said Estela, 'that's just what I need.'

'Me too,' breathed Bèatriz, alight with excitement. Someone called her name from the doorway and the needlework she hadn't touched was abandoned on the stool behind her. 'I must go.' Like a butterfly drunk on spring, she zig-zagged across the room and out. Estela watched her go, older by two years and a chasm.

Sancha touched Estela's arm and said, inexplicably, 'That was well done.'

Estela ignored her heartbeat as it drummed arrhythmically, 'Return to Paris, return to Paris, return to Paris...' She herself of course now belonged to Ermengarda and was going nowhere. With anybody.

CHAPTER SEVENTEEN

Hardened by sun and exercise, Dragonetz led his men back into Narbonne. Their tight formation gave the impression that the control would have been the same on open plains as through the meandering streets of the city. Horses gleamed, armour shone, even the men looked polished and no-one doubted the keen-ness of their sword blades. This was a deliberate show of force, the mailed fist wielded by Aliénor's silken power and let no-one forget that this was the army of a Queen. A Queen paying a friendly visit to a much-respected ruler, a Queen keeping her dogs of war on a tight leash, but a Queen nevertheless and her dogs were showing their teeth.

A handful of Ermengarda's men observed the triumphal entry from the Palace gates but Sicres was not among them, nor was there any attempt to meet military splendour with equal show from the City Guard. Which made its own point, acknowledged and approved by Dragonetz, who dismounted in one fluid movement and tossed his reins to an anonymous stable-hand. Dragonetz made sure the stable-hand remained anonymous, not worth one glance. That way he wouldn't have to kill him if the wrong stable-hand came within range. He left his officers to disband the men, organise fodder, lodgings and duty rosters for beasts and humans and he strode into the

Palace to make obeisance to Queen and Viscomtesse, strictly in that, officially correct, order.

The interview took longer than he had hoped, each ruler demanding a lengthy explanation of events in the Jewish Quarter a week earlier. The version that Aliénor received was remarkably similar to the version given to Sicres, that Dragonetz' men were going soft and needed to pit their skills against an adversary, that surprise had been essential for the exercise and that of course Dragonetz had to tell the Guard that he was acting under Aliénor's orders to avoid unpleasant consequences. Yes, he appreciated that he had a nerve asking for Aliénor's authorisation after the event. Yes, he was duly penitent. No, he wouldn't do it again.

Then came the matter that had really galled her. Was it true that Ermengarda's Captain had defeated Dragonetz one to one, as everyone said? Dragonetz gave her his steadiest look in response. What did she think? Her gaze dropped. Lesser mortals, he told her, needed trivial imaginary victories. She could hardly berate him after that so he rescued her. Had she seen her troops entering the city? She had. Was she satisfied with them. She was. Oh yes, she was very satisfied with them. So he had been right to test their mettle and return them to battleworthiness. He had been right. But he should have discussed it with her beforehand. Of course.

Once out of Aliénor's sight, Dragonetz smiled. It couldn't have gone better. His promise of new songs and and his best ever performance as troubadour at the planned evening of entertainment had sealed their understanding. It was perfectly clear between them that Ermengarda must be left in no doubt that Aliénor had the best fighting men, the best troubadours, in a word the finest court in Europe, which meant in the world. Then Aliénor could return to Paris happy with all aspects of her sojourn in the south.

There was no need of such ego-dancing with Ermengarda. What had passed between them had left behind a freedom of speech and thought, and Dragonetz knew that Ermengarda valued Narbonne and its citizens above differences of race or creed. As he'd hoped,

Raavad had already spoken to her and outlined the situation but the mercenary band of provocateurs was a new factor.

'And you have no idea who was behind this?' Ermengarda's perfect high forehead was crumpled in thought.

'All I can say for sure is that they intended to start civil war in the streets of Narbonne, Jew against Christian, and they came damnably close to succeeding. And that it would have pleased them to add my corpse to their success. There is no doubt they knew who I was and were hoping for a big fat reward from their employer. So that gives us the usual suspects.'

Ermengarda nodded. 'Anything that hurts Narbonne pleases Toulouse. And it is possible that Toulouse holds you condemned, as Aliénor's Commander and perhaps there might be personal grounds too?'

'I know of none, my Lady. But that doesn't mean they don't exist.'

'You weren't over-friendly with his mother, perhaps?'

Dragonetz laughed aloud. 'God forbid! I'd have remembered.'

'Of course,' she said.

He looked at her then. 'I will always remember,' he said. And she received the words graciously as they were meant, a last gift between ex-lovers.

'Toulouse this, Toulouse that – he is an easy answer and I am sure the right one for some of my city's problems. But' she hesitated, 'I have a concern I hardly dare speak aloud.' He waited. 'There is also someone who increasingly disputes my legal rights and tries to move land and judgement boundaries to his financial advantage, someone who would very much like to cleanse Narbonne of heretics and heathens. I can imagine him hiring your band of thugs as a way to get Jews out of Narbonne. What I can't see is why he would care about you, unless I envisage some wholesale Church conspiracy against either Aliénor or you or both.'

'Your Archbishop,' Dragonetz confirmed.

'Narbonne's Archbishop,' Ermengarda corrected, 'and it is clear he would prefer a different Narbonne. He preaches of the weaknesses in a woman as ruler, and of course all the sins embodied in our sex that have been the downfall of so many good men; he preaches the Crusading spirit and the corruption of living shoulder by shoulder with unbelievers; and of course he practises invasion and deceit in all aspects of his jurisdiction in my city! But he is the Papal Nuncio, the representative of the Pope himself, God's holy messenger and I dare not use his own methods against him, nor strike at all without proof. I must be a better Christian than he!'

'Not difficult,' was Dragonetz' short response. 'I cannot say whether he is involved but yes, he has reason to ill-wish me. To connive at my death seems a little extreme, I must say, but I shall think about it and take precautions.'

'We understand one another,' Dragonetz was told by the second powerful woman in one morning but this time he was holding nothing back when he agreed. Meeting over, he barely stopped to take water and a day's rations before commandeering a fresh horse, from a stable-hand whose very existence Dragonetz denied firmly to himself. He was too recently back from the company of stars, night breezes and hard, physical work to enjoy the constraints of Palace politics and it was with a sense of escaping that he spurred his horse onto the river path and out towards his paper mill, where, he sincerely hoped, he would find al-Hisba supervising the enterprise of his dreams. With al-Hisba he could discuss paper and polyphony, plan an export route and prepare his new songs, while working shirt-less alongside men, and men only. Perhaps the Archbishop had something right in his sermons after all. Life would certainly be simpler if.

The smell of rotten eggs reached Dragonetz several leagues before he could see the tanks, beams and mill-tower with its wheel turning; the smell of the sludge in the holding pond, the smell of the future. Drag-onetz jumped out the saddle and, throwing his reins and a nod to the worker who greeted him, sought out al-Hisba. The robed, turbaned figure was easily identified through an open door, gesticulating near a tank where two men were raising a metal screen, the deckle, with its sheet of yellow matted fibres.

Paper, thought Dragonetz, with rising excitement as the words Al-Hisba had taught him came back to mind. Macerating, pulping, couching on the felt, deckling with mould and deckle, then pressing. Dragonetz frowned. It looked to him as if a new stage had been added to the process since he last visited. Every new stage added time and cost so he hoped whatever it was that al-Hisba was doing was worth it – and worth the smell of rotten eggs.

'One sheet at a time,' al-Hisba was instructing. 'Take a few sheets between the wooden rods and dip them into the size, then press them here.' He indicated the rack beside the vat. 'If the two of you take turns, you'll get into a rhythm once you're working.' The two men, sweating in their leather aprons, each picked up two wooden sticks, clamped them around a few sheets of deckled paper and the first one dipped his sheets into the viscous liquid in the vat, which was the colour of rancid butter. He swore while laying the sheets on the press.

'Be careful!' Al-Hisba said, without noticeable annoyance. He shrugged as he turned to Dragonetz. 'There will be wasted sheets. There always are. That's why the sizing place is known as 'the Slaughter-House'.'

'So why are we doing this? What's in the vat?'

'Raw paper soaks up water like a flower in the rain. The moment your nib touches it the ink spreads like ripples from a stone in a pool and writing is impossible. So we size the paper, coat it to repel liquid enough that the ink will stay on the surface and not spread. The easiest way is brushing with sugar starch.'

'But that's not sugar starch. So? There is a reason we are using whatever that is?'

Al-Hisba nodded. 'Starched paper deteriorates very quickly. This is a gelatin and alum mix.'

Dragonetz couldn't help taking a sharp breath.

Al-Hisba nodded again. 'I know. Expensive. Complicated.'

'If this ends up as expensive as making parchment, we might as well import the animal hides and be done with it! Gelatin and alum! Suppliers?' Dragonetz snapped.

'The tannery downriver for the gelatin, at a good price. Colour varies so the sheets come out cream, yellow, beige according to what we get from the tanner. Alum –' al-Hisba paused. Dragonetz was well aware that the only alum mines were in the control of the Ottoman Empire and Venice held the monopoly of the alum trade in Europe. So either al-Hisba was breaking trade laws with direct Moorish contacts or he had bought at Medici prices, for that powerful family *was* the Venetian alum trader.

'Tell me the worst.'

'It is the best size there is. The alum acts as a mordant to bind the gelatine to the fibres. And I have a contact who gets alum to Narbonne direct from Venice, without middle-man prices.'

'Convince me.' Dragonetz told him and the rest of the morning passed in account details. Unwillingly, al-Hisba divulged his Narbonne alum contact and Dragonetz felt less uneasy when he knew the route his alum took from a merchant in the Venetian ghetto to the Jewish Quarter of Narbonne. He had given his steward responsibilities and freedom to use his own judgement and in return the accounting was to be full and frank. Al-Hisba bowed his turbaned head and gave no cause for criticism.

In fact, Dragonetz knew that if the Fates had not brought him this genius of an engineer, with all his foreign wisdom, the paper-making dream would have rotted in its first vat. And there was no doubting al-Hisba's own pride in the mill's efficiency as they strolled round the processes, giving a word of quiet praise where it was due, and, according to al-Hisba, it was due to all of the workers in their different ways, each named and acknowledged. Dragonetz duly admired everything that was pointed out to him, from the well-greased shaft mechanism to the deckled edges of the final product.

He fine-tuned the plans for shipping the finished paper, in its 14" by 20" stacks, the size of the mould. He agreed a shipment to a merchant in Venice's Jewish Quarter, where the paper was to be marbled in the secret expertise of that city and no doubt sold on at a hundred times the price paid for it. That was the world of trade; take a product and add value, then sell it on. The other recipients of the first export of paper from the mill were duly listed and a meeting arranged with a Bookbinder, to discuss a personal project Dragonetz had in mind.

And every time he was near paper, whatever stage it might be in, his long, tapering fingers touched the fabric, whether the mushy mix of rags or the weave of the finished product, in which he could trace the grain. He must speak to al-Hisba about the possibility of some kind of branding, something unique to their mill, so that even when rivals set up their Mills, his paper would be distinctive. Maybe if a symbol was coated before the paper was sized, the brand would remain distinct on the sheet? There must be some way and if there was, al-Hisba would think of it.

Breaking fast at mid-day, Dragonetz speared a loaf and gnawed on it, alongside his men, not even aware of the silence. He contemplated the water clock, idly. If he attached further rings to the clock, say with figures attached, he could get the figures to move at designated times, make a fancy for a gift. Perhaps he'd try it with some wire birds. Not that he had anyone special in mind to give it to. His mind drifted with the one cloud in a blue sky until the same clock was referred to by the Supervisors to call the men back to work,

Only one exchange between the two men marred Dragonetz' visit. 'There is a problem with Estela,' al-Hisba said, hesitating, his eyes glancing sideways away from Dragonetz as they had done when he was unsure of the reaction he would get over the alum. 'We have been rehearsing for the banquet. The Queen wants the performance of your lives.'

'I know.' Dragonetz was curt.

'Estela has lost her music. Oh, her technique is better than ever. And she will pass muster singing satires and religious faradoodles. But her love songs are as flat as the desert. No life in them at all. I cannot tell her that there is no feeling or she will lose even the notes that she still has. I cannot give her feeling, my Lord. I don't know what has happened or if anyone can but you could try.'

'It was probably just an off-day,' Dragonetz said lightly, 'It will be fine.' His stomach lurched and called him a liar but he saw no way out. They would have to sing together at the banquet anyway. 'I will see her.'

Estela told herself how excited she was about the coming performance. In a few months she had got everything she wanted; she was a singer at the most refined court in Occitania, with the Viscomtesse as a generous patron. In al-Hisba she had musical tuition that combined expertise and patience with a twist of the unexpected. She had the security and freedom given by her marriage, without any unpleasant duties attached to this state. She had a chamber to herself – unheard of! She had silks, lace and jewels in the latest fashion. She even knew what the latest fashions were. She was happy with the way she looked. She didn't need her mirror to tell her that her eyebrows were a delicate trace of black in a permanent arch of enticement. Her skin was still the unfortunate golden colour she had been born with but it was smooth with rose-water and glycerine, scented with attar and musk. Her body had filled out, too much in her view, but at least the curves had stopped rounding further and she had grown used to a woman's hills and valleys. Her teeth showed the benefits of the daily rinsing, rag-rubbing and fennel-chewing that she had learned from her mother along with other herbal lore.

What is missing? Estela asked herself for the umpteenth time. And once again refused to acknowledge the answer. She had thought this emptiness would pass with her monthly courses, which, after the initial relief, had brought her pains in the belly as if kicked by a horse. It was hardly surprising that she had not been her best in music lessons, even having to excuse herself and retire with a concoction of lemon balm and ginger, an antispasmodic she had seen al-Hisba use when Dragonetz had stomach cramps after the poisoning. But her time of the month was well over and a dragging ache, a void, still remained, changing to something more painful when she received the summons to a music lesson, with both her mentors. It would be the first time she had seen Dragonetz since the stable incident, as her thoughts termed an event about which she refused to have feelings. If, that is, she thought about it all. And surely no knight worth the name would refer to such an incident, so all she had to do was get past a little awkwardness between them and find the common ground that had always been there in their music.

With face and lips more carefully rouged than usual, camou-flaging any trace of extra pink in the cheeks beneath, Estela swished her silks and clicked her pattens towards the alcove in the allotted Hall, where her eyes caught immediately on the tall figure that unfolded on her arrival, a mere silhouette back-lit against the window but unmistakeable. She greeted Dragonetz formally, accepting the token brush of his lips on the back of her hand and turning quickly to al-Hisba, who bowed in his Moorish fashion, hands clasped as in a winter muff. Firmly avoiding eye contact with Dragonetz, Estela tuned her mandora and chatted breathlessly about the proposed programme for the banquet. With an artificial giggle that wouldn't have been out of place among the Queen's Ladies, she proposed that Dragonetz sing and she listen, as she would surely learn more that way.

'I've practised myself to absolute shreds for weeks now, with al-Hisba spurring me on, so I'm sure I'm ready and it would be more useful for me to hear you and model myself on your interpretation.' She drew breath and Dragonetz cut in.

'No. We'll sing the whole programme. I start with the nightingale song, you come in with the glory of our Lord in nature, then me again with the youth voyaging, we try a Cervantes to sharpen the wits, then the Tenson.'

'I know the programme!' She ought to. Al-Hisba had made her repeat every line of it until her dreams were full of witty puns and rhyming couplets. 'And we finish with the Dawn Song as a duet.'

'Of course.' His voice lacked all inflection, emotionless, until he lifted his own lute, rested one knee on a stool and, standing, became a nightingale. Estela had wondered why he didn't give her the nightingale song, so obviously better with a woman's voice and she had her answer, the liquid melody flowing like nectar through all her defences, through the tangle knotting her core, through her veins until she felt she could fly if he told her to. Instead, his fingers danced their last chord on his lute and he nodded once to her, and the music skipped lightly from him to her and back again, then between them until she could shut her eyes, finding the notes with her hands and her heart, feeling words as laughter, light, tears and shadows.

Estela had no idea when al-Hisba left as there had been no-one but Dragonetz and her from the moment the nightingale sang and she was deep, deep in a world where a knight kept his promise through temptation and trial, where the sea-monsters and land demons snatched maids from their mothers, and where love was secret and everlasting. Dragonetz *was* what he sang, inviting Estela to join him in the song, to lean out the window of her tower prison to hear the nightingale better, to spurn the buffoon with her foot, to accept the lover kneeling at her feet, fingers still caressing the strings as he offered her his words in the Tenson and waited for her reply, his eyes on hers, black haunted with hope, deep with need that speared her like an arrow. They were acting, murmured the voice in her head as the flower of her body opened of its own volition to the murmur of 'Dous' amor privada'.

'C'aisi vauc entrebescant
Los motz e-l so afinant:
Lengu'entrebascada
Es en la baizada'

I twine the words and the melody
Like two tongues in a kiss,' sang Dragonetz and as he knelt in front of her, his mouth on her hand was no courtesy but a lazy, circling continuation of the song's promise as he waited the response that missed not one beat, thanks to the hard work put in by al-Hisba.

His smile pure mischief, Dragonetz acknowledged her cool timing, her control and his demise, rejected, was such a study in pathos that she would have wept laughing had she not her next lines to sing and her own performance to give, regret and sorrow lacing the slowed movement of the verse.

Reviving with remarkable speed, the dead lover told her briskly, 'Straight into the Aubade,' and there they were, fresh from a night sleepless with passion, naked, in bed, fully awakened to what could never be and sharing the last minutes before their enemy the Dawn parted them forever. Estela was so in tune with her partner that his kiss on her mouth was as natural as her fingers on the lute. His lips carried the sweetness of the night they had spent together and the pain of parting and if she clung to him to keep him against her, to hold him a moment longer, then so it would have been, surely. And if the mouth on hers hardened, became demanding, exploratory, wanting to renew known pleasures, that too, would have been in the Aubade. Her head was swimming as he broke off and stumbled away from her, his eyes dark as when poisoned.

'We go too far.' She hardly heard the words. She didn't need to hear his words to feel what he felt. And finally, unequivocally, she knew what she wanted.

'Come to me tonight,' she commanded him, tall and straight and proud.

'I can't.' He held himself as if bound in rope, lute discarded, arms by his sides. His eyes begged her.

Her confidence wavered and she could feel ordinary Estela replacing this magical lady she had been for just a precious moment, a moment she would never forget. She would not cry. 'Ermengarda,' she stated blankly. She had read the signs between them wrong. He had been acting. 'You don't want me.'

His eyes blazed and his hands jerked at his sides. He said nothing but he couldn't hide his response, not from her. She had not been wrong.

'Then come to me tonight. Or you insult me forever.' She turned and mustered what dignity she could to stalk off and reach her chamber before her shaking legs gave way. She left too quickly to hear his low, ragged reply, 'It is both that I fear, my Lady, but we have already gone too far.'

At whatever cost, Dragonetz lingered in the Hall, easing any suspicions that might have arisen in onlookers by showing off his comedian's skills, giving a parody of familiar court faces, showing his facility in switching from one part to another. Satisfied that his acting talent and outrageous humour had left more impression than his musical rehearsal with his student, Dragonetz too sought privacy, where he often sought it, in a small shrine, where he could commune with his God.

Kneeling on the cold stone, his head bent on the cross of his sword, the knight felt the tumble of his thoughts like a mill race churning and chopping. Impossible to put to one side the warmth of her golden skin on his mouth, the way she had opened to him. Impossible for a man of his experience not to imagine what was freely offered and what he knew he should deny them both. From his first sweet induction at fifteen in a hayfield with a laughing farm-girl, he had known glut and abstinence, peasant and princess, hessian and silk. He had never forced a woman but then he had never been refused. He had rutted like any other soldier and paid court to a Queen. From the moment he realised his effect on women he had fine-tuned it to an art, given generously to the moment and walked away with an appropriate expression of courteous regret. How could it be otherwise? The sparks lit by flesh on flesh must always burn out and he had never waited till there were just ashes.

And then there had been Damascus, a girl who felt what he didn't, a girl whose father told him proudly how she'd withstood all attempts to torture information out of her, about him, died for his sake. Dragonetz had watched a man's tears, offering a general's tawdry compensation for his daughter's death – and for what anyway? For a campaign doomed by Aliénor's caprices! Aquitaine would be the richer for its men and goods if they had all stayed home and the Duchesse had just randomly executed one in ten of her warriors! However much he turned his guilt on Aliénor, Dragonetz knew his real crime. He had murmured pride, thanks, the importance of her gesture to this bereaved father and he had racked his memory to find a picture of the girl.

Nothing. No name, no face, not even a cleft between thighs remained as a memory of her passage in his life. And yet he had ended hers. Shame filled his dreams with hair of all shades and lengths, eyes that were blue, hazel or green, all accusing and he denied himself the sweet thing that had meant so little. And so much. His body had woken to Ermengarda like a desert to the rain and he knew he would become dangerous without slaking those needs as Raoulf considered proper. Without Ermengarda, he could no more stay away from Estela than live without drinking. Perhaps his father was right and he should have married long since. Better to marry than burn. Perhaps, but it was too late and burn he must. He had no choice. He knew what Raoulf would say. 'Scratch the itch and be done with it.' But there was no chance that it would be done with, or mean so little, not this time.

If he left now, as he should, she was young and would get over it quickly. He never would. He wondered how long he had known this, how long he had denied it. Had it been there at the start in a song by a ditch, or later in blood and broken glass, in a blue token, in straw from a stable, in a million glances? He pictured himself riding away. He couldn't stay in Narbonne and stay away from her so he would have to return with Aliénor to Aquitaine, give up the paper mill. No, he would leave al-Hisba as overseer. He pictured her lying in bed that night, waiting for him, growing tired, weeping perhaps, finally sleeping, knowing he had not come, thinking he didn't want her. He pictured them both growing old, separately, remembering a might-have-been with gentle nostalgia. His knees creaked as he sighed and rose, suddenly cold in the gloom of the chapel. He lit two candles, one for each soul that must suffer this night, crossed himself and left. Decision made. This was how it had to be, in all chivalry.

So Dragonetz himself could never afterwards explain how, in the first hours of night, the flicker of sconces on the Palace Walls witnessed him tapping a quiet rhythm on the door to Estela's chamber. He was answered by a growl and a whisper, then the door opened. Following instructions, he stepped around the great hound that blocked the doorway and watched him suspiciously, though without further comment. Automatically, Dragonetz bent and let the beast sniff his hand, and then he turned his attention to the mistress. She glowed in the candle-light, the thin white linen of her nightgown emphasising the contours of her body rather than concealing them even though the laces across her breasts were modestly crossed and tied. Although the summer night was warm enough that Estela was barefoot on the stone floor, she was trembling.

He took her hand gently and raised it to his lips. 'I will go if you want me to,' He searched the eyes raised to his, all depths and shadows.

'Please stay,' she breathed and offered her mouth in continuation of the kiss begun that morning.

He held her at arm's length an instant longer. 'Estela, I will go as slowly as I know how and I will try to stop if you ask me to but there will come a moment when I won't be able to.'

'I won't stop you,' she promised and then she was in his arms. 'Boethius,' he said desperately, stupidly, breaking off. 'Harmony between humans.' He had to fight the desire to take her there and then, half naked against him and it took all his experience and self-control to hold her away from him long enough to calm his breathing. Boethius would help, for a short while. She smiled back at him, her hair floating about her in a cloud of black silk over the white gown. 'The music of the Spheres,' she responded. Of course, she had spent time with al-Hisba, talking philosophy and music. He stroked a tendril of her hair with the back of his hand.

'Turn around,' he ordered her quietly. It was the way she froze, like a deer before a hunter, that told him. 'I should have killed him,' he spat, his desire churning instead to white fury. 'What did he do to you? What did you think I was going to do?' Suddenly wary as a forest creature, her eyes round as saucers, she watched him, rigid, motionless. Mastering himself with difficulty, he spoke carefully to her, moving slowly away from her to the ledge where her toilette stood. 'I wanted to brush your hair.' He picked up the brush, its tortoiseshell back gleaming brown and gold. He could have left then, would have left then but she nodded wordlessly and sat down on the clothes chest, back towards him. The great white dog had looked up but now it thumped its head back down to rest and sighed, losing interest.

'The first being cosmic music, concerned with the movements of the heavenly bodies and the cycles of nature,' he said conversationally, placing the brush on her hairline and drawing it down deep below her waist, below the rim of the chest. He had to bend to take the brush to the end and then straighten to start again from the crown. His voice thrummed alongside the brush. 'The second being human music, the harmony between soul and body and that between people.' He found a rhythm and the deft strokes trailed a wake of sparks in their passing. 'And the third being the technique and practice of instrumental or vocal music.' His voice found the timbre he used in his ballads, half-crooning, half-hypnotising, modulated, musical. Her hair made fiery points in the candle-light.

'Don't stop,' she murmured and he felt her shoulders slacken, her body arch again under the gentling brush.

'As my Lady wishes,' he whispered, tirelessly tracking bristle through the gleaming black tresses. 'The earth and all upon it which has material existence is subject to time and therefore to change. Nowhere is there stability. The four elements commingle and separate in constant flux.' Her hair crackled from the brushing. He touched it lightly with his free hand and the crackles stung him and disappeared into his own body. He moved his left hand in contrapuntal accompaniment to the right, ever brushing. 'Our world is at the centre of the universe, surrounded by crystal spheres that fit perfectly and spin, enclosing in each one a heavenly body.' As his hand stroked down the length of her hair, he could feel the warmth of her back through the fine cloth. 'Outside of these is the firmament of fixed stars, not susceptible to time or change.' He parted her hair at the neck, kissed the bared, young bone, pressed himself against her and his hand followed its natural course down from her shoulder to curve under her arm and gently cup her breast. He waited.

'More,' she whispered.

'The firmament is stocked not with material things but rather with perfect forms.' His fingers traced the bud hardening under his touch. 'Free of material existence,' he purred, 'these exist in eternity. Through reason or in his very soul, a human being may contemplate and observe the eternal. Estela.' He returned the brush to its place and raised her, turning her to face him. 'Undress me.' With his help she removed his tunic and loosened the gatherings so that his under-breeches fell to his feet. She reached out, curious, and he let her explore, her touch shy and hesitant. Then it was his turn. He untied the laces across her breast, loosed her shift, paused and queried, 'Dagger?' earning a laugh. Then her nightgown joined his under-breeches in a discarded heap. His mouth found the scar noticed so long ago but now was not the moment to ask. There would be time, later, to know everything. Now he ached with restraint and could hold back no longer. She moved to blow out the candle but he stopped her and his eyes never left hers as he lifted her onto the bed. Once sure that there was a welcome for him between her thighs, he murmured, 'Guide me, Estela. Make it your choice to take me in.' And then the great music of which the world is made took him over, beyond thought, beyond control until he heard her cry his name and they fell together off the edge of the world.

He held her like a child till she slept, tears drying on her cheeks, 'Jouissance,' her last word. Then he carefully extricated himself, dressed quietly and stood, a silent silhouette against the window, as much guardian of her sleep as the white fur in the doorway, snoring. Whatever doom came upon them, they had known this night and when first light showed, he stirred and stroked her cheek to wake her. 'I have a gift for you and then I must go,' he whispered, watching her eyes wake from what dreams he could only imagine, to confusion at his presence, followed by a flush of emotion. He stood aside so she could see the window and gestured. 'The present.' Even through the small window the perfect dawn tinged the sky with cream, gold and red from the first rays of the sun. Her face lit up with her own awakening and he was amused to detect the return of desire. 'I must go, really. People shouldn't see me here.' He detached himself gently, and reluctantly, from her questing hand.

'I don't care about people!' she flashed.

'But you must, my Lady.' He put space between himself and the bed and gave her his most charming smile. 'Or it will be difficult for me to come to you again.' Then he stepped over the dog and left, while he could still force himself out the door, banishing from his mind the raspberry tips of her full breasts, the curves of her hips and thighs, the opening folds and secrets of the sweetest place in the whole of the universe, an endless present.

CHAPTER EIGHTEEN

Bleary-eyed from lack of sleep, Estela passed the next few days of routine duties in a satiated daze, alive only in her lover's arms at night. Reprise by reprise, their encounters added laughter and experiment to a mix that was already heady enough to leave both of them intoxicated. The geography of her own naked body had become the study of a cartographer as meticulous as any of Ermengarda's log-keeping navigators and he wanted the history of the tiny burn mark on her calf – a childhood accident with a bonfire – and of the weal he kissed on her left shoulder, twisting a hank of hair to one side as he traced the raised edge of the scar with his mouth,

In this man's arms she could say or do anything and so she told him how her father's new wife had dazzled fourteen-year-old Estela with her pretty yellow hair and dainty manner. How she had encouraged the girl to grow into her womanhood and leave behind the smithy and the knife games that had been her refuge as a child. Equally enamoured, her brother was shaped by a smile here, a compliment there, into smoother behaviour and taking his duties as squire more seriously. Until the trap sprung, the day her father's wife invited Estela to look through the spyhole to the great Hall, from the inner Sanctum of the new Private Bedchamber. While Estela was standing agog at watching the bustle below her, men and maids all oblivious to the young spy, her father was sent for. His wife suddenly started screaming at Estela who was apparently a viper in the bosom and a thief. Bemused, Estela saw her father arrive on this scene and comfort his distraught wife, who said she'd found Estela snooping in their Chamber, where she was not allowed, and that her worst fears were proved true. Of course, the wife's missing bracelet was found under Estela's pillow and, white-faced, her father took a whip to her.

'It got worse,' Estela told Dragonetz. 'Everything was turned against me and I finally realised that she wouldn't be happy till I was dead. I got out.'

'And your brother?'

'Didn't believe me either,' she said shortly. 'But his turn will come. She will secure her future and her children's future, should they be so lucky as to be born, by killing him or marrying him. Either is possible. Anything is possible. If she spoke to you, it would take seconds and you would believe her too.'

He took her head in both hands. 'Never.' And he took her mind off the past with a wildness that took them both to new heights. There was something untamed about him, an unpredictability that sparked fire between them. Just when she thought the flames were tamped down, temporarily, he told her, 'The Church has a useful edict detailing all that is forbidden.'

'I am aware of it,' she replied, lowering her eyes demurely.

'I propose we work our way through the entire list so as to have a better understanding of sin and repent more fully, unless of course you find anything distasteful or painful.' As he was already engaging as promised in an activity that was definitely on the Church's proscribed list, and was very very pleasurable, Estela made a noise in response, which seemed to be taken as assent.

Afterwards, he murmured as he lay beside her, 'Why, I do believe I am repentant after all. I have never been as tired in my life. And as it is you who have been wronged, you must declare a penance for me.' She did. 'When I'm recovered,' he whispered, and kept his promise. She learned to make his body her playground, trading scar for scar, discovering a warrior's closest escapes etched in his skin. With her eyes shut, she could distinguish between each type of hair on his lean body, silky under his arms and tapering down his back, thicker tufts on his chest. She knew how many handspans measured the distance up his spine or between the ridges of his shoulder-blades. She knew the exact tension of his thigh muscles against her own and the fit of him to her, in the shelter of her arm, in the curl of two spoons nestling, his hand on her breast, in passion, over and over.

They were exhausting each other. She ached inside and out and could think of nothing else. They could not continue at this pitch. They couldn't stop. They had to stay awake in order to sing together at a banquet.

Arnaut had never seen a banquet like it. He was sure he was full at the end of the second course, gorged on herring, mutton in wine sauce, chicken in almonds and all of it flavoured with any combination of ginger, sugar, vinegar, wine, raisins, mace, cloves, cumin, cardamom, cinnamon, pepper, and honey. If he had not visited the kitchens beforehand, he would not of course have recognised any of the meats either by taste or appearance, so transformed they were by food colourants of indigo, red and yellow.

There was no mistaking the meats of the third course and even those accustomed to the French court gasped as the servers brought in the platters, fifteen more dishes to delight the eye and the stomach. The long-tusked boar was laid on the table with due ceremony but remained disappointingly ordinary until carved open to reveal the cockerel roasted inside it, which in its turn revealed sweetmeats in its recesses, to general applause around the Great Hall as the various dishes were displayed and duplicated on the crowded tables.

Arnaut found that a man's appetite could revive with an appropriate appeal to his senses and for him, it was the glazed pilgrim that awoke his abused stomach to demand more. The biggest pike he had ever seen had been boiled at the head, fried in the middle, roasted at the tail and was served in heraldic pose alongside a roast eel, on an edible background of the colours of Narbonne, with the black of burnt bread crumbs etching the lines. Ermengarda's cooks must have prepared for weeks, commandeering cart-loads of hens, herrings, rabbits, game birds and sheep, and five thousand eggs was probably an underestimate.

Arnaut helped himself to one of the fruit dishes (plums baked in wine and spiced with cinnamon) that accompanied the boar, pike and venison, and let the conversation drift around him. As bellies warmed, anticipation of the evening's entertainment was growing and amongst discussion of the food was comparison of the various troubadours who had passed this way. The title of 'Best' kept returning to two men. Marcabru had his devotees but it was generally agreed that Dragonetz was his equal as a lyricist and beat him for range and performance. It would be something to tell one's children. And of course this would be his last performance as he would be off back to Paris with the Queen. As for this protégée of Aliénor's, tutored by Dragonetz, she was a treat for the eyes and the ears, if not of the same quality. You wouldn't expect it from a woman, would you.

Beside Arnaut, al-Hisba kept the same discipline in his thoughts that he had in his eating habits, hiding all emotion in the foreign swathes of cloth that marked him out in the company he kept. As usual, he hadn't touched the wine and had even been abstemious with the glorious feast spread before him. Arnaut felt a stab of irritation with al-Hisba, who showed no amazement at the final subtlety, each course having been followed by these marchpane fancies.

The last one was a full-size table-piece sculpted as a merchant ship with a likeness of Ermengarda as figure-head, extending the blazon of Narbonne to a crowned figure, flying impossibly, attached to the whole only by Ermengarda's hand. The symbolism of friendship and alliance was obvious but it seemed to Arnaut that Ermengarda came off better than Aliénor, whose giddy flight was all too true to life. In following Dragonetz, Arnaut had followed Aliénor, in all her crazes, through Courts and Crusades.

Someone was brave enough to break off the two rulers and the marchpane circulated. Arnaut chewed absently on the sweet almond paste of Ermengarda's finger. He had followed Dragonetz and felt he was part of his inner circle. Recently he had felt more and more shut out. At first he had been an equal at the mill but al-Hisba's obvious expertise had left Arnaut more and more dispensable until he had stopped trying to keep up and went there only under orders.

Fighting in the Jewish Quarter, exercising in the woods, sleeping under the stars, Arnaut realised what he was losing. He washed down the sweet with another glass of wine. Who was al-Hisba anyway? It wasn't like Dragonetz to let someone into his life like that. It had taken Arnaut years, campaigns together, fighting back to back, earning his place. He hoped Dragonetz wouldn't regret it. Moors weren't like Christians, however good they were at channelling water. He was definitely not going to use his trencher again and he slipped the hunk of dried bread under the table to a willing dog.

Tables were cleared, the buzz was rising and it was time for the performance to start. Arnaut saw Dragonetz and Estela leave the top table, take their place in the limelight, tune their instruments. From the first note, there was no doubt that this was to be a virtuoso performance from a master, who drew tears and laughter from his audience, as he wished. Only to be expected, the satisfied expressions of his audience suggested. But what no-one anticipated was the quality of his little protégée, become his antithesis, his counterpoint, his muse, his follower, his leader, his lady, his star, his equal. Outstanding as each was alone, in their duets the connection between them charged the Hall with magic. At first, Arnaut let the music carry him to a world of love and loss, courtesy and conflict, the two voices interweaving with his very soul,

'I don't know what he did but it worked,' murmured al-Hisba. 'She is superb.'

'I know what he did!' Whether it was al-Hisba's words, or some heightened intensity between the singers that opened Arnaut's eyes, he couldn't say but suddenly he knew. Pike, venison, boar, plums and marzipan nearly returned onto the table as he controlled his reaction. Had he looked that way, he would have seen the Viscomtesse of

Narbonne as pale as he was, and for the same reason, however much her expression showed the appropriate pleasure and appreciation, but all Arnaut's attention was focused on escaping. He untangled himself clumsily from the bench and shouldered aside anyone in his way as he lunged towards the back of the Great Hall where he found his father blocking the exit, on guard duty. Instinctively, Arnaut's hand went to his chest, covering the place where his token as Estela's knight lay beneath his tunic over his heart.

'I'm off to a tavern,' he told Raoulf. 'I'm de trop here.'

'When will you grow up!' He eyed Arnaut's hand, knowing full well what lay beneath it. 'Such a fuss for a woman!'

'He could have had anyone!' Arnaut's sense of injustice blazed with all the fervour of its fresh flames. 'Why did he have to take her?'

His father shrugged his wide, capable shoulders. 'So what if he did. She's just a woman. He's your liege Lord, my boy and if it was you instead that he wanted, Viking fashion, why you'd just have to bend over and take it.' His eyes narrowed and he pushed his son in the chest. 'Or is that the real problem. *She* could have had any man she wanted and she chose *him*.'

Arnaut felt the bile rise. 'Leave me go.' He pushed back while two voices threaded their plaintive chant behind him.

'Aissi-m te amors franc
Qu'alor mon cor no-s vire...'

'Love holds my heart so clear and true
That I see no-one else but you...'

The big man stood aside, watching Arnaut stumble into the night. 'It's not real!' he yelled after him but his son had gone.

Unaware of Arnaut's absence, Dragonetz and Estela made obeisance to the Queen and Viscomtesse, receiving as their right the evening's rich gifts, armour and jewels, alongside the plaudits. The evening had clearly been too much for the girl's social skills as she managed to knock the goblet out of the Queen's hand and a pitcher beside it, while accepting a gift. There was a furore of servants mopping up, and some gracious words from Aliénor smoothed over the clumsiness and all was perfect. A night to remember. Only Dragonetz and Ermengarda were close enough to hear Estela's low words of explanation to Aliénor.

'The infusion reeks of pennyroyal, my Lady.' She lowered her voice still further. 'It is an abortificient and can poison the mother too.'

'I've only had a sip. I asked for a digestive tisane – it smells of mint.'

'There is a similar freshness,' Estela agreed, 'and mint wouldn't harm you but this isn't mint and whoever used it knew exactly what he – or she – was doing. Don't worry – you'll be fine,' Estela assured her, ' – both of you. It's a lot harder to do harm at this stage anyway.'

'There are hundreds of servers here – we will never trace it back! You should have been safe here, Aliénor. I am so sorry!' Ermengarda was as helpless as she was anguished and it was Dragonetz who took control.

'Pretend,' he instructed them. 'We don't need the puppet, we need the puppet-master and we will draw him out before you leave for Paris!'

And so they pretended. As did Dragonetz and Estela, separating for the night with mutual praise in public – and, not much later, mutual pleasure in private. Neither of them gave a thought to Arnaut, who was deep in his cups, trying to ignore some loud-mouthed stable-hand nearby. The lad was as drunk as Arnaut, hoping to make a fortune by selling some love-token from a drab he'd deflowered. Gratitude from some easy lay. Arnaut snorted in his wine. He'd be lucky if his token was worth another jug of wine and he'd probably regret it in the morning. As, no doubt, would Arnaut himself. He caught hold of a passing female haunch, squeezed it in a friendly manner and ordered some more wine.

It was growing harder, not easier, to part at dawn. This time was even worse.

'Of course you must go,' Estela told the man kneeling at her feet, his lips on her hand, seeking her permission to leave Narbonne. He gathered her to him and kissed her more intimately and she shivered, not with cold, although she was naked. It was indeed growing harder to part. They separated because they had to.

'Only for a few days,' Dragonetz told her. 'I must draw this assassin before the Queen returns to Paris.'

'Before you return to Paris,' she said, banning all emotion from the words.

He looked at her sharply. 'I thought you knew.' Her eyebrows arched in query. 'I told the Queen I was staying in Narbonne.'

Because of her? The thought was dismissed as quickly as it had fluttered hopes in front of her. Then why? In the same expressionless voice she asked. 'How would I know?'

'I thought it would be common gossip. I'm sorry.' He weighed up what she hadn't known. 'And yet you asked me here anyway. Or was that the point? That I would be leaving.' His tone mirrored hers and she felt she walked along a ridge in the fog, ravines either side, and only the touch of a hand to guide her, his hand. How far did she trust that touch?

'If you don't know the answer to that, nothing I say will convince you.' She stroked his cheek to soften the words, to remind him. Was this what love did? Pierced all armour, made steel vulnerable and ice melt? Of course. He was staying for Ermengarda. It made no sense but it was true. She tried the words on her tongue to see how they felt and they had a bitter taste. 'You are staying for Ermengarda.'

His eyes held hers, pools with depths she could never read, though she felt every ripple that shadowed them. 'In a way,' he stated, 'but not as you mean. The paper mill is important to me, part of something bigger, something I can realise in Ermengarda's domain.'

'And how did Aliénor take it?'

Unexpectedly he laughed. 'Very badly. But most of the damage has been repaired. I remain her knight, of course.'

'Of course. And Ermengarda's man.'

'Yes.'

'You lead a complicated life.'

'You don't ask what your place in it is?'

'If I have to ask, then I don't deserve one.' She summoned a smile and gathered the love-words he scattered around her like autumn leaves. Summer always ended.

'So, you start at Douzens?' She brought them back to the practicalities.

'The first attempt was after Douzens. I might pick up a trail there and if Raymond is involved, Carcassonne might know the gossip. Six days away, I think. The road is shorter without carts and baggage, even on borrowed mounts.'

'You'll miss the Court of Love.'

'I know all the answers.' He gave his lop-sided smile and she was lost.

'Six days is nothing,' she reassured him and herself, as she pressed him to leave. The sun was already higher than was safe, with the bustle of servants starting their work in streets and hallways. What was a week?

If nothing else, Dragonetz' absence at least gave Estela the motivation to face up to one of her own monsters. If she were going to escape the city for a few hours, with some safe company like Arnaut, she would need a horse, and it was ridiculous to keep avoiding the stables. There had to be a first meeting, after... after what had happened, and she would make it clear that in fact, nothing had happened. She would be absolutely normal. She would even smile and be gracious. If she saw him at all, of course. It was always possible that he would be elsewhere and some other stable-hand would help her mount. She flushed even at the thought of such contact with him. This wouldn't do. Her days spent with the Ladies had not been wasted after all, she thought, as she applied a layer of chalk powder, painted it delicately with water, then added some diluted indigo to trace the pale blue veins demanded by current fashions and of course abhorred by the church. Today, Estela had no qualms about wearing a mask and if she should have to choose her Confessor carefully afterwards, why then she would be following Queen Aliénor's lead in that too.

Suitably painted, mantled and shod in pattens, Estela tripped out the Palace across the Courtyard, which was already reflecting the heat of the summer sun. She was rehearsing her calm request to have Tou saddled and ready for her in the afternoon, by which time she would have found Arnaut to either accompany her or propose a substitute, when she noticed her friend in person, with a detachment of his men, armoured and active in front of the stables. As she grew nearer, she noticed that his complexion had a green tinge, his eyes were bloodshot and his movements nervy. His words when he saw her were sharp enough though.

'Estela! You can't go in. You're not to see the boy.' Estela flinched at the command, outraged beyond shame, for the moment. Only one person could have set Arnaut to guard the stables and prevent her going near them. How could he! What did he think she was going to do there? How could he make something so private the talk of a regiment! As Dragonetz wasn't there, she glared instead at the young man blocking the stable entrance.

Far too quick for Arnaut, she ducked under his arm and swished her skirts and clacked her heels from ringing stone onto dusty earth and straw, into the dark smell of leather, wax and fusty fodder. It was strangely empty, no hoof-clinks, snort-breaths or shifting movements. No horses. Instead a stillness, a wrongness that smelt of a thousand punishments Estela had seen inflicted on criminals at her father's keep. The iron, screaming smell of bloody judgement. Estela stepped back, too late to make her eyes return their vision to the darkness, Arnaut's arms supporting her, too late to make any difference, as he murmured, exasperated, 'I tried to warn you, to stop you, Leave it, turn round.'

Mechanically, she obeyed orders, but his attempt to comfort her sparked some instinctive repulsion that was not his doing. She saw the hurt in his eyes and his voice and she should have said something to put it right. But when Arnaut said, 'I'm sure you'd rather *he* were here,' and withdrew from the stable, she merely stumbled after him, speechless, blinking in the light, seeing nothing but a human form hanging from the wooden beam at the top of the partition that separated the first stall from the second. It shouldn't be possible to see so much detail in seconds. Peire's brown hair was undamaged, flopping like that of some marionette above the smashed face, its empty sockets accusing Estela of she knew not what. The head was twisted at no living angle, familiar to Estela from every death by hanging passed along a roadside. But she had never before seen a man's hands, tied together in ironic supplication as he swung, holding five objects. His empty sockets identified the two balls, slimy as old fish. It was the gouges hacked out his blood-stained jerkin, at groin level, like a carcass in a butcher's, which told Estela what else he held. But the worst amongst the flesh and flies gathering to feast was the glitter of gold and emerald.

Nausea fouled her mouth and she crumpled to the ground, her head buried in her gown between her knees as she fought to keep control. 'Tell me what happened,' she demanded through gritted teeth. Anything to engage her brain, anything to diminish the image that recurred.

Still cold and formal, Arnaut did at least reply. 'We don't know. One of my men found the boy like this.' He hesitated. 'I think I might have seen him in a tavern last night.' Arnaut hadn't stayed at the banquet? 'He was trying to sell some jewel, presumably...' He didn't have to finish his sentence. They both knew where the jewel was now and that robbery had not been the motive for this killing. 'If he spoke truly, he had the jewel from some wench so no doubt this is payment from her parents.' Estela raised her head then, watching his face, seeing no irony, understanding that he didn't know, after all. And if it wasn't Peire he was referring to, then who? Her stomach looped. 'The jewel and manner of his death suggest he paid for an act of lechery with his betters.' Arnaut shrugged. 'My Lady, it is unpleasant and I wish you had not gone against me. But he was just a stable-hand. You must put it out of your mind and not let it spoil your day.' Hesitantly, he held out his arm to her and she took it, shaking out her skirts as she stood.

'I think a man's death in such a manner deserves my thoughts for one spoilt day,' she said quietly. 'Any man's.'

'Worse happened in the Crusade, both to our men and done by them.' His eyes glanced off hers. 'As Dragonetz could tell you.' The name was a double-edged blade between them and Estela let it lie. 'This is no place for a lady. Two of my men will see you safely back to the Palace.' Estela made no objection as he gave his instructions. 'And inform Dragonetz,' Arnaut added to her bodyguards.

Estela opened her mouth to speak but the grizzled soldier with even less teeth than hair spoke first. 'Sire, he left word for you this morning. He is abroad for a week on a mission from the Queen.' Estela's mouth was firmly closed but her eyes gave away that she knew. Arnaut's lips tightened. 'See that my Lady is tended to,' he said curtly and turned to deal with the remains in the stable.

CHAPTER NINETEEN

The dog lay in his usual place against the door, more than happy to do so during daylight hours and even more contented to have his mistress pressed against him, crouching against his belly, between his outstretched front and back legs. If she were silent and shivering on one of the hottest days of the year, it was only one more human oddity and need not prevent him sleeping. With one ear open, just in case.

Estela felt behind her back the rhythm of Nici's breathing, the rhythm of life itself, calm and regular. Like this they had lain in a ditch together but then she had been asleep too. She wondered whether she would ever sleep again, she who had wished to lose her innocence. Nothing made any sense.

She had no reason to connect Peire's murder with herself, or any threat to her, but the jewel in its bloody bed made a connection, along with what had happened previously in the stable. What she had made happen. And that only one other person knew about. *I should have killed him* ran through her brain. She forced herself into a lonely catechism. Had Dragonetz acted on his words? She knew – who better – the maelstrom under the ice. If Arnaut could become a stranger, could assess a man's bloody remains with a professional eye as 'just a stable-hand', then surely his leader was at least equally a warrior, able to dispatch life when he chose. Estela had seen him do so. Did he love her enough to kill for her? She knew beyond doubt the answer. But kill in such a way? Of this she was equally certain, but of the opposite response. No, a thousand times no. And this time her head and her heart were in accord. Even if he had been the kind of man who would do such a thing – and her every instinct screamed against this – he would hardly have killed Peire and left the only link between her and the boy for all the world to see. The jewel had hardly got there by accident.

If not Dragonetz, who? Why? Was it linked with her or was she just assuming guilt for other reasons? If Arnaut chased his wild geese of offended parents might he find the thread that led to her? She supposed it all depended what Peire had said in the tavern and who had listened. But Arnaut had been there, had listened and had no idea how close he was to the wench of Peire's bragging. Her young body was already reasserting control, the shaking had nearly stopped, when Nici gave a low growl and footsteps stopped outside the door.

'Estela,' came the husky voice of Sancha. 'Let me in. I have al-Hisba with me. Arnaut thinks you might need something for the shock.' Estela pulled to her feet, smoothed out her crumpled clothes and ran a licked hand across her face, which was presumably smeared with make-up but would have to do as it was. 'Friends,' she instructed the great beast, who rolled enough out of the way to allow the door open and who kept a lazy eye on those who came in.

Estela sat on the bed and her visitors pulled up stools. She didn't want to talk about what she'd seen. 'Dragonetz is retracing his steps to find out if he has missed any clues to the assassin's identity.' Now that she had been told officially by Arnaut's man, there was no harm in discussing it.

'He sent word,' al-Hisba nodded as he brought out his medicine pack and flask of water. A good physician, he ignored the attempt at distraction and firmly grasped the nettle. 'Arnaut told us what happened and he regrets that you were there. He says he forgot the weakness of your sex in discussing the situation with you and that you need one of my potions to calm you.'

Any truth in this only stoked Estela's indignation. Perhaps she did want to talk after all. 'I'm used to seeing bulls and horses gelded and finding their sweetbreads on my plate but I'm not used to seeing a dead man carrying his own lights in front of the chopped remains of where they used to be! And he used to have blue eyes you know? Blue! And you know what was left of them?'

'Estela!' Al-Hisba cut across her. 'There *is* at least *one* lady present!' Sancha was definitely paler than she had been and Estela thought with a pang of remorse of what she must have been through Oltra mar. Perhaps suffering didn't always toughen you up.

'I'm sorry, but anyone would have felt a bit sick at the time. Arnaut was wrong and I don't want anyone fussing over me. I'm fine now. In fact I've been thinking and I'm starting to wonder whether there is some link between this death and the assassination attempts.'

'A stable-hand?' They both looked sceptically at her. 'Why?'

'I don't know,' she owned. 'I just have this feeling. Arnaut was in the same tavern as this boy last night.' May God forgive her for pretending she didn't even know his name. 'Maybe someone mistook the stable-hand for Arnaut, or for someone else, if he was carrying a fine jewel.' She warmed to her theme. 'I'm sure that's it. Someone thought he was one of ours.'

'Wearing a leather apron and smelling of horses?'

'He wouldn't be the only one of Dragonetz' men to smell of horses,' she retorted.

'Maybe you're right,' Sancha conceded. 'But there's nothing we can do for now and we can't contact Dragonetz till he's back here next week so we might as well forget about it for the moment. I have a message from the Queen for you; she hopes that you will be well enough to attend the Court of Love tomorrow.'

'Of course I will.' A wave of exhaustion suddenly chilled Estela.

'There is water here.' Al-Hisba offered her the flask and she took a deep draught and then another. 'What have you given me?' she asked him. 'Not white poppy, I hope.'

He smiled. 'No, my Lady. That would be far too strong for you, dangerous even. It is just valerian, hops, St John's Wort.'

'To prevent the melancholy induced by certain sleep-inducing herbs,' Estela added mechanically. 'If it's really just gentle somnifores it won't take effect for a couple of hours.'

'I added a little something.' al-Hisba's white teeth gleamed, dancing like laundry in the river as Estela lay back on the bed and drifted downstream. 'Not sleepy,' were the last words Estela said.

The Hall Ermengarda always used for public audiences had extra benches along the sides to accommodate the knights and ladies there for the show. As always, Ermengarda's carved throne was on the High Dais facing the doorway from the far end. For this occasion, two chairs with almost equally ornate backs and arms flanked the Throne of Narbonne. Two? Estela wondered, from her bench seat amongst Aliénor's Ladies, She had watched Ermengarda's judgements often enough as part of her duties to know that the supplicants waited in the ante-chamber, the lucky ones on a bench, the majority standing in a patient line against the wall, waiting for hours to see their ruler and often being turned away for lack of time, only to start queuing again the next day. Usually the judgements were on questions of land, bonds, alleged thefts and neighbours' disputes, as tedious to Estela – and probably Ermengarda – as they were crucial to the supplicants themselves. In her naiveté when new to the court, Estela had wondered why Ermengarda fought the Archbishop to keep such a say in such trivial matters but she quickly realised that, aside from establishing her authority, when Pardons were given they drew a steady income into the Palace coffers – and away from the Archbishop's.

Today's judgements would be very different however and the Hall itself bore witness to that change. Red satin cloths swathed the walls in huge loops pinned with extravagant cloth of gold rosettes. However impressive the roses on the wall might be, they were rendered ordinary by the red path-way from entrance to High Dais. The velvety carpet was indeed rose, or rather rose petals, in every shade of red, fire and sunset, passion and blood, crimson, vermilion, scarlet and maroon, orange and terracotta. Never, not even in the baths scented with eastern essences and oils, had such a heady fragrance dizzied the Palace of Narbonne

The very walls, old stone a metre thick, were so saturated with rose that they breathed out sweetness. As if the strewn roses were not riches enough, the path was bordered with shrub-roses, each in a large tub, in the style of al-Andalus. Alternating red and white bushes, love and purity, human and divine, the flat single flowers in silken clusters were closer cousins to the briars than were the large petals underfoot. Truly it was the Season of the Rose, and this its finest hour. 'Essence of rose against heartache,' Estela murmured her herbal to herself, the difficulty of course being the quantity of roses needed for just a tiny amount of oil. 'For happiness and love.' Surely there were enough roses here to put it to the test.

Then the music began, not this time the flourish of trumpets for a triumphal entry but rather the strands of psalter, the instrument of saints and angels, accompanied by the rebec, flute and viol. Harping on the same string as the symbolism of the roses, the mingling of human and divine. Like woodland nymphs, floating on their floral carpet, Ermengarda, Aliénor and – of course, the third throne – Bèatriz, entered the Hall. The young Comtesse de Dia came first, in Mary-blue, a vision of spirituality, followed by the white rose and the red rose incarnated. Aliénor was incandescent in deepest red and Emengarda beside her ethereal in white and gold, all three glittering with jewels that matched their robes, sapphires, rubies and pearls. Behind them, an escort of three youths, the flower of chivalry indeed, strutted their sword-belts and their slashed white tunics, revealed the silk of their Ladies' colours underneath.

Each stood beside a throne as the Queens of today's court took their places. Perhaps it was no bad thing that Dragonetz was absent. Estela imagined him in his accustomed place at Aliénor's side and a new feeling curdled her veins. Would he have glanced round the Hall, seeking her, perhaps smiled as he found her own gaze fixed on him, the current between them secret and strong as that driving the cams in his beloved paper mill? The curly-haired knight who was in fact at Aliénor's side gave a wide smile in Estela's direction and she could have sworn he winked.

'What do you expect if you stare like that at the man, today of all days,' remarked Sancha beside her, her voice light with laughter.

Estela was mortified. 'I was day-dreaming,' she excused herself.

'I shall enjoy hearing you explain that to him,' Sancha continued to tease.

Estela risked another look but hastily dropped her glance again when she found that the man's gaze was still fixed on her. 'Who is he?' she asked, having studied him long enough to observe a crop of honey-coloured curls, shorter than was fashionable, and framing a mischievous face, sparkling with laughter and intelligence.

Sancha sighed. 'Eventually, you'll learn how to use those ears for more than making music. All three escorts are by Ermengarda's invitation and I don't think it's a coincidence that men of such calibre – or their sponsors – just happen to be passing through Narbonne today. The Viscomtesse attracts troubadours like a honeypot lures flies. Your gallant beside Aliénor is Peire Rogier.'

'I've heard of him! From the Auvergne? New on the scene last year with some clever internal dialogues about love.' She quoted,

'*que joys m'a noirit pauc e gran;*
e ses luy non seria res,'

'joy has so shaped me that
without it I am nothing'

He's the perfect poet for today!'

'Yes, from Clermont in the Auvergne,' Sancha confirmed. 'He left the canonical life as it didn't suit him.'

'I can imagine!' Estela had not been immune to the heat in the look that came her way. 'Looks like his hair's still growing out.' She was now free to indulge her curiosity as Peire's attention had moved to the youth beside Ermengarda, in an exchange that made the women laugh as much as the men.

'They know each other,' Estela observed.

'All three,' confirmed Sancha. 'Beside Ermengarda is young Guiraut de Bornelh, protégé of the Viscomte de Limoge, already making his mark and learning fast from Peire.'

'Why didn't I know they were here? Why wasn't I with them?' burst from Estela's lips, with no thought this time for their looks, as a second rush of the deadly green sin flooded her like wormwood.

'You perform like an angel but these – these,' Sancha nodded towards the glittering youths, 'are troubadours.'

Estela's hands clenched and she swore to herself, by everything from her dead mother to her hope of having children, that she would finish her secret compositions and join this élite.

'Then,' continued Sancha, 'beside Bèatriz, is the youngest of the three, Raimbaut d'Aurenja. Youngest but in no way lagging behind.' Even Estela knew the background of the heir to Aurenja, who must be about the same age as the girl he accompanied, carrying the same weight – a future kingdom – with the same grace. Born to it, trained for it and ready for the day he would gather his own court about him in the Chateau de Courthézon, near the ancient Roman-founded town of Aurenja, just as Ermengarda did here in Narbonne. At the cusp of manhood, his chin and upper lip lightly shadowed, his court manners were perfection and yet he seemed lithe and dark as some forest creature, always escaping.

Of the three men, all younger than her Dragonetz, it was Raimbaud who reminded her of her lover and opened her eyes to what might otherwise have passed her by. Estela had seen Bèatriz flushed with excitement over her music, over a pet marmoset, over a special occasion but this time it was not merely the occasion that lent the serious face unconscious beauty. Her deep brown eyes, enlarged with no need of belladonna, drifted politely over others as they spoke but returned like a dog on a string to her young escort, who clearly took the duties of the day very seriously.

What is love? Is it jouissance, the fireworks after the sparks? The tempering and melting after the sword meets the anvil? The song of songs? A private look in a public place? And – the question of questions – is it forever? All this and more, Estela wondered, her restless imagination chasing its own tail, trying to ignore complications. How did Sancha fit in? Or not. How had her own mother loved? Or not. Apart from loving her children, of course. Was it 'of course'?

She started as Ermengarda's cool, carrying voice seemed like her own thoughts spoken aloud. All three of the day's Queens were standing, Aliénor tallest and her gown let out once more, flowing large about the hope of France; Bèatriz still girlish despite the ever-hardening veneer of courtly behaviour, and a stockier build already than the figure beside her. However slim she might be, no-one would ever ignore the presence of the Viscomtesse of Narbonne, her kingdom knitted to her very bone when she was four years old. How could Estela be jealous of the time this vision had claimed Dragonetz as hers? She might as well be jealous of a ray of sun that touched his skin and passed on.

'What is love?' Without any effort, Ermengarda's every word reached the back of the Hall. 'And how should we best live by its precepts, governing our relations with courtesy, choosing aright when we have difficult choices to make? As God's representatives on earth, we, your rulers, are channels for divine judgement, and by His Grace we offer our judgements today on matters of the heart, in this Court of Love, where we all seek the true path, among thorns as well as roses, knowing that one day we must all answer to the divine judgement. Let conscience meanwhile be our guide and let the laws of love, as decreed here today, guide our conscience. May love rule this day!' As she opened the Hearing with these words, the three gallants flung themselves to their knees in front of their Ladies, offering one perfect red rose to each one.

It was a magnificent, tongue-in-cheek walk along the tight-rope between blasphemy and frivolity, and any listener could understand why an Archbishop might frown on the Lady of Narbonne and her cultured court. No cleric had been foolish enough to put himself in the position of listener and if the Archbishop felt his ears burn that day, he would have to wait his own turn for the throne on Sunday, to preach hellfire and damnation against all women, a doctrine for which he felt very special affection. Many of the same courtiers enjoying the Court of Love would also be present at the Archbishop's Sermon, including Ermengarda herself, if only to stare him down, but that was all part of living in the world. And of being young. There was time enough to repent. Meanwhile, there was a spectacle to enjoy, with some intellectual sport and a thousand opportunities for a woman's glance to cross a man's, full of promise.

The first supplicant entered and the Hearing began. Estela suspected that the knights and Ladies kneeling before the thrones were acting a part rather than bringing their own problems for public judgement – or even those of their friends – but it didn't prevent her from being caught up in asking herself 'What would I do if? Or 'What is the right thing to do?'

Kneeling before the Queens, a knight posed the first question. 'Suppose that a chevalier has gained permission from his dearest love to marry another and after the wedding he keeps his distance for a month. He then returns to his first lover, saying that he wished to test her constancy and is overjoyed to find her true. She however now rejects his advances, saying that his love is no longer worthy and he has the liberty he sought from her. Is she right?'

There was a conference between the three women and then Aliénor was chosen to give judgement. Gravely, she stood and pronounced. 'It is well-known that true lovers often test each other by pretending they have found someone else so it is an offence against love itself to refuse a lover's caresses on such grounds. Unless there is some other reason, this Lady lacks courtesy. Where there is no jealousy, there is no love.' A ripple of comment and polite applause greeted the verdict as the Knight bowed his thanks, left and a Dame trod the rose path.

'These two men are equals in birth and in honour, with only one difference,' declared a lady petitioner, the two unfortunates so described looking suitably hopeful and worried. 'Their wealth. And I don't know whether it is more courteous to choose the richer or the poorer.' She shrugged her delicate shoulders.

Gravely the three Queens murmured between themselves, then Ermengarda took the judgement on herself. 'If a poor man is well-bred and noble, then there would have to be a very good reason for a rich, noble-man to be chosen instead, rather than the poor, who needs the money this Lady would bring. Indeed, a Lady blessed with all attributes, including wealth, is very likely to be right for a poor man, especially as nothing is more painful for honourable people than to see other honest people in want. So it is laudable for a rich Lady to seek a poor but noble lover. One of the best pleasures of love is to provide for a lover's needs.

However, if the Lady herself lacks wealth, she had far better choose the rich lover. Otherwise, if both lovers find themselves in want, their constancy will be strained beyond bearing. Poverty is a shameful topic for all honest people; it leads to obsessions and to tormented nights that chase out love.'

The petitioner replied, 'I thank my Lady for her wisdom. And if the two men should be equal in all ways, including their homage to the Lady and their hopes to become her lover? Which one then should be chosen?'

Ermengarda didn't hesitate. 'Then he who asks first should win the Lady. Or if it so happens that they ask at the same moment, then the Lady is free to choose whomsoever of the two her heart desires more.'

Next, a young girl asked, 'Suppose a lady leaves her lover because she has married and the lover says she is behaving dishonourably to him.'

Aliénor replied. 'Marriage in no way interrupts or interferes with the right to love and be loved so the lover is right. Unless his Lady gives up love itself, she has no right to leave him.'

'And,' continued the same girl, 'is love a stronger feeling between lovers or between spouses?'

Aliénor responded to some whispering behind her and sat down graciously to allow Bèatriz, quiet but self-assured, twelve and single, to show what she had learned. 'Affection between spouses and true love are completely different and opposite in nature. The word 'love' should not therefore be used of the two relationships but merely confuses discussion. No comparison is possible of a situation where each has a bodily duty to the other and a situation where a joyous gift is made and where each strives to be worthy of the other.

On the other hand, one should not seek the love of someone whom one would be ashamed to marry. This would be dishonourable.' Bèatriz sat down again with an almost audible sigh of relief and was rewarded with a reassuring hand on her shoulder, a hand that her own stole up to touch lightly, a mere polite acknowledgement of a gentleman's service. The sort of touch that was allowed. The sort of touch that awakened womanhood, to burn its slow way into the light, sometimes in an hour, sometimes over years.

Another Lady, older. 'The lover of a Lady has been gone a long time, on an expedition Oltra mar. She has given up hope of seeing him again as have all those around her, so she seeks a new lover. But a friend of her first lover reacts violently to what he sees a betrayal. She argues with him, citing the fact that when a man dies, his Lady is allowed to love again after two years so why should this not be so in her case, after she has passed more years than that with no word. Which of them is right?'

Aliénor again. 'A Lady does not have the right to break off with her lover unless he has broken faith. This is even more the case when the lover is absent by necessity or for a reason that does him great honour. Nothing should make the Lady gladder than to receive news from far countries of her lover's prowess in battle. The fact that he has sent no messages is trivial in view of the great mission he accomplishes and it also shows his discretion for he is not willing to confide knowledge of their love to another.

True love is by its very nature secret and private, never to be spoken of to anyone other than the lover.' Estela enjoyed the whispers and exchanged glances around the Hall as known liaisons were highlighted with mere allusions and a knowing look. Then she flushed as she wondered if some of the knowing looks and allusions were directed at her.

A man this time, dragging one leg, whether for real or not, Estela couldn't say. 'A lover has lost an eye or a leg in brave combat. Is his Lady right to refuse him because she now finds him ugly?'

Ermengarda. 'Such a Lady has no honour in rejecting an infirmity which shows valour. In fact, true Ladies find such a man more desirable!' Amongst the usual rustle as Ermengarda sat again, Estela saw Peire lean across Aliénor and she half-heard, half read his lips before he bent to kiss Ermengarda's hand. 'I never thought I would regret having two legs and two eyes, my Lady.' His next words were hidden in the kiss but Aliénor laughed aloud and Ermengarda suddenly looked as young as Bèatriz, her face turned like a flower to the mischief brimming over beside her. Catching his eye, Guiraut smoothly changed places with Peire, paying court to Aliénor, who seemed to be enjoying the comedy on the Dais as much as that in the Hall.

Next. 'What presents should lovers give each other?'

Once more, Bèatriz plucked up confidence, reciting, 'A handkerchief, hair ribbons, a gold or silver coronet, a platter, a mirror, a belt, a purse, cords, a comb, embroidered sleeves, gloves, a ring, perfume, fastenings, are examples of appropriate presents between lovers.'

'And if the present is expensive, say, a horse or amour, and from a Lord, and a Knight has no need of it, how may he turn such a present down without offence?' This was beyond Bèatriz and she allowed Aliénor to replace her.

'In such a case, a knight or a Lady may say their thanks and ask the Lord to keep it in their care until such time as they should need it.'

Another Lady. 'Suppose a Knight of unquestioned honour, valiant in war, chivalrous at court, sans pareil in the musical arts, makes duets at night that lack all harmony and his lover is a drab from a ditch, it is surely the duty of any friend with honour to chase the drab back to her ditch and rescue the Knight from his false note. The drab of course thinks she can become a Lady by climbing on a man's horse and riding him to death.'

Estela blanched and then blazed with fury, restrained only by Sancha's firm grip on one arm and low murmur, 'Don't let her win. She's no-one. There's someone behind this.' Estela shook herself free but had already regained control and was thinking fast, one hand reassuring itself against the steel in her under-shift. Sancha was right; this woman was no different from all those who had preceded her, modest and well-attired, primed with her question, but this time by someone with a different and specific target. Amusing allusions were one thing; this was a crude and direct attack. Estela stood up at the same time as Ermengarda and the two women, united in their knowledge of a man who was not there, looked steadily at each other, over the head of the supposed petitioner. The silence in the Hall had changed; it scented blood now.

Cool as spring-water, Ermegarda spoke, 'We Queens have given many judgements, and have more to say, but you speak of music. I have three of the greatest troubadours to-be gracing this day with us.' She indicated the three youths behind her, all merriment wiped from their faces. 'But they will forgive me if I ask someone else's view for as a musician I know of none better qualified to speak, in the absence of my Lords Dragonetz and Marcabru.' The ripple at the name Dragonetz needed no explanation to Estela. She knew exactly what was being said and she conjured her mother's shade to keep the steel in her back and not turn to that in her skirts. Was this tribute or execution, Estela wondered briefly as she curtseyed and felt three hundred eyes prick her like a pincushion. Did Ermengarda trust her to deal with this or was she herself a 'friend of honour' who wanted to to see the ditch drab driven out?

'My Lords, my Ladies, my Good Dame,' Estela began, hoping her voice was free of vitriol. 'I think the petitioner confuses two issues in one here. To deal with them one at a time: There seems to be a complaint regarding dissonance in night music and yet we are told that the Knight is a perfect musician so how can this be? It can only be that the complainant's knowledge of music is inadequate and that she – it is 'she' I take it that you represent?' The figure gave an involuntary movement and Estela smiled to herself. That meant yes. 'She mistook the perfect fourths for an error. Is that not so?'

'I don't know,' was the muted response. Ermengarda's expression had the merest hint of a smile but it was enough to encourage Estela. She had been right; this was a mere messenger, spewing undigested filth. She understood nothing of music and nothing of her message, although she clearly knew it was meant to do harm. Whatever she'd been paid, it wasn't enough.

'And the second question has already been answered here today so I merely quote my Lady Ermengarda in brief. If the Lady you describe as a drab in a ditch is merely poor, but otherwise well-born and well-educated, in every way a suitable match for a marriage *it is laudable for a rich Knight to seek a poor but noble lover. One of the best pleasures of love is to provide for a lover's needs.'* She bowed her head towards Ermengarda in acknowledgement of the earlier judgement.

Sulky in defeat, the woman did try a last challenge. 'But is she well-born and well-educated and worthy of marriage?'

Now Estela smiled, clear and full at Ermengarda, who pronounced clearly, for the Hallfull to hear. 'Oh, yes, she is all of that, and much much more.' The Viscomtesse turned a less charitable stare on the woman kneeling before her. 'Tort-n'avetz, you are wrong,' she said, pronouncing each word separately, like a death sentence. Then, unexpectedly, she turned to Peire behind her. 'What do you think on this question of music?'

Ablaze with mischief, he came forward to stand beside her. He put a hand to his chin in the mummers' gesture of deep thought, he held his head as if the thinking hurt and then he pointed at the petitioner. Emphasising each word, in perfect mockery of Ermengarda's grave tones, he repeated 'You are wrong!' There was another silence throughout the Hall, no-one daring to react and then a sound few had heard pealed out. Ermengarda laughed out loud.

'Go home, old crow,' Estela heard Peire tell the kneeling woman, while relieved, embarrassed laughter broke out all round the Hall. 'Be grateful I don't pluck your feathers one by one and name them all in song.' As the woman hurried out, Estela was vaguely aware of

Sancha disappearing too, but her attention quickly returned to what was now an open debate, the three troubadours matching their wit against that of the three Queens for the entertainment of all. And as they set the Laws of Love, each outdid the other, to cries of appreciation from their audience. 'One can be loved by two people' pronounced Aliénor, to be capped by Guimaut with 'but one cannot have a liaison with two people at the same time.'

If Estela was ambivalent as to whether she'd wished Dragonetz there with her, she was definitely glad Arnaut wasn't! As it was, he was on duty and she didn't have to school her face in its reactions to the flow of Courtly Judgements. She too was weak with laughter. And if it looked like the fun was flagging, Peire only had to say, 'Tort-n'avetz' and waggle a finger at Ermengarda and the whole Hall held its sides with mirth. Everyone knew how fond the Lady was of the phrase and no-one had seen it used against her to such effect. And what's more, she was enjoying it.

The memory that had been nagging Estela finally surfaced. Bleakness of heart, night, a low-ceilinged house in the Jewish quarter, with Aliénor giggling like a toddler in a mud-pit. The Gyptian and some cards. What had Ermengarda been told? Something upsetting about a child. Then something about a lover and she, Estela, had thought it meant Dragonetz. Bleak-hearted, she had told him to go to hell. What had the Gyptian said? It was the words Tort-n'avetz that had sparked off the memory. Yes, that was it. 'Be happy in this, you shall know love, with one who sings and plays for you, my Lady Tort-n'avetz, My Lady 'You-are-wrong'. Not Dragonetz after all but Peire Rogier, who was leaving soon, thought Estela in amazement. It couldn't be, could it? And then she tried to remember what else had been said over those cards. What had she herself been told? She remembered that the Pathfinder brooch had blocked the woman's magic – or so she said.

At that moment there was stir in the Hall and a man pushed in, rushing up the rose path with Palace Guards chasing behind. Everyone thought it was all part of the show and there was only a slight dulling of the merriment. He didn't seem very merry though.

Two guards caught him roughly and were going to bundle him out when Ermengarda motioned them to wait and stand back. Unlike all the other supplicants of the day, the man was dressed as a peasant, a rough burlap tunic over woollen leggings probably knitted and just as badly darned by his wife. His garments were holed and dirty, his face bearded and smeared with travelling. What drew the eye first though was a recently cauterised stump where once his right hand had been, the sign of a thief.

'Tell us your petition and we will see whether there can be pardon on this auspicious day,' commanded Ermengarda, rendered magnanimous with pleasure.

Realisation hit Estela as the peasant opened his mouth. 'Gilles,' she breathed and moved leaden feet towards him, bruising past those in her way, as his words drew all laughter from the day.

'I seek Roxane de Montbrun,' began the deep voice with its local bur that had warmed her childhood. 'I was told to come here, that she calls herself Estela—'

'—de Matin,' said Estela, looking to Ermengarda in apology before raising him to his feet. On this day she had earned the right to such a gesture before asking permission. Close-up, the stump of his arm smelled of ash and roast pork. She felt sick. When she last saw him, his right arm had been a tree trunk. 'Gilles is my man,' she said, finding the shortest route to the truth. 'He saved my life. What has happened?' she asked him. *A Lady has no honour in rejecting an infirmity which shows valour.*

'After you left, I kept my head down, worked hard, but the Lady, your father's wife, was only biding her time. She accused me of theft and –' he held up what was left of his right forearm. No further explanation was needed. Ermengarda listened but said nothing. 'I was turned out.' Everyone knew that was a death sentence for a man disabled and branded a thief. 'I was told where to find you and to give you two messages. This is one.' He held up the arm again. 'She said you should have got the other message already.' His eyes were full of pride, as if she were still twelve and he were checking on her target practice. 'I didn't recognize you with your hair high and your fancy clothes. It does me good to see how well you're doing. I just wanted to see you once and then I'll be on my way.'

'No.' Estela looked to Ermengarda, her Liege Lord, hardly knowing what to ask her for. It was Peire who spoke. 'Such a day needs *someone* to be pardoned, my Lady.'

Me, thought Estela, may God forgive me for what this man has paid on my behalf. And already she was starting to realise what the other message had been, the one she had already received. She no longer tried to remember the Gyptian's prediction for her. The sight of Gilles' arm had been all it took to recall the words she wished she could forget again. *You drag other people in your wake, the highborn and the lowborn, and someone will not survive the knowing of you.* Yes, she had a very good idea what the other message had been. *Hurry home, Dragonetz, and stay safe,* she prayed.

Ermengarda said, 'Your man may take his place among the serving men in the Lower Hall. The Guards will see to him.'

'My Lady.' Estela recognised the tone and said no more. 'Gilles,' she instructed, 'I am glad you are here. I need a man and we will talk tomorrow.'

'What use is a manservant with no right hand,' someone sneered.

Gilles stood up, broad and patient. 'Just as well he's left-handed, that useless manservant,' he told the air. 'My Lady,' he bowed to all present and limped off between the Guards. Was it pity in Ermengarda's eyes as Estela too made her farewells and left? *Someone will not survive the knowing of you.* A message she had already received and not understood. But now she knew.

CHAPTER TWENTY

Estela opened the cloth, pulled out a loaf and two small rounds of goat cheese. She drew her dagger, sliced the loaf in two and passed a speared hunk to Gilles, then put a cheese on a broad leaf beside him. He sat with his back against the wind-sculpted oak that offered them shade and munched into the fare offered. Estela spread her fine skirts heedlessly on the parched ground and followed suit. 'No!' she told the great white dog questing titbits. Nici had latched onto Gilles with frenzied recognition, and been allowed to come with them out of the city, into the peace of the fields. The only sound was cicadas tuning up. Azure skies burned bright through the sheltering branches. Still chewing, she mumbled, 'How long since we did this?'

Gilles ruminated. 'Probably your father's wedding day.'

A hollow behind a wall. The prospect of best clothes and best manners, brushed hair and bruised heart. The woman who was to be her new mother. And Gilles, always there for her to run to, until even he was banned from the cage her life became. '*You are too old for that. A woman must... patati patata.*' 'What if we'd killed her then and there?'

'Costansa?' Gilles considered it. 'She was a pretty thing.' Estela grimaced. 'For all we knew she could have been the best thing to come into your life since your mother died. Tibau needed someone.' Tibau, her father. A shaggy black bear, whose rare hugs crushed all breath from his little blackbird. Whose hands were hard as bed-boards. Who saw no-one but Costansa from that day on. 'Your father chose the wrong knife, Roxie.'

'The one that glitters but is ill-forged,' Estela acknowledged. She watched him put his crust down so he could pick up the flask with his one arm and drink, deeply. He had to put the flask down again to wipe his mouth, this man who had taught her brother all he knew of stringing a bow, of sword thrust and tilting, of how a knight should conduct himself. And not just her brother. Thanks to Gilles, she not only had a dagger but she could use it. As could he. A whir as he pulled out his own weapon and stabbed it into the tree trunk.

'Hung for a murderer instead of this?' Gilles raised his blunted arm. 'No. But she'll shatter one day and I don't mind helping it happen.' He retrieved his knife and stuck it viciously back, lower down. 'The further away from her you are, the better.'

'How's Miquel?' Estela reached for the flask and took a draught of the watered wine herself.

'You know your brother.' Gilles' deeply wrinkled face was grim. 'He never could choose a knife. He thought if a pretty one smashed, he just chose the next prettiest and so on till he found one that didn't break. Which of course he did. So he never worked out that you could test the pretty one and prevent mistakes.'

'You didn't tell him?' A challenge rang in her tone.

'Not about knives, nor about Costansa. He wouldn't have believed it and if he'd come to resent me, the one thing I was good for was finished.'

'I was going to ask why you didn't leave. After I did.'

'As a runaway bondsman? That's no life. And yes, I thought I could protect Miquel but Costansa has drawn him too close.'

'Close enough for it to be my father who needs the protection?' *Sing for me, little blackbird. Her mother smiling encouragement. In better times, in times that were dead.*

'Maybe.' They took turns with the flask. 'He serves his turn in your father's bed. Forgive my coarseness.'

'Between us, there can be no coarseness. Only honesty. What happened, Gilles, after I left?'

'It went as we planned. After Mada told me she'd heard the mistress paying someone for your accident to-be, and I told you, and we did the swop. I took some of that lavender water you used, spilt it on your clothes that you'd given me and rubbed them on the ground every now and then, left a trail for the dogs. Dragged a shoe along at first for good measure then walked heavy footed, like I was some skulking bastard who'd got your body over his shoulder.' She reached out a hand and caressed the silken ear of the dog lolling beside her.

'I buried the clothes then, with some butcher's left-overs in them,' Estela winced. 'And made enough scraping and fresh-turned earth to suggest a dozen boar or something worse, to anyone looking for a buried body. Then I stomped away from the scene a bit, took my boots off, walked a bit barefoot and ran home. Your father couldn't track Toulouse's army, never mind find a slip of a girl. Next morning, as we expected there was a hullabaloo and I ran round with everyone else, only it was easier for me to act like I was worried about you because I was. Costansa's face was a picture between worrying that something had gone wrong and she'd be denounced for planning to kill you, and hoping that her man had gone ahead and done it. She'd told him she didn't want details so she could be more convincing when it happened. She even came with us, tracking with the dogs and of course, I took a little time but with some help from the dogs I found just the route poor little Roxie must have gone.'

'The first part of it, I did go!'

'That was one of the danger spots – making sure the hounds took the wrong trail with me but some dried pork scraps and a lot of enthusiasm and it was surprising how definite the dogs were about which was the right trail. So I gave out the story as I studied the tracks and we went along till we found the pile of dirt. The dogs started scrabbling and I left it to others to yell, 'There's something there' and all the obvious. I felt a bit bad for your father then, wondered what he felt when he thought his baby was about to be uncovered dead.' He shook his head.

'You don't have to tell me.' Estela's voice betrayed her. 'When he took his belt to me, he ended feeling. He sees some Roxie figment of his wife's imagination and I see nothing. Costansa's puppet.'

'So Costansa did some wailing and screaming and nearly fainted at the sight of bloody remains but I think she was disappointed there wasn't more there, so she still had this little doubt. Your father and Miquel were fully occupied dealing with Costansa and everything muddled its way back to the general agreement that you were dead, the body dug up and destroyed by wild animals, and we wouldn't find more evidence than that. People hardly noticed that Miquel kept saying that his dagger had been stolen but when they did, the view was that it must have been the criminal who'd taken Roxie. So far, so good. And according to Mada, Costansa had some kind of hold over the murderer so the payment would be her leaving him alone, and she didn't want to see him again afterwards. So that was fine. She assumed he'd kept his word and he was hardly going to come round shouting that it hadn't been him who'd killed you, now was he!

All was carrying on with only the usual ordinary nastiness when things changed, about three weeks ago. Your father grew grimmer again and I'd catch Costansa looking at me all the time, as if she'd figured something out. As if they'd had word you were alive.'

Guilt washed through her again as if she hadn't already known it was her fault. 'I know what happened. I had to give my real name to get married. Word must have got back.' And after they'd heard, Costansa had sent someone to Narbonne, someone who'd talked to a young man in a tavern, plied him with drink, found out the name of the girl who'd given him such a jewel. Someone who'd thought she truly cared about the youth and so they'd sent her a message. A mutilated corpse with his jewels in his dead hands. Someone who'd take instructions from Costansa but was capable of taking that sort of initiative. Her stomach lurched as she realised, from all Gilles had told her, who was the most likely person.

'Married,' Gilles stated, flatly, as if her being married was as ordinary as having fish on Fridays. In fact, it probably was.

'I'll tell you later. You first.'

'You've heard the rest. Costansa's usual trick – hide something, accusation of theft, this from your father.' Gilles gestured once more with his right arm and Estela instinctively felt for the scar on her shoulder. Branded as thieves, both of them, by the same injustice. 'And I was let go, with the message for you.'

'They hoped you'd frighten me, that I'd run away and that you'd die in a ditch.' As she might have done herself, as one-handed as Gilles, if she hadn't sung a song at dawn for Dragonetz. 'But I am not the Roxie of Costansa's imagination.'

'You're your mother's daughter,' Gilles told her, bringing a lump to her throat. 'So, your turn now. How did my little tomboy turn into a Great Lady and an Artist, who's allowed to go traipsing about the countryside with ne'er-do-wells just because she fancies it. Married.' He shook his head in amazement this time. 'And what, in the name of God, is this dog doing here?!'

And so she told him everything. Or almost. As the Court of Love decreed, *'No-one should be privy to the object of someone's love without a very urgent reason.'*

Sancha was waiting for her at the Palace and the moment Estela confirmed that Gilles could be trusted, she shared her discovery with both of them. Estela had almost forgotten about the vitriolic petition at the Court of Love until Sancha announced, with deep satisfaction. 'I tracked her down to one of those backstreet shops in the leather quarter. Husband's a shoemaker and wife a seamstress, open to diversifying her trade, I gather, including little missions between knights and Ladies. She's a good enough seamstress to act the honest woman and her job gives her access to all levels. She responded very positively to the suggestion that her trade would benefit from confiding in me the details of her latest commission.'

'Benefit as in continue at all,' Estela had taken Sancha's measure by now.

'Indeed,' the older woman acknowledged. 'A purse and a threat and the woman's bought and sold to the latest-come. She neither knows nor cares anything about the messages she carries but we have come to a very good understanding. We have a meeting tomorrow afternoon at our friend the seamstress' house, where we can enquire directly of her patron in person, the reason she tried to hurt you. I suspect we will find the same person was behind the broken glass too. Who knows? Maybe we've found our spy too, the informer behind the assassination attempts,'

'Do you have a name?' Estela held her breath.

'Oh, yes.' Sancha was grim. 'I have a name.'

Dragonetz knelt alone in the chapel, head resting on his hands, seeking guidance from the figure at the altar. He had wasted four precious days on eating, drinking and discussing Templar politics, none of which furthered his search. Peter Radels had once more tried to recruit him and the two commanders had tried to draw him on the subject of the next Crusade but there had been no evasions on their part, no signs of guilty consciences. It had been obvious that the leaders avoided any reference to Dragonetz' mill, suggesting that they knew that it was a paper mill, disapproved, and were too polite to say so. Hardly the behaviour of men involved in a conspiracy to kill him! They were far more concerned with the Pope's precarious situation, his relationship with Clairvaux and how this would affect the stability of their banking arrangements. Interesting as this was, it didn't help Dragonetz at all.

He was painfully conscious that he was leaving Aliénor and Estela exposed to the very murderer whose tracks he was hoping to spot, although he couldn't for the life of him understand why Estela should have been targeted. He, himself, and Aliénor had any number of political enemies but the smashed glass in the bathroom didn't fit. It was vicious without being an attempt at murder. Over and over, he organized the facts, going back to the first attempt on his life. A message to Arnaut with his Commander's password, instructing him to ignore the arbalestier on the road between Douzens and the Abbey at Fontfroid. The solitary assassin with crossbow attempting to kill Dragonetz himself, presumably, or just possibly Estela, or, even less likely, al-Hisba, and carrying safe pass from Aliénor. Someone in their entourage who could have overheard his password and gained a safe pass from Aliénor. Someone innocuous. Someone so much taken for granted he – or she – was invisible. It kept coming back to one of the Ladies but so far Sancha and Estela had found nothing. Whoever it was could only be a puppet and the most likely Puppet-master was Toulouse so where was the connection between a Lady and Toulouse? Dragonetz was a short ride from Carcassonne, in lands owing fealty to Toulouse. Perhaps a visit to Raimon in the walled city itself would open up new information. He felt he was close to something if only he could find the right questions,

'Can I help you, my son?' A brother with hair as white as his robes interrupted him gently.

Dragonetz smiled ruefully, rising to his feet. 'I fear no-one can.'

An earnest furrow crumpled the shiny round face as the priest sat on the hard bench and motioned Dragonetz to join him. 'In myself I am nothing but sometimes I am the vessel for something bigger. It hurts nothing to try.'

'It is more mortal help that I need,' Dragonetz told him gently. There was something in the other man's calm, in the set of his clasped hands, the open-ness of his expression that forbade mockery. This might be simplicity but it was no simpleton.

'Of course. Brother Hugues,' the man introduced himself. 'And you have no need of introduction. The whole Commanderie has been stirring with hopes that you will take the cloth and join the order, preparing for the next Crusade. You are the legendary Dragonetz los Pros.'

'I believe the song has grown somewhat in the singing,' Dragonetz laughed. 'And no, I am not here to become a Templar.'

'But you do have dreams?'

'Yes, I have dreams.'

Hugues hesitated, his gaze fixed on Christ crucified rather than on the man beside him. He was even older than Dragonetz had first thought, the newly-washed shine of the face misleading by a decade or more. The folds round eyes and mouth told a different story. 'I was a Crusader. This might shock you but I would be in no hurry to fight in the Holy Land again.'

Startled, Dragonetz looked at the serene profile. He didn't have to ask why. Anyone who had been on the Second Crusade had a thousand blood-red reasons to hold back from another such. 'But that's heresy,' he observed.

'Perhaps.' The tone remained calm. 'And perhaps today's heresy will be tomorrow's reason. It has been known. You see, my Lord Dragonetz,' he turned his mild unblinking gaze full on the visitor, 'I too have a dream. I have seen Jerusalem, I was there when we reclaimed it, and I could not find the Holy Place I sought. I fought the Muslim dogs and the Jewish dogs and it seemed to me that we were all fighting over the same bone. Worse, because more fragile than a bone, so we were destroying what we fought over, not reclaiming and cleansing it. Perhaps we will win next time, perhaps not, but I would like us to build our Jerusalem here, a land fit for Our Saviour, a heaven in the here and now. If Our Lord can be here with us, so can the Holy Land.'

'There will be another Crusade.' Dragonetz stated the inevitable.

'Yes. But, God willing, I will be too old to kill.' The ambiguity hung in the air. 'I have told you my dream, my Lord Dragonetz. What is yours?'

'Paper,' was the short, honest answer.

As if continuing a full exchange, Hugues commented, 'There are songs come from Cymru, the Welsh lands. Have you heard them?'

'Bleris,' Dragonetz nodded in recognition. 'I heard him at Poitiers. A strange accent but a true, sweet voice and his stories twist in the gut. Aliénor approved of him, sent token with him on his travels back north and to his own country. Tales of a King sit better in the west and north.'

'Arthur,' nodded Hugues, 'and his Queen and his knight Lancelot, a knight who dreamed.' Dragonetz said nothing. 'A knight who dreamed of finding the Holy Grail but for all his searching, saw no more than a vision.

Because in his heart, instead of the love of God, was the love of a woman.'

'My Quest is more earthly, Brother Hugues.' Dragonetz was still gentle, even as he resisted the one-sided conversation.

'So you said. But there are only two certainties in this world and we are alone for both of them but for our Faith. The time between birth and death is all about the Quest, whether we acknowledge this or not.' Dragonetz remained silent. 'The Moor used to talk of these things with me when he came to tend and collect herbs for his medicines.' It took Dragonetz a heartbeat to realise who the priest meant. 'I suppose he's back in al-Andalus now?'

Confused, Dragonetz replied, 'How could he go back? He is my bondsman. The Commander signed him to me.'

As gentle and implacable as Dragonetz had been, Hugues contradicted him. 'No, my Son. The Commander might have signed him to you, in good faith, but that was because the Moor himself allowed it. He was the third Moor to bring us his skills as part of the agreement for relinquishing the Afonso inheritance but I came to understand that he was no bondsman. He chose to place himself here and he served us well but he was always a Free Man and respected among his own people, whether those here knew it or not.'

'But you knew it.'

A humble nod. 'Certain information comes my way. It is the nature of my work but I am not always at liberty to disclose what I know.'

'Then what was al-Hisba doing here?'

Hugues' smile was slow and sweet. 'Is that what you call him? I think you must ask your Moorish Everyman for the answer.' He winced and rubbed his thighs. 'Stone and hard wood do me no favours these days.'

A week, Dragonetz had said he would take, then he could return to Narbonne and remove the question of al-Hisba from his unsolved mysteries. Two more days then. Time to go to Carcassonne. 'Brother

Hugues, I am wondering if I should visit the new Lord of Trencavel as I am so close but I am wary of the welcome likely to be given Aliénor's Commander. I hear things have changed since Roger died.'

'You mean that Carcassonne under Raimon has bowed to the nearer liege and Toulouse trumps Barcelone.'

'Exactly.'

'And the House of Toulouse holds no love for Dragonetz los Pros.'

'So it seems,' Dragonetz hesitated but what was there to lose? 'It seems the Comte de Toulouse might go so far as to wish me, personally, dead.'

'Of course,' was the strange reply.

'Of course?' Dragonetz queried.

'I told you I have been Oltra mar. My son, was there nothing you did there that lies heavy on your conscience, heavier than killing Infidels?' He searched Dragonetz' eyes, attempting to read their depths.

'Too much to confess, Brother, in a week of Sundays. Like you, I vowed obedience and like you, I did what a higher authority required of me.'

'Aliénor,' nodded the priest. Dragonetz let his face be stone and his eyes reflect nothing but the kindly, puzzled face quizzing him. Hugues sighed, gave up, returned to the question Dragonetz had asked. 'You are out of touch with Trencavel. He and a few other vassals went to pay allegiance to Toulouse a few weeks back and something happened. No-one knows what, but Trencavel came back changed. He will go to any lengths to stay within his new walls and avoid contact with Toulouse, and all talk of his daughter marrying young Raymond has stopped dead. He brought her back with him, quite ill.' Dragonetz' thoughts raced. That put Trencavel out of the picture for the puppeteer and although it made Carcassonne safer to visit, it also sounded less likely to offer results. To buy time and keep thinking, he prompted, 'Raimon's daughter?'

'Alis,' said Hugues, surprised. 'But you know her. She joined Aliénor's Ladies at Toulouse, where she'd been at Court for some months. And,' he was patient, as with some dull schoolboy, 'she was unofficially affianced to young Raymond until a couple of weeks ago.'

'Then there's no need for me to go to Carcassonne!' Dragonetz could have saddled the nearest horse and galloped back to Narbonne to test out his theory.

Hugues took his response at face value. 'Unless you want to see for yourself the relations between Carcassonne and Toulouse?'

'No, I believe you! That's been very very helpful.'

'My pleasure.' The priest stood, easing his stiff limbs back into use. 'You said paper,' he stated slowly.

'Yes.'

'I hear many things in my work, tending to the sick. Even the rich get sick. Even God's workers get sick and speak out in fevers. Give up paper, my son. This Quest is beyond you. Paper is Muslim temptation, the work of the Devil corrupting Christian tradition. Imagine scribes being unnecessary, the Church cast to one side and people writing as and when they wish! This way lies chaos!' Earnest brown eyes fixed Dragonetz.

'Do you believe this?' he countered.

The eyes didn't falter. 'What I think is worth less than the husk of an ear of corn. I am a little man who talked about herbs with the man you call al-Hisba. I belong to the Church and I have made my vows. My Church has a view about this new development of paper and the changes it will bring, and so it is. But I warn you it is not just about trade and competition. It is deep-rooted hatred of this heresy. Powerful men will finish you, my Lord Dragonetz. Very powerful men will protect this land from the heresy of paper and if you stand in their way, they will think nothing of protecting the world from you too. Think about what I've said. Find a Quest worthy of you.'

'You won't see Jersualem built here in your life-time,' Dragonetz observed. 'Will you give up laying the foundations?'

Hugues didn't need to reply. 'I am sorry. You carry such a weight on your conscience.'

'You tried,' Dragonetz assured him. 'And you have helped me much more than you know.' Dragonetz watched the stooping figure shamble his anonymous way out of the chapel. This was no little man. And as for the man Dragonetz called al-Hisba? Hugues then had another name for him. If the Moor had given his name to this Brother, that was no ordinary discussion of herbs between them. One more mystery to take back to Narbonne. Dragonetz whirled into action, rounded up his followers, organised packs, mounts and curtailed farewells, and was pounding dust up the trail back to Narbonne, cursing the slowness of hacks and wishing he had his own Seda beneath him once more.

CHAPTER TWENTY-ONE

stela closed the door firmly behind the figure that swished her silk skirts into the room, then blocked it with her own body. 'Alis,' she said, wondering how she had not known.

All colour left the pale girl's face and Sancha nodded, then ran her hands over the slight form, checking for weapons. Estela was conscious of her own dagger but Alis carried nothing. 'Sit down.' Sancha indicated a stool and Alis sat. 'You may leave now,' she told the neat, curious seamstress who scurried out, hiding her face from the poisonous looks thrown her way.

'Ladies,' Alis greeted them, wand-thin and straight-backed, dignified despite the green tinge to her face.

Estela's professional response was instinctive; red meat to restore colour and garlic to fight demons. Her sympathy must have showed as she caught a sharp look from Sancha, who opened their planned interrogation. 'Let's not waste time. We know you paid this woman to drag my Lady Estela's name through the mud in public.'

Alis made to stand up, shrugging the delicate shoulders, from which her gown hung in loose folds. 'She's used to being dragged through the mud.' The sharp little voice was more like the Alis Estela had heard a hundred times, telling her stories of hangings and omens. Sancha pushed the girl back down onto the stool. She barely needed to touch her. It was as if she couldn't really touch her. There was no more physical resistance than in a cushion. Estela had the impression that someone could have punched or kicked this silk cushion and it would have taken on the shape it was pushed into. She felt confused. Was this the enemy?

Sancha too seemed to be holding back more, cool in her questioning.

'We know everything.'

'Then I can leave.' But this time Alis stayed still, waiting, only her sarcasm showing what spirit she had left. A creature clinging to frail spite.

'You have tried to harm Estela before, with broken glass.' Alis' smile was confirmation enough. 'You knew the Queen was with child and you, one of her trusted Ladies, had the Queen's glass dosed with herbs that would endanger her baby – that isn't just malice, that's treason.'

'Alis the Malice,' the girl half-sang dreamily. 'Why would I do such a thing?'

'That,' Sancha was grim again, 'is what we are trying to find out. Let's start with the easy bit. Why are you trying to harm my Lady Estela? She has done you no harm.'

Blue eyes opened wide, guileless and empty and in that same sing-song tone, Alis chanted, 'Her father loved her dearly, her mother called her sweeting.'

'But,' Estela interrupted.

Sancha shook her head and mouthed, 'This isn't about you.'

'Long hair, long gold hair, daddy's little angel, full of promise,' then her eyes flashed and, with bile in her voice, 'Promises!' She seemed to focus on them once more, or rather on Estela, and there was no mistaking the hatred in her eyes. Why?

Estela instinctively shut her eyes and there it was, the precise mixture of musk and hate, a false apology after kicking her when she had first joined Aliénor's company; the same scent and spite amid her triumphant début at the banquet.

'I'll tell you why.' Gobbets of spittle flecked Alis' rosebud mouth as she spat the words at Estela. 'You have it all, don't you! With your looks and your talent! Married! Free! Who wouldn't hate you! Taking you down a peg would have been a pleasure but no! Your knight came riding to rescue you!' Her laughter was a blade run along an open wound.

'But,' Estela tried again, unable to describe the loveless mess her life had been until Dragonetz came into it. Then it struck her. 'But how could you feel like this when you first saw me?' For she knew it was true. The dainty boot had been a statement of intent, against a stranger found in a ditch. It made no sense.

The blue eyes mocked. 'As if you don't know. As if you didn't see the way he looked at you.' Estela's stomach lurched. She hadn't seen. She hadn't known. Was that too there from the start? 'No-one has ever looked at me like that. And now no-one ever will.'

She turned to Sancha who listened, impassive. 'Why should she have him? He didn't even notice me! The chivalrous knight rescues the Lady! Well, it only seems to work for some Ladies. Her sort of Lady. You have no idea what it's like!'

Estela winced but Sancha just replied, 'More than you think. And the Queen?'

'Why would I do such a thing? I have a secure place amongst Aliénor's Ladies. Why would I risk that?'

Suddenly Estela had had enough. She felt sick herself, as if green worms lived in her most precious memories, eating them away. 'Look at her,' she told Sancha. 'She can barely hold herself together. Forget the other things. She's not capable of that. She's probably telling the truth about the Queen. There's no grand plan here, just petty spite turned vicious.' She addressed Alis. 'I'm sorry for you and you're ill. I don't know what you've been taking but you need help. I have herbs that could help.'

The girl flinched from Estela's pity as if lashed. 'Keep your herbs. It was probably you that dosed the Queen!' Then, retreating once more into her own world, she murmured to herself, 'Too late now, too late.'

Sancha looked a question at Estela, who nodded. 'Let her go. She is her own worst enemy now. She can't be helped unless she seeks it.'

Sancha stood back to make it clear to Alis that she was free to leave but she warned her, 'Any act against Estela, so much as one word, and Aliénor shall know all this sorry history and you can forget your secure post then.'

Alis smiled, singing to herself as she tripped down the steep staircase, ignoring the seamstress and ignoring Gilles, who had defied orders to wait at the end of the street and was passing the time of day with the cobbler, one eye and ear for noises upstairs, his one hand always at his mistress' service.

No-one followed Alis, who click-clacked along the cobbled streets, past Ermengarda's Palace and on to that of the Archbishop, who was expecting her.

Pierre d'Anduze, Archbishop of Narbonne, was used to making difficult decisions. As Papal Nuncio he had the direct authority of the Pope to make those decisions and of course the Pope had direct authority from on high, God being reinforced by the more earthly connection of Bernard de Clairvaux and the entire order of Cistercians. The Pisan-born priest now known as Pope Eugene III had become the first Cistercian to achieve such greatness and, as a former disciple of Bernard of Clairvaux, was only too willing to lend his office to Clairvaux' direction.

The little matter in hand for the Archbishop of Narbonne this afternoon was a mere irritant compared with his delicate negotiations with the King of Sicily, which would shake the Western World and return the Pope to Rome, and of course also return some of the status to the Archbishop from the cursed Cistercians. There were certainly disadvantages to the appointment of a genuine innocent to the Papal throne, as Clairvaux himself had complained at the time, but needs must use those very qualities to advantage – as Clairvaux too had decided.

The Cistercian must be champing at the bit over the Pope's warm support for Aliénor's marriage. But for Eugene, the accusations of consanguinity would have won out and Clairvaux would have been rid of the whore. Not that a whore as Queen caused problems; a powerful, intelligent whore was another matter. He should know. He had another such in the neighbouring palace, chafing his daily duties, the whore to whom his brother had sold the family respectability in a marriage that mocked God daily.

A slight figure was escorted into the gloom of the side-chapel where he waited. He was too accustomed to the saints watching his movements to recognise the irony of Saint Brigit in her niche, offering a reminder of charity to all women. He sighed again, thinking back over the private message he had received that very morning from the Comte de Toulouse, and motioned his young acolyte to bring the girl to him. The mess was never-ending and not of his making, although he had to clear it up. He had of course made sure the messenger was dealt with but he did so hate the inefficiency of all this.

'Father,' she curtseyed low. 'I have sinned.'

If the acolyte was surprised at the Prelate hearing confession himself from someone who by her dress was clearly one of the Palace women lambasted regularly from the Pulpit, he gave no sign but bowed silently and left them. It was common for confession to be taken with Priest and penitent side by side on a bench, like this, rather than screened, and no-one would have been surprised to see the young golden head bowed and tears falling while the old man beside her nodded sagely. Their words however might have aroused a different reaction.

'I have tried to do everything the Comte asked,' Alis was saying. Her voice faltering slightly on 'everything'.

The Archbishop had a fair idea of what 'everything' might involve.

'I am sure you tried your best,' he reassured her.

'It wasn't my fault that someone saved Dragonetz from the cross-bow. I did everything to make it work. I hired the man at Toulouse before we left, I put the safe pass in with documents Aliénor was signing for the Master at Douzens and then gave it to him afterwards.

I sent the message with the password to Arnaut. That was easy enough to get – I might as well have been invisible round the camp! And it was all for nothing. Nothing!'

'You were remarkably clever, my dear. I'm sure the young Comte de Toulouse understands,' he soothed. To judge by the message he had received that morning, the young Comte de Toulouse understood completely. And so did he.

'You don't know him.' Alis' fear was rancid in the air and d'Anduze fought the urge to cover his nose with the fine lawn of his handkerchief. 'I put the belladonna in the water. It should have killed him!'

'Another unhappy accident spoilt your good work. I know, I was there, you remember.'

'Yes, Father, and without your encouragement I should have taken my life there and then. But Raymond told me you would be at my side.'

'Indeed, indeed. As I am now.' The deep voice conveyed the security of stone foundations, the love of the father. Alis trusted fatherly love.

Alis' voice sank to a whisper. 'I tried to kill the baby.'

Like the grand chapel bell, the Archbishop's voice rang with assurance. 'We live in the world and must sometimes do things that are not of God, for the greater good.' *And the real sin, my dear, was that you failed. Not once but in everything.* He smiled at her.

'I don't know what to do,' she confessed. 'Two of the Ladies are suspicious, Sancha and that whore of Dragonetz' but I've played dumb for all but the pranks.'

'What pranks?' He saw straight away that the sharpness was a mistake and he put it right, smoothing the question. 'For a minute I thought you had betrayed us but of course you mean girlish pranks.'

'Exactly,' she sweated relief. 'But it made them curious about other things. It's not safe any more for me to try again. And anyway,' her voice was blank with despair, 'I don't know what to try.'

'Well now, you wipe up those tears because I have the answer.'

She dabbed damp hands across her smeared face, hope lighting her eyes. 'You do?'

'I believe so.' He gave his most benevolent smile. 'I think it is time for me to take over. You were given a burden too heavy for you and I can't watch it burying you so it is time for you to let go. I will look after everything. All you have to do is forget about it.' He gave his most benevolent smile and moved his hands in benediction as he offered formal absolution.

'Is there hope for me, Father?' Her upraised face reminded him of a snowdrop on its fragile stalk. When she opened her eyes, they shone with a vestige of the girl she once had been.

'Of course, my child.' He fed on her gratitude, a welcome reward for his priestly duties, and, as soon as she had been escorted out by the priest who'd responded to the little bell, he ordered incense to be shaken to remove the smell.

He had spoken the exact truth. He would now deal with every-thing and Alis would indeed forget all about it. That, he could ensure. He then summoned a mercenary in his pay, leader of a small band who had earned his displeasure for failing on a previous job and who would make every effort to ensure he was satisfied this time. And the next. And he could give the reward due for the morning's work at the same time.

Travel-stained and sweat-streaked, Dragonetz waited for private audience with Aliénor, noting the bustle of servants as they carried crates and bundles from the Queen's chambers out of the Palace. The return to Paris was then imminent and his revelation all the more urgent. If he was right, Aliénor would travel with one less Lady-in-waiting than she had arrived with. Two less, if you counted Estela.

His chest constricted by irrational panic, Dragonetz wasted no more than a quick obeisance to the Queen before demanding, 'I need to see Lady Alis, Trencavel's daughter. I think she arranged the attempts against us.'

Aliénor's usually mobile face didn't change. Not a flicker of shock, not even surprise at the betrayal Dragonetz was revealing. Her words were slow, measured as if she and Dragonetz were living at a different pace. Where Aliénor lived, time no longer mattered. The tightness in his chest increased as Dragonetz listened to Aliénor's words. 'You can see the Lady Alis. She is in her bedchamber. And I believe you are right about her trafficking. For Toulouse, I suppose?'

'Yes. She spent a long time there before she joined our company. Rumour has it that she was his paramour and expected marriage, that he

treated her unkindly. I don't know why I didn't see it sooner!'

Aliénor shrugged, smoothing the folds of damask over her ever-growing belly. 'Her uncle was ever strong against Toulouse, her father requested a place for her among our Ladies and we must always draw such people close about us. I learned much that was useful from her. But it seems Toulouse drew her closer and her father's allegiance was not as his brother's.'

'He is a weaker man than Roger was, more grateful for the legacy of thick walls his brother has left him than for the legacy of defying Toulouse. I think there is more to it, some hold that Toulouse has over Trencavel and his daughter. That's why I want to talk to her.' And to find out exactly why Toulouse wanted him, personally, dead, not just because he was Aliénor's Commander.

'That won't help you.' Still that same slow tone. 'She's dead. She killed herself yesterday. She's laid out in her chamber before burial tomorrow morning. So we have what amounts to an admission of guilt but you won't get any more answers.'

Dragonetz felt time slow for him too. 'I will see her all the same,' he decided.

'Be warned. Lady Sancha and Lady Estela are keeping vigil. They believe it is their doing. That they pushed a fragile mind over the edge with their questioning. They met with her yesterday, forced her to admit to petty misdemeanours against Estela and they think she feared they would catch up with her for the bigger crimes. She left them, went to her Chamber and stabbed herself. They have taken it very badly. Tread gently.'

Teeth set, Dragonetz steeled his weary body and brain to its task.

There was no reason to look at a corpse, no reason to face another death that was his responsibility. If Sancha and Estela had not been tracking the infamous spy for him, they would never have taken things so far. He could go and bathe, change his clothes, emerge after the burial. His feet followed the page boy who led him to the open door of a bedchamber. He paused on the threshold, looking in.

Pale blonde hair, brushed to silk, flowed over a brocade cushion and onto the bed linen underneath the fine blue stuff of Alis' gown, a new gown showing no tears, just a reddening around her breast from the wound beneath. She had been prepared tenderly for viewing, her face coloured with pink on cheeks and lips belying the chalk-white skin. In eternal repose, her face was childish, too thin for the curves of infancy but exuding innocence, enhanced by the blue robe, a white angel in Mary's colours.

Dragonetz entered the room. In the silence that seemed to spread from the corpse herself, sat Estela and Sancha, hands clasped, each deep in her own thoughts. Neither stood when they saw Dragonetz but their eyes gave him subdued welcome. Death makes criminals of the living, life itself a crime, and all its pleasures guilty. Especially such a death. Dragonetz crossed himself and quietly broke the silence.

'I have spoken with Aliénor. I found a connection between Toulouse and Lady Alis.' Somehow it seemed respectful to call her by her full title. 'It seems that her conscience was too heavy.' Where had he heard that recently, and not of Lady Alis? 'You can't blame yourselves.'

Estela turned huge red eyes on her lover. 'We don't,' she told him.

Confused, he waited and it was Sancha who explained. 'A servant found her and brought word to Ermengarda and Aliénor. The Queen defied the demands that she be thrown into an unmarked grave straight away and decreed that she was still a Lady and her friends had the right to mourn her, whatever the Church laws on suicide. The Archbishop is blazing but Aliénor won twenty-four hours. We asked to prepare her body, thinking we owed her that. Estela got fresh clothes, took off the old ones. They were already sticking to her body where the blood had pooled, on her chest and on her back.'

Dragonetz was quick. 'On her back,' confirmed Estela. 'I already wondered why a woman in despair would buy new hair ribbons.' She opened her hands to show scarlet satin ribbons. 'She didn't have these when she met with us so she must have stopped to purchase them before returning to the Palace.' She shrugged. 'And the dress she died in was green. She wasn't planning to wear the ribbons with that dress. I washed the blood from her and knew for sure. There was a deep wound in her back as well as the one in her chest. She didn't have a dagger either when we met her.'

'We searched,' agreed Sancha briefly.

'I think she was stabbed from behind, with either a sword or a dagger, then someone made it look like she'd killed herself, stabbing her chest and placing the dagger in her hands.'

'Why?' Dragonetz mused aloud, accepting instantly the facts Estela had given him.

'Who?' Sancha responded. 'We are worse off than before we realised what Alis had done!'

'She has paid.'

'You haven't told Aliénor that it was murder?' Dragonetz asked.

'We have talked about it for hours. You didn't hear the exchange between Aliénor and the Archbishop! It seems that Alis made confession with one of his Priests after she left us and although he cannot break the secret of the confessional, he has said that she was agitated and depressed, that he is not surprised by her carrying out an act against God, despite his counsels.'

'So she confessed, on the verge of suicide, then bought hair ribbons!'

'The Archbishop has declared it suicide.'

'But the wound in her back is a fact!'

'A fact that would pit Aliénor against the Archbishop,' observed Sancha. 'Aliénor is returning to Paris, where she is the irritating wife of the King, not the loved Duchesse d'Aquitaine, where Suger and Clairvaux will pounce on any opportunity to diminish what little power she can wield there. Add the Papal Nuncio to her enemies? I think not. She has already braved his fury to gain a day for goodbyes, a day's respect.'

'And then tomorrow, the ditch lies open for her.' Estela's eyes filled again. 'She envied me even my ditch. And now that is all she will have.'

Dragonetz knew the church laws regarding suicide. Everyone did. An earth hole outside the city wall, with at best a wooden marker declaring the inmate unclean, doomed to damnation. 'Her father?' he asked.

'Word went yesterday.' They must have crossed on the road, Dragonetz realised. 'But the Archbishop is adamant that this charade as he calls it, finishes tomorrow morning, regardless of whether her people come or not. And he will not let them take her body for fear they give a Christian burial.'

'You should hear him! I think he has sermons for months on demons disguised as women, on God's mercy misdirected – he's enjoying himself!'

'Then there's nothing we can do?' Dragonetz was surprised to hear his own words and to know their desperate sad truth.

'We can pray for her,' said Sancha. 'And then we can find out who did this.' In silence, Dragonetz took his place beside them, for another long vigil, and if his eyelids drooped and he slipped into sleep, his dreams kept fitting company for a corpse.

No-one was surprised at the absence of Lady Alis' family the following morning when a scattering of Aliénor's followers witnessed the girl's body dumped like a rabid dog. To be there was guilt by association with one of the worst crimes against God, taking your own life. It was expected that Alis' name be erased from the book of Trencavel and from all conversations in Carcassonne, as if she had never existed.

This did not prevent a wagon stopping outside the walls of Narbonne that night, well after curfew, by the fresh mound of earth.

Two men with shovels dug up the body and the man directing them jumped off his horse, swaddled the dead girl in white linen, like a baby, and lifted her into the covered vehicle. A well-paid guard called no alarum from the Watch-tower but observed the cart being driven back along the road it had come, away from Narbonne and back to Carcassonne.

Raimon Trencavel swore through his tears that he was finished playing the beetle under the feet of great Lords. Toulouse would not crush another of his children in this game of Kingdoms, nor would Barcelone back him into a corner. He would out-think them as long as he could but if it came to it, he would say no and die a man, never again what he had been in that torture chamber where he had said nothing, while a sweet girl's life hung with her body. He had made the wrong decision. Trencavel dashed the tears from his eyes as he rode through the night, slowed by the burden dragging always behind him.

Now that she knew Dragonetz was staying in Narbonne, Estela could watch the preparation for Aliénor's departure with equanimity. Their reunion the night of Alis' burial had started with exhausted sleep in each other's arms and woken them to healing pleasures. Luckily daytime brought physical constraints and time to talk, to hear about Douzens and tell of Peire's murder and Gilles.

'You don't know what it's like to be responsible for something so terrible,' she told him.

'I do know,' he replied and wrapped her in his arms, giving her love's absolution. Alis had been right to hate her. She did wrong and her punishment was this man in her life, this miracle. It was unjust.

Somewhere between kisses and sleep, Dragonetz remembered something, some mystery about al-Hisba that he wanted to follow up. 'He's been staying out at the mill,' Estela told him. 'He said he would be unavailable for music for a few days.' As it was all too much trouble to leave the Palace and go to the mill, Dragonetz put it out of mind for the moment. For the extremely consuming moment. Somewhere between kisses and sleep, Estela remembered how oddly Arnaut had been behaving and wondered whether she should mention it to Dragonetz, but she decided it would be embarrassing for her friend and better left to heal itself. There was talk of Toulouse and plots but they had no new ideas and nothing happened.

Both Estela and Dragonetz were in the Great Hall, among Ermengarda's courtiers, for the formal farewell to Aliénor and her company. With surprisingly little awkwardness, Aliénor had informed her troops that Dragonetz was staying in Narbonne and instructed Arnaut to continue in charge until her new Commander arrived to take over. Her one petty act of revenge for his desertion was to withhold the name of his replacement from Dragonetz, who stood impassive at Estela's side, ready to officially start his new life as a Narbonnais landowner. He no longer tried to hide his relationship with Estela nor did he flaunt it. The simple rightness of their partnership flowed between them though they never touched in public. Quickly understanding what Estela had not told him during their picnic, Gilles had been very quiet after Dragonetz' return but still dogged Estela's footsteps, retreating to the servants' quarters only when completely sure his mistress was in good care. Nici definitely qualified as good care but it took a few days, and several inquests in the servants' quarters over a jug too many of wine, before Gilles finally gave his judgement on Dragonetz: 'Well-tempered. No doubt you think he's pretty too.' Estela had just smiled but there was relief in it. She owed Gilles too much to fall out over her lover but woe betide anyone who tried to part them now. That included Arnaut, who still kept his distance and showed no sign of making so much as a polite goodbye speech to her. Ignoring the guilty ache, she told herself it was for the best. He would be on the road soon, heading for Paris.

It was therefore with a feeling of security that Estela watched the new Commander stride into the Great Hall, tall in his own right, bulky with greaves and breastplate, greying hair and black eyes, swarthy skin and a scowl, all visible beneath his mail coif. Bowing to

Aliénor and Ermengarda as best his armour allowed, he begged their excuses for a personal moment and stomped directly towards Estela, removing his gauntlets as he walked. He didn't walk round people, he walked through them and stopped in front of Estela. She felt the swoosh of air as a mailed glove smashed across Dragonetz' mouth, leaving a trail of blood. He wiped his mouth, rigid and silent, as he had been throughout.

'Not even man enough to take the challenge,' the stranger sneered. 'Not even a little Dragon but a puppy who squeals 'enough' and abandons his liege lord to play with – what is the boy playing with this time?' He glared at Estela 'This the latest whore is it? One in a long line,' he told her, 'and not the last, believe me.'

Estela flushed and waited for the eruption from her knight, which didn't come. Pale but controlled, he finally spoke. 'My Lady Estela, allow me to present my esteemed father, Dragon de Ruffec. I gather my mother has been nagging him about my refusal to marry. This is his way of expressing himself.' This time Dragonetz caught the hand swinging again for his mouth and held it firmly, in mid-air, sinews bulging in both men's arms. The older man was breathing heavily, as red as Dragonetz was pale. 'Father, may I present to you the celebrated musician of the court of Narbonne, my Lady Estela de Matin, protégée of Queen Aliénor. Sire,' he pointed out politely, as if their hands were not locked in struggle, 'it is considered discourteous in this court to strike a father – or a woman.'

The Baron's hand dropped as Dragonetz released it. 'I wasn't going to hit her!'

'Your charm with the fair sex is unparalleled.' Dragonetz swept a mocking bow to his progenitor.

'Just because I don't have your fancy ways and nickname.' Estela flinched, half expecting a fist to really come her way as Dragon made her a passable bow and stated in his gruff voice, 'Misunderstanding.'

'That's an apology.' Dragonetz translated.

'For her, maybe. For you, I wish I'd used the back of my hand more when you were smaller and I wouldn't have to put up with you now.'

'And my mother is well, I take it?' Dragonetz' mouth was already beginning to swell and Estela wondered where her arnica balm was. People in the Hall had started talking again now it looked unlikely that breathing fire would progress to full dragon-fight and there was a growing restlessness near the Queen, who was after all waiting to take ceremonial leave of the Court of Narbonne.

As if suddenly aware of this, Dragon answered shortly, 'I'd have told you otherwise, before I hit you. Ride away with me so we can talk.' He read his son's eyes. 'I know. You're staying here. I really mean it, just ride a short way with me.'

'I'll catch you up.' Dragonetz agreed as his father returned to duty and with due ceremony, and somewhat jarring fanfares, escorted Aliénor from the Hall, with all her company. Tall enough to carry the extra breadth to her frame and barely show it, Aliénor shared a farewell embrace with her sister ruler, an embrace longer than was required by protocol. Estela had only a faint notion of the world Aliénor was going to, a Frankish country where women had no rights, where the men and the weather were equally cold. Whatever the weaknesses of this Queen, she had mettle and it was thanks to her judgement and her passion for music that Estela was alive and not dead in a ditch. There but for the grace of God. She shivered as a ghost with a name walked over her grave.

'Sweet,' Dragonetz was saying softly.

'I know,' she told him. 'You'll ride with them a way. You'll come back?' She searched his eyes.

'Half a day. No more.'

'You have an interesting relationship with your father,' she observed.

'He worries about me.' He smiled. 'My mother's the tough one.'

'I worry about you too,' she told him.

'Don't,' he told her. 'You're a match for my mother.' He kissed her hand and disappeared, as adept as his father at making his way through a crowd but rather more subtle.

CHAPTER TWENTY-TWO

Pierre d'Anduze shook his head at the effrontery of the man being escorted to his private ante-chamber. He had thought to intimidate him by having him led past the Christian treasures of the Archbishop's Palace, the jewelled triptych and gilt paintings from Byzantium, the silver chalice large enough for two hundred to partake of the Blood of the Lord, the great brass incense shakers and marble plinths. The man showed no sign of being anywhere unusual. He trod his usual calm pace as if this world was an illusion and his current surroundings equal to the mud hut where no doubt he had been born.

It was true that the Palace building was not as impressive as its contents and the Archbishop promised himself that the Glory of God would be better served in the future. He was pleased with the statue of Charlemagne in the new cloisters, not least because this representation of Narbonne's mythical founder bore a marked resemblance to d'Anduze himself. His architects were already offering him plans for the Great Archbishop's Palace that would one day grace Narbonne thanks to the careful management of wealth which was d'Anduze's talent.

And this robed servant approaching, insulting him with his

covered head, was necessary to the careful management of wealth and the eradication of the devil's work. He sighed. The tools were not always worthy of God's work but he had to make do with what was available. The Commander of the Brothers Templar at Douzens had assured him that this man had given loyal service throughout his years there. He put aside the urge to cover his delicate nose from the smell of a brown skin and smiled benignly.

'Be seated, al-Hisba.'

There was no answering smile and the Archbishop wasn't in the mood to waste time on a nobody. 'There is no need for lengthy discussion. We have spoken of it often enough and the Brothers Templar assured me of your good faith to do God's work.'

'I do indeed do God's work,' the turbaned moor answered gravely. Somehow, coming from his lips, the words didn't sound reassuring.

'It would have been easier if you had allowed our problem to disappear.'

Al-Hisba nodded his understanding. 'I am a physician. It is not permitted to me to kill nor to let someone die.' The Archbishop winced at this crude expression of his meaning. He did not want a theological debate on the Ten Commandments at this juncture.

'Quite so. But you accept the necessity to solve our problem another way.'

Al-Hisba folded his arms, hiding his hands up his sleeves for all the world as if he would produce a dozen knives and juggle with them. 'If there is no other way.'

'There is no other way.' Silence built layers of mistrust between them. The Archbishop skated across it. 'It must be now. Today. Directly. We have waited long enough.'

'So be it. I go directly from you to set fire to Lord Dragonetz' paper mill and burn it to the ground, ensuring that nothing remains of his venture. Then you inform the Brothers Templar that I have carried out a mission of great importance for the Church and you have personally granted my freedom, to return to al-Andalus, safely far from Narbonne.' The Archbishop flushed crimson. The man was a savage!

How dare he speak to him, the Archbishop, in such a fashion! Some matters were better left unsaid as any civilised man would know. He controlled himself, remembering why it was important that al-Hisba carried out his orders straight away, remembering the orders given to his mercenaries two days earlier.

'Yes,' he said.

The man didn't know when to leave well enough alone. 'And the men who work there? And Lord Dragonetz himself should he be there?'

The Archbishop waved a fat, be-ringed hand. 'I am sure you will devise something that allows you to do only what is permitted.' He indulged in a sarcastic edge but there was no reaction. The Moor put his hands together and bowed his head in the slavish manner of his kind, and left, barely allowing the Archbishop time to summons an acolyte to escort the man out.

D'Anduze felt much better after he had sent two message-boys; one to the mercenary leader and one to my Lord Dragonetz los Pros. He twisted his large signet ring, musing on how much Raymond de Toulouse owed him and how pleasurable it would be to collect his dues.

The late afternoon sun glinted on Estela's Pathfinder brooch and she turned to avoid the glare, gazing absent-mindedly across the Palace Courtyard. Dragonetz was due back and her heart hung on every movement at the gate. She had tried passing the time more constructively but she lacked patience with Bèatriz and had excused herself before she drove the girl to tears. It was especially unfair as the young heiress of Dia had fast become Estela's equal and her lyrics, like their composer, had lost their girlish awkwardness, pricking Estela to envy. She knew she could find the songs within herself but so far what had she done? Only the songs of others. When things were settled, the songs would come, she promised herself. When Dragonetz was back to stay. She gave up all pretence of activity and waited, watching.

Her eyes registered the anomaly before her brain as she watched a robed, turbaned figure riding out the gates. Al-Hisba had said he would be at the paper mill and had certainly been absent from the farewell ceremony. What was he doing in Narbonne? Was something wrong at the paper mill? Had he been looking for Dragonetz? The Pathfinder rune glinted again, pointing her wayward imagination to action. Better to find out what the problem was, and perhaps help solve it, than agonise here for every minute waiting. For all she knew, Dragonetz had accompanied the party further and was spending a night with his father, knowing she'd understand. In the time it took to change to riding boots and send for Gilles, Estela was heading to the stables, too pent up to feel the usual lurch associated with the place.

That's when she had a second jolt. Grim and busy, Arnaut was giving orders to a handful of Dragonetz' men, looking more set-faced if anything when he saw Estela.

'My Lady,' he said curtly.

'I thought you were gone with Aliénor's company,' she blurted out, too surprised to be tactful.

'Sorry to disappoint you but my Lord Dragon detailed a group to remain with my Lord Dragonetz los Pros. Unfortunately I am one of them, along with my father.'

Rue, thought Estela, and a posy of pansies, but she could not find words to work the healing needed. 'And Dragonetz in this?'

'Had no say in the matter.'

She hesitated but she had to try. 'I am sure he would have only your best interests at heart.'

'As always. If you'll excuse me, my Lady, there is work to do re-organising our accommodation when we have settled horse and pack. I take it you're riding?'

She searched his face for the times they'd ridden side by side but his eyes refused to meet hers. She was going to tell him about al-Hisba but she suddenly felt foolish in her fears. 'I'm going to show Gilles the paper mill.'

'I'm glad you have a suitable companion.' Arnaut left her. Gilles had already found two mounts from among those still saddled and offered a hand to Estela, who put Arnaut from her mind and vaulted into the saddle. The inexplicable urge to hurry overtook her and as soon as they were out of Narbonne, she kicked her mare into a passable canter, accompanied always by Gilles, whose one-handed horsemanship was more than her match.

In the Palace courtyard, a grubby urchin caught his breath beside a man removing his helmet. 'Please Sire, can you tell me where to find Lord Dragonetz los Pros? I have a message for him.'

'Take it to him,' pointed the knight. As Dragonetz was not back from the road that they should have been on themselves, Arnaut could deal with whatever it was. An assignation no doubt, knowing their liege lord.

Arnaut had seen to the horses and was about to take his foul mood into the Palace when the boy ran up to him. 'Sire, sire, I have a message for Lord Dragonetz los Pros. Are you he?'

'Yes,' snapped Arnaut.

The boy shut his eyes and screwed up his face, the better to repeat word for word what he had rehearsed. 'The Infidel is going to set fire to the Paper mill.' Ducking expertly to avoid the mailed arm snaking out to catch him, the boy hared off into the warren of streets, well used to the rewards of his chosen profession.

'The bastard!' It wasn't the boy Arnaut meant as he smote the stable wall. And Estela was heading towards the mill with a one-armed man as her only protection. He swore again, sent curt messages after the men he'd just dismissed to take their ease, including his own father with whom he was barely speaking. Like Estela, he found a mount ready saddled, tore its reins from a protesting burgher and pounded the path along the river.

Also known as al-Hisba, Malik-al-Judhami of the ancient line of the Banu Hud, disinherited Emir to the Taifa of Zaragoza did not hurry as he poured oil onto the wood of mill-house, mill-race, shafts, presses. He had dismissed all the men so that the mill was peopled only with ghosts but even they could shake his detachment, perhaps shake even the resolve itself. Like any surgery, this must be performed with precision, and this time he was not detached enough. On this stone, he had broken bread with Dragonetz and solved problems of lubrication and rotation, mathematics and mechanics. They had talked of harmonies and export duties, absolute truths and cartwheels.

The mill was a monument to an alliance between two opposed cultures and two men who were friends. Would Dragonetz ever forgive him? Would a man believe that his physician friend had amputated and cauterised a limb that was doomed anyway? Malik struck sparks from the tinderbox and lit the fire. He ripped off wooden struts and used the brands to torch the furthest corners. Sweat streaked runnels down his soot-grimed face as he worked to destroy the domain where he had been the king he could never be in Zaragoza, not while Aragon and the Christians claimed his country as theirs.

Malik had tested the wind before starting the great blaze, relying on the water channels and the river to keep the fires contained, and he had not erred in his calculations. All the paper made in their mill – *their* mill – had been carted and shipped the week before, their receipts carefully lodged with Raavad but of course Dragonetz could not know this, not until after he had been saved from himself. In the springtime, when the payments came in, he would be a rich man.

Meanwhile, some token sheets burned to cinders, fizzling into the vats that blackened and spluttered themselves. He had held out as long as possible, driving production as hard and as efficiently as he knew how, but he had felt the end coming, heard the impatience in the Archbishop's voice in their rendez-vous. He had prepared Raavad. All was in order. Whether Dragonetz understood or not, his remarkable and much-loved friend would be alive, to follow his destiny.

And he, Malik, was free to return to his people in al-Andalus, with all that he had learned, and all the secret alliances he had forged in Occitania. He was free to return to his wife and five children, having done his duty. If Dragonetz had been other than he was, Malik would have slipped away as planned, forgotten by the Templars after they sold him, forgotten by his new 'owner' after disappearing.

A quiet ship from Narbonne to Barcelone and then home, to continue working for his people, squeezed between the Christians and the Almohads, with their fundamental intolerance. But Dragonetz had not bought him, had offered him choice, had shared his dreams and in return he, Malik-al-Judhami, had bought him a summer and taught him and his young protegée all he could. Insha'Allah. As God wills.

And then Malik was given a brutal reminder that Allah's ways take no account of a man's planning, however meticulous. Riding towards him were Estela and her henchman. She threw herself off her horse, ran at him, a dagger in one hand. Had she chosen to throw it rather than stab him with it, she would have caught him but he had enough warning to twist the attacking wrist so the blow was harmless. As he restrained her wrists, she kicked and bit, using anything but ladylike language and he was hard-pressed to hang onto her while keeping an eye on the man approaching. Malik had little choice but to hold Estela in front of him as a shield, earning another mouthful of abuse while she kicked and screamed.

To his horror, another rider came into view, dust spraying round his hooves. This one was in armour. Dragonetz? No, on first impression maybe, but a friend recognized the difference, a shade less in height, a nuance in carriage. Malik hardly had time to recognize Arnaut before he saw the trap sprung round him – five men who must have been lying in the undergrowth, biding their time.

'No!' hurled Malik at the treacherous skies. He pushed Estela at her man, who stumbled, caught off balance, giving the Moor time to pass them and pick up his scimitar from its resting place. He had not thought to use it this day but he would not stand and watch, especially as he could hazard a guess at whose doing this misbegotten ambush was. With the ancient war-cry of his people he charged at Arnaut, who was already fighting for his life, grounded by men who'd hacked his horse to its knees. His eyes widened as Malik came towards him wielding the great curved blade but then he understood and turned his back on him as he had a thousand times with Dragonetz, only then it had been scimitars they fought against.

Malik was seconds away from changing the odds to two against five, soon to be three against five, now that Estela's man had read the situation, but a second was all it took. One of the five blades slipped between coif and hauberk at the neck join, bubbling blood after it as the assailant jerked it back and Arnaut dropped to his knees, then to the ground. Satisfied that their work was done, the ragged band ran off.

Malik pulled the coif off Arnaut's head and moved the mail of the hauberk to one side. He put pressure on the wound to stem the flow of blood, but could not stop it completely. Estela threw herself down beside him. 'Is your medicine box on your horse? Can I get it?' He just shook his head at her, the verdict absolute.

Arnaut opened his eyes, a spasm of pain chasing across the otherwise clear gaze, no trace now of bitterness. 'It's all right Estela,' he slurred and she had to bend to catch his words. They all felt the thunder of approaching hooves. 'Go, al-Hisba,' Arnaut told him. 'Dragonetz will kill you.' Malik hesitated but Estela repeated, 'Go,' and moved Arnaut's head onto her own lap, moving the Moor's hand aside and pressing her own fingers against the wound to buy a few more minutes. 'I am Malik-al-Judhami of the Banu Hud,' he told them, bowing in respect to Arnaut. 'Peace be with you, brother in spirit. May we meet again in Paradise.'

'Go,' Estela told him flatly, and the Moor took to his horse, racing past the newcomers with a nod to their leader. It was indeed Dragonetz, with Raoulf and others of his men.

'My Lord,' Arnaut greeted him. 'This was meant for you.' He made a faint effort to raise his arm to the wound in his neck. 'Five armed men, the leader red-haired and pock-faced, and all of them without honour.'

'I know them,' Dragonetz told him. 'They will pay.' He took Arnaut's hands in his own. 'I wish it *had* been me!' Then he moved aside for the man whose son this was, who couldn't speak but rubbed the cold hands over and over, trying to create this precious life a second time. Raoulf pulled at the mail hauberk. 'Too tight,' he said stupid with grief. 'It's too tight.' And he caught accidentally at the chain under the hauberk, revealing Estela's token, still worn next to Arnaut's skin.

As if reminded of something, Arnaut spoke again. 'Estela?'

'I'm here,' she told him, stroking the bloodless forehead where blonde hairs escaped from the iron hooding his head. 'I'm always here.'

'What sort of song would I be?'

'The best kind,' she told him. 'A song of love and courage and friendship.'

'Of honour,' Dragonetz added, 'and skill in battle and fighting back to back.'

'You were wrong,' Arnaut breathed, eyes dimly on his father.

'I was wrong,' Raoulf agreed brokenly, crushing his hands tighter. It was as if Estela's ribcage was crushed by those desperate hands, the waste of it all choking her, until suddenly she flooded with *the Song of Arnaut*, words glittering and honed to a fine blade, the rich, bloody poetry of one man's life and death singing itself to her open heart. *This will be my first song,* she promised her friend, silently, *You will never be forgotten. Where troubadours sing, across time and space, they will remember Arnaut, who gave his life for his friend.*

'Feet out of stirrups,' Dragonetz told his friend, leaning over to close the sightless eyes. He gently untangled Estela from Arnaut, forcing her to let go, raising her to her feet. She couldn't take in that it was over. 'Leave them,' he said to her, supporting her arm. Incapable of moving by her own volition, Estela allowed herself to be led away from the tableau of father and son. Still holding her, Dragonetz gave orders to his men, told them he needed to return to Narbonne as soon as possible to ensure the murderers were caught. The fires were already running out of fuel, dying safely to ashes around the razed mill-works and Dragonetz barely glanced at what remained of his dream as he hoisted Estela up in front of him. Gilles kept them company during a sombre return to the city, in which much was said about a man they had not known, whom they had called al-Hisba.

CHAPTER TWENTY-THREE

E rmengarda listened, sharp-faced and still, astute as ever in her questions when Dragonetz completed his accusation. 'The same five as tried to start civil war in the city and to kill you in the Jewish Quarter?'

'Yes.'

'And you suspect someone who would benefit from ill-will towards the Jews in my City, and from preventing the invention of paper taking over Church functions and Church money?'

'Yes. I believe he was also behind the attempt to kill me at the Viking Games. Employing the Lady Alis and perhaps in league with Toulouse.'

'But there is no proof against the Archbishop?'

'Nothing that wouldn't disappear with bribed witnesses.'

'Your man al-Hisba's role in this?'

'I don't know,' admitted Dragonetz. 'Estela and presumably Arnaut saw him set fire to the mill but Estela and Gilles swear he didn't expect the assassins and would have given his life for Arnaut's. It makes no sense to me. All I know is that he was never my man. Who he is, I have yet to learn. All I have is a name but that is more than we knew before.'

There was a reflective silence and Dragonetz knew better than to

JEAN GILL

break it. 'You will need to speak with Raavad,' commented Ermengarda at length. 'You cannot but renege on your contract as you have no mill and no merchandise, so he must call in his dues.'

Dragonetz flushed. 'I have some payments owing from shipments already at sea but the uncertainties of weather and travel means I have no sureties. I can only hope that Raavad is willing to wait and that I come across a miraculous well of good fortune.' This time the silence was heavier. Dragonetz was asking whether Ermengarda would offer him a loan – or more. He knew the answer. What the woman might have given, the Viscomtesse of Narbonne dare not. She had made that clear when they had first made their private pact.

She held his gaze, steady, without apology. 'I too hope that Raavad will be generous to a debtor.' Dragonetz nodded. It was no. Ermengarda had realised how far the Church would go to prevent paper changing the world and her priority was her city and its existing trade, not some possible future goods dependent on the vision of a madman. 'I believe that the Commander of my Guard can find your mercenaries, given your description.' Dragonetz gave cautious assent, waiting.

'They will have to be questioned,' continued Ermengarda. Meaning tortured and mutilated. Dragonetz still waited. 'They will certainly hurl all kinds of false accusations against a respected prelate, a citizen of Narbonne, which we will report to him, along with our amazement that criminals should think us so stupid as to suspect him of conspiracy and murder.' So d'Anduze would know that Ermengarda was well aware of what he'd done and that she would hold it over him for the future. He would owe her a favour for not making his life unpleasant. She could certainly have done that much even if she could never have proved his complicity.

'If we could have tied him to the crossbow attempt, he would have also broken the Church's ban on the use of bolts against Christians.'

Ermengarda nodded. 'That too will be held over him. He is, after all, my brother-in-law so I must proceed against him with caution. It is hard to believe that I welcomed his appointment!' She ruminated

306

further, then, 'I have a feeling that the murderers are Jewish,' she declared.

Now she had lost him. 'Jewish?' he queried.

'It will be impossible to recognize them after the inevitable results of questioning but their confessions and our reports will show that they are the Jews behind all the recent, regrettable acts against the good Christian citizens of Narbonne. And their fellow-Jews will of course cast out these vile saboteurs, and will be only too pleased that we make an example of them from the gibbets on the Hill at Ad Fiurcas. What is left of them that is. And our good Jewish citizens of Narbonne will likewise be able to continue their lives in peaceful trading and discourse, the cause of the malady having been rooted out.' So the Christian community would have its Jewish scapegoats, the Jewish community would be protected, peace would be re-established and a band of mercenaries would die an unpleasant death, with of course the full blessing of their very Christian employer.

Dragonetz looked at her in total unfeigned admiration. This was why she was Viscomtesse of Narbonne. 'Words fail me,' he told her, truthfully.

She gave one of her rare smiles. 'I shall take that as a compliment. And would you please present my respects to Raavad and inform him that he must break all the details of the sad news to the Jewish community, to ensure that there is a suitable reaction to the death of five of its members who have sadly let down their race.'

A thought struck Dragonetz. 'And the families of the five criminals?'

'They have done no wrong and any such family we discover will be generously enabled to start anew life elsewhere.'

'My Lady.' Dragonetz bowed low and took his leave.

In the dark study of the philosopher and businessman known as Raavad, Dragonetz found he was expected. As with any two men of affairs, they exchanged pleasantries first, then Dragonetz passed on the message from Ermengarda, which was quickly grasped, with a quiet, 'Please thank the Lady Ermengarda,' in return. Then they got to the crux of the visit. Before Dragonetz could make his proposals however, Raavad drew out some sheets of parchment, covered in a flowing hand, and passed them over to Dragonetz.

'A friend of yours deposited this with me at the same time as you took out your loan. He instructed me to give it to you on just such an occasion. I will leave you to digest the contents in peace.'

Dragonetz' eyes had already skipped to the signature, Malik-al-Judhami of the Banu Hud. He had no problem in reading the beautiful Arabic and if his eyes blurred from time to time, it was not from problems with the language or script.

Friend of my mind,

It was my intention to accompany the first traveller from Douzens who asked for such a servant, as a way of leaving the Brothers without arousing suspicion. They have no cause to complain of the years I served them but as you now know, I am no bondsman. My grandfather was king of Zaragoza and I hope one day to return that country to its former greatness. You would have loved the libraries and the gardens, the architecture and of course the paper mills. We are in a bad time between the Christians of Aragon, who take more of our rights every day, and the Muslim Almohads, who have no concept of right, and are even worse than the Almoravids before them.

My people in al-Andalus have suffered the consequences of your Christian Crusades and I needed to find out what was planned and whether the last victory had diminished your enthusiasm to invade Oltra mar. We both know that this is far from the case and with a heavy heart I have now learned all that I can and must return to my people and protect them within my means. I also know, dear friend, that not every Christian feels pride for deeds in the Holy Land.

When you gave me the right to say no to taking your bond, you laid a burden of honour on me. When you were attacked, I saved your life but felt the burden even more for I knew there would be further attempts. When you talked to me of music and irrigation, I saw a fertile field and I held the seeds in my hand. How could I throw them to the winds? In my Lady Estela too there is a rare spirit and talent. It pleases me to watch your music-making and there is something in your harmonies together that makes me long for my own beloved and our children, left these five years to face this uncertain world without me. But I will stay to seed the field and I hope we will have a marvellous crop before the storm. Unlike you, I know the storm must come because the Archbishop has already found me, tested whether I will kill you – I will not – and tested whether I will destroy the paper mill that is not even five planks of wood yet! I will, friend of my mind, I will destroy the paper mill because I can think of no other way to protect your life from these Christian curs. They will stop at nothing. I will do my best to give us the harvest before then.

Insha'Allah.

Malik-al-Judhami of the Banu Hud

There was a long postscript, clearly written recently and in haste.

In the next world, you and I will talk of all that separates us in this one. Arnaut waits for us there and I take heart that his last words showed more understanding of my actions than I deserve. He was a good man and a brave comrade.

The harvest was good my friend, better than you can understand at this moment when you know you cannot fulfil your contract with Raavad in two months time and that your land will be forfeit. He and I have an arrangement which cannot be shaken. He will explain to you what is required and you have no choice. I place this burden on you from love. You must leave until the world moves on and there is a place for your dreams in it. Until then Narbonne is your death sentence. Believe me, if there was another way I would not constrain you.

I beg of you that you accept the gift of friendship I leave for you.

'Bring me a horse, a bow,
a book, some poems
A pen, a lute, dice, wine, a chess set too.'

Until we meet again.
Malik

Unseeing, Dragonetz stared at the sheets, unable to make out their meaning. The quotation from the old poet was no more cryptic than the way in which everything he thought he had known was turned upside down. Al-Hisba was right about one thing. There was no way he could repay the 15% he owed on the Kalends of November and according to the contract he had signed, his land was forfeit and that left him bankrupt. He would not turn to his father for aid so he must at least listen to the proposal he was being pushed into.

Raavad made him jump when he spoke. 'I understand you will need time to take all this in but sadly,' he opened his hands in that Jewish gesture of apology which laid the blame on God. He went to a large chest, rummaged among some robes and withdrew something wrapped in oiled sailcloth. 'You cannot pay your mortgage dues,' he stated. 'The terms on the contract were very precise.'

Dragonetz bit his lips. He remembered the terms very well and how confident he'd been of the repayment.

'Your land will of course be forfeit. But as Malik – al-Hisba – has stated, he has come to an arrangement with me in advance, that I will pay you the exact sum that you borrowed from me to purchase the land, if you carry out an errand for me.'

'You will pay me the worth of the land with a working paper mill, when I owe you the land in any case. It makes no sense. An errand.' Dragonetz was ironic. It seemed that everyone but him was responsible not just for people but for *a* people.

'Malik was generous. Also, it is a dangerous errand,' Raavad admitted. 'This,' he opened the oilskin to show a book, 'is no longer safe here. I need someone to take it to the Holy Land and deposit it with my brethren.

'Oltra mar.' Dragonetz laughed outright.

'Jerusalem,' Raavad clarified. 'It will be safe there.'

Return to the scene of his greatest failures, his greatest crimes and carry a precious Jewish book across enemy terrain into the Holy City. Was this a sick joke?

'With the next Crusade gathering force and Nur ad-Din's army probably outside the city walls already, waiting their moment to take Jerusalem back!'

'The book will not stay in Jerusalem but from there it is no longer your concern. Please, Dragonetz. If there was another way, we would take it' That was another phrase Dragonetz had heard too often and it was not the book's safety that worried him.

'Do I have a choice?'

'There is always a choice,' Raavad said gently. 'But this is the only honourable one being offered.' He placed the book carefully on the table and opened it, revealing old parchment pages, each with three columns of even script, footnotes, and neat annotations in the margins.

Dragonetz studied the page, which looked upside down to his Christian eyes.. 'You can at least tell me what this is, given that I am likely to die for it.'

'It is the Keter Aram Sola,' Raavad stated simply, then seeing that Dragonetz was none the wiser. 'a very old Torah, our Bible, perhaps the oldest we have. These,' he pointed with reverence to the squiggles in the margins, 'are the work of Aaron Ben Asher and they represent years of work and study by a brilliant mind. They tell us not only how to read the Torah but how to sing it.'

Dragonetz looked with new interest at the marks which must be a form of musical notation. How al-Hisba would have pored over this treasure.

'This Codex,' continued Raavad, 'is the sacred guide to the Torah and must be preserved. It has been stolen, ransomed and given into my care. It has fed the learning of my people in Provence and I have great hope that something special has been born here, thanks to this book. But it is no longer safe in Narbonne, or even in Occitania. It is perhaps the only copy after the desecrations of the last decade in the Holy Land and it must go back there, all four hundred and ninety one pages still in one piece, to somewhere safe. *'Blessed be he who preserves it and cursed be he who steals it, and cursed be he who sells it, and cursed be he who pawns it. It may not be sold and it may not be defiled.'*

Dragonetz bowed understanding and listened to the detailed instructions on who, how and where.

'We will not be ungrateful for the service nor will we forget the cost to you,' Raavad told him and the words rang déjà vu in Dragonetz' mind. The Gyptian Fortune-Teller? No, not her, but the other one, the mystic Jew. Raavad had not been there but Makhir had. Was this the service Makhir had in mind?

'Have you spoken of this to others?'

'The nine,' he acknowledged, 'and to those who seek the truth. Knowledge is not for burying.'

'Tell that to those who had my Paper mill razed to the ground!'

'Which is why it must be you. You care about wisdom. You understand why we must pass on what we know. I told you the book is no longer safe here. I know there are rumours growing that I am the keeper of something precious. There are those who guess at it. You must go straight away. And give some other reason for going.'

Dragonetz nodded. Then he was walking to the door, concealing the book in his jerkin. 'Should you wish to contact Malik, I can reach him,' Raavad told him. 'And one other thing, Dragonetz. The gift of friendship is waiting for you in the stable. May Yahweh guide you and be with you.'

What else would be waiting in the stable? That it was a horse only surprised Dragonetz when he thought of the effort of getting this horse to Narbonne. What amazed him however was the quality of the destrier before him, a black stallion, finely bred from Arab lines. It must have been shipped from al-Andalus and it had cost a fortune, no question.

'Bring me a horse, a bow,
a book, some poems,
a pen, a lute, dice, wine, a chess set too.'

'Sadeek,' the stable-hand told him. 'That's what he's called Sire. The man who left him for you said you'd like that.'

'Yes,' said Dragonetz. 'Sadeek.' The Arabic for 'true friend'. And now he must see someone he wanted to spend his life with and to whom he could offer only one night.

'However long we have will never be enough,' Estela told him, stroking his naked shoulders with her curtain of hair. The shadow of Arnaut and of their parting deepened their coming-together, mixing desperation with desire. At one point Dragonetz turned his face from her. 'What?' she asked him.

'Ghosts,' he replied and once more they chased away the ghosts with the dance of hands and lips and skin.

'What if I come with you?' she asked.

'Don't think I don't want you to! You know what I face Oltra mar. Do you think I could bear what might happen to you? You know what Sancha has seen. And I don't think you're safe here either. Go with Bèatriz when she returns to Dia. You'll be out of reach of those in Montbrun or of his Eminence here in Narbonne and you can be the trobairitz you've always wanted to be. And I will find you there. I will find you wherever you go.'

She knew he was right. 'But when you come back,' she couldn't phrase it as 'if' even to herself, 'we'll be old, perhaps thirty, wrinkled and paunchy, our teeth falling out. How will you love me then?'

'Like this,' he told her. 'Shut your eyes. It's about touch not the tricks our eyes play.' His hands made their deft moves on her body, proving his point. 'While we can touch each other, our bodies can profit, whatever our eyes tell us. But that's for when we're old. My eyes are perfectly contented with what they see now.' She opened her eyes to find the black gaze intense on her own, holding her, drawing her in till she no longer knew where she ended and he began.

The dawn was starting to tinge the sky with unwelcome pink when he turned to her, serious. 'I could be away years. I don't expect you to be faithful to me. I don't expect to be faithful to you with my body. But with my mind – I see no help for it.'

Trying to master the lump in her throat by teasing him, she said,

'And when you come back, if I don't want to give up my new man for you?'

'Then I will kill him,' he told her, his eyes blazing and she believed him, in his arms, as the sun itself became visible, gilding the clouds.

He knelt before her, kissed her hand in fealty and took off his signet ring, with his crest engraved in the heavy gold. 'Keep this for me and if you should be in need, show that you are under the protection of Dragonetz los Pros, or send it to me and I will come to you no matter where I am or what I do.' She slipped the ring on the chain given to her by Arnaut's father, the chain that had once held her bangle on it.

They clung to the last moments of night until neither could pretend any longer. It was time. They had sung it a thousand times together. Aubade. Dawn Song, in Dragonetz' own words that had reached out to a girl growing up in Montbrun.

He spoke them softly to her now.

'My sweet, my own, what shall we do?
Day is nigh and night is over
We must be parted, my self missing
All the day away from you.'

Then he kissed her and left.

EPILOGUE

I t was October and the leaves were starting to turn. The road north would be blocked by snow in a few weeks and the party had delayed as long as was prudent before bidding Narbonne farewell and taking the Via Domitia towards Dia in the Vercors mountains.

Estela fiddled with the chain round her neck, feeling the ring swing against her breasts under her gown, and she responded absently to Bèatriz' chat as she rode beside her, accompanied by Gilles, Raoulf and a large white dog that seemed to think it belonged with her. One man's stump and the other's bleak eyes accused her equally for their losses but all she could do was watch over them as they, in every word and gesture, watched over her.

In her panniers, wrapped in cloths to stop the wires from breaking, was a gift that had been sent her from a foreign port, made on shipboard by a traveler stopping there on his way to Oltra mar. It was a marvelous invention that consisted of a blue jar and wired attachments circling it. When filled with water, and placed in its stand, the jar kept time, performing three times daily, at tierce, set and vespers. Each wire circle would jump into motion as the water leaked through a small hole. On the first wire circles were the planets, on the second two little human figures, whose mouths opened and shut as the wires turned and on the third were musical instruments, recorder, lute and rebec, in fine detail. 'Boethius,' Estela had smiled through tears, accepting the present.

The other precious gift hidden in her pannier was a perfect bound book, presented to her by the book-binder of Narbonne, whose work with parchment usually went to the scribes of the Archbishop and the Viscomtesse. This was, however, not a parchment book. It was a rare and beautiful book of paper, leatherbound with marbled endpapers imported specially from Venice. 'From Malik-al-Judhami of the Banu Hud to his friend Estela de Matin,' the bookbinder had told her. From the first moment she saw the book, Estela knew that this was where she would record her first song, *The Song of Arnaut*, which sang always in her heart.

In the Cité Palace of Paris, which had been extensively redecorated in a doomed attempt to please its Queen, that same lady was screaming in a bedchamber, attended by her midwife and carefully chosen Ladies. Those present were disappointed when the midwife finally announced, 'It's a girl.'

Aliénor was not disappointed. She was incandescent with rage. 'Take it away,' she ordered and the unfortunate baby was rushed out of sight. The Queen sent for her husband, who tried to take her hand and soothe her.

'Never mind,' he told her.

'I want a divorce,' she replied and turned her back on him. She had already decided who she would have for her next husband.

HISTORICAL NOTE

When actual historical figures appear in the narrative, I used historical fact whenever I could find it, and then added detail which fits with historians' research. The 12th century left little in writing so both fact and interpretation are widely disputed by historians, leaving room for a novelist to explore what might have happened. There is no record of Aliénor visiting Narbonne but it is certainly possible in the dates I have suggested, and it seems likely that she and Ermengarda would have formed an alliance. Also, the notion that Aliénor brought sugar back from the Crusades and made it part of Narbonne's trading goods has some evidential support, linking Aliénor strongly with Narbonne.

Aliénor is of course known in English as Eleanor but I have tried to keep the flavour of the period by retaining French or Occitan names, unless this confuses the narrative. Spelling of names was arbitrary and every other male ruler in Occitania was called Raymond so I have used the different language spellings to try to distinguish between the various Raymonds, who would in fact all have enjoyed every spelling possible at the time.

Although Estela and Dragonetz are completely fictional characters, they live in the real world and events of the 12th century, which I have recreated to the best of my ability. All the lyrics in the book are from existing texts attributed to different troubadours but where the historical troubadours appear in the narrative, such as Marcabru, his lyrics are indeed his own. Again, he could have been in Narbonne at this time. Amazingly, the Prince of Orkney did indeed call at Narbonne and write heroic verse for Ermengarda at roughly this date.

In Occitania (now the south of France and north of Spain) it was a time when Muslims and Jews shared their amazing science, medicine, engineering, technology and even philosophy. Some Christians, like Dragonetz, recognized the future; others preached hellfire and damnation. Among the heathen inventions which drew the wrath of the Church, threatening its coffers and its monopoly on the word, was paper.

The medieval Church was so successful in stamping out the production of paper in Christian Europe that it took 200 years before the knowledge of the 12th century re-appeared, leading to that freedom of thought across time that we call a book.

Historical sources that were particularly useful were:

Troubadours et cours d'amour – J Lafitte-Houssat
Ecrivains anticonformistes du moyen-âge occitan – René Nelli
La Fleur Inverse – Jacques Roubaud
Voix de femmes au Moyen Age – Danielle Régnier-Bohler
Les Troubadours – Henri Davenson
Ermengard of Narbonne and the World of the Troubadours – Frederic L. Cheyette
Eleanor of Aquitaine – Alison Weir
Blondel's Song – David Boyle
Holy Warriors – Jonathan Phillips
The Crusades – Thomas Asbridge

HISTORICAL CHARACTERS APPEARING IN THE NOVEL

- *Aliénor of Aquitaine/ Eleanor of Aquitaine* – Duchess of Aquitaine and Queen of France
- *Abraham ben Isaac/ Raavad II* – Jewish leader and famed interpreter of the Torah, father of Abraham ben David, a Jewish leader in Nîmes
- *Alphonse nicknamed 'Jourdain'/ 'Jordan', Comte de Toulouse*, father of Raymond, killed by poison in Caesarea in 1148
- *Alphonso, King of Castile, Emperor of Spain* – died in 1144 leaving his estate to the Templars
- *Archbishop of Narbonne, Pierre d'Anduze,* brother of Ermengarda's husband
- *Archbishop Suger* – royal prelate in Paris, Adviser to King Louis
- *Bèatriz,* the future Comtesssa de Dia / Comtesse de Die and famous troubairitz
- *Bernard of Clairvaux* – influential Abbot leading and reforming the Cistercian order, whose preaching helped launch and bless the disastrous 2nd Crusade
- *Bernard d'Anduze* – Ermengarda's titular husband, brother of the Archbishop of Narbonne
- *Ermengarda/Ermengard* – Viscomtesse of Narbonne from four years old
- *Jarl Rognvaldr Kali Kolsson, Prince of Orkney*
- *Louis VI – King of France,* married to Aliénor
- *Pope Eugene III*
- *Raimon Trencavel,* brother to Roger and Comte de Carcassonne on his brother's death in 1150
- *Ramon Berenguer,* Comte de Barcelone, Prince of Aragan and Overlord of Provence
- *Raymond V,* Comte de Toulouse

- *Raymon of Antioch,* Aliénor's uncle and rumoured lover, killed by Saracen troops in 1148
- *Raymond and Stephanie of les Baux,* rulers of Provence
- *Roger Trencavel,* Comte de Carcassonne, died in 1150
- *Sicard de Lautrec,* ally of Toulouse
- ***Troubadours*** – Marcabru, Cercamon, Peire Rogier from the auvergne, Raimbaut d'Aurenja / Raymon of Orange, Guiraut de Bornelh
- ***In charge of the Templar Commandery at Douzens*** – Peter Radels, Master; Isarn of Molaria and Bernard of Roquefort, joint commanders

ACKNOWLEDGMENTS

Many thanks to

my editor, Lesley Geekie.

Kaye for her constructive criticism
and John Green for his impeccable translation of Marcabru's poem
'Pax in nomine Domini'. I know he will run round in lustra at some of
my wilful interpretations.

the Dieulefit Writers' Group, for existing, and especially to Laurent
for constructive criticism of *Song at Dawn*

and to the like-minded souls on authonomy.com for their support and
helpful comments

ABOUT THE AUTHOR

I'm a Welsh writer and photographer living in the south of France with two scruffy dogs, a beehive named 'Endeavour', a Nikon D750 and a man. I taught English in Wales for many years and my claim to fame is that I was the first woman to be a secondary headteacher in Carmarthenshire. I'm mother or stepmother to five children so life has been pretty hectic.

I've published all kinds of books, both with traditional publishers and self-published. You'll find everything under my name from prize-winning poetry and novels, military history, translated books on dog training, to a cookery book on goat cheese. My work with top dog-trainer Michel Hasbrouck has taken me deep into the world of dogs with problems, and inspired one of my novels. With Scottish parents, an English birthplace and French residence, I can usually support the winning team on most sporting occasions.

www.jeangill.com

facebook.com / writerjeangill
twitter.com / writerjeangill
instagram.com / writerjeangill
goodreads.com / JeanGill

The follow-up to her memoir *How Blue is My Valley* about moving to France from rainy Wales, tells the true story of how Jean

- nearly became a certified dog trainer.
- should have been certified and became a beekeeper.
- developed from keen photographer to hold her first exhibition.
- held 12th century Damascene steel.
- looks for adventure in whatever comes her way.

BLADESONG

1151: THE HOLY LAND

If you enjoyed *Song at Dawn,* don't miss
the further adventures of Dragonetz and Estela
in Book 2 of *The Troubadours Quartet*

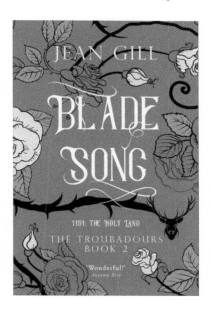

CHAPTER 1 SAMPLE

BLADESONG

His world was a small white chamber, dazzling him with light after days in the darkness of a blindfold. Large cushions of rich, silk brocade offered ruby-and-ochre relief from the whiteness, and rest for his body. An empty pail for his needs in one corner, clean rose-scented water and a towel in another, were the only other furnishings.

Stripes of sun and shade slanted through the arched window, filtered by the vertical iron bars rooted in the stone sill. The room was well protected from invaders. Wrought in the iron were flourishes of spear and ball but the man was in no mood to appreciate the exquisite craftsmanship of his prison and cared not whether someone could attack him from outside.

His enemies would come through the door, not through the window. Wearing black robes and swathes of black around their heads and faces, speaking soft Arabic, they would bring some kind of spicy pottage. They would untie his hands so that he could use them to stuff the mash into his mouth and they would give him a cup of water. He'd be allowed to wash his hands and face. Then they would bind him again and bow before taking leave of their 'honoured guest'. Strange hospitality.

Escape attempts had failed so far, although it was a compliment to his perseverance and ingenuity that three anonymous attendants always stood outside the door with their curved swords. Rubbing bonds against the rough wall merely fretted his skin to bleeding, as did the shattered fragments of his water-cup after he'd kicked it against the wall. After that, they'd not left the cup with him.

Biting into the cushions and scattering their contents – feathers – advanced him no further than when he'd kicked over his chamber pot. Unless disgust in his jailers' eyes counted as an advance. Fasting for a day while they were absent and lower mortals cleaned his mess, struck him as no advance at all but he added their obsession with cleanliness to his observations on the fine scimitar blades. The filigree patterns on the steel were no ordinary pattern welding and they teased his memory. Who knew what would be useful, or when.

His hands were tied and his balance was badly affected, but he was starting to adjust. Lying on his back and repeatedly scoring the wall under the window-sill with a big toe, he could mark the passing of nights, a dirty smudge for each, without it being noticed by the guards. The toe-marks tallied twelve already but he couldn't guess at time lost before he started counting. Time when he also lost his clothes, his precious horse and the book entrusted to him by a wise Jew; the book he was supposed to guard with his life and deliver to Abdon Yerushalmi in the dye-works in Jerusalem; the book on which his own future depended. His ideas about that future were changing rapidly in the white chamber but it was still possible he might have one. If they meant to kill him, they would have done so. Wouldn't they?

He crouched and straightened, exercising his calves and thighs, rotating his ankles, strengthening his riding muscles. His hands bound behind his back, he could do little for his arms but stretch them sideways or lie prone and arch hands towards feet but whatever use he could make of a cushion and a wall in keeping active, so he did.

For his restless mind, his usual release was unhampered and he shut his eyes, breathed deeply and sang. He roved through spring-time and kisses, goat-girls and fatal sword-thrusts. When memory threw him lines last sung as a duet with the sweetest partner he'd ever known, he accepted the pain and let it flow into the song of morning-after, the aubade and a lovers' farewell. Discipline for the heart as well as the mind.

Another lyric, not his own, floated into his mind; a song born in Occitania and carried into the crusade by its maker.

Lanqand li jorn son lonc en may,
M'es bels douz chans d'auzelhs de lonh,
E qand me sui partitz de lay
Remembra.m d'un amor de lonh

'When days are long in May
I hear
the sweet-tongued birds so far away
And near
Things leave me dreaming
Only of my love so far away'

The far-away lady-love of the poet, Rudel, had been here, in the Holy Land, although he had never seen her. His fancy had been fuelled by stories of a matchless beauty, the Comtesse de Tripoli. The captive knight mouthed the plaintive Occitan.

Iratz e gauzens me.n partray
S'ieu ja la vey l'amor de lonh,

'I would leave in joy but also pain
Should I but see my love so far away
Just once, again,'

He deliberately altered the words, thinking of his own Estela, no unseen, unknown lady.

'I know not how nor when,
The lands between so far away,

The roads uncertain to her door –
No more!
I cannot speak! Insha'Allah!'

He sang the Arabic, ironically, instead of *'Diau platz.'* It seemed to him that the God of the Muslims held more power over him at this moment than the God of the Christians.

He let the sounds of the street below accompany his first attempts at shaping a new lyric, clashing tin pans for a tambour and a muezzin's call instead of the plaintive flute, to the rhythm of a rolling cart. Everything was a song if you knew how to listen.

Whatever the anonymous guards thought of such music, nothing showed in their demeanor as they entered the room, seemingly in the appointed way, at the appointed time. When they'd taken off blind-fold and gag, after a head-splitting journey, the first thing he said was, 'If you harm my horse, may God, Allah and Yahweh spit on your children's future, and on their children's future, to the thousandth generation.'

Milton Keynes UK
Ingram Content Group UK Ltd.
UKHW041400121123
432429UK00003B/202